The Matchmaker

SAMAN SHAD

VIKING
an imprint of
PENGUIN BOOKS

VIKING

UK | USA | Canada | Ireland | Australia
India | New Zealand | South Africa | China

Viking is part of the Penguin Random House group of companies whose addresses can be found at
global.penguinrandomhouse.com

Penguin
Random House
Australia

First published by Viking in 2023

Cover design by Debra Billson
Cover images courtesy of Denis Cristo/Shutterstock, Shaheer Ahmed/Shutterstock,
Marza/Shutterstock, Greens87/Shutterstock
Author photograph by Joe Chan
Typeset in 12/17 pt Adobe Garamond Pro by Midland Typesetters, Australia

Printed and bound in Australia by Griffin Press, an accredited
ISO AS/NZS 14001 Environmental Management Systems printer

A catalogue record for this
book is available from the
NATIONAL
LIBRARY   National Library of Australia
OF AUSTRALIA

ISBN 978 1 76104 469 4

penguin.com.au

We at Penguin Random House Australia acknowledge that Aboriginal and Torres Strait Islander
peoples are the Traditional Custodians and the first storytellers of the lands on which we live and
work. We honour Aboriginal and Torres Strait Islander peoples' continuous connection to Country,
waters, skies and communities. We celebrate Aboriginal and Torres Strait Islander stories, traditions
and living cultures; and we pay our respects to Elders past and present.

For Matt, Milan, Kaiden and Nyle

Chapter 1

A mehendi-decorated hand gripped Saima's arm tightly and almost pulled her off the chair. She looked up to see a bejewelled woman smiling kindly at her.

'Why are you sitting in the back? You must be in the front!' the woman exclaimed.

'No, Aunty,' Saima protested, but her voice was drowned out by the thumping drums that were getting louder with every beat. By the time the noise became deafening, she had given up resisting and was on her feet, wincing in her sparkling, too-tight new heels as she was led through the crowd of aunties and uncles, toddlers and teenagers, men and women; faces turned towards the parquet dance floor where the grand entrance was about to take place. The vaguely familiar woman who had pulled her into the crowd now let her go and was swallowed up by the surging mass of guests with their phones – and the occasional iPad – raised, trying to capture the scene. Saima ran through her mental Rolodex, trying to place her. She was sure she must be a close relative of the couple that were getting married.

In front of her, standing in the middle of the Bexley community hall, a group of turbaned men with slick beards thumped their bare palms on large dhols that swung from around their necks.

1

They wore elaborately embroidered jutti on their feet, and the overhead fan billowed their white silk kurtas.

'Balle, balle!' one of the drummers shouted. The thumping picked up in pace and ferocity. The crowd hollered with appreciation and excitement.

The drummers moved to the side of the dance floor and abruptly stopped. For a second, there was silence, punctuated by a cough and a screeching baby, and then the speakers came to life, blasting the opening chords of a popular Bollywood wedding song.

As the singer began to whistle, many in the audience joined in. Saima smiled. She'd heard the song hundreds of times before, but every time, the sweet whistle at the beginning made butterflies churn in her stomach.

This would be her fifth wedding this year and it was not yet March. And yet she couldn't help but enjoy it as if it was her first wedding. It was probably why she did what she did.

The groom flew in the face of tradition and walked into the hall by himself. Throwing his arms open, the spangles on his embroidered pagri glimmering in the spotlight, he began to lip sync to the lyrics to *Ban Ja Rani*. He called to his lady love, asking her to become his queen. And then his queen appeared through the doorway, an enormous smile on her face as she approached her groom.

Saima estimated that the ornate red bridal lehenga weighed around ten kilos, decorated as it was with all that heavy zari and stonework. The dupatta that covered the bride's head would probably be another seven kilos. Desi brides really needed to do strength training, she'd always thought. They wore garlands of flowers around their necks, lavish necklaces underneath, then the dupatta, the lehenga, the teeka and armloads of bangles, with ears weighed down by earrings the size of small plates. But beneath it all, the brides never seemed to mind. This was their time to shine, and when it came to shine, Pakistanis didn't do things by halves.

When the bride and groom were side by side, hands clasped together, they walked to the podium, where the emcee offered them a microphone each.

'Thank you everyone for being a part of our special day,' the groom began. As he spoke, the crowd began to wander back to their tables. Saima headed to her seat, which, thankfully, was at the back of the hall and close to the exit. She liked to observe the weddings she'd helped to arrange from her vantage point and not interfere in the proceedings. It also meant she could leave quietly when she was ready.

'Aunty!' The bride suddenly exclaimed loudly into the microphone. Saima ignored her, assuming she was calling out to one of her relatives. 'Saima Aunty!'

What? Saima stopped in her tracks. The blood rushed from her face. *She* was the aunty?

Was this the moment? That pivotal moment where she went from being a young woman going about her business to being lumped in with the 'aunties' and all the connotations – gossip and excess arm fat included – that went with it?

As she turned around, she noted, for the most part, curious, smiling eyes, but also some that were narrowed and beady – the eyes of women twice her age, running their gaze up and down her body. The women's hushed whispers rang loudly in Saima's ears. *I'm only thirty-three!* she wanted to yell.

By the time she looked back at the bride, she had composed her face into one of serene graciousness.

'I just wanted to start off by thanking Saima Aunty here. Though, sorry, I really should be calling you baji, shouldn't I? I never know how to get that right. Who's a baji, who is an aunty, it's all a bit confusing, am I right?' The bride laughed self-consciously. 'It was Saima here – is it okay if I call you Saima? – it was Saima who brought us together, which was why I wanted to thank her first. Without her matching us up, this guy next to me would still be living at home, getting his mum to wash his chuddies.' The crowd erupted with laughter. 'And I would've risked becoming the career woman who never found time for love.' Warm applause.

You're only twenty-four, Saima wanted to reply. *You've got nothing but time on your side.*

But she knew that by traditional South Asian standards, by twenty-four you were expected to be married and contemplating giving birth to your first child, if not your second. Small wonder that at thirty-three, she was being seen as an aunty.

'So, anyway, if you're looking for a matchmaker, I say give Saima a go, 'cos she's really good at what she does and I'm sure she'd appreciate your business.' The bride smiled beatifically at her for a moment before moving on to thank the many friends and family in attendance.

Saima's face felt hot. Not just content with calling her an aunty, the bride had also mentioned her business. Usually, the couples she matched didn't thank her in their wedding speeches at all. If they did, they just mentioned her in passing. And they most certainly did not refer to her services as a business that needed actual clients to keep going.

She felt dozens of eyes on her. Her head began to throb in time to the pulsing in her feet as the straps of the new shoes dug into her toes. She started moving again towards her table. She could quickly eat the entrée, which would arrive soon, and head to the exit. The thought of throwing off her heels, putting on a pair of PJs and burying her head in a giant bag of chips and a binge on Netflix presented itself in her mind like a shimmering mirage.

4

Another woman accosted her on her way back to her seat.

'So, you're a matchmaker?' She had tasteful blonde streaks through her hair, cleverly concealing any sign of greys against the black, enormous eyelash extensions and fierce eyebrows. She may well have been over fifty, those eyebrows suggested, but don't you *dare* go and call *her* aunty.

Saima pinned a vague, pleasant smile on her face, thinking longingly of her seat and the exit beyond. The woman let her laser gaze run the length of Saima's body, gathering facts on age, weight, height and complexion. Saima could almost hear her thoughts:

Somewhere around thirty years of age. Though the bride called her aunty, so maybe closer to thirty-five.
Could lose a couple more kilos, but not too skinny, that's good.
Five foot four. Good height.
Very tanned, but a few weeks indoors with the right skin cream could fix that. Probably a wheatish complexion under that sun damage.

Her mental cataloguing complete, the woman asked, 'You are here with someone?'

'No,' Saima replied.

'Oh!' The woman couldn't hide her shock as a group of teenage girls walked past. 'A single woman like you, matchmaking? I've never heard of such a thing. You didn't arrange a match for yourself?'

Saima was used to this question, but it didn't mean she didn't find it annoying. A matchmaker, most people assumed, would be a middle-aged woman, probably with adult children, who had enough time on her hands to arrange marriages as a hobby. They didn't expect a young(ish) single woman who did matchmaking as an actual job. In fact, it was her full-time profession. And she'd been doing well at it, too – until recently, at least.

'Are arranged marriages even *legal* in this country?' one of the teenagers asked her friends loudly as she walked past, sending the rest of the group into fits of laughter.

'Arre, you'll see in a few years when your mother starts to fix you up!' the woman shouted at them as the girls quickly scarpered. 'Honestly, our young people think they are above our cultural traditions,' she said, turning back to Saima. 'But they don't know what's good for them. I myself have learned a fine lesson these last few years. I have been too patient, some would say. But enough is enough.'

Saima knew there was probably a story there, a hook for her to reel in a client who was just waiting to be brought onto her books. But her head was throbbing too severely, she had just been called 'Aunty', and the last thing she wanted to do was pull out her sales pitch. She said nothing, just continued to smile vaguely, hoping that she might make a break for freedom soon.

'Where are you from?' the woman suddenly asked. When the question was asked within the South Asian community, they were either trying to pigeonhole each other by religion, ethnicity, caste, or the hastily drawn boundaries Britain had carved on a map many decades before she was born, or they were trying to figure out if they had family or friends in common.

'Here,' Saima answered wearily, refusing to rise to the bait.

'Yes, my son would say the same. But you both know you're not *really* from here, are you? The goras won't let you forget.'

In the background, the groom's brother had taken hold of the mic and was regaling the audience with a supposedly hilarious tale about how he and the groom had once gone fishing and ended up with a boat operator who reminded them of Quint from *Jaws*. Saima was only half-listening, but she could tell that the anecdote had gone on for far too long, and you probably had to be there to find it funny in the first place.

'Anyway.' The bride chirpily cut her brother-in-law off. 'Let's get this party started!'

The hall began thumping with loud Bollywood beats and the crowd livened back up after the too-long speeches. The woman with the blonde-streaked hair continued to talk, but she was quickly drowned out by the noise. Saima decided this was her chance to make her apologies and leave.

'My son isn't here yet, but I want him to meet you,' the woman said. Saima mimed that she couldn't hear what she was saying.

'My son!' the woman shouted. 'He will be here soon!'

'Too loud,' Saima mouthed back.

'He needs someone to set him straight!' the woman persisted. She waved her arms in the air, as though that would help Saima hear her better. Saima deliberately misunderstood it as a wave.

'Bye, Aunty!' Saima waved back and started to walk away. There seemed no other way to get rid of the woman. As she made her way back to her table, she was aware again of the painful ache pulsing in her temples and feet.

A platoon of waitstaff was now manoeuvring big trays between the tables, expertly placing alternating plates of entrées in front of expectant guests. Saima's stomach growled. She could do with something to eat, and perhaps that would make her headache go away. But seconds away from her table, a familiar face appeared.

'Saima! It's been so long!' Laila exclaimed.

As Laila's hand fell on her shoulder, long-buried memories began to bubble up inside Saima. Before they could overwhelm her, she pulled Laila into a hug.

'Laila Aunty, so nice to see you,' she said. 'And how lovely you look!'

Laila patted the thick bun at the back of her head and shyly looked away. Purple glass bangles dangled down her arms, matching the heavily brocaded sari in the same shade. The colour highlighted her warm skin tone and Saima noticed that she was wearing make-up – something she couldn't remember seeing Laila do before.

'The purple eyeshadow is too much, isn't it?' Laila asked, self-consciously. 'I see you staring at it.'

'No, no, it's perfect! I was just admiring how nice you look.'

'I shouldn't have listened to Zana when she wanted to do my make-up for the evening. Me, who only ever wears vaseline and sorbolene! You remember Zana, don't you? She's got children of her own now. Can you believe I'm a grandmother?'

Saima smiled and nodded. 'That's amazing, Laila Aunty, you must both be so happy.' The last time Saima had seen Zana, she had been a scowling teenager, angry at Saima and her mother for staying in her house. Saima shook the thought away. She wanted to only remember the kindness Laila had offered them in that previous life, not any of the unpleasantness that had gone along with it.

Laila let her fingers trail along the thick gold necklace that gleamed brightly at the base of her throat. 'I am, we are, beti, thank you. And tonight, when Zana said, "Ammy, it's time to focus on you", I let her dress me up like a doll!' She giggled like a teen, and Saima had to laugh with her.

'Well, she's done a beautiful job, Aunty.'

As Laila continued speaking, catching her up on how her kids were now doing, Saima could feel the pulsing in her head becoming stronger. She'd also lost feeling in her toes. All her senses seemed to be heightened. The smells of the food and the heady mixture of perfume and attar combined, and she found herself taking shallow breaths. The noise seemed to pick up, too. The bass from the music vibrated in her stomach, and the chatter – gossiping tongues, laughter from merry lips – seemed to echo loudly in her ears. She felt unsteady on her feet.

'Are you okay, beti?' Laila asked suddenly.

'Yes, of course!' Saima said, even as nausea surged. 'Except, Aunty, I'm so sorry, but I do need to go to the bathroom. Please excuse me!'

'Make sure you tell your ammy I send her my salaams!' Laila called at her retreating back.

Her head down, hurrying towards the seat where she'd left her handbag, Saima barely heard Laila's parting words, but she waved vaguely to acknowledge them. She fished out her phone and noticed the battery was about to die. In her rush to get ready for tonight, she'd forgotten to charge her phone. She quickly scrolled to the Uber app and ordered a car. While the food looked amazing, at this point she just wanted to get home.

'The driver will be there in one minute,' a notification dinged.

Saima pushed the doors of the function room open and immediately appreciated the relative silence of the reception area. The wedding, with all its noise and smells and intensity, was now a buzzing in the background. Out here, a man pushed a cooing baby in a pram, willing it to sleep, and a young couple had thrown all convention out the window to flirt in a corner.

A light breeze from the open door to the street stroked her face. She reached down and pulled off the heels that had been torturing her all night, basking in the instant relief.

The nausea settled a little too, though the throbbing at her temples remained. She hurried towards the entryway and was relieved to find the Uber already waiting outside.

'Your driver will be in a blue sedan,' the app had said, before her phone gave up and carked it.

She ran down the stairs, shoes in one hand, bag in the other, and opened the idling car's back door. She seemed to have startled the driver – he jumped when she got inside and turned to give her a confused look.

'Hi,' she said as she did up her seatbelt and sank into the seat, closing her eyes. 'Just take me home, please.'

The car didn't move. She flung her eyes open to find the driver still staring at her, an unreadable expression on his face.

'I don't mind which route you take, though I usually go via the Eastern Distributor. The roadworks around St Peters are a nightmare right now,' she said firmly.

'O-kay,' he said slowly. 'Home it is. So . . . I'll head towards the Eastern Distributor . . .'

'Yes, please.' She tried not to sound impatient. She was well aware of how hard these drivers had it. Many of them drove Ubers as a second job or were on student visas, and despite the long hours spent behind the wheel, they barely made minimum wage.

After another moment of hesitation, the driver released the handbrake and pulled away from the kerb. She opened the window and closed her eyes again, already feeling a little better.

Chapter 2

The night should not have ended with a strange woman jumping into the back seat of Kal's car. Krista, the woman he until recently had considered his girlfriend, had been texting him all night. At least now he had an excuse to stop replying to her messages. Without thinking too much about it, Kal just started driving through the dark, to a location he hadn't as yet worked out, especially since the stranger in the back had promptly shut her eyes and folded her arms across her chest.

The logical, *normal* thing to do would have been to ask her to get out of the car as soon as she'd gotten in. To have told her straight away that he wasn't the Uber driver she had clearly been expecting. In another context, Kal might even have had some pointed things to say about assuming that all single desi men sitting behind a steering wheel were Uber drivers. But tonight, freshly smarting from the fight with Krista, looking for a reason to avoid the wedding his parents had demanded he attend with them, he didn't automatically do any of those things. Instead, he'd stared at her in surprise as she seemed to settle in for a nap. If she hadn't opened her eyes, he might have sat there staring at her for longer.

Which sounded creepy as hell, now that he thought about it.

In any case, he couldn't quite say what had stopped him from correcting her misunderstanding, or what made him steer the car in the direction of the motorway. The night had not started out great, and now it had gotten weird. And so he found himself just going along with it.

As he drove silently in the direction of the airport, his phone buzzed again. Krista's name impatiently flashed across the screen. He pictured her tapping her foot, irritated.

The more he thought about it, the more he considered bringing out the 'It's not you, it's me' line. Because it *was* him. Or rather, it was his parents.

He hadn't introduced her to them because he knew the first thing they would do was deliberately massacre her name. And Krista would politely correct them and his mother would give her an apologetic smile through narrowed eyes and a clenched jaw. And as soon as they had a private moment, she would refer to her son's partner as 'Kirsty', and he would say, 'It's Krista', and she would say, 'Not only do all these white women look the same, but they also have the same name: Krista, Kirsty, Kirsten, Kristy, Kristina'. And he would shove his hands in his pockets so she couldn't see how tightly he'd clenched them into fists.

He knew all this because it would be far from the first time a meeting between a woman he was dating and his parents had gone exactly this way. And for Krista, he had wanted better.

The woman in the back seat was still silent, her eyes firmly shut, and he wondered if she was actually asleep, or just pretending to be so she wouldn't have to make the smallest of small talk with her driver. Kal reflected that if he *had* been an Uber driver, he'd have preferred his passengers to be quiet, too. Their level of chattiness would probably affect the rating he'd give them. He imagined driving passengers around Sydney on nights like this, when the roads were quiet and there was the static weariness in the air of a city that had shut down for the day.

He wound down his window a little and let the gentle night breeze waft in, the last of the summer humidity giving way to cooler evenings. Yep, he probably *could* do this for a living. Just a man on the road with his thoughts, ferrying Sydneysiders all over the city he loved. It almost sounded romantic.

His phone buzzed again. There were already a dozen unanswered messages from Krista in his notifications. 'Take the hint,' he mumbled under his breath.

'Sorry?' The stranger in the back suddenly spoke. He jumped, having forgotten for a second that she was there.

'Nothing,' he said, and then, after a moment's hesitation, 'Actually, do you mind giving me your address again?'

She looked at him strangely. 'It's in the app.'

'The app's down, there have been some system errors recently.' Kal surprised himself with how easily the lie came out.

She shifted in her seat uncomfortably, and he could almost see the wheels turning in her head as she went over all the usual safety things she hadn't done before getting into his 'Uber'. He should just come clean. Or would that make things worse? He didn't have any explanation for the last twenty minutes, and there was nowhere to pull over on the motorway if she freaked out. *When* she freaked out.

'It's just in Ultimo, on Jones Street. But you can drop me off at Broadway and I'll walk up from there,' she said, eerily calm.

'You sure?'

'Yeah.' Her eyes were wide open now. He looked at her in the rear-view mirror, but she didn't meet his gaze. He supposed she was quietly grasping the handle of the car door, ready to make a run for it.

13

Well, in for a penny, in for pound, I guess. He did what came naturally to him when faced with clients who were a little edgy or unsure. He made small talk.

'How was the wedding? Beautiful night for it.'

'How'd you know it was a wedding?'

A bead of sweat started to trickle down his neck. He pulled the window down a bit further.

What he should say now was, *I was meant to be at the wedding myself, but I was stalling because of a fight with the woman I'm seeing because she wasn't invited. And I couldn't face my parents who were inside, and then* you *got in the back seat of my car.*

'Your outfit,' he said. 'I just assumed.'

She looked down at her clothes and self-consciously let her hand run down the length of the kameez.

'It's not *that* flashy, is it?' She seemed genuinely concerned. 'I didn't want to show up the bride. Not that I ever would, I mean. God, I sound conceited. I thought I was being understated by wearing this.'

'You are!' he blurted. This conversation was turning into quicksand.

'I am?' She was looking back at him now through the rear-view mirror.

The bead of sweat worked its way down his back. He wanted to say that he knew nothing about what women were meant to wear to desi weddings. He generally avoided them like the plague – he was only at tonight's event because his mum had been particularly insistent about it. Women at these weddings all seemed to dress up to the nines, so her outfit didn't look out of place to him. It occurred to Kal that he was much better at making small talk in boardrooms than talking to strange women in his car. He probably wouldn't have made it as an Uber driver after all.

14

'I mean, the outfit looks fine. Not that I've looked. Um. You know what I mean.'

'How long have you been driving for Uber?' she asked, out of nowhere.

'Um, just a few months.'

'But your accent . . . You're from here.'

'So?' Here was an opportunity to claw himself out of the pit of awkwardness. 'Are you saying all Uber drivers are fresh off the boat?'

'I'd never use such a term,' she said indignantly, but he knew he'd got her there.

They fell silent again, the sound of the odd passing car punctuating the quiet while they sped along the Eastern Distributor. Kal had forgotten to turn on the radio, as most Uber and taxi drivers usually did. Though talk radio was something he'd shunned his whole life, he could have plugged in his favourite Spotify playlist and let himself drift in the nostalgia of nineties RnB. But he couldn't do it now. It was the absolute wrong vibe for the current situation.

His phone buzzed. Krista. Again.

'Someone's really trying to get a hold of you, huh?' she commented.

'Yeah, she is.'

'Your girlfriend?'

He didn't respond. Was Krista still his girlfriend? After the last fight, he wasn't sure if they had broken up. Or whether they were even supposed to be together, especially after—

'Sorry, it was rude of me to ask. It's none of my business. I'm just having a strange night.'

'You and me both,' he replied.

'Oh yeah?'

'She's not happy with me. You know how it is. Our culture gets in the way.' He'd revealed far more than he intended. He felt damp patches in his armpits.

'Does it?' She moved forward in her seat and was raising an eyebrow at him in the rear-view mirror.

'Well, it certainly complicates things,' he said, trying to walk back his comment, but not fully retreating.

'Perhaps,' she conceded. 'But then, all relationships are complicated.'

'I don't know, I sometimes feel like if things were meant to work out, they'd be easy.'

'Nothing good in life comes easily.' She sank back into her seat. 'But then, I guess we all have different lives.'

'Why? You think I've had things easy?' He didn't know why her comment riled him up so much.

'No, of course not. I'd never assume . . .' She wound down her window some more, closing her eyes as they stopped at a traffic light. They listened for a moment to the sounds of a group of drunk guys heading along Cleveland Street.

'How many brown guys have you seen bring white girls to desi weddings?' he asked. 'None, I bet. And even if you did, they'd be sat in the far corner, sweating with awkwardness, making polite conversation while trying to ignore the fact that everyone's gossiping about them.'

And it was *that*, and the stupid wedding he was meant to be at tonight, which had started the whole argument with Krista in the first place, he wanted to tell the woman in the back seat. When he'd told Krista that he couldn't meet up tonight because of a prior commitment, she had naturally asked him what the commitment was. After much needling, he'd admitted to her that he was actually going to a wedding – with his parents.

'But shouldn't it be me? Shouldn't I be the plus one going with you?' she'd asked. And he'd changed the subject.

But she hadn't forgotten, and then she'd done something completely unexpected. She had gone and bought herself a sari. In actuality, it was just a really long sarong that she'd paid way too much for. She had wrapped it around her body, letting the end of it fall over one of her shoulders. No blouse. And she'd been so proud of herself when she revealed the outfit to him, but all he had been able do was stare at the gold bindi on her forehead, and wonder how he could tell her that bindis weren't part of Pakistani culture.

He hadn't been able to square the fact that, despite the lack of an invite, she had walked into that new-age store in Newtown that always smelled too strongly of sandalwood, and had bought an overpriced extra-long sarong with an 'Indian print' that no desi would've been seen dead in. He may have known little about what desi women wore to weddings, but even *he* knew that wasn't it. She looked like she'd come off a beach in Bali.

He hadn't said any of this, of course. Thought he was doing the polite thing by keeping his mouth shut. But his silence was what had upset Krista the most. 'You don't even care that I tried!' she'd said. And then she'd said . . .

But he didn't want to think about that right now.

'I'm sorry,' the woman in the back seat said. 'I know it's hard. But if you really like her, don't let the judgey uncles and aunties put you off.'

'Nah, it's not them that put me off. It's the whole damn culture.'

'That's a big leap to make, don't you think?'

'Is it? I was born here. I've been to Pakistan only a few times in my whole life. So why the hell should that place mean anything to me now? Just because my parents insist that it does?'

'Are you embarrassed of your roots, then?'

'Embarrassed?' He shot a quick, disbelieving look over his shoulder. 'I'm not embarrassed. I just don't give a shit about it.'

His face was hot. He avoided catching her gaze again in the mirror.

They spent the last few minutes of the drive in silence. Kal swerved into an empty space on Broadway, near a Japanese noodle shop opposite UTS. A few students sat on the plastic chairs outside, slurping down late-night snacks.

'Well, thank you for an interesting conversation,' she said as she gathered her bag and opened the car door. 'The one good thing about our talk was that it helped rid me of my headache.'

The one good thing. The words stung him, even though he was unlikely to ever see this woman again.

She got out of the car, but just as she was about to close the door, she ducked her head to meet his eye.

'You know, you can hate your culture all you want, but you can never get rid of it. Just like you can't wash the brown off your skin, as much as you may want to. Oh, and you can forget about your five-star review.'

And with that, she slammed the door shut.

He pulled out from the kerb and hit the accelerator, his wheels screeching slightly as he sped away into the night.

He was moments from calling Krista back when a sparkle caught his eye.

There, on the back seat, was a pair of glittering high-heeled shoes the stranger had left behind.

Chapter 3

The woman incessantly laughing on her phone was the last straw. Saima got up and moved from the top deck of the train carriage to the bottom one. Her mind was churning. The day after the wedding, the whole Sunday, she had reminded herself over and over that she was a savvy woman who had looked after herself for actual decades.

She'd read any number of stories about Uber drivers who had kidnapped and assaulted their passengers. These were awful, frightening scenarios. But something much worse could have happened to her on Saturday night – for, as she discovered when she finally reached her apartment, the man who got her home hadn't even *been* an Uber driver. He'd just been some guy whose car she had stupidly gotten into without checking that his numberplate matched the one on the app.

She had plugged in her dead phone to charge, so she could give the driver his deservedly low rating after their strange, tense conversation. But before she could, she saw the actual Uber driver had already left her zero stars for being a no-show. He'd apparently waited almost fifteen minutes and sent her a few messages before driving off. Her heart started to race and she went into a small panic as she realised that a complete stranger – for god knows what reason – had just given her a lift home. Literally anything could have happened.

When things got overwhelming, Saima's default was to disengage. She'd done this on Saturday night, calmly removing her make-up, changing into her freshly washed pyjamas, brushing her teeth for a full two minutes and getting into bed without once thinking about her contact with a probable psychopath. Any errant, panic-inducing thoughts that broke into her mind, she pushed into her Too-Hard Basket and firmly closed the lid, and eventually, she managed to fall asleep.

All of Sunday, too, Saima had busied herself, swatting away any thoughts of the man she had inadvertently carjacked. And then, she remembered her shoes.

He still had her shoes.

She hadn't even missed them when she'd angrily walked barefoot all the way from Broadway to Ultimo.

What would he do with her shoes? *Hopefully he'll throw them away*, she thought. *Otherwise, I got driven home by a shoe-stealing weirdo.* And somehow, that would make everything just that little bit worse.

'The next stop will be Parramatta.' The automated announcement interrupted her thoughts. Saima whirled into action. As she moved towards the train door, she firmly put all thoughts of the not-Uber driver into the corner of her mind, where all the other disturbing thoughts lived, hoping never to be brought up again.

The bustle of Parramatta hit Saima like a wave as soon as she stepped out of the station. The sea of humanity had become part of the soundtrack to her daily commute. Schoolgirls giggled as they sipped bubble tea, businesspeople in tailored suits spoke briskly on their phones as they rushed to meetings, parents lazily pushed prams on their way to story time at the library. The faces were much like her own, speaking languages she understood – English, Urdu, Hindi – and plenty more she didn't, but which still sounded familiar. These were her people, this was the area where she had grown up.

It was this sense of familiarity that had made her turn and run into the comforting arms of the inner city where nobody knew who she was. There, everyone was equally anonymous, and no-one looked you in the eye to judge you, because you were just another obstacle on their way to somewhere else. She'd made Ultimo her home when, a few years ago, a friend had moved out of a small studio apartment inside a refurbished wool factory and asked if Saima wanted to take over her lease. The rent was definitely on the steep side for a studio, but Saima's matchmaking business was just taking off; she was flush with success and tired of living with her mother, so there was no other answer but yes. The commute to Parramatta, in the heart of her clientele's community, was an easy express train from Central Station.

'Where's your head at, girlie?' a voice shouted behind her.

Saima jumped. 'Oh my god!' She picked up the pace to get away from whoever was screaming at her. She looked over her shoulder to see Jess bent over, giggling.

Jess eventually straightened and ran the few paces to catch up with her.

'I'm sorry, but that was just too funny. Your face! But seriously, are you okay? And if you're not, will coffee help?' Jess didn't wait for an answer. She grabbed Saima by the arm and pulled her the short distance to their regular café, tucked in a laneway behind one of the fancy new high-rise office buildings behind the station.

As Jess sipped her flat white and Saima her long black, they walked to the co-working space they shared and talked about their weekend.

'I can hear myself becoming a nag and I hate it,' Jess said. 'Rob's a grown man. He should be able to pick up after himself. And yet there I am most of the weekend, telling him to throw his dirty laundry into the basket. If I wanted to pick up after a coddled man-child, I'd have kept sharing a house with my brother.' It was one of Jess's favourite topics: her boyfriend Rob, whose messy habits drove her up the wall but whom she completely adored. 'But *then* he'll come back from his run with a pastry and a coffee for me and not say anything, just give me a kiss and hand them over. How can he be the sweetest and also drive me crazy?'

Saima smiled and quietly sipped her coffee. She had learned a while back that all Jess needed was for someone to listen, not give advice.

'And you? What did you get up to?' Jess asked.

'Nothing much, just another wedding.'

'Oh yeah, just *another* evening of getting glammed up, eating incredible food and dancing the night away,' Jess said, rolling her eyes comically. 'Weddings are meant to be exciting, my friend, but you make them sound boring. No offence.'

'You should never say "No offence" in any sentence, ever,' Saima returned. 'It's like starting a sentence with "I'm not racist, but ..." It's a hundred per cent going to cause offence if you say "No offence".'

'Geez, Saima. What happened at that wedding? You seem off.' Jess held up her hands quickly as Saima shot her a look. 'Sorry, just calling it like I see it.'

They walked in silence for a minute before Saima spoke.

'No, I'm sorry. I'm just ... preoccupied, I guess.'

22

'You sure you're okay?' Jess asked, and Saima was filled with warmth for her friend.

'Nothing some sweet treats can't fix. I brought some ladoo for afternoon tea,' she told Jess.

'Ah, love me some ladoo.'

'But it's really gulab jamun you've got a soft spot for, right?'

'Yes, but honestly don't bring me more gulab jamun, or I will end up looking like one.'

'Girl, your spray tan is lovely, but you're not brown or sweet or shiny enough to be a gulab jamun.' They laughed.

For Saima, the best thing about where she worked was that Jess shared the space. They worked in adjacent rooms, each of them operating their own small business, along with one other tenant. Jess worked as a virtual assistant for various companies, and the other tenant, Dave, ran a quiz and puzzle website. The co-working space was inside a small renovated cottage. The landlord had converted the bedrooms into office spaces and they shared the kitchen, bathroom and tiny reception area. The cottage sat on a busy road, nestled between a South Indian restaurant on one side and gleaming towers filled with state government offices on the other, just one block away from the banks of Parramatta River. When it was a nice day and she'd had enough of dealing with clients, Saima could walk down to the river and unwind. On days like today, when it was warm and sunny, the big windows of the cottage made it seem more spacious than it actually was. For Saima, having her own enclosed office rather than a communal open-plan workspace was especially important when seeing clients.

As they approached the front door of the cottage, Jess scrunched up her nose.

'I don't know why we continue to work here,' she said as they entered. 'The place is falling apart.' The floorboards managed to be especially creaky under each step she took, and she stopped and bounced emphatically on one spot.

'They're only this creaky today to prove your point!' Saima said, laughing.

'I guess it's why the rent's so cheap,' Jess admitted.

Saima bit her lip. 'It could be cheaper.'

'What are you talking about? I mean, have you *been* to the new co-working spaces that have opened up over near Westfield? Or in the city?' Jess continued. 'They have espresso machines, ergonomic chairs, meeting rooms and some seriously hot guys.'

As if on cue, Dave padded by, wearing a particularly woolly beige jumper with a seventies argyle pattern across the front. He waved politely at them as he made his way into the kitchen.

'Why is he even wearing a jumper? It's so warm!' Jess whispered.

'Thought you said you wanted a hot guy around,' Saima quipped. 'Anyway, you've got Rob. What do you need hot guys for?'

'Everyone needs some eye candy to help them get through the working week. Even you've got to admit that!'

'I hadn't really thought about it.' Saima had other problems to think of – like making this month's office rent. She wanted to tell Jess that her finances were starting to spiral out of control and she was facing the prospect of all her hard work coming undone; that her client list was getting smaller, and her wedding invites drying up. But even thinking about it made her feel sick, let alone the prospect of talking about it. So into the Too-Hard Basket it went.

'Oh, Saima?' Dave called out as he ambled back towards his office with a steaming mug in his hand. 'You've got a couple waiting for you.'

'Are you sure?' Saima asked. 'I wasn't expecting anyone.'

Dave shrugged, blew into the top of his mug and took a sip as he kept walking.

'Bet that's Horlicks in there,' Jess said, with a shudder.

Saima let out a sigh and waved to Jess as she marched off.

She recognised the blonde highlights immediately. There, seated in one of the plastic Ikea bucket chairs in her small office, was the aunty who had accosted her at the wedding on Saturday. Today she was accompanied by a man Saima assumed was her husband. The two of them turned towards her when she entered, their eyes appraising her as she moved towards her desk.

'Hello,' Saima said, smoothing down the front of her kurta.

The couple were both impeccably dressed. Uncle wore a crisp navy shirt and his trousers sat snugly on surprisingly slim hips that showed no sign of the telltale middle-aged paunch most uncles acquired post-forty. Aunty looked like she'd had a fresh blow-out at the hairdresser that morning. Her make-up was understated; she appeared fresh, as if she'd just had a facial, and the diamonds at her ears, fingers and throat caught the sunlight and glinted back at Saima.

Uncle, when he spoke, had a vaguely British accent. 'Saima, am I correct? We got your details from . . .' He turned to his wife.

'Oh, I can't remember her name. It doesn't matter,' she responded.

'In any case, we hear you're very good at what you do,' he continued.

'Oh, thanks—' Saima began, sitting behind her desk.

'We are Mr and Mrs Ali,' he interrupted. 'I don't know if you've heard of us or our family, or if that sort of thing is important to you. I run the Liminal Group. For the most part, we are in the business of producing cooking oil, but we have a few other business interests, such as investing in commercial property. We have offices all over the world, but our headquarters are here in Australia—'

'Yes, though really the company started in Pakistan,' Mrs Ali added. 'That's where our heart lies.'

25

'Well, I don't think *that* needed mentioning,' Mr Ali said to his wife.

'Okay, but it's good for her to know our roots, no? Anyway, you were giving her all this talk about headquarters and such.' Mrs Ali sniffed at her husband before turning back to Saima. 'His great-grandfather began a shipping company in Karachi and then his grandfather expanded the business into cooking oil—'

'And the rest is history,' Mr Ali finished, a little impatiently. 'Look, all you need to know is that we are doing well and that the company is a tightly held, well-established family business.'

'O-kay . . .' Saima said, mystified. She didn't know what they expected from her.

'We are only telling you this because it is important to us that our son is properly settled. He's our youngest, and our only son. His elder sister is married and living in London,' Mrs Ali said.

The two of them stopped talking and stared at her in silence. Saima was caught off guard.

'. . . So you want him to take over the business at some point?' she asked after a moment.

Mr and Mrs Ali looked at each other and broke into howls of laughter.

'Oh, no,' Mr Ali said.

'No, no,' Mrs Ali added, reaching into her Louis Vuitton bag and pulling out a handkerchief to wipe away her tears.

'Can you imagine?' Mr Ali asked his wife.

She shook her head as she dabbed at her eyes.

'The boy is, how shall we put it, a bit bewaqoof,' Mr Ali said.

'Oh, he's not a bad sort,' Mrs Ali hastened to add. 'But no, he's not the type to run a big company. His sister, though, she might one day do that.'

'Maybe,' Mr Ali said thoughtfully, nodding and turning suddenly serious.

Saima gazed at them silently, still unsure how she was meant to respond. Then Mr Ali sent his wife a look that Saima didn't have any trouble interpreting. He was questioning his wife's judgement for approaching Saima today, and Saima for some reason was finding herself caught on the back foot.

What was wrong with her? She wanted to grab a drink of water and start all over again, but that didn't seem possible, so she took a deep breath and remembered her sales pitch. Here were some clients waiting to pay her; all she had to do was reel them in and close the deal.

'Okay, Uncle, Aunty. You're here because you want to see your son properly settled with a good partner. I can certainly help you with that.'

Mrs Ali reached inside her bag again, pulling out a sheet of paper with a photograph stapled to it. 'His biodata,' she said. 'I've made it a bit more modern, kind of like a dating profile they make in the apps, yes? But it has all the usual information in there as well, height, weight, education—'

'Dating profile in apps?' Mr Ali interrupted her. 'How do you know about that?'

'I googled it. What, you think I'm going around making profiles for myself? Darling, I don't need the apps to get men if I want any.' Mrs Ali let out a tinkling laugh and looked at Saima with smiling eyes as she handed over the biodata.

Saima took it but didn't glance at it.

'Thank you for this, Mrs Ali, and it's great you made this biodata,' she said. 'But I must tell you that I usually make one of my own for my clients after having a proper interview with them. I know that's not the usual way, but it's how I manage my business.'

'Oh, call me Ruby!' Mrs Ali exclaimed. 'And this is George. Unfortunately, it won't be possible for you to interview our son.'

'I beg your pardon?'

'Yes, this is why we came to you especially,' George said. 'We want you to, uh. Well. How do I put this? We want you to *approach* him.'

'That's right,' Ruby said, taking charge of the conversation. 'He would never agree to it otherwise, and I know it's not how you usually operate, or how most matchmakers would work, but that's why we came to you. You of all people we thought would be open to matchmaking in an unconventional way.'

'Oh? Why do you say that?' Saima asked.

'Well, look at you! You certainly don't look like other match-makers. You are not too old, you still have some of your beauty.'

'Thank you,' Saima said dryly, but Ruby did not catch her irony.

'We also know how hard it has been for you and your mother,' she continued.

'My mother?' Saima felt her heart rate picking up.

'Yes, well, we had to do our research before we came to you with such a request, especially when it came to our son. We wanted to know that we could trust the person we were asking to do such an important job.'

'And what exactly did you hear about me?' Saima asked. She could feel her back getting sweaty now. *This is why I moved away from this area*, she thought. *Everyone is always in everyone else's business.*

'Oh, it doesn't matter what was said.' Ruby dismissed the question with a wave. 'But we know how hard it must have been for you and your mother to strike out on your own. And for you to take the unusual step to become a matchmaker – of all things! – without getting married yourself.' Ruby's tone suggested that she was a little put out and unaccustomed to explaining herself. 'But

28

it now makes sense to me why you yourself decided to not have a relationship.'

'And why is that?' Saima asked, her voice wavering only a little.

'Why, so you could focus on finding matches for your clients, instead of being distracted by your own marriage. Isn't that so?' Ruby tilted her head innocently.

George shifted impatiently in his seat. The Ikea chairs were clearly not what he was used to. 'So, what we are asking, Saima, is that you casually approach our son, maybe bump into him somewhere, and then – well, I can see you're a smart woman, you can work out how to talk him into signing up for your services as a matchmaker.' He sat back in the chair, satisfied that all had been properly explained.

Ruby clearly thought otherwise, leaning forward conspiratorially. 'You see, Kal has spent *years* with these, these – well, to put it politely, *time-wasters*,' she said. 'As you can tell from his photograph, he's a handsome boy. He finds it easy to attract women.'

Saima's eyes at last fell to the biodata now sitting on her desk.

And then she saw him.

She picked up the paper from her desk and stared at his picture, her heart turning a somersault in her chest.

His face. Those eyes. She had flashbacks of them looking at her through the rear-view mirror on Saturday night. Her hands trembled.

Khalid Ali, she read. *Son of Rubaiyah (Ruby) and Ghulam (George) Ali. Age: 30. Height: 6 foot. Complexion: Fair. Profession: Management Consultant.*

Very much *not* an Uber driver.

'You know him?' Ruby asked, registering the expression on Saima's face and edging further forward in her seat.

Saima shook her head.

'He was meant to be at the Shah wedding on Saturday,' Ruby explained, moving back in her chair again. 'I thought maybe you might have seen him there . . . but then he didn't turn up.'

'Even though he texted me at one point, saying he was outside and just looking for a parking spot,' George grumbled.

'Well, what did you expect?' Ruby said. 'You know how he feels about weddings.'

'How does he feel about weddings?' Saima asked, finally looking up from the biodata.

'He hates them, of course,' George said. 'No doubt in no small part because his mother is always trying to fix him up with any girl she meets.' He raised an eyebrow at his wife, who waved him off impatiently.

'Not *any* girl.' Ruby began counting off on her beringed fingers. 'She has to come from a good family, be young – twenty-eight years old at most, twenty-five would be perfect – and be fair-skinned, have a nice figure. Slim, but not too slim, tall, but not too tall, good upbringing, good job, but nothing to distract from family life, obviously will want children . . .' She was running out of fingers. 'Maybe you should be writing this down?' she said pointedly to Saima.

Saima wasn't really listening. Her eyes kept dropping to the photograph stapled to the biodata, the unsmiling-yet-still-friendly face looking back at her. It looked like a corporate head shot, a LinkedIn profile pic. On one hand, she was relieved. He probably hadn't intended to kidnap her – she'd jumped into his car, and, rather than explaining the error like any rational person would've done, he had driven off, probably to avoid going into the wedding lion's den where his mother waited with a parade of single girls. She couldn't blame him for wanting to run away from that. On the other hand, she wished that he had acted sensibly, because it would have saved her a lot of panic in hindsight. Easier perhaps for him in the moment to start driving and hope that the evening would sort itself out, but things just as easily could have gone from bad to worse, particularly if she'd worked out her error before he dropped her off.

'What we propose,' George now said, calling Saima's attention back to the couple seated in front of her, 'is that you bump into Kal, casually, nothing suspicious, and convince him to sign up and meet at least a few of the girls you have on your list. Ultimately, you see, we want him to settle with a nice Pakistani. Or maybe even an Indian bride.'

'We are quite open-minded like that,' Ruby said, smiling. 'But we're both Muslim, so we want her to be Muslim too, of course.'

'But we don't want a hijabi or anything,' George added quickly. 'We're not exactly what you'd call practising. It's a cultural thing, you understand.'

Saima tensed at the familiar hypocrisy of certain Pakistani families who would one minute scream blue murder at the thought of their child with a Hindu or Sikh partner on the basis of religion, then cheerfully organise an open bar at the wedding that an Imam had nevertheless been called upon to officiate.

'Most importantly,' Ruby said, 'she needs to have good values and come from a good, established family.'

'Yes, we don't want a gold-digger,' George said bluntly. 'We want a respectful girl who is educated, smart.'

Saima's stomach turned. She wanted to tell them that their son already had a girlfriend. A white girl, a gori. He had mentioned that he felt uncomfortable bringing her to desi events, and Saima honestly could sympathise if this was how his parents thought about his future partner. But there was no way to say any of this to the Alis.

She quickly got up, startling them both. 'I'll be back in just a minute,' she said, and dashed out of her office before they could reply.

'Ladki theek hai?' she heard George mutter dubiously to his wife behind her.

Saima escaped to the kitchen. Jess wandered in a few minutes later to find her there, standing with her eyes closed, breathing deeply.

'What's going on?' she whispered. Saima nearly leaped out of her skin and barely stopped herself from yelping in fright. 'Whoa! What's happening?' exclaimed Jess.

'I don't know!' Saima hissed back. 'Everything's been so strange since the weekend. Maybe even before that. I haven't been feeling myself . . .'

'Is it your period?' Jess asked.

Saima rolled her eyes. 'Are we teenagers now?'

'I know I feel off sometimes when I have mine.' Jess sniffed. 'Is it your mum?'

'No, she's fine.'

'Is it work?'

'No. Yes. Maybe . . .' Saima bit the bullet and admitted, 'I don't think I can afford the office rent anymore.'

'Oh shit! Why didn't you tell me? I could give you a loan.' Jess looked concerned.

'No! No way! I love you, but friendship and business don't mix. Anyway, I don't know if it's that. You know I got called Aunty at the wedding? I'm Aunty-old now. And then I saw this aunty, Laila . . . We knew her well when I was a kid, she was an old family friend.'

'O-kay,' Jess said slowly, trying to follow.

'And then I got talking to this guy . . .'

'Okay, so now we're getting to the real deal. It's a guy. *Of course* it's a guy. Money problems – hey, you've worked through those before. But men problems? You need to call in the experts.'

Saima huffed. 'I *am* the expert. I'm a matchmaker, in case you've forgotten.'

'A matchmaker who's never actually been in a proper relationship herself,' Jess pointed out.

'Why is everyone harping on about this all of a sudden?' Saima asked wearily.

'I'm just saying, you're basically Drew Barrymore in *Never Been Kissed.*'

'Oh, please! I'm going to be Drew Barrymore in *Charlie's Angels* if you keep this up.'

Jess snickered. 'Also had no luck with guys. I'm sensing a theme.'

'*Anyway*, it's the money problems I should see someone about. I might not even be able to make rent on my apartment this month. What if I have to move back in with my mum?' Saima struggled not to shudder at the thought.

'Chill, girl. Chill. Aren't those clients waiting in your office? Surely they're a quick solution to your money problems?'

'Well, that's the thing, what they want me to do is . . . ridiculous.'

'What do they want you to do?'

'They want me to set their son up with a woman.'

Jess stared at her. 'Um. Isn't that what you do?'

'No, this one's different.' Saima started rubbing her temples.

'Is it the kind of woman they're after, then? Like a jewel thief or something?'

'That would probably make things easier. They want a normal desi woman—'

'Riiiight . . .'

'—but they don't want me to tell him that they're setting him up. I need to bump into him on the street or something and convince him to become one of my clients.' Saima stopped rubbing her head and was now squeezing her eyes shut. The thought of doing such a thing was beyond her.

'Wait, *really*?'

'Yes! And it gets weirder. Their son – he's the guy I met on the weekend.' Opening her eyes, Saima looked back at Jess with concern.

Jess lit up at the news. 'Ooh, I like this! This just took a turn from weird to properly interesting! So you'd like him for yourself, then?'

Saima sighed. 'Okay, not *everything* is about me being desperately single, Jess. Look, he mentioned he already has a girlfriend.'

'Seriously, Saima, I don't see what the problem is. If you're not keen on him yourself—'

'I'm *not*.'

'Hmm, sure – *if* you're not keen on him yourself, why does it matter if you bring him onto your books?'

'It's dishonest, for one thing,' Saima said.

'Yeah, okay, a *tiny* little bit. But you're not forcing him to do anything, you're not tricking him into marrying some rando. You're just fudging over the details of how you came to find him, right?'

Saima tried to put her unease into words. 'Maybe it's everything put together that's freaking me out. The business isn't doing so well recently, and now there's this couple who want me to trick their son . . . It's not who I am, Jess. It's not who I want to be, and I think I'm having some sort of panic attack . . .'

'Look, I get it,' Jess said sympathetically. 'You're all about honesty with your clients, I know that's super important to you.'

'And isn't it so bizarre that the same guy I met on the weekend is the one they want me to fix up?'

'Is it *that* strange, really? Your business is marriages, and you were at a client's wedding. It's not outside the realm of possibility that you'd cross paths with future clients at these events – you've done it heaps of times before.' Jess shrugged. 'Anyway, sometimes the universe is mysterious, and sometimes it's just one big coincidence. Now, put on your big-girl pants, get back in there, take the job, and charge them through the roof to do it. These seem like desperate people – desperate, *rich* people. Both your problems will be solved.'

The floorboards in the corridor creaked as Ruby poked her head into the kitchen.

'There you are!' she said. 'I wondered where you had gone.'

Jess smiled politely at Ruby, gave Saima's shoulder a squeeze and walked out of the kitchen.

'We have somewhere else to be, so I thought I would see if you were interested in our proposal,' Ruby said when they were alone.

'Ruby . . .' Saima's mind raced for an appropriate response. What did it mean to take on this strange job, and how much should she charge to do it?

'Beti,' Ruby said, with unexpected kindness. 'I know it mustn't have been easy growing up the way you did. This is why I'm so keen to help you now.'

Her kindness made Saima want to tell Ruby to keep both her money and her help. *Keep your head held high*, her mother had said to her time and time again. When they'd had little else, they'd still had their pride. But was her pride now getting in the way of her success? She considered this for a moment before taking a deep breath.

'Okay, Ruby,' she said. 'Let's talk.'

Saima watched from the front door as George and Ruby got into their sleek black car parked outside. She had quoted triple the cost of her usual services, added a day rate and expenses on top, and neither George nor Ruby had flinched once before signing the paperwork.

Perhaps I've been underselling myself, she thought. Either way, the landlord was sorted for the next little while.

As her new clients pulled away from the kerb, Saima turned to find a beaming Jess standing in her doorway.

'That's my girl! Next coffee's on you.'

Chapter 4

On Sunday morning, Kal's phone woke him at 7 am. He hit snooze and slept till the alarm rang again at 7.30. He hit the snooze button again and again. Each time, he fell straight into a dream where he was stuck at a train station, unable to get to the right platform to catch his train.

Eventually, some time after 9 am, he dragged himself up. He felt hungover, for some reason, even though all he'd drunk the night before was a Diet Coke while glaring at a pair of shoes that glittered accusingly at him by the front door where he'd dropped them. The sight of the heels beside his own shoes had made something inside him shift strangely. He'd blamed it on indigestion from downing the fizzy drink so quickly, shrugged and gone to bed.

He picked up his phone now and texted Tom.

Hey. Wanna do brunch?

Tom still hadn't responded twenty minutes later when Kal got out of the shower. *Probably still sleeping off a big night,* Kal figured. He thought about sending a text to Lachie, but since Lachie and his girlfriend Nicole had moved in together, they usually preferred to do couple things on Sundays, and he wasn't in the mood to third-wheel.

He scrolled through his contacts, past the one name he was trying to avoid.

Krista.

Her name was like a siren call, tugging at him, urging him to open her dozens of unread messages and fall down the inevitable rabbit hole. Krista would be the easiest option. He could call her, apologise for the argument – which she'd probably accept – and then they would ignore the elephant in the room and continue with the relationship that, until yesterday, had him honestly thinking that she might be the closest he'd get to The One.

Maybe he was wrong to feel so strung out and disappointed in Krista. One part of him reasoned that it had only been six months since they'd begun dating in earnest.

Six months is your longest relationship to date, another part of him pointed out.

Surely an actual relationship shouldn't be so fragile as to blow up after one argument, though? It should be stronger than that. Should he be fighting for a relationship only six months in? Then again, *shouldn't* he be fighting for a woman he had started thinking about settling down with?

Before he could go any further, he stopped himself in his tracks, typed out a quick text to Lachie and hit send.

Half an hour later, he was sitting at the café that was conveniently located right next door to Lachie and Nicole's place, figuring he may as well go to them rather than do the back and forth of trying to work out where to meet. He had tried in the past to persuade them to come over the bridge to one of his local spots, but he didn't have the energy to have that argument again today.

As Kal ordered the big breakfast board, Lachie opted for chia pudding and Nicole for buckwheat porridge – which, when it arrived, looked like sludge.

'That does not look appetising,' Kal commented. *Probably why the place is deserted,* he thought to himself.

'Don't let looks fool you. Porridge done right is absolutely delicious,' Nicole said, but as soon as she took a spoonful of the porridge, she pulled a face of deep regret. 'Um. This might not be done right.'

'I don't mind sharing,' Kal offered. 'This breakfast board is probably too big for just one person.' He was glad he had gone with his choice. Couldn't go too wrong with eggs and fried potato gems and sausages.

Nicole smiled, slightly screwing up her nose, and shook her head, soldiering through a couple more bites of her porridge.

'Okay, I'll just put these potato gems in this corner, and if they fall onto your plate, so be it,' Kal said, feigning innocence.

Lachie was meanwhile working on his chia pudding with a look of dogged determination.

'Lachie?' Kal said. 'Potato gem?'

Lachie mournfully shook his head.

'Not sure if Lachie told you, but he's trying to lose weight,' Nicole explained helpfully.

Kal tried not to laugh, but he choked on a bite of toast.

'It's not that funny,' Lachie mumbled.

'Kal, can you please tell Lachie that he doesn't need to lose weight?' Nicole said, starting on the potato gems. 'He doesn't listen to me!'

'You know you don't need to lose weight, right?' Kal said. 'And I'm not just saying that because Nicole asked me to.'

'My abs are gone!' Lachie moaned. 'Where there was once a six-pack, now there's just one keg!'

'When did you have a six-pack?' Kal asked. Lachie flipped him the bird.

'Anyway, I told you I like my men soft and cuddly!' Nicole said with a smile.

'I'm not a teddy bear!' Lachie said indignantly. 'And I'm not ready for a dadbod! Not till I'm a dad, at least.'

'Whoa. You guys are talking about having kids?' Kal blurted. As soon as he spoke, he realised that it made perfect sense that once they moved in together, they'd start all the steps most couples naturally progressed through – joint accounts, marriage, kids, mortgages, wills. Kal shuddered involuntarily at the thought. How could his friends be thinking about creating a new life together while he felt like he hadn't even properly started his own?

'Well, we aren't having kids just yet,' Nicole said, though she couldn't quite meet his eyes. 'We just moved in together.'

'You're blushing,' Kal pointed out.

'That's just Asian flush, don't be rude,' she said smiling.

'Uh-huh,' Kal said. 'But you're not even drinking.'

She picked up a potato gem and threw it at him, laughing. It landed on the table.

'Don't waste these, they're the only thing worth eating here,' Kal said, popping it in his mouth.

Lachie stared into his chia pudding, pushing his spoon around, but Kal could see he too was looking flushed. 'Anyway, not ready for a dadbod,' he muttered.

'Fair enough,' Kal said, not pushing further. 'There's got to be easier ways to stave off that nightmare than eating glue for breakfast, though.'

'And you?' Nicole changed the subject as she ate another potato gem. 'What's going on with you?'

'You mean on the girl front?' Kal asked.

'Not necessarily. But Krista did call last night to say that you'd had a big fight.' She looked frankly at him. 'You want to talk about it?'

He sighed. 'I don't know. Me and Krista, that's a whole other matter. I think we might be done.'

'You think? You don't know?'

'It's been twenty-four hours,' he said dryly. 'Give me a minute. But I've also been wondering lately if maybe turning thirty is messing with my head.'

'Ah, come on. You're so focused and ambitious,' Nicole said. 'Everyone's entitled to an off day or two.'

'Yeah,' Lachie chimed in. 'Out of all of us, you always seem to know what you're doing.'

'Hah! Looks can be deceiving. I'm winging it like everyone else.'

'Bull.' Lachie gave up on his chia pudding and grabbed a thick slice of wholemeal toast from Kal's breakfast board. 'You're killing it at work, you're in a great apartment, you've got your pick of the ladies.'

'Okay, that's hardly the case,' Kal protested. 'I do all right, but I'm not Tom.'

'So what's the problem?' Nicole asked.

'I honestly don't know. It just feels like – well, we're all hitting our thirties now, right?'

'Unfortunately,' she replied with a grin.

'It's like the peak time for engagements, weddings and' – he raised an eyebrow at her – 'baby announcements.' Nicole rolled her eyes good-naturedly and gestured to him to continue. 'And meanwhile, I feel like I spend my time wondering how to progress on *Red Dead*.'

'What was that you said to me at your thirtieth? "All work and no play makes Kal a dull boy"?' Lachie asked as he swiped one of the sausages. 'Sounds like a bit of *Red Dead* wouldn't do you any harm.'

Kal pushed the breakfast board into the middle of the table and Lachie fell on it like a man starved.

'It's good that you're not at work as much. You just need to expand your horizons,' Lachie said, focused on the food.

'And how do I do that?' Kal said. 'I mean, I'm either at the gym, or I'm at home playing video games. That's if I'm not scrolling on my phone. There's got to be more to life than this.'

'Okay, first of all,' Nicole said patiently. 'This isn't a "you" thing, Kal.'

'Huh?'

'I should say, it's not a uniquely "you" problem. It's totally normal to have one of those "what am I doing here" crises when you hit a milestone like your thirties.'

'Did *you*?'

'Probably. Why d'you think we moved in together?' she said as she gently nudged Lachie.

'Well, if a turning-thirty crisis is what it took . . .' Lachie said, kissing her on the cheek.

'Anyway, it's like Lachie said,' Nicole continued. 'You just need to shake things up. You're in a rut, so do something different.'

Kal looked over to where Lachie was cutting a path through the grilled mushrooms. 'Just like you guys are?'

'Well, we've been together for ages,' Nicole said. 'Since—'

'—'leven years,' Lachie supplied around a mouthful.

'Yep, since uni,' Nicole continued. 'And we are shaking things up. We're renovating the bathroom!'

The three of them laughed.

'So how do *I* shake things up? Any hints? Apart from home renovations?' Kal asked.

Lachie shrugged. 'Find someone to settle down with?'

'You sound like my mum.'

'Well, your mum's right.'

'And if not with Krista,' said Nicole, with a wry smile, 'then maybe with someone else. Or maybe give dating a break altogether. Maybe you need space to clear your head and decide what you *really* want. Either way, you need to let Krista down gently, and soon,' she added. 'I've told her I don't want to hear too much about what's going on with the two of you. I feel stuck in the middle of whatever is happening because I met her through you.'

'Sorry about that. I tried not to mention her today,' Kal said.

'The fact that you didn't, when you apparently had a massive fight,' Lachie observed, 'should tell you something.'

Kal thought about what Lachie said and it told him all he needed to know.

Kal rang Krista on the way home.

'Finally!' she said by way of an answer. 'I've been trying to get hold of you for *ages*.'

'Yeah, I saw the missed calls and messages.'

'Well, why the hell didn't you call me back?'

Kal sighed. 'I needed some time to think. Listen, Krista, I think we need to talk.'

'Don't you dare,' she hissed. 'Don't you dare give me a "we need to talk" after what you said yesterday.'

'What *I* said?'

'That I wouldn't be welcome at that fucking wedding.'

'I just said it'd probably be best if you didn't go.'

'But *why?*'

He sighed again. 'Look, I don't want to rehash all of this. I'm sorry you were so upset yesterday, and I'm sorry I didn't appreciate your efforts properly. And I'm sorry my parents are . . . well, they're my parents.'

43

'Thank you,' she said, sounding slightly appeased.

'And you know you're great, right?'

'Yeah . . .' She was sounding wary now.

'But I don't think this is going anywhere.'

'*What?*'

'I'm sorry,' he repeated. 'Really.'

'Where is *this* coming from?'

'I've thought a lot about it and I don't think we're a good fit for each other. The fight yesterday just made that obvious.'

'Are you doing this because of your parents?'

'I—yes, because of my parents.' *And the gossip and the culture and when you said—* He cut off that train of thought. 'But it's not just because of them. Let's just say it's not going to work out.'

'Babe,' she said in a soothing tone, 'we can work through this. I'll meet your parents and they'll love me and you'll wonder why you ever thought it was going to be a problem.'

'That's the thing, though, Krista. That's not how it will go. Trust me. And whether we break up now or six more months down the track, it'll still end the same, and every time this fight happens – and it'll happen again, I promise you – things will be just that little bit worse. Better that we call it a day now.'

'Can we at least talk about this face to face?' she said, sounding more annoyed than anything else. 'Do you want to come over?'

Kal thought about it. He could go over there and try to rationalise what he'd been thinking about all day, but he knew they'd likely just end up in bed and he'd have sent exactly the wrong signals. One thing that was never a problem between him and Krista was their sexual chemistry. 'I don't think that'll help, sorry.'

'So that's it?'

'Sorry.'

'This is bullshit, Kal.'

44

'I know. But I think it's the right thing to do.'

'We're going to talk about this whether you want to or not,' she said. 'I deserve the right to say what I need to say.'

'We can do that right now—' he said, but Krista had already hung up.

Later that day, as Kal sat playing Xbox, Tom finally returned his call.

'What time do you call this?' Kal asked, setting the controller on the coffee table.

'Sorry,' Tom said, sounding groggy. 'Late night. Only just got up. Thought you'd come out after that wedding your parents were making you go to?'

'I didn't end up going to that,' Kal said. Onscreen, a Wild West gun battle was under way, frozen mid-scene.

'Then why didn't you come out?' Tom asked. Kal heard a toilet flush in the background.

'I met a girl.' The words popped out before he could stop them.

'Whoa, what about Krista?'

'We just broke up.'

'What? Are you sure?' Tom yawned loudly into his phone. 'Sorry. Still waking up.'

'Anyway, it doesn't matter,' said Kal. 'That girl – I won't see her again. And Krista . . . yeah, look, I don't really want to talk about it.'

Tom let out another yawn. 'Complicated.'

'Yeah.'

'Too complicated for me. I'm going back to bed.'

'You're a mess, man. Go back to bed, then. Hey – remember we've got that meeting about the new account tomorrow morning. Don't be late!'

'Yeah, yeah. See you then.' Tom hung up, no doubt already half-asleep.

Kal picked up his controller again, and the gun battle raged on.

When he next emerged from the game, the windows showed the grey light of dusk. So this was how time would pass him by if he let it slip away without paying attention. He saved the game, put down the controller and sat back in his armchair, the light from the screen illuminating the room.

Once, he had asked Tom if this was all there was to life – work, nights out and girls. Tom had laughed and said, 'If you're lucky.' Which, when he thought about it, was a very astute answer, for all that Tom had been half-cut when he said it. They *were* lucky to have what was basically a charmed life. He'd thought he was on the brink of something new with Krista, but that had gone tits up without warning. Maybe he wasn't cut out to settle down. But was the old charmed life enough?

As he pondered that question, the light outside fading into darkness, a shimmer caught his eye.

The shoes.

He should've thrown them in the bin last night. For some reason, though, he hadn't.

And now, he looped his index finger through the heel straps, carried them carefully to a corner of his closet, placed them in there and closed the door. Maybe he'd chuck them in a clothing bin sometime.

He would focus on getting into the right headspace for what looked to be another big week at work. All that other stuff could wait.

At least for now.

Chapter 5

After the meeting with the Alis, Saima hadn't slept well. Sitting now on a Tuesday-morning train on its way to the suburbs of the Lower North Shore, her palms slightly damp, heart racing, she tried to stay calm and alert by taking in the unfamiliar commute north of the bridge.

The views were certainly nicer than the generic stream of suburbs she usually observed on her way to Parramatta. After emerging from the tunnel cutting underneath the CBD, the train glided under the steel arches of the Harbour Bridge, the sunshine glittering brightly on the water far below. From her upstairs seat Saima had a perfect view of the curving white sails of the Opera House and all the boats and ferries sailing across the blue expanse, in and out of the bays and inlets of the sparkling harbour.

A hazy childhood memory bubbled up. Her parents were sitting on either side of her as she pointed excitedly from a train window at this same view. She scanned her brain for more details – what had her mother looked like? What had her father said? Her brain failed to provide any answers and the memory drifted away.

Saima focused instead on the task at hand.

Kal's parents had told her that he lived over on the North Shore, in St Leonards, and had a fairly regular morning schedule he

47

stuck to. They had given her the details of the local gym where he usually headed first, as well as his favourite café near the station.

'How do you know all this?' Saima had asked at one point.

'You'd need to get to the café by 7.30 am or so.' Ruby simply ignored the question and bulldozed on, leaving Saima to wonder whether they had hired someone to tail their son or if George and Ruby had actually followed him around themselves. Neither scenario was particularly comforting, but both seemed fairly plausible at this point.

She glanced at her phone as the train pulled into St Leonards to see that it was already 7.45. She was running late. She ran up the stairs to the busy station plaza, weaving around a group of chattering high school kids in pressed uniforms and boater hats clutching McDonald's breakfasts, off to their private schools on the Upper North Shore.

Her plan now seemed worryingly vague. She started to run through it in her head – first she had to engineer a way to bump into Kal, after which he would most probably recognise her from last Saturday night and naturally be awkward about it, giving her an opportunity for an introduction and an icebreaker all at once. And somehow – here was the gap in her plan – she would mention that she was a matchmaker and casually ask whether Kal might be interested in using her services, particularly while she had a special no-fee promotion going?

Saima stopped walking. *This plan is ridiculous. It's* Notting Hill *levels of contrived. Without Hugh Grant to pull it off.* She fought the urge to call off the whole deal, turn around, head home and spend the day in bed, but then she remembered the letter that had been patiently waiting on her desk after the Alis had left. The Alis' advance had helped pay for her apartment, but there was still a reminder from her office building management that she was a

48

month behind in rent. She had already downgraded her phone plan and cancelled one of her streaming subscriptions. What next? No internet at home? Or worse, trying to get her mum to remember what her wi-fi password was when she moved back in with her?

When she arrived at the café, Kal wasn't there. *Dammit.* She ordered a coffee while she regrouped.

'I'm looking for someone, one of your regulars maybe,' she said as casually as she could to the barista. 'Do you think you could help me, please?'

'I can try,' he said, as he punched in her order.

'Oh, thank you! Okay, he's, like, six foot tall,' she started. 'Has one of those designer beards, I guess he might be some kind of hipster.'

'Like me?' the barista asked with a grin.

'You're probably a genuine hipster, but this guy I'm looking for, he's got short-long hair. You know what I mean? I don't know how else to describe it.'

'Mm-hmm . . .' The barista started to get her coffee order.

'He has dark eyes, nice teeth . . .' She realised that she hadn't properly observed Kal's face, aside from what she'd seen through the rear-view mirror in his car and the standard profile pic attached to his biodata. 'He's quite handsome?' she finished unconvincingly.

'So, what you're telling me is that you're looking for a tall, dark and handsome stranger, is that right?' the barista said, placing a large cup of coffee in front of her. 'Aren't we all, honey?'

Saima shook her head with a laugh. 'Fair enough. Thank you, though.'

'Pleasure, love. Good luck with your manhunt.' He turned to the next customer with a ready smile.

On a whim, Saima decided to try walking by Kal's apartment building, seeing as she'd already made the trip out. Maybe he was still there, working from home, running late or something. She typed his address into her phone and began to follow the blue arrow. The tall buildings of St Leonards created wind tunnels that transformed the warm breeze into sudden billowing gusts. Her summery choice of dress was turning into a bit of a Marilyn Monroe nightmare as she juggled her phone and coffee in one hand and held her dress down with the other. When one particularly frisky blast of wind blew up her dress, she managed to drop first her bag, then her coffee, and then, horrifyingly, her phone, which spun in almost slow motion before smashing onto the pavement. The contents of her bag scattered everywhere – stray receipts, a few tampons, lipstick and a flurry of her business cards. The coffee, miraculously and perversely, stayed intact, dribbling gently out of the lid and slowly into the gutter.

'Your destination is approaching on your right,' came Siri's distorted voice from her phone.

Saima stared at the carnage. The whole scheme – this whole day, in fact – was a complete bust, and it was barely 8 am. She should have followed her instincts and gone straight back to bed.

'Are you okay? Do you need some help?' a quiet voice came from beside her.

She looked up and saw it was him. Of course it was him.

Kal's eyes immediately brightened with recognition and he broke into a smile.

'Hey!' he said.

'Oh! Hi,' she said. The banter she had planned out earlier blew right out of her mind. They gazed at each other for what felt like a bubble in time. Everything seemed to stop. 'Hi,' she said again. His smile grew wider.

She hurriedly began to shove her belongings back into her bag.

'You're here,' he began inanely, bending to help her. 'I mean, what are you doing here? Sorry, wait, that's none of my business. I just didn't expect to see you here. You work around here?'

His obvious nervousness made her relax a little as she gathered up her business cards.

'I'm just here to see a client,' she answered.

'Oh, cool, cool.' Another silence.

'You have arrived at your destination,' Siri suddenly repeated, making them both jump slightly. Saima picked the phone up off the pavement and finally took in the extent of the damage. 'Shit.'

'Can I—' Kal reached towards her, then hesitated. 'Sorry, can I take a look?' She handed it over. 'Yikes, this screen is toast.'

'I know,' she said with a sigh. 'It'll probably cost hundreds to fix.'

'You may as well get a new one.'

'But I *liked* this one. It's done me well for years. It didn't deserve to go out like this.'

'I mean . . .' he turned it over. 'I think it's probably well past retirement age? I can't remember the last time I saw an iPhone 5.'

'It's hardly a museum exhibit,' she said defensively. 'I'm not the sort of person to dump something just because a newer model comes on to the market.'

'Yeah, but it's a phone. Not a person.'

They both stood on the pavement, looking down at the phone still clasped in Kal's hand.

'So, how come you didn't tell me you weren't my Uber?' Saima blurted at last.

Kal blushed. 'Oh god. I was hoping you wouldn't bring that up.'

'Did you expect me to not mention what was basically a kidnapping?' she asked with a slightly incredulous laugh.

'Hardly a kidnapping. More like a carjacking, really; you were the one who got in my car . . .' he quipped back. 'Look, if you want to know the truth, I was trying to find a reason not to go to that wedding. When you jumped into my back seat, it felt like the perfect excuse.'

'That . . . that doesn't make any sense,' she pointed out.

He held up his hands. 'I know! I know. It's the only explanation I've got, though.' His face turned serious. 'I'm sorry. Really. It shouldn't have happened, and there's no scenario where I don't sound like a weirdo.'

Saima was a little taken aback at his upfront earnestness. It disarmed the slightly harsh words that she'd had lined up on her lips about their encounter on Saturday night.

'I'm sorry, too,' she finally said. 'I shouldn't have accused you of being a kidnapper.'

He laughed ruefully. 'I don't think you have anything to apologise for, but thanks. Anyway, listen,' he said, handing her phone back to her, 'there's a repair place next to the station, if you wanted to take this over there.'

'No, that's okay. They probably haven't seen phones from the Jurassic Age before. Thank you, though.'

'Ooh, does this mean today is the day you'll be going for an upgrade, then? Am I about to witness a historic moment?'

Saima laughed. 'Afraid not, sorry.'

'You're just going to stick with the broken phone?' he asked, eyebrow raised.

'Nothing wrong with being a little broken,' she returned. 'Have you heard of kintsugi? It's the Japanese art of repairing broken pottery with gold. The flaws become a thing of beauty, and they add to the piece's history.'

'Right,' he said, smiling. 'So now we just need to find someone who'll fix your phone with gold.' He put his hand in his pocket and brought out a business card. 'I hope you don't mind, but I picked up one of these from the footpath.' Saima realised it was one of hers. 'Saima Khan. Matchmaker,' he read out loud now. He glanced back up. 'So that's the mystery woman's name. Nice to officially meet you, Saima. I'm Kal. Well, Khalid, but everyone calls me Kal.'

Saima bit back a laugh when she realised she'd never introduced herself. Everything about this conversation seemed to be backwards. 'Lovely to meet you, Kal.'

'Wow, a matchmaker,' he said next, flipping the card over to the plain design on the back. 'You don't have any social media channels or a website? You should pop them on the card so people can do their research.'

'I don't need to,' she explained. 'People do their research before they come to me. It's all through word of mouth, through the community.'

'Oh, okay. But what about people *outside* the community? How do they find you?' Kal shook his head. 'Sorry, it's probably not my business. I just do this sort of thing all the time in my day job, and it's a bit automatic.'

'Not many people from outside the community are looking for my services.'

'But surely you'd want them to? If you want to expand your business, that is.'

'Yeah, because so many other Australians want arranged marriages, right?' she sniped, slightly scornful.

'You clearly haven't been watching those awful reality shows,' he said with a grimace.

'Yes, but they aren't about arranging a marriage,' Saima replied. 'They're about fame-hungry wannabes and their fifteen minutes. It's theatre. It's not about love, family or long-term healthy relationships.'

He bit his lip. She could tell he had a lot more to say, but then he looked at his watch and swore. 'Shit, I'm late! I'm meant to be in a meeting in the city in ten minutes.' He pulled out his phone and quickly began typing out a message.

'I should let you go,' Saima began, but she couldn't give up this opportunity. It was as close to her vague game plan as she was likely to get. 'Um, do you want to get a coffee sometime?'

He looked up from his phone with a quizzical smile. 'Coffee?'

'I'd love to know more about your thoughts on trashy reality TV,' she said. She could feel her cheeks turning deep red.

'And what else would we talk about?'

She began to return his smile and caught herself. Oh no, she was giving him the completely wrong idea. 'Maybe we could talk about whether you'd have any need for a matchmaker,' she said, briskly switching to a more professional tone. 'You mentioned you had a girlfriend the other night, but in case you were – I mean, it sounded like it wasn't, you know, working out. Which, um, I was sorry to hear, of course.'

'You don't need to apologise,' Kal said. 'Krista and I broke up the day after I met you. It was for the best.' His phone chirped urgently. 'Shit, sorry, I've got to get to the office,' he said. 'But it was nice to see you again, even though we started on a completely weird foot.'

'Oh,' she said, slightly discouraged.

'Look, to be honest,' he continued quickly, 'things between me and Krista just – I mean, I don't think it's the right time for me to get into anything new. Or any*one* new.'

'Oh, I wasn't—' she began.

'I appreciate the coincidence of us bumping into each other again, but I'm not looking for – uh, this is awkward – it's just that I'm not looking to date anyone right now.' He looked like he wanted the ground to swallow him up whole.

'I'm not – I'm not trying to *hit* on you.' Her words were thick with embarrassment, and when she heard it, the familiar irritation she had felt on their Saturday drive began to brew inside Saima.

'I just thought, after our first meeting, that perhaps you hadn't met the right desi girls. Someone who could change your mind about your own culture, help you appreciate it.'

'My own culture?' Kal repeated. His tone shifted to something colder and harder than she'd heard before. 'What exactly is that? Honestly, let's not get into this again.'

'Your parents are Pakistani, right? Doesn't that mean something to you?' Saima couldn't help herself.

'Aside from the fact that my skin is brown? No.'

'That's kind of tragic. That you won't go deeper than the colour of your skin.'

'You don't know me,' he said, unable to hide his exasperation, 'and yet you seem to think you have me all figured out after a few minutes.'

'I've known enough guys like you to have a pretty good handle on how you think, yes,' Saima snapped.

'Yeah, we must all be the same to you.'

'A desi man living in this country, chasing after white girls?' She feigned shock. 'No, I've never *heard* of such a *unique* person.'

'Well, this has been so lovely,' Kal said sharply. 'But I need to get going. Good luck with your phone.' He turned abruptly and strode off.

Saima thought about going after him to apologise. This had not gone at all like she had planned. If anything, it was the opposite. She watched the answer to her financial troubles walk away, but her feet refused to move. Her pride, as always, stood in the way like a mountain.

She took stock of her morning's achievements. She didn't have a phone. She had antagonised her biggest would-be client and he couldn't get away from her fast enough. In her mind's eye, she could see the dominoes falling – her office, her apartment, her business.

She fought the uncharacteristic urge to hurl her belongings back onto the ground and have a big cry. But all the tears in the world would not stop the worst from happening.

Saima threw her broken phone into her bag and walked decisively back towards the station.

Chapter 6

Kal found it impossible to focus on work. Saima's business card weighed heavily in his pocket as he finally made it to the office – only twenty minutes late – and into the meeting that Tom had been winging on his own. The card bothered him throughout that meeting, and after he and Tom had finally ushered their clients out the door, he found himself taking it out and fuming silently while he stared at it.

What was it she'd said? *A desi man living in this country, chasing after white girls.* How dare she presume to classify him into a type? The colour of his skin and that of the women he went out with *didn't* matter. That *wasn't* why he found those women attractive. Anyway, weren't they meant to be living in a post-racial society?

Kal stuffed the card back into his pocket.

'What the hell happened?' Tom asked. 'Did you sleep in or something?'

Kal groaned. 'I'm sorry, man. I got held up on my way in. Thanks for starting the meeting without me.'

Tom shrugged. 'All good, it was basically in the bag anyway. But we better hustle, we're going to be late for the all-staffer.'

As the staff meeting dragged into the midmorning, Kal found himself oddly conscious for the first time that almost everyone around him, except for Tom and one of the juniors, was white. Did that matter? They were just people at a management consulting firm, and they were there because they were great at their jobs. But an insidious thought came creeping into his mind, one he thought he'd buried years ago. *Am I also in this room because I'm good at not being 'too brown'? Because I've learned over the years how to fit in by wearing a mask that doesn't threaten the whiteness of these rooms?* He glanced over at Tom, sitting beside him. *His* connection to his cultural heritage seemed to begin and end with his appreciation for Japanese whisky.

Kal was suddenly irritated. He'd never thought about masks, or about how brown or Pakistani he was, or how other people might look at him. He'd never thought about being anything other than Kal, plain and simple.

Tom nudged him sharply.

'What do you think about that, Kal?' one of the execs asked him from across the table.

Kal had lost the thread of the conversation at least five minutes ago and now blanked completely. 'Well, Charles, that's an interesting question,' he stalled, and then, thankfully, Tom leaped to his rescue once again.

Later, as Kal was leaving the meeting, the card still strangely heavy in his pocket, he briefly thought about putting it in the bin. He pulled it out and let it hover above the rubbish bin before having second thoughts, so he transferred it into his wallet, wedging it between a credit card and his gym card.

Afterwards, when they were walking back to their desks, Tom nudged him again.

'All right, seriously, what's going on?' he asked. 'You were late to the meeting this morning, and not gonna lie, it was noticed. And just then, when you drifted off in front of Charles, that probably wasn't the smartest move. I'm sure he'll be having a word with Linda about it, and then she'll come down hard on you. You're off your game, man.'

'It's nothing, don't worry about it,' Kal insisted.

'Is it something to do with the break-up?' Tom pressed.

'No.'

'Then what is it?'

'What's it matter?' Kal replied tersely. He appreciated his friend – today even more than most days – but he didn't need Tom's intensity right now. It was barely 11 am.

Tom looked a little taken aback by Kal's sharp tone. Despite any impression he might give, with his tall, solid build, party-hard life-style and the tattoos across his upper body carefully concealed by his slightly too-closely-fitted business shirts, Tom was quite sensitive.

Kal sighed and rubbed his face. 'Look, I'm sorry. I appreciate you having my back in there and out here as well.' He clapped his friend once on the back. 'It's nothing, I swear. Just an off morning.'

'Sure?'

'Yep.'

'All right, then. Just . . . get it together, yeah?' With one more dubious glance, Tom slunk off.

Back at his desk, Kal found his father had emailed his work address.

Subject: *Coffee or lunch?*
Dear Kal,
Will you be free to meet me for a coffee today? Or perhaps if you have time, we could have lunch? I know you are busy, but I was going to be in the city anyway and I was hoping you could find space in your schedule for a quick meeting with your father.
Best regards,
Papa

Not today, old man, Kal thought. *It's been too weird a morning already*. He fired off a quick reply.

Hi Papa, sorry I'm quite busy this week. Let's try and schedule another
· time. Kal

Just as he was about to hit 'Send', he sensed someone standing beside him. He turned to find his manager Linda right there. She moved around like a cat, coming up quietly behind you to catch you at the most inopportune moments.

'Fobbing your dad off, huh?' she said.

Kal fought a blush. 'Yeah,' he said, closing his laptop screen. 'What can I do for you, Linda?'

'Just checking in. What happened this morning? You were late.'

If Linda was going to dress him down, he didn't want to have this conversation at his desk, where everyone could hear everything. Kal got up, grabbed his mug and started walking towards the kitchen. Linda followed silently behind.

'Nothing happened, just a little hold-up on my way in.'

'Hmm' was all Linda said. Kal's patience fractionally slipped.

'Linda, is it that big a deal that I was late one morning when I've been on time for the last seven years?' he asked her quietly when they were in the kitchen. 'I let Tom know I was running late, and he got things started great without me. It's not like the clients were kept waiting.' He scanned the cupboards in vain for something non-caffeinated. 'Honestly, the amount of money we make for this company, you'd think they'd be stocked up with some proper drink options.'

'Just drink coffee like everyone else, for the love of god,' Linda said.

'I'm trying to cut down.'

'And you've been late before. Don't think I've been fooled by those hungover phone calls pretending you were sick.' Linda moved a little closer towards him and lowered her voice. 'But I'm telling you to be careful right now for a reason. It's not been officially announced yet, but Charles is going to take over as head of department. And one of the first things he wants to do is some restructuring. "Get rid of dead wood", as he calls it. I'll put in a good word for you, of course. But you need to be on your guard, because people around here have a tendency to talk.'

'Oh. Thanks for the heads-up,' Kal said, his heart starting to race. 'But I think I'll be fine. My job is to make the clients happy, and as far as I know, that's been going off without a hitch.' *So why*, he asked himself, *do I suddenly feel under threat?*

His phone rang. 'It's my dad.' He took quick steps out of the kitchen as he answered. 'Papa-ji, I saw your email – I can meet you for coffee right now, if you like.' Kal hustled towards the lifts before Linda could collar him again.

'Great news!' his father said jovially. 'Because I'm already downstairs.'

Kal's father always liked to be centre stage, like a man who was used to being in command. As Kal walked out of the lifts, there was George, standing tall, a curious smile on his face as he observed the hustle and bustle of office workers streaming through the revolving doors in and out of the marble-clad lobby.

Kal took a moment to appreciate his father's sense of style, which did not look at all out of place among the sharply dressed Barangaroo crowd. Unlike a lot of other Pakistani men his age, George still watched what he ate, went for forty-five-minute walks every day and, through the luck of genetics, had managed to retain most of his hair, which was now streaked with grey, giving him the air of an elder statesman.

Or a silver fox. Kal clocked a young woman, probably around his own age, turning to check out his father. George caught her glance and returned her smile, looking a little too pleased with himself.

'Papa!' Kal called loudly.

His father headed over to him, and rather than offering a handshake as he usually did, wrapped him in a hug. Kal was taken aback. They were not a touchy-feely sort of family, especially in public.

'What's happening? You okay, Papa?' Kal asked after his father had held him for a moment too long.

'Yes, of course. Just because I give my son a hug doesn't mean anything is wrong,' George said, finally releasing Kal. 'Come, let's get that coffee.'

They walked down to the sparkling water's edge at Barangaroo, the slick corporate district at the western edge of the Sydney CBD. Trendy cafés, polished cocktail bars and expensive restaurants lined the waterfront, as tourists strolled up and down taking photos with their families.

Kal and George sat on faux–French provincial rattan chairs in one of the cafés as the waitress came to take their order.

'I'll have a chai latte, please, young lady,' George said, after Kal had ordered a decaf flat white. 'Did you know that "chai" in our language means "tea"?' he told the waitress. 'And "latte" is Italian for "milk". We're basically bastardising two languages with this drink. What is "tea milk", anyway?'

The waitress smiled and shook her head.

'I suppose it's a sight better than chai tea, which is literally "tea tea",' George continued. 'Did you know that?'

'Yes, sir,' she said, then took their menus and left rather quickly.

'Bet she spits in your drink for giving her a hard time about it,' Kal said.

'I wasn't giving her a hard time! I was just making conversation,' George protested. 'Is talking to waitstaff giving them a hard time, now?'

Kal just shrugged and remained quiet. At some point, there was no point arguing with anyone in his parents' generation.

They waited in silence for their drinks, looking out at the water. These days, whenever Kal met his father, they had very little to say to each other. Only Ruby's presence ever made them talk. Otherwise, they would be perfectly comfortable sitting quietly, usually scrolling on their phones, and then going back to their lives.

'So why the rush to meet me?' Kal asked as the waitress brought over their order.

'You know, I'm turning sixty this year,' George said, still staring towards the water. 'I've been reflecting a lot about what that means. I'm going to have to retire soon.'

'I don't believe you could ever retire. You wouldn't know what to do with yourself.' The only version of his father Kal had ever known was a workaholic with little time for anything else – hobbies, leisure, children.

'Well, I was hoping I could spend more time with you and your sister. Maybe even some grandkids. Amna is finally talking about having children, much to your mother's relief.'

'Is she?' Kal asked noncommittally. He hadn't spoken to his sister in a while. They had a cordial but distant relationship, despite their two-year age gap. She had moved to the UK for uni straight after she finished high school, met a guy, and remained there ever since. Save for the odd birthday greeting or reciprocal 'like' on social media, they weren't inclined to chat.

'But you, though,' his father continued. 'You still haven't found your place yet, Kal.' George said this so matter-of-factly, like it wasn't even up for debate. Kal resented his certainty.

'I've worked at the firm for the last seven years. I'm doing pretty well, in case you hadn't noticed. I've bought my own apartment, my own car. That's what it all comes down to, doesn't it, *Dad*?'

'That's the least you should have achieved after the fortune we spent on your private education and all those silly extracurricular things you liked to do. That world tour you went on with your rugby team? Ridiculous! I only agreed to it because your mother insisted.' George sniffed dismissively. 'And for what? Did you end up becoming a rugby player? Of course not! By thirty, I was hoping at the very least that you would be part of the executive team at a big firm, not still working for some small "boutique" company where they refuse to promote you.'

Under the table, Kal's hands clenched and unclenched. 'Did you turn up in the middle of the workday to lecture me? You could've saved yourself a trip and just done it over the phone.' He finished his drink and moved to get up.

'No – no, I didn't. I – I apologise for all of that,' George said quickly. 'Please sit down, Khalid. None of that was what I came here to say.'

Kal tried not to stare. Never in his life had his father apologised for anything, not even when he had called his son an 'underachieving waste of space' because Kal had been let go from his first job fresh out of university, doing temp work at a firm owned by one of George's friends. Both men had learned a lot from that incident. Kal never again approached his father for help, and George never again offered it. As he got older, Kal appreciated the distance, because it made him feel like he'd achieved his own successes.

'I've been seeing a psychologist,' George said suddenly. 'She's helping me see many things in a different light. I know I haven't been the best father to you or Amna over the years.'

Kal couldn't believe what he was hearing. Not only had he apologised, he was admitting to seeking professional help. This was unheard of among desi fathers.

'I know I've been hard on you,' George continued, 'but it was because I wanted you to do better. Perhaps that wasn't the best way to go about it. But I want you to know that everything I did was so you could have a better life than me.'

'Papa, you literally went to a private boarding school in Switzerland.'

'That was only for a few years. And after spending that time away from my family, I knew I never wanted to send my own children away.'

'Just because Amna and I never went to boarding school doesn't mean we saw much of you, though,' Kal pointed out.

'That is something I regret in hindsight,' George said quietly. Kal had never seen his father look so subdued.

'Are you dying or something?' he blurted out.

'What? No!' George was offended. 'I'm still young! Just because I'm turning sixty doesn't mean I'm ready for the grave! I'm fighting fit!' He struck his chest. 'Even women your age find me attractive!'

'Great, what does Ammy think about that?'

'What's your mother got to do with it? I'm just saying that I'm years away from my deathbed.'

'Well, that's good to know, I guess?' Kal was beyond confused at this point.

'Look, the reason I wanted to speak to you was because I have been doing some thinking about my past, about how I have been as a man, as a father. And you know what I realised? One of the best things I did was marry your mother. Before that, I was loafing around, not knowing what I wanted from life. I didn't have direction, I didn't have purpose. And then my parents introduced me to her, and I got to know her, and I *knew*. I just knew she was the one I had to marry. Let us find you someone like that, beta. When you find the right girl, everything else will fall into place. I just know it.'

The penny finally dropped. This wasn't the first time Kal's parents had brought up marriage, of course, but it was usually his mother on his case. The way his father was speaking to him now, openly and honestly, was a first. *That psychologist must be really good*, Kal thought.

'Papa, you know I was dating someone,' he started.

'These gori ladkiyan are no good for you, Khalid. They don't understand us, our culture.'

This again. Why was this suddenly all anyone wanted to talk to him about?

'*What* culture?' Kal asked, exasperated. 'What do we do that's so different from what everyone else does? You literally changed your name to George! Ammy calls herself Ruby! If we aren't the poster children for assimilation, I don't know who is.'

'Oh, those name changes are nothing,' his father said with a casual wave. 'They're basically for business purposes. It's just easier to call ourselves that in this country. No, what I'm saying is, find yourself a good desi girl. She doesn't even have to be Pakistani! Let us help you.'

Kal had had enough of lectures today. 'Look, I have to get back to work,' he said sharply, getting up and reaching for his wallet. His father did the same, both of them in a race to take care of the bill before the other. As Kal whipped his credit card out of his wallet, Saima's purple business card flew out along with it, landing squarely, perfectly, in front of George.

George picked it up and looked at it briefly. Kal froze, bracing himself for questions. But none came. His father just smiled, dropped the card back onto the table and briskly walked to the counter to pay the bill.

There was little else Kal could do other than tuck his credit card back into his wallet and pick up Saima's card off the table. He thought again of throwing it away but he couldn't do it. The card wouldn't let him. He stuffed it back into his wallet, waved at his father and headed back to the office, telling himself tersely not to think of Saima or the card again.

Chapter 7

'We tried calling you, Saima baji, but we kept getting your voicemail.' The young woman sitting opposite Saima had eyes so large that she looked like a Disney character.

'And so I told Haniya, let's just go see her,' added Faisal, the groom-to-be, a lanky man with a prominent Adam's apple and a gentle voice. 'Sorry we're so early.'

'Of course, no worries at all.' Saima smiled. 'And I'm sorry you couldn't reach me. I'm having some phone troubles.'

'What trouble, baji? Can I help?' Faisal asked.

'I doubt it,' she said with laugh, and reluctantly pulled out her phone to show him the smashed-up mess.

'I think that phone is dead,' Haniya said as Faisal examined it carefully.

'If you like, I can get you a good price on another one?' he offered.

Saima wondered how to tell him that she couldn't afford the expense of a new phone right now, whether with a good price or not.

Possibly reading her expression, Faisal said, 'You know, baji, I have so many phones, I can just give you one I'm not using. Just so you have something till you can get a new one.'

'That's so kind of you,' Saima began, 'but—'

'Oh, yes, you must!' Haniya exclaimed. 'He has too many phones. Too many!'

'I can't help buying them,' Faisal admitted sheepishly.

'He is *addicted* to technology,' Haniya said with a giggle. 'Maybe this is something I should be worried about.'

Faisal looked at her in alarm. 'Wait, no, no, it's just a hobby! Some people collect stamps, I collect smartphones.'

Haniya squeezed his arm reassuringly and turned to Saima. 'You may as well take one of those phones of his, baji.'

They were both so sweet, and easily two of Saima's favourite clients. The generous insistence to accept extravagant gifts was quite common among desi communities, and it could be tricky to navigate when you simply admired someone's jewellery and they insisted that you take it from them. 'Please, there's no need,' Saima tried again, but she knew it was already a lost cause as Faisal got up.

'Look, I'm going to go get the phone I've been carrying around in my car for who knows how long. I don't even use it.'

'Please, sit down, Faisal,' Saima insisted.

'No, baji, let him go get it,' Haniya said. 'It's been in his glove box for ages. I think he even has the charger in there!' Faisal was out the door in a flash.

Haniya looked at her with shining eyes. The flush of first love made her skin glow.

'You look well,' said Saima with a smile.

'Only because of you, baji,' Haniya replied. 'I never thought I would feel this way about a boy. Well, a boy other than Harry Potter.'

Saima laughed. 'I didn't think you still read Harry Potter.'

'I don't think I'll ever stop,' Haniya said earnestly. She surveyed the room while they waited for Faisal to return. Saima wondered what her office looked like through Haniya's eyes – the crumbling paint on the walls, the patch of damp on the carpet and the strange musty smell, which usually made Saima light a candle when she had client appointments. Though she seemed to be having a run of her clientele popping in unannounced lately.

'Are *you* doing okay, baji?' Haniya asked. 'The old man who saw us in – is he the caretaker of this place?'

Dave had brought Faisal and Haniya into the office, padding past Saima when she arrived to mutter pointedly, 'I didn't think working here would mean I'd end up being your receptionist.'

'Oh, that's just Dave,' she said to Haniya now. 'He runs the business in the office next door. And me, I'm doing fine, thank you. It's sweet of you to ask. But the whole reason we're meeting is so I can ask you how *you* are doing. I want to make sure that you and Faisal are happy to go ahead with the marriage, now that you're six months into your relationship.'

Haniya broke into giggles again. 'Ammy finds it hard to say that he and I are in a relationship at all,' she said. 'I could never say that word to her face. She calls him my "friend". "Are you seeing your friend today?" she asks me.'

Saima joined in her laughter. 'There are worse things than marrying your friend!'

'Definitely! I'm so glad you have a policy that the couples you bring together have to see each other for at least six months before they get into a marriage. Faisal's, like,' she sighed happily, 'my best friend, but even better.'

'I'm so glad. That policy exists to make sure no-one is rushing into a relationship they don't really want.'

'It's very modern of you. Ammy even complained to Abbu about it. I overheard her asking him, "Why are we letting Haniya go about with a boy she's not married or related to? Is it not haram?" I swear I had to hold back a laugh! Abbu was great, of course.

70

He said, "Just let the girl do what she needs to." I'm so glad I have a dad like him.' She faltered, then started to blush. 'I'm sorry,' she said like a kid caught passing notes to a friend in class.

'What for?' Saima asked.

'Because of your dad . . . Ammy told me to not say anything.'

Saima injected her voice with a breeziness she did not feel. 'It was a long time ago,' she said. 'Anyway, I know my methods aren't for everyone. I'm glad your parents agreed to them.'

'Yes. Even though there's been talk—' Haniya bit her lip and broke off again.

'What sort of talk?' Saima asked, perhaps a little too sharply.

'Oh, you know.' Haniya looked startled. 'That maybe you are too modern. That you pair up couples who maybe shouldn't be together. You ask too many questions and expect too much from the families who have their own traditional ways . . .' She trailed off, then continued in a smaller voice. 'It's maybe why some of them won't come to you?'

For the past few months, as her clients had started drying up and the steady depletion of her finances had begun, Saima had suspected something like this was going on. Gossip was a powerful weapon in the community, and if it had turned against her, she was in deeper trouble than she had imagined. Haniya was the first person to mention the rumours directly to her. She felt her cheeks heat up, but didn't want to let on how this information affected her in case Haniya stopped talking.

Too late.

'I'm talking too much!' Haniya exclaimed. 'Honestly, what's wrong with me?' She started fidgeting with her sleeves, pulling them over her hands as though she was sitting in the principal's office, waiting to get told off. 'I wonder what's taking Faisal so long,' she mumbled at last.

71

'Anyway, things are going great with you and Faisal?' Saima asked, trying to lift the mood and get back to the point.

Haniya lit up. 'Oh, yes! They really are! We're definitely going ahead with the marriage, Saima baji. We wanted to tell you in person today. We've booked a ballroom for November. My khala is looking at bridal ghararas in Karachi and I get to choose who I want to design my outfit. I've been looking at so many shaadi websites!'

'I have some shaadi websites I can recommend too, if you like?'

'Oh yes, please send them to me!'

'This is all wonderful news, Haniya – no wonder you're glowing!'

Haniya blushed rosily just as Faisal walked into the room carrying what looked like a brand-new iPhone.

'Faisal, this is still in its box,' Saima said. 'There's no way I can take it.'

'I haven't taken it out yet, because it's another colour of the model I already own,' Faisal said cheerfully.

'Honestly, baji, he just buys different colours of the same phone. He has to have the red one, the gold one, the black one.' Haniya took the box from Faisal and placed it on Saima's desk with determination. The look in her eye said that there was no way they were going to let Saima refuse this gift.

'This one's red, which I thought was perfect because of what you do. Red for shaadi, right?' Faisal looked at Haniya as he spoke, making her blush even more.

'I heard about the wedding plans,' Saima said to Faisal, trying not to look at the unopened box in front of her. 'Congratulations to you both, I'm so happy to hear everything is going so well.'

'Yes, it's better than I ever expected,' Faisal said seriously. 'I never thought that a girl like Haniya would come into my life.'

'What do you mean, a girl like me?' Haniya asked shyly.

'You know, the daughter of a lawyer being with someone like me, the son of a cab driver.'

'Faisal, stop!' Haniya's shyness turned into indignation. 'How can you think like that?!'

Faisal tried to sound matter-of-fact, but he clearly felt at least a little vulnerable about this. 'It's the truth. I know there's been talk already about our match.'

'But we've never made you feel like – I mean, your family has always been treated well by mine, haven't they?' Haniya anxiously asked him.

'Oh, yes, every time!' Faisal rushed to reassure her. 'But without Saima baji, do you think the two of us would even have met? Our parents hardly move in the same circles. We may as well come from different planets.'

'Maybe we *came* from different worlds,' Haniya said, 'but we're together now!'

'Because Saima baji here doesn't care about all that. It didn't matter what my parents' professions were, or whether I went to university or not. Without you, baji,' he said earnestly to Saima, 'we wouldn't be sitting here, telling you we're getting married.'

'I'm just happy to play a part in bringing you two together,' Saima said. But Faisal was not done.

'Even my father said, when you brought Haniya's profile to us, that someone like her would never even agree to meet a family like ours,' he admitted.

'He did?' Saima was taken aback.

'But after he met Haniya he saw what a decent, kind, wonderful human she is, and how happy she makes me. And he knew things like what he did for a living didn't matter. All that mattered was love.' Faisal and Haniya gazed at each other with such adoration that Saima had to look away.

The main reason she had a six-month check-in with her matched couples was to gently remind them that marriages needed constant maintenance. That even arranged marriages, where there was so often pressure for couples to remain together for the sake of appearances, needed work. That they wouldn't be in the first flush of love forever, and needed to dedicate themselves to maintaining a strong foundation so one day they would be celebrating their golden anniversary happily hand in hand. It was basically a pre-marriage counselling session.

But as she looked at Haniya and Faisal, dreamy-eyed and euphoric, Saima couldn't bring herself to burst their bubble with any cold realities.

Eventually, the couple remembered where they were, and blinked back at her. She noticed them surreptitiously holding hands under the table, still rather scandalous behaviour in some parts of the community. Very likely, she thought, they would have done nothing more than hold hands even in private, and the innocence of this touched her rather more deeply than she expected.

'Congratulations to you both, again,' she said with the gentlest smile. 'I'm so pleased to see how happy and hopeful you are. It's a great place to start the rest of your lives.'

'Thank you, baji,' Faisal said.

'You know I'm here if you need anything at all, of course.'

'Yes, baji.' Beaming, Haniya grabbed her bag. 'Anyway, we should get going now. We showed up early because we have a lunch booked with some of Faisal's colleagues. He's finally decided to introduce me to them!'

'I wanted to introduce them the moment I met you,' Faisal protested. 'I just didn't think you wanted to meet the boring people I work with.'

'We're going to try those famous triangle dosas in Harris Park,' Haniya told Saima.

'Oh, they're delicious, you'll love them,' she replied. 'The ghee masala one is to die for.'

'We'll send you our wedding invite in the mail,' Faisal said. 'You'll be the guest of honour!'

'Oh, don't be silly! I just played a small part in all of this. But you've reminded me, can you please send the invitation to my home address?' Saima jotted it down.

'You're planning to move from this place?' Haniya asked. 'That makes sense. It's a bit run-down, right? Probably more suited to the old man who smelled of Vicks. Though the lady with the eyebrows was nice.'

'You mean Jess?' Saima asked.

Haniya nodded. 'We had a chat about microblading,' she said. 'Her eyebrows are *amazing*.'

Saima smiled and shook her head. 'Most of that is genetic, sorry to break it to you. Jess lights a candle to her yia-yia every night in thanks.' She held up the box holding the new phone. 'Before you go, please take this. I really can't accept it.'

'Oh, but it's yours now,' Haniya said with a finality that Saima couldn't argue with.

Saima saw them out of her office, watching as Faisal took Haniya's hand before opening the front door for her. Footsteps creaked up behind her.

'How gorgeous are they?' Jess said.

'Absolutely precious,' Saima agreed.

'I saw them waiting in your office and popped in for a chat. They're so excited about their wedding.' Jess said. 'She even asked me where I got my eyebrows done.'

'I gave away your secret, sorry.'

'Oh man, you told them about Yia-yia?' Jess waggled her eyebrows. 'I want everyone to think these are the result of hard work and sorcery.'

Saima laughed. 'Okay, I promise I won't tell anyone else!' She walked into her office while Jess followed behind.

'Where are you off to?' Jess asked, as Saima grabbed her bag.

'Back to Officeworks,' Saima replied quietly. 'And I don't want to talk about why.'

'Okay, now you're going to absolutely have to tell me why.' Jess had a look that Saima knew meant she wasn't going to let up till she told her what was going on.

'Well, if you really want to know . . . I'm going to grab some boxes. It's time I packed up and stopped working out of this office,' Saima answered with as much resolve as she could muster.

Jess grabbed her arm. 'No. I absolutely refuse to let you leave this place.'

'You have no choice, I'm afraid. I blew it with the rich couple's son yesterday, and I can't in good conscience keep their money. I did some thinking when I went into Officeworks this morning.'

'Oh yes, I've heard a number of philosophers talk about how they do their best thinking in the promised land of office stationery.'

'No, seriously! I was in there for some ringbinders, and then I saw the flat-pack boxes and I realised that just because life isn't working out the way I want it to doesn't mean that everything is lost.'

'Was that printed on the side of one of the boxes or did you see it in a motivational Instagram post?'

'It wasn't Instagram.' Saima huffed with exasperation. 'Don't you see? The flat-pack boxes were a sign and they got me thinking. Anyway, you're meant to be encouraging me here! You're meant to say, "Yes, absolutely! You're so right!"'

'But you're giving up without a fight! Give things a chance to work themselves out, Saima.'

'I feel like I've been fighting for years, Jess. I'm exhausted.' Saima threw herself into her chair and spun for a bit. 'When my phone smashed yesterday and I worked out I didn't have the money to fix it, I knew I'd reached the end of the road. This whole matchmaking lark was a good experiment, but ultimately it just isn't enough to keep me going.' She sighed and looked at her pinboard filled with wedding invites – weddings she'd helped to arrange. 'It was nice while it lasted,' she said wistfully.

'So, what then?' Jess stood with her hands on her hips. 'You'll move back in with your mum, get depressed, go back to that admin job you hated, and spend the rest of your life totally miserable?'

'I won't be *totally* miserable. I'll have those motivational Instagram posts to hang on to.'

'Stop making jokes!' Jess said. 'If you're really that broke, why do you have this fancy new phone sitting on your desk?'

'That young couple basically forced me to take it.'

'You see?' Jess pointed her finger in triumph. 'The universe always provides. You just need to give it a chance. It's when all hope seems well and truly lost that the biggest opportunities appear.'

'Wait, do you follow the same Instagram accounts as me?'

Jess smirked and then forced her face into a determined scowl again. 'So, you had a shit day yesterday. But look, today is different and somehow you managed to get a brand-new phone! One I'd love to own myself! And just because you think you blew it with the rich couple's son doesn't mean that's what actually happened.'

'I was there – pretty sure that's exactly what happened.'

'Yes, but you tend to fixate on the negative. Sorry, but you do.'

Saima abruptly lost the urge to joke. 'Excuse me?'

'I'm not trying to be a bitch—'

'—got bad news for you, then—'

'—but you're a bit of a pessimist, Saima. Everything's always worst-case scenario with you.'

'Oh, I wonder why that is?' Saima snapped.

Jess rolled her eyes. 'God, don't start on this again. Plenty of kids grow up with divorced parents, Saima. It's hardly the world-ending origin story you seem to think it is.'

'Fine! Let's fast-forward, shall we? Let's talk about that admin job and the absolute psychopaths in that office.'

Jess yawned theatrically. 'Oh wow, a shitty office job, never heard of that before.'

'And then I finally got together the money to start this place.' Saima leaped to her feet. 'And damn it, I am good at this!' She stalked over to the pinboard and began yanking invitations down. 'Happy couple!' She flung one at Jess, then another, and another. 'Happy couple! Happy couple! What's this? Oh, it's *another happy couple!*' Jess yelped as one flying card caught her on the cheek. 'I'm not just good at this, I'm fucking brilliant!' Saima said, now tearing down handfuls. 'And just because people are too small-minded to see what I'm doing, it's all going to shit! Everything I've built! And – and—' her legs folded under her and she crumpled in a heap, surrounded by fluttering wedding invitations. 'And I don't know how any of this is going to get better,' she finished, with a quiver in her voice. 'So no, I'm not "fixating on the negative", I'm actually at the end of the road.'

'Oh my god, you're going to cry,' Jess said in disbelief as she rushed over to her. 'You never cry! *Please* don't cry. I didn't mean to make you cry!'

'I'm not crying!' Saima said, red-faced but dry-eyed.

'I'm such an arsehole! Honestly! Rob is always telling me that I speak before thinking!' Jess said, kneeling by Saima's side. 'Of course you don't fixate on the negative!'

'I'm not a pessimist!' Saima sniffed. 'I'm just trying to be realistic.'

'No, you're not, you're not a pessimist,' Jess repeated soothingly. 'I'm so sorry. Please forgive your bigmouth friend. I panicked when I thought about you leaving and I said thoughtless things. Can I give you a hug?' she asked Saima tentatively.

Saima wasn't much of a hugger. Then again, she thought, looking around at the mess, she didn't think she was given to tantrums either. She turned towards Jess's embrace.

'I can't afford to keep paying the rent here,' she finally said, her words muffled into Jess's shoulder. 'Hence the cardboard boxes.'

'What happened with the rich guy?' Jess asked, getting back to her feet and pulling Saima up with her.

'It started with him thinking I was hitting on him and ended with me yelling at him.'

'Wow. That's some quality work for one morning.'

'Some of my best, yeah. I don't know, Jess. There was just something about him . . . He irritated me.'

'How did he do that?'

Saima couldn't quite recall. 'Just some things he said.'

'It's weird that he managed to get such a strong reaction from you when you don't even know him,' Jess said curiously.

Saima just shrugged.

'Okay, so what about the couple who were just here?' Jess asked next. 'They seemed to appreciate what you've done for them.'

Saima thought about everything Haniya and Faisal had said and sighed. 'They did. They were really sweet. There'll be some money coming in from their parents, yes, but it's not enough, and it's just putting off the inevitable. The groom's family, at least, have been super positive about the whole relationship.'

'Not the bride's?'

'I'm not sure, to be honest. I got the impression that maybe the mother of the bride wasn't completely chuffed, but the dad seemed pleased.'

'And that's how you've always done things, right?' Jess pressed. 'For six years now, you've had happy couples and their families recommend you to other would-be clients. What's gone wrong specifically now?'

'I didn't quite know until talking to that couple just now,' Saima admitted. 'But I think, in a nutshell, my methods have finally caught up with me.'

'What do you mean?' Jess sank into one of the chairs.

Saima sighed again. 'It's like this. Among desis, class and social caste is pretty much everything. Like sticks with like, do you see?'

'More or less, yeah.'

'Okay, so.' Saima began to pace behind her desk. 'Nowhere is that more important than when people get hitched. I mean, it's all a bit muddy when couples meet and date and marry on their own in love matches, but *arranged* marriages? If you've got the son of a posh family in Mosman, he should be matched with a posh girl from – well, from somewhere swanky, like Vaucluse, for example. Middle-class, business-owning families marry into other middle-class business-owning families. Professionals marry professionals. Blue-collar families marry into families like theirs.'

'Gosh.'

'There are a bunch of other reasons that are too complicated to get into.'

'I'll take your word for it. And I do get it,' Jess said. 'Mum's Theia Chloe wanted to marry some guy from the wrong village and caused a heap of drama that people still talk about.'

'And there are other prejudices and other types of pigeonholing, too, and don't even get me started on the religious side,'

Saima went on. 'Being a matchmaker means keeping all of those traditions and expectations in your head when you're setting up matches.'

'Wait, you *do* that?'

'No, that's exactly it,' Saima said, sitting down at last. 'I don't. I haven't. I've been focusing on the actual compatibility of my couples all this time.'

'But that's a good thing!' Jess protested.

'It's a *great* thing,' Saima corrected her. 'My parents were "properly" matched and that was a disaster. I know so many other couples in their generation and mine who are in exactly the same boat. So, I decided when I started that I wasn't going to get bogged down in community expectations. I was going to think about compatibility and longevity and match up my couples based on that.'

'Why have we never spoken about this before?'

'Honestly?' Saima blew out a long breath and stared at a brown patch in the ceiling plaster. 'I didn't really think about it after I made that decision. I knew there'd be talk – there's always talk – but I thought I could stay above it, especially if I had a great track record to show for it. But now . . .'

'But now?'

'The balance has tipped. That rich couple on Monday were the first proper clients I've had in months. And something Haniya – that sweet bride-to-be – said just now makes me realise that the gossip about how I do things is beginning to outweigh any goodwill about my results.'

Jess contemplated this in silence for a minute. 'Well, shit.'

'Yep.'

'Okay, but wait. If the balance has tipped out of your favour, couldn't it tip *back*?'

'How?'

'I don't know, but it could, right?'

'Is this another "universe will provide" thing, Jess?'

'Don't discount the universe, Saima. No, I'm being serious! Nothing you've said makes me think it's curtains for your business just yet. What you need is a bigger cash injection to tide you over while you work out a game plan to get the clients flowing again.'

'That could take ages. Where am I going to get an indefinite cash injection?'

'Please just take a loan from me to tide you over, at least to help you pay the rent on this place,' Jess begged.

'Nope.'

'Well, surely you don't have to move out straight away. Haven't you paid in advance?'

'I'm in arrears. I owe them for last month and this one.'

'Didn't that rich couple pay you in advance?'

'Yeah, and I used their advance to pay for my apartment so at least I'm not going to be homeless for the next few months. But now that I've blown it with their son, I'll need to pay them back.'

And as if on cue, the floorboards squeaked rapidly down the corridor.

'Looks like you have another client coming, Saima!' Dave shouted from the other end of the cottage.

'Thanks, Dave!' Saima shouted back. 'He's being passive-aggressive about my client visits recently, even though they're so infrequent,' she said to Jess, who rolled her eyes.

'Probably the most interesting thing that's happened to him in years,' she muttered.

Ruby Ali popped her head round the door.

'Knock, knock!' she said cheerfully. She faltered as she took in the aftermath of Saima's meltdown. 'Oh . . . is this a bad time?'

Saima hastily got to her feet. 'Mrs Ali! Um, please do come in.'

Jess gently kicked a few invitations under Saima's desk as she made for the door. 'You okay?' she mouthed from behind Ruby.

Saima gave her a surreptitious thumbs up.

'The universe,' Jess mouthed again, pointing upwards as she backed out the door.

'Sorry about the mess,' Saima said, gesturing Ruby to a chair. 'It's been a bit of a hectic morning.'

Ruby came inside the office. 'I tried calling you, Saima. But your phone kept going to voicemail.'

'Yes, my phone had an unfortunate accident. But I've just got a new one.'

'Okay, good.' Ruby settled into a chair and gazed benignly at Saima.

'I, uh . . .' Saima began, unsure what to say. She was not used to failing her clients. In fact, this would be the first time she was admitting defeat as a matchmaker.

'I was telling George earlier that we don't give the girls from our community enough credit,' Ruby interrupted. 'Everyone makes out that you are simple, naive girls, but as you've shown me, you are anything but.'

'Mrs Ali, you've got me all wrong. I didn't mean to—'

'No matter how impossible the task, you will find a way. I admire that.'

'If this is about the money—' Saima began doggedly.

'Yes, you are right. It *should* be about the money.'

'Okay, but Mrs Ali—'

'Ruby, please.'

'Ruby, I didn't expect for me and Kal to—'

'You and Kal! Amazing for me to even hear that! How you did it, beti, I don't know. And so quickly!'

Saima wondered if she was ever going to be permitted to finish a sentence. 'Ruby, please. In terms of the money—'

'We keep coming back to money. In other circumstances, I would say that it was a bit vulgar, no? Talking about money like that.' She looked around Saima's office. 'But I understand for someone like you and the situation you're in, money is important. So how much extra are we talking?'

'Extra?'

'Yes, I appreciate that you are asking for more, and I have no problem paying for such excellent service.'

'More?'

'Okay, Saima, you don't need to play simple for me. I understand that this is a strategy that has worked for you before. You keep people's expectations low, and then you surprise them with what you achieve.'

'What I achieve?'

'Arre ladki, stop repeating what I'm saying like a parrot! How much extra are you asking? I realise we probably underpaid your deposit considering what we were asking from you. But then George met Kal yesterday and saw with his own eyes your card in our son's wallet! Just one day after we hired you!'

Saima couldn't believe what was happening. A new phone on her desk, a rich woman with a chequebook at the ready, willing to pay her anything. Oh god, maybe Jess was right? Maybe sometimes the universe *did* provide?

Or maybe Kal just forgot to throw your card in the bin after you yelled at him in the street, her natural cynicism suggested.

'Have you started thinking of the sorts of women you will introduce to him?' Ruby asked.

'Uh no, not yet,' Saima said. *Likely not ever*, she added silently. 'Ruby, you do know that Kal was just dating someone?'

'So what sort of money are we talking about?' Ruby blithely ignored her question, pen and chequebook poised in her hand.

84

'Ruby, did you hear?' Saima pressed her. 'Kal just broke up with his *girlfriend*.'

'I'm only fifty-five, darling. I can hear you perfectly well.' Ruby put down her pen and sat back in the chair. She looked at Saima and sighed. 'Darling, that gori he dated shouldn't stand in the way of you earning what you truly deserve for the work you're doing. So let me put it this way. I'll pay you a fair price now for what you've already proved yourself capable of. And if Kal ends up committing to one of the girls you propose, well, then, we can talk again about a bonus. If he marries the girl, you'll get your usual percentage.'

Saima's ethics grappled with her pragmatism. What had the Alis asked her to do? Bump into Kal and introduce him to her matchmaking services. Well, she'd done that, and Ruby was now offering to pay her fairly for it. Was it so wrong to take the money?

She thought of Haniya and Faisal. If she could keep her business going, she could continue to help people like them. Sure, there were members of the community who didn't like that she brought people from different backgrounds together. But Ruby's offer would buy her time to regroup, at least for the short term, and she could work out a way to get ahead of the gossip again.

And even if, as she suspected, Kal wasn't going to have anything more to do with her, well, then, the Alis weren't going to be paying for that, were they? And she could deal with their disappointment later.

'Okay, Ruby,' she said, and named an exorbitant price. Ruby agreed to it without hesitation.

Chapter 8

'Yo, turn that up!' Tom called to the DJ. It was 11.30 pm, and they were still at the King Street Wharf bar they had headed to after a late night at the office, finishing up a proposal. Kal stifled a yawn, and Tom turned back just in time to catch him in the act. 'This is what happens when you turn thirty,' he said to Kal with disgust. 'You wanna be tucked up in bed with a warm cup of cocoa, rather than listening to some banging tunes with a bunch of beautiful girls.'

'Guess you can look forward to that soon enough,' Kal retorted. 'Yours is just around the corner.'

Tom shuddered. 'Never, old man! Imma sleep when I'm dead.' He tossed back the remainder of his drink, accidentally bumping the blonde girl sitting beside him in the booth.

She turned, smiled stiffly at Kal when he held up his hand and mouthed an apology, before turning back to her friends. Kal leaned closer to the oblivious Tom. 'Mate, I think they're just with us because you're buying the drinks.'

'Are you just hanging with us because we're buying you drinks?' Tom shouted over at the girls. He was clearly half-cut, because any sense of volume control had blown right out the window.

86

'No, of course not!' said the brunette sitting at the end of the table. Kal couldn't remember any of their names, or whether they'd even offered them at the beginning of the night.

They had meant to go out for some beers to unwind after the last-minute tight deadline, but somehow, as tended to happen with Tom, a quick after-work drink soon snowballed into a big night. Kal wasn't feeling it like he used to.

'I'm going to jet,' he said to Tom.

'No way! Not yet!' Tom put a friendly arm around him and leaned in too close. Yep, definitely *more* than half-cut. 'You're my wingman! And I'm yours! That's the deal, right?'

'And what if I said your wingman wants to call it a night?'

'I'd say you need another drink.' Tom poured him a glass of Hakushu. 'Get that in ya.'

'Mate, don't waste it on me. I'm done,' Kal insisted, pushing the glass back towards him.

'I was joking about the cocoa, you know, right?' Tom blinked at him dolefully. 'Come on, man, don't bail on me. I was just kidding.'

'Yeah, of course. It's just, all this,' Kal said, gesturing around him. 'It isn't doing it for me anymore.'

'Nah, I don't believe it. You're a single dude again! You can't tell me that a top night of booze and girls is not your scene anymore! Not yet. I've seen you in action over the years. Something's off about you. Come on, spill. Tell Uncle Thomas all about it.'

Perhaps Tom wasn't as drunk as Kal had assumed. His expression had suddenly changed into a more serious one and he eyed Kal shrewdly.

Before Kal could line up an answer he didn't even know himself, the DJ changed the track. A couple of their companions whooped and leaped up to dance. The brunette from the end of the table had some serious moves. Tom and Kal watched her for a while.

SAMAN SHAD

'Come on, that's got to do your soul good,' Tom said. 'Go and show her how all those jazz ballet lessons your mum made you do have paid off.'

Kal sniggered. 'Yeah, nah, I'm good.'

Tom downed Kal's untouched glass of whisky and followed his own advice, getting up to dance with Brunette. Before long, they were grinding on each other. One of her friends pulled out her phone and began to film them both.

'You'll be so horrified tomorrow!' she shrieked.

'Don't 'gram it!' Brunette shouted, laughing and continuing to grind with Tom.

Kal closed his eyes against a budding headache. A few years ago, he'd have been right in there, but right now, he just felt . . . tired. Maybe *that* had been the lure of Krista, the promise of finally settling down and being at rest instead of continuing the frenetic pace of his twenties into his thirties.

Something was placed on the top of his head. He opened his eyes and jerked forward, and a shot glass toppled into his lap. Tequila dribbled from his head onto his clothes. The girls shrieked with laughter.

'That's what you get for falling asleep on us!' one of them said.

Kal got up and grabbed his things. 'I'm off!' he shouted over to Tom.

The girls booed. Tom snagged his arm as he passed the dance floor. 'No way you're leaving now, bro!' he said, then leaned closer to hiss, 'I think I've got a good chance with her.'

Kal looked over at Brunette, who was now swaying to the sound of the music with her eyes closed. She looked nice enough, he supposed, but she also seemed very drunk. As did Tom. Both of them would likely regret anything further that happened that night.

88

'I reckon you leave it now, mate,' he said. 'Get her number. Call her tomorrow.'

'It's so on right now, though,' Tom wheedled. He was starting to slur a bit. Kal quickly thought through the likely scenarios if he left his friend on his own tonight.

'You know what, man?' He waved his phone. 'I just got a call from Linda. She wants us to come back into the office to go over a few things.' Kal gathered up Tom's discarded jacket, hoping Tom wouldn't realise what time it was.

'No way! I'm not heading back to the office now! Tell her to go home!'

'Come on, mate.' Kal took him by the elbow.

'I'm never going to the office!' Tom declared.

'He's never going to the office!' the girls shouted, breaking into peals of laughter.

'If he never goes to the office, he won't be able to shout your Piper,' Kal said to them. They booed again. He went over to where Brunette still swayed. 'Hey, we need to head off, but maybe you can give my man Tom over there your number?' he said over the thumping music. 'He likes you, maybe he can call you tomorrow?'

She stared at Kal with sleepy eyes and wrapped her arms around his neck, resting her head on his shoulder. Her friends whooped, their phones at the ready.

'Oh, I get it now!' Tom shouted. 'You wanted her all along!'

'Don't be stupid!' Kal hissed.

'Don't call me stupid!' Tom said angrily.

Kal could feel the situation spiralling out of control. He disengaged from Brunette, propping her up on one of her friends, and seized Tom's arm just as a mountainous bouncer appeared at their side like a genie.

'Now, boys, we don't want any trouble. I think perhaps you both need to cool off.'

'We were just leaving,' Kal said quickly. He didn't wait for Tom to respond, instead dragging him towards the exit. When they were outside, he rounded on his friend. 'What the hell?'

Tom was now swaying unsteadily on his feet. 'Sorry, man,' he mumbled. Drunk or sober, he was always quick to apologise. Now he sniffed once, looking about ready to cry.

There was a chill in the air. The wind blowing across the water brought the promise of rain. The sudden drop in temperature from the sweaty bar sent a shiver through Kal as he slung his jacket back on. That hot cocoa increasingly sounded like a good idea.

He hailed a taxi, threw Tom into the back and clambered in beside him.

'You almost got us into a lot of shit back there,' Kal said as he buckled his seatbelt. When he looked over at Tom, he was passed out. Great. He buckled Tom's seatbelt and gave the driver his friend's address in Milsons Point, only a couple of suburbs away from his own. Once there, Kal managed to drag a legless Tom out of the taxi and through the front door of his apartment, leaving him in the recovery position on the couch with a box of ibuprofen and a big glass of water on the coffee table.

The half-hour walk home in the cool night air did wonders for his headache. Kal took the lift up to his apartment, dropped his keys and phone on the kitchen counter, pulled off his shoes, shirt, jacket and trousers into a pile on the ground, and collapsed on the couch in a dreamless sleep.

He woke with daylight beaming through the open blinds and his alarm blaring for another workday. *Shit.*

It wasn't until he was on the train that Kal checked his phone to see a bombardment of messages from Krista.

Who TF is the girl?

Didn't take you long to move on!

Asshole

What was she going on about? Clearly Krista had gotten the wrong end of the stick about something and was blaming him for it. What girl was he supposed to have moved on with?

Unbidden, Saima Khan's face popped into his mind.

His phone began to buzz. He eyed it gingerly, expecting it to be Krista, and breathed a sigh of relief to find Lachie's name on the screen.

'Hey.'

'Hey,' Lachie replied. 'So, how long have you and Tom been going out without me, then? An invite would be nice next time so I can see what I'm missing.'

'What?' Kal asked.

'And I thought you were taking a break from girls right now? Or have you found The One?'

'What?'

'Nicole saw her friend's Instagram story. You really looked into that girl.'

Kal suddenly remembered Brunette from last night, and the few seconds she had clung to him. 'Wait, those girls know Nicole? Is that why Krista—'

'Oh shit, did Krista see it too?' Lachie exclaimed.

Not for the first time, Kal was reminded of how practically everyone in Sydney was only one or two connections removed from each other. Sometimes it felt more like a village than a big city. 'Didn't they post the story of the girl and Tom dancing?' he asked, annoyed.

'Nope. Was she dancing with him too?'

'Yeah, for ages. She was pretty drunk. So was Tom. I just went over to get her number for him before we left and she kind of fell on me. I can't believe her friends posted that online.'

'I dunno who took the vid, but she was the one who posted it. She even captioned it "steamy nights with a hot guy".' Lachie started to crack up.

'That's not funny,' Kal said. 'She didn't actually say that, did she?'

'Nah, I think she said, "He was the wind beneath my wings".'

'It's too early for your comedy routine, Lachie. Did she say that, or are you taking the piss?'

Lachie was clearly enjoying himself mightily at Kal's expense. 'If I tell you what she said, you'll be mad about it,' he sniggered.

'Just tell me already.'

'She said – are you ready for this? – she said, "Met Dev Patel last night".' Lachie was in hysterics.

'Yeah, all right, be a dick about it.'

'No, really, she did! Her account's on private but Nicole could screenshot it for you.'

Kal was gobsmacked. '*Dev Patel*?!'

'I know, I know, not all brown guys look the same,' Lachie said hastily. 'But c'mon, she compared you to Dev Patel. No way I'd be mad if someone said "bumped into Chris Hemsworth last night" about me.'

'Ha, you wish. Anyway, doesn't matter if Dev Patel's hot. He's probably the only Indian guy she can think of – and I'm Pakistani! It's like we're all the same to them.'

'Right, right. It's important that people know you're Pakistani, not Indian.' Lachie was definitely just humouring him.

Kal thought of Saima again. She would probably tell him it was his fault for disconnecting from his cultural roots among his friendship circle or something. Or perhaps she wouldn't. Perhaps she would acknowledge what it was like to grow up brown in this country. Immigrant kids like them seemed to fall into two camps – the ones who fully embraced their heritage and bought into the whole desi culture, and those who didn't.

He pulled himself up. Where had *that* thought come from? When he was younger, he'd ignored thoughts like these whenever they'd arisen. His teens and twenties had been spent making himself as much of 'one of the guys' as possible. He took the occasional comments about 'terrorists' and 'curries' on the chin, laughed along, told himself he didn't care. That the people those comments referred to didn't include him. But it was starting to matter.

'Kal, you there? Did you hear what I said?' Lachie was saying.

'Yeah, man.' Kal snapped back to the conversation at hand.

'So, you're okay to meet up with Krista?'

'Wait, what?'

'Ugh, you *weren't* listening! I said, Nicole is hating being in the middle of the two of you, and Krista's adamant that you can't break up without her getting to say her piece. We thought maybe we could get you both together so you could talk it out.'

'Oh god, I don't know,' Kal hedged. 'It's not going to change the outcome.'

'It won't be that bad, I promise,' Lachie said.

'You absolutely can't promise that. But look, I'll think about it.' Fingers crossed he wouldn't have to and the situation would go away on its own.

After he hung up, Kal stared blankly out the window. For the first time in a long while, he didn't feel like going to work today. He briefly contemplated staying on the train and letting it take him wherever it went. *Is this depression or something?* he briefly wondered. He chalked it up to his hungover brain and tried to shake the feeling off.

At Wynyard, he moved on autopilot up the escalator and through the gleaming underpass towards Barangaroo. Hordes of fellow commuters hustled past the illuminated billboards. He felt like he was travelling in slow motion. As he emerged into what had turned into a drizzly morning, rather than heading along the pedestrian plaza towards his building, he instead found himself moving in the opposite direction, to a bookshop he had often walked past but never entered.

The store played loud jazz as the bald guy behind the counter set up the till. 'Good morning!' he said with a broad smile. 'Let me know if you need help with anything.'

Kal hovered uncertainly in the entryway. 'Hi, do you have books on, uh, I don't know, feeling like you're in a funk?'

'We've got a great self-help section,' the man said, gesturing towards the back of the shop.

'Thanks.'

'No worries!'

Kal made his way over to the shelves that showcased how much life could go wrong at almost every juncture. There were books about anxious kids and child psychology, books on career paths, on finding your life partner, books on how to organise your family life, your finances, and then books on coping with infertility, depression, parenthood. And a big row of books on what to do after a divorce. Book after book on how hard life could be. It made him feel a little queasy.

He gravitated towards the travel section. He wasn't much of a traveller himself – he liked the idea of it, but the thrill of actual travel had long ago drained out of him after an early childhood tagging along as a family whenever his father travelled for work.

It was here that Kal noticed a book on 'Third Culture Kids'.

He started to flick through the pages. 'They are citizens of everywhere and nowhere,' he read, 'finding it hard to identify with one place, one culture as their own.' Intrigued, he read further. Third culture kids were adaptable, did well in social situations, made friends easily. They were not of one place but of many. But despite all the positives, third culture kids often felt alone, not knowing where exactly to call home, or which culture to identify with.

His phone chimed a ten-minute reminder for his first meeting of the day. He rushed to the till and bought the book, clutching the brown paper bag as he legged it to the office.

Much later that day, he took a brief break from the client proposal he'd been elbows-deep in. The paper bag caught his eye from where he'd stashed it under his desk.

On a whim, he pulled Saima's card out of his wallet and stared at the number written there. Before his brain could question what he was doing, he fired off a text. He hoped by now she had at least gotten herself a new phone.

My culture it seems is no culture. I'm a third culture kid.

Regret crowded in as soon as he hit 'Send'. Why had he felt the need to tell her that? He supposed it was because her comments had settled like sediment in his mind, and he couldn't push them out. Or maybe he figured, more than anyone else around him, she might understand what it meant to feel like you belonged everywhere and nowhere.

His phone pinged back almost immediately. He was almost scared to read what she'd written. She would probably be wondering who the hell had texted her, since, he realised too late, he'd made no attempt to identify himself in his message.

He winced as he opened her reply.

It feels like everyone knows everyone, but no-one knows you, she said.

Another message came in as he read.

Incidentally, who is this?

He grinned widely as he texted back. I bet you say that to all the guys you carjack.

Only the ones I yell at in the street, came her swift reply. There was a pause, during which Kal's heart rate picked up pace as he stared at the three bouncing dots on the screen. He felt strangely on the edge of something extremely important. After what felt like an age, his phone pinged with her next message. Would you like to get a coffee tonight and tell me more about your third culture?

His thumb flew over the screen without hesitation.

Sure.

Chapter 9

The middle-aged Pakistani couple sitting in Saima's office wore sombre expressions that became even more pronounced as she spoke.

'Aunty, Uncle, I won't be restricting myself to women under thirty for your son. There are plenty of wonderful, accomplished women older than that who would be a more suitable match for a forty-five-year-old man.'

'Yes, but he will want children,' Aunty said plainly. 'Do you think a thirty-year-old will be fertile enough?' She didn't wait for a response. 'No, of course not. And we do not want all this fuss women go through with these doctors and clinics, trying to get pregnant. All everyone will think is, why didn't she just have children when she was younger?'

Saima wanted to ask her the same. *Why didn't your son have children when he was younger?* She pressed her lips together against the words. 'And you've written here that you want someone with a university education, but would prefer if she doesn't want to work. Is that right?' she continued.

'We just want grandchildren,' Uncle interjected. 'My wife won't say it, so I will. We want our beta to have children and we want our home to be blessed with the laughter and life that they bring. A good wife will understand that.'

'And is this what your son also wants?' Saima asked. 'As you know, I have to speak to him as well.'

'He doesn't mind,' Aunty said, looking away.

'And has he had any relationships in the past?'

'Maybe. We don't know,' said Uncle.

'Chee-chee!' Aunty exclaimed, touching both her cheeks. 'How can you ask that? Our son is a good Muslim boy. He has done no fooling around! He's been busy with work, that's all. He's very focused on his career. You need to write that down.'

Saima found that highly doubtful. When she spoke directly to the person a family was trying to set up, she usually winkled out the information that they hadn't – or couldn't – tell their families. Information like an existing relationship with someone 'unsuitable' – someone of the same sex or outside the community – or a lack of interest in marriage and families altogether. All in the strictest confidence, of course. But the foundation to her business from the beginning was to ensure that everyone she helped was in it for only the right reasons.

'You're meant to be a good matchmaker,' Uncle now said. 'We heard the Alis approached you recently about their son. This is why we came to you. Just find us a good girl for our son. Twenty-five years old would be perfect, but we could accept a year or two older. And I would prefer if she stays at home to look after the children after they are born.'

'And I suppose you would also prefer that she's good at cooking and keeping a house?' Saima said before she could stop herself. 'Ironing, cleaning, that sort of thing?'

The couple opposite her didn't seem to appreciate the sarcasm. 'Yes, yes!' Aunty agreed enthusiastically. 'At my age, it would be good to have someone take over all the work I do at home. So many girls these days don't understand that. It will still be my home and

I will run it, of course, but I want a girl who will feel comfortable taking over the labour.'

Saima was trying so hard not to roll her eyes that her head ached. She'd had versions of this conversation so many times, and each time, she was tempted to ask whether the parents who came to her were really looking for a wife or a servant.

'Aunty, Uncle, you must know that I have certain rules in my matchmaking. It's why hardly any of my couples have separated over the years, because what's most important to me is that I bring the right people together. With all respect, if you want a good match for your son, you have to be a little more open-minded about the sort of women I would propose. They may not be exactly who you imagined your son would settle down with, but I assure you, they will be women most suited for a marriage with your son.'

They listened to her with strained patience, before Aunty protested, 'But we *know* who will work best for our son. He needs a good, traditional girl. Parents know best.'

'Yes, Aunty, but—'

'Beti, listen, if you continue this way, you will have absolutely no business coming to you,' Uncle said grimly. 'There is already talk in the community. Maybe you're not aware of it, or you choose not to listen. We heard many disturbing things. They say you brought together a taxi driver's child with that of a lawyer. Another family found out the man you matched their daughter with has epilepsy? The couple is going ahead and getting married, but you must realise that this is wrong. This is not our way. Your methods may look good to you, but they are not good for the families. But we thought, maybe, if the Alis were trusting you, that you might not be a bad option. But now I see you have no respect for the way things should be done.'

'Maybe we should go.' Aunty gathered her bag. 'This has been a waste of time.'

Saima had been speechless with angry disbelief throughout Uncle's self-righteous diatribe. 'Uncle. Aunty,' she bit out. 'My priority is to make sure your son is happy at the end of the day. That he finds someone he wants to spend the rest of his life with. Is that not what you also want?'

'Our son,' Uncle thundered, 'will find happiness through the happiness of his parents. Not through your besharam ideas!'

They stormed out of her office, slamming the front door loudly as they left.

Saima took a couple of deep breaths. *It's fine. It's no loss. They are not people I want to do business with anyway*, she told herself. But the day stretched out ahead of her, grey, raining and depressingly empty of any other appointments.

She decided to head out of her office and spend the rest of it with her mother.

Rahat Begum still lived in the small two-bedroom flat in Guildford where she and Saima had eventually moved following her divorce. The building backed onto the railway line, and the apartment balcony overlooked a section of the tracks. As a child, Saima had fallen asleep to a soundtrack of wheels over tracks. Clickety-clack, clickety-clack.

The building had become dilapidated over the years – the residents more transitory, the surrounds dicier as the gentrifying developers passed over the old apartment blocks to focus on the other, 'more desirable' side of the tracks. It was not the sort of place Saima wanted to see her mother in, but Rahat refused to consider moving, particularly when the rent was so cheap and she could save so much money. Saima had only found out what her mother had been saving her money for a couple of years ago, when she was cleaning under Rahat's bed one afternoon and discovered a suitcase. Inside was a complete set of bridal clothes – lehengas, cholis, dupattas, shalwar suits, saris and all – as well as an ornate gold bridal jewellery set, including two whole armfuls of bangles, all wrapped carefully in plastic. Rahat had bought a bridal outfit and a full trousseau for Saima. She even had extra cash set aside to pay for the wedding.

'Ammy, what on earth is all this?' Saima had exclaimed with a bemused laugh.

'Don't laugh, it's my duty as your mother,' Rahat had replied sternly.

She'd hugged her mother and told her to keep her money. 'If I ever get married, Ammy, I'll pay for it myself. And as for the clothes, well, hopefully I can wear some of them at an event sometime.'

Since then the suitcase had continued to gather dust under the bed.

The flat was Rahat's space through and through. The walls were hung with photographs of Saima; as a toddler, in her various school uniforms, in her graduation robe. The sofas were strewn with worn-out throw cushions, a sheen of yellow coated the sink from years of fresh turmeric ground into paste, and the smell of spices had sunk into the kitchen walls, which no amount of scrubbing would ever shift. One day, Saima hoped she could buy this apartment for her mum. She might not be the best daughter, but she still clung to a desperate hope of making her mother proud. She could hear the Hindi soap opera blaring loudly from her mother's television even before she had her key in the lock. When she got inside, Rahat was sitting on the frayed couch with its dated floral print, staring at the TV set.

'Assalaamu alaykum, Ammy,' Saima called loudly over the sound of the dramatically weeping young woman onscreen.

Rahat spared her a glance. 'Wa-alaikum as-salam,' she said, before turning back to the soap. A generously proportioned older woman bedecked with jewels was shouting at the crying woman while the rest of the household looked on with shocked faces. Saima could have sworn exactly the same scene was playing out the last time she'd been over. She took the opportunity to examine her mother closely.

Rahat's face was gaunt, the skin clinging tightly to her cheekbones and jaw. Her skin was free of make-up as usual, her nails unpolished and blunt. The only skincare routine she had followed for years was sorbolene cream and turmeric paste. Once, as a child, Saima had asked Rahat why she rubbed turmeric into her skin so regularly. Her mother had sharply told her to mind her own business. She realised much later that her mother probably believed that turmeric would lighten her complexion, which, Rahat once said, was as dark as the soil of the earth from the land she had left behind.

'How are you, Ammy?' Saima asked politely.

'Good,' Rahat replied shortly.

'Have you eaten lunch?'

'Hm.' Which meant that very likely she hadn't.

'I know eating isn't your most favourite thing in the world to do, Ammy,' Saima said for what felt like the thousandth time, 'but please, you need to take care of yourself. I'll fry up some bhindi. What do you think?'

She went into the kitchen and pulled out a packet of okra from the freezer and some spices from the cupboard.

'No, let me do it,' Rahat said, coming in behind her as the credits rolled on the soap. 'You don't know how to make bhindi like I do.'

Saima happily let her mum take over. For all that she didn't enjoy eating, Rahat was a far better cook than Saima could ever be.

Rahat fried the okra in hot oil, then added onion, garlic, ginger and spices, eyeballing the amounts for each. Whenever Saima asked her mother about the exact measurements in her recipes, her mother would always shrug vaguely and say, 'You just judge by the eye.' To go with the okra, Rahat mixed some atta with water to make roti. She kneaded the dough, then separated it into small balls that she rolled out beautifully round and as thin as paper. Saima heated up the tava, ready for the first roti Rahat slapped on. It puffed up like a balloon.

Watching the roti inflate, Rahat smiled at her daughter. 'You're hungry.'

Saima smiled back. If the roti inflated, Rahat always said, it meant that whoever was going to eat it must be very hungry. And, she supposed, it *was* true, because she was always hungry when her mother was cooking.

She grabbed a couple of plates and Rahat piled hot roti and crispy okra onto them. They ate with their fingers, taking small pieces of roti, wrapping them around the bhindi and popping the whole thing into their mouths. Rahat watched Saima as she ate, delighting in the pleasure her cooking brought her daughter.

'It's good, yes?' she asked, eyes shining.

'Perfect, as always. Just the right amount of crunch,' Saima said with a blissful smile. Before her plate was empty, Rahat loaded it with another roti, then another.

'Ammy, please stop,' Saima begged, after eating three. Eating at her mother's table was always like this, and for the most part Saima overate just to see Rahat happy.

After they were done eating and Saima had washed up, she turned on the kettle for some chai, strong and sweet in equal measure, just how they liked it. They took their tea from the same mugs from Saima's childhood, now faded and chipped, and sank onto the living room sofa, its sagging cushions long ago moulded into the shape of their bottoms. Only then did Rahat turn to Saima and ask, 'So, when are you getting married?'

Saima almost spat out her tea. 'Where is this coming from? You know my answer, Ammy!'

'I know, I know. But still, a mother has to ask. Two nights ago, I had a dream you had met someone. You said you hated him, but whenever you looked his way, your face lit up and my heart fluttered at the sight of it. When I woke I thought, one day I want to see my Saima smile like this. It is my life's goal.'

'*Ammy*,' Saima groaned. 'Please tell me you haven't taken out that suitcase again and started getting ideas in your head.'

'No, no, of course not,' Rahat said, but like a child telling fibs, she was unable to meet Saima's gaze.

'I knew it was a bad idea to leave it under your bed,' Saima joked. 'It's infecting your brain.' She sighed, then smiled at her mother. 'I haven't met anyone yet, Ammy. But who knows? Maybe one day.'

'Arre, chup! You're not going to fob me off again with that. You deserve happiness, Saima. Oceans and oceans of it.'

Saima liked the thought of oceans of happiness. A train rattled past in the background. She sipped her chai. A warm comfort drifted through her, and she didn't want to spoil it by telling her mother she would likely never marry because frankly, she didn't trust anyone enough to tie herself to them for life. 'Ammy, if I meet someone, I promise I will tell you. But until then, please, stop asking me.'

'Have you even had a boyfriend, Saima?'

'Ammy! What a question! When would you have let me have a boyfriend?'

'I assumed since you're living by yourself now that you'd be doing that. A pretty girl like you, alone in that flat.'

'Sorry to disappoint, Ammy.' Saima thought about the few guys she'd dated, none of whom she could really classify as boyfriends. There was the Indian guy at her last office job. They'd spent months chatting casually in the tearoom and hanging out after work with other colleagues before they had finally gone out for drinks. But they had never moved beyond friendly banter and she'd never felt a spark. Clearly, neither had he. The first guy to ask her out had been at uni – he'd asked her a few times. Eventually, she'd said yes and they had gone to the movies. But when he had put his arm around her shoulders in the dark cinema, she felt an overpowering desire to shove him off and tell him to keep his hands to himself. Needless to say, that hadn't progressed much further either.

'There's no shame in dating,' Rahat was saying now. 'We are modern women, you and me. And I . . . I want you to have more than this.' Her mother gestured across the space in front of them, taking in the weathered couch, the peeling paint on the walls and the fading photographs of better days gone past. 'You deserve more,' she said simply.

Saima didn't want to tell her mother that marriage didn't necessarily mean something more. 'You deserve more as well,' she said instead. 'Let me help you find somewhere else, somewhere better.'

'You'll not find better, not for the amount of rent I pay! I told one of Mark's patients how much I pay and her eyes nearly popped out of her head! She said, "Rahat, never let go of that place. You can't even rent a garage for that much in Sydney these days."'

'A dental assistant can probably do a little better than a garage, Ammy. Especially if Mark paid you properly,' Saima said. 'When was the last time he gave you a pay rise?'

'He takes care of me, don't you worry about that.' Rahat's jaw clamped resolutely. You could never utter a bad word about Mark around her mother. He was the dentist who had taken a chance and given her a job when she'd been qualified for nothing, and she had repaid him with her unbending loyalty for almost a quarter of a century.

Rahat turned the TV back on. This was how she spent most of her days. She worked five days a week from 8 am to 4 pm, and

105

spent the rest of her time watching Hindi soaps on a slightly dodgy streaming service that Saima had set up for her a couple of years ago. *At least*, Saima thought, *that job gives Ammy a productive way to fill her time*. If she didn't have the job, Saima imagined her mother might waste all her time in front of the TV, pining for the day her perennially single daughter got married.

The opening credits of the next soap faded onto a dramatically miserable, handsome man overdosing on anxiety medication as his wife stormed out of their opulent house.

'This is ridiculous,' Saima said, after watching a few moments. 'Ammy, this is going to rot your brain.' Rahat shushed her, and Saima started searching for her bag. 'I suppose I should be getting home.'

'It's still early. Stay a bit, watch this show with me.' The music onscreen rose to a crescendo. Saima winced.

'Some other time, maybe.'

'How is work going?' Rahat asked, as if Saima hadn't gotten off the sofa.

'Work is fine.'

'I heard from Laila.' The words pulled Saima to a halt. 'Remember how we stayed with her for all those months, sleeping on the sofa bed in that study? It had a big spring in the middle that poked you if you rolled on it. Remember? I had a backache for weeks.' Rahat said this as cheerfully as if she was remembering a luxury holiday, rather than the time they were one step away from moving back into a women's shelter. Luckily, Mark had offered Rahat a job just in time.

'Yes, I remember.'

'Anyway, Laila mentioned something about your business being in trouble.' Rahat finally looked away from the TV and back at her daughter.

'Why would she say that?' Saima hedged.

'She said she saw you at a wedding a few weeks ago. The bride told her you didn't have many clients.'

'I just told her to pass on my card to any interested parties!' she protested. 'That's how it works, it's word of mouth.'

'You must've said more than that.'

'The way tongues wag in our community, honestly. You'd think nobody had anything better to do.'

'What does that mean? Tongues wag? Laila said the bride told her you worked from a sad office.'

'It's not sad. It's a charming little cottage near the river. It has character, history. You saw it when I first moved in, remember?'

Rahat shook her head. 'No, I don't recall. But your business, I thought it was going well?'

Saima sighed and decided to come clean. 'Look, Ammy, it was. But some people in our community don't like the way I match couples. They care too much about class, status.'

'They always have.' Rahat sniffed. 'Laila was one of the few who helped when everyone else acted like they didn't know us.'

'Anyway, I'm going to handle it,' Saima assured her. 'So please don't worry about it. And I'm glad Laila has gotten back in touch. It's good for you both to catch up.'

'Yes, she also said she wanted to have us over for a meal one day. I said I would ask when you're free and then get back to her.'

Saima would rather go back to being lectured by the uncle from this morning. 'Don't worry about me, Ammy. You just go.'

Whenever she thought of Laila, which was rarely, Saima was reminded of the painful and confusing time after they had unexpectedly fled from their home. She and Rahat had gone into freefall, ending up in a women's shelter. Laila, sweet, kind Laila, had convinced them to stay with her, but that had had its own issues. Saima wanted to revisit that house and those memories over lunch with Laila about as much as she wanted a hole in the head.

'I should never have lost touch with her,' Rahat was saying now. 'I was a stubborn woman. All that time we lived in her house, and I didn't know how to repay her. I felt so embarrassed and guilty because I couldn't thank her for all that she'd done. I'm so glad she called me again.'

'Even more of a reason for you to get together without me as a distraction.'

But Rahat was adamant. 'No, tell me a day when you're free and we'll go over. After all that woman did for us, Saima, the least you can do is make yourself available for a meal.'

Saima's phone chimed before she could answer. The message was from a new number.

My culture it seems is no culture. I'm a third culture kid.

She paused for only a beat. It had to be Kal, though he was the last person she expected to hear from, particularly after their previous encounter. She re-read his message and a vague memory pinged of an article that referred to Barack Obama as a third culture kid. She googled the article, copying a quote to text back to him before gently roasting him for the anonymous text, grinning at his reply.

'Who are you texting, beti?'

'Oh, just a friend, Ammy,' Saima mumbled absent-mindedly.

'Oh, this must be a very good friend,' Rahat observed. 'You suddenly went quiet, and I've not seen you smile like that before. Tell her your ammy wants to meet her!' Saima looked up in alarm to see her mother reaching towards her. 'Show me your phone. I'll tell her myself.'

Saima dodged away from her mother, horrified. 'No, Ammy, sorry, it's not a friend, my mistake! It's work, it's a client.'

'What could a client say to make your face light up like that?'

'My face didn't light up! This is how I normally look.'

'Beti, I've know that face from the moment you were born. That's not how you normally look.'

'Sure I do, I'm always happiness and light.' She ignored her mother's snort. Kal had messaged her out of the blue. Was this an opportunity to earn that second cheque Ruby had handed her last week? It felt too good to be true, but maybe this was Jess's universe, providing. She thought of the irate couple this morning, her dwindling client numbers, the gossip nipping at her heels. Before she could talk herself out of it, she surprised herself and fired off one more text to Kal.

Would you like to get a coffee tonight and tell me more about your third culture?

His swift response brought unexpected butterflies low in her belly. Rahat was eyeing her knowingly.

'Ammy, I have to go,' Saima said hastily. 'I'm meeting this client after work today.'

'Okay, ja, ja,' replied her mother. 'Tell *the client* I said hello.'

Chapter 10

Saima had chosen a second-hand bookshop in Glebe for their meeting. Kal thought it an odd location, but after he made his way past shelves of dusty books, he found a charming courtyard out the back. It was crowded with potted plants and trellises with fairy lights hanging between them, and a cute little fountain in the centre of the courtyard. The walls were painted with bright murals by local artists, overlooking small tables dotted with tea lights. A singer was setting up to one side. One of the idling young waitstaff smiled at him as he walked in.

'Hi! Sorry, we're full at the moment,' she said.

'Oh, I'm meeting someone,' Kal said, scanning the tables. He spotted Saima sitting in a far corner, unencumbered by any devices. Instead she stared straight ahead, seemingly lost in her own world.

'Saima,' he called as he took quick steps towards her, a smile spreading unconsciously across his face.

She blinked, startled. 'Oh, hi!'

He pulled out the chair across from her. 'Sorry I'm a bit late. It's been a bit full-on at work.'

'Oh, no worries. I've been enjoying my—' She looked down at the glass of table water in front of her. 'Oh. I ordered an iced tea. Didn't even notice that they hadn't brought it.'

'You seemed lost in thought,' he said.

'Did I? I can't even remember what I was thinking about. Possibly my mother. I just got back from visiting her.'

'I hope she's doing well,' Kal said politely, pouring himself a glass of water as well.

'Yep, just her usual self.'

He felt a prickle of awkwardness speaking to her in person after their last meeting, and casually glanced at the drinks menu to hide it.

'They have wine and beer, I think. If you want a drink,' Saima said.

In fact, they had two choices of wine – red and white. And three choices of beer. The tea list, however, was extensive. He turned around and immediately caught the attention of the waitress who had greeted him.

'Out of the red and the white, which one would you recommend?' he asked her.

'Neither,' she replied with a grin.

'Thanks for the warning!'

'Can I make a suggestion?' She hitched her hip slightly on the table. 'You look like a guy who would appreciate a negroni.'

'Probably yes, but it's not on the menu?'

'Doesn't mean I can't make you one, though. Trust me, I make a good one.'

He smiled at her and she flushed perceptibly. 'That would be great, thanks.'

As the waitress turned to leave, Saima spoke. 'Excuse me, I ordered an iced tea a little while ago? I never got it.'

The waitress barely gave her a glance as she made her way towards the kitchen. 'I'll check for you.'

'Sure you will,' Saima muttered.

'Do you want me to call her back?' Kal asked.

'No, no, that's fine,' she said, shortly. 'I'm sure she's on top of it.'

Kal reached for something to say, feeling defensive without knowing why.

As if reading his mind, Saima said, 'So my invitation must've seemed out of the blue. You probably wondered why this angry lady asked you to coffee?' Her tone was casual, but he detected an undercurrent of nervousness that he found reassuring.

'To be honest, I think curiosity got the better of me.' Kal smiled and she laughed.

'You know what they say about curiosity,' she said.

Before he could reply, the young waitress arrived with his drink. She put it down and hovered. 'I want to see what you think.'

Slightly self-consciously, Kal took a sip. The bitterness hit him first before the taste mellowed in his mouth. He eyed the glass in faint surprise. 'This is excellent,' he told her. 'You should be mixing cocktails at a fancy Surry Hills bar.'

She blushed. 'I'm training to be a mixologist,' she said. 'I've been doing some shifts at a couple of bars in the city, but I don't think I'm good enough to be with the big boys yet.'

'I think you could show them a thing or two,' Kal said, taking another sip.

Saima had been smiling fixedly through this whole exchange. She now cleared her throat. 'Excuse me,' she said. 'My iced tea?'

'Oh yes,' the waitress said, her gaze not leaving Kal. 'I'll just check on that.' She lingered.

'Would you mind seeing if my friend's tea is ready yet?' Kal asked.

'Your friend? Sure,' the waitress said. 'Let me know if you guys would like to eat anything.' At last she turned and headed back to the kitchen.

112

'She's going to write her number on something and pass it to you,' Saima predicted. 'And I'm never going to see that iced tea.'

'You think?' Kal said, sipping the negroni again. It was very good.

'I'm interested in what life must be like for the beautiful people. Do you get so used to the attention you don't even notice it?'

'You think I'm beautiful?' Kal smirked.

'Oh, please,' Saima scoffed. 'Try to be less of a cliché.'

'I think you've called me a cliché before,' he said, and she looked briefly stricken. He decided to change tack before they could revisit their street-side argument. 'Hey, do you think I look like Dev Patel?'

Saima exploded into laughter. 'Oh, get over yourself!'

The waitress reappeared and placed a glass of orange juice in front of Saima. 'What did you think of the drink?' she asked Kal.

'Easily one of the best negronis I've had,' he said. 'Sorry, I think my friend asked for an iced tea?'

'Seriously, don't worry about it,' Saima told him. An evil glint came into her eye. 'Hey, can I ask you a question?' she said to the waitress. 'Do you think he looks like Dev Patel?' Kal quirked an eyebrow at her but said nothing.

The waitress took the question very seriously. She appraised Kal's face for a while, before saying, 'Maybe a little bit. But I'd say you look more like Riz Ahmed.'

'Oh dear lord,' Saima muttered and her shoulders shook with suppressed laughter. Kal tried to ignore her.

'Thanks. I didn't *think* I looked like Dev Patel, but someone recently said that I did.'

The waitress gazed at him a bit longer. 'Well, if you grew your hair longer and got a goatee, then maybe . . . Yeah I can see that, definitely.' She was twirling her hair around her fingers and didn't move.

113

'We'll let you know if we want to order some food,' he told her gently, and she drifted off at last.

'So what's with the Dev Patel question?' Saima asked, prodding her glass with an unimpressed look and pushing it away with a sigh.

'Someone I met the other night compared me to him. It annoyed me,' he said.

'Is being compared to one of the most handsome men in Hollywood that annoying?' Saima sniped. Kal gave her a look and she quickly shook her head in apology. 'Sorry. I can't help it. The sarcasm just seeps out of me.'

'I hadn't noticed,' he replied dryly, and she grinned appreciatively. 'I just don't like the insinuation that all brown guys look the same. How can I look like both Riz Ahmed *and* Dev Patel? It's almost as if white folks can't distinguish us from each other.'

'To be fair, she would've agreed that you looked like Brad Pitt *and* The Rock if you asked her. In her eyes you're the handsomest of them all.'

'Stop it!' Kal said with a laugh.

The singer began to play a folksy acoustic version of 'Wrecking Ball' and the two of them fell silent for a time. He wasn't sure if it was the music, the fairy lights or the booze, but Kal found himself marvelling at the romance in the air.

He glanced over at Saima and saw that she was lost in thought. As the song finally came to a close and the patrons applauded, she looked back at Kal and shook her head as if coming back down to earth.

'You okay?' he asked.

She took a moment to respond. 'Sorry, I've had a weird day. I must be hungry or something,' she said, snapping out of it.

'Same, don't think I've eaten anything since midday,' he said. 'Do you want to go somewhere else to eat?'

'Sure.'

Kal downed the remainder of his drink as they stood up. 'I've got this,' he said.

'Please, don't be silly,' she protested.

'Look at it this way,' he said. 'I'm paying for the drink I had, rather than you paying for the one you didn't.'

Saima laughed. 'Fair enough. Thank you, then.'

The singer had started up a lively cover of 'Call Me Maybe' when they made their way to the till. The waitress looked disappointed that Kal was already leaving. As she ran his card through the machine, she glanced at Saima, standing a little behind him, and murmured softly to Kal, 'Call *me* maybe?' She scrawled her number on his receipt.

Kal ignored Saima's triumphant grin as he took the receipt and put it in his pocket.

'This has been very enlightening for me,' Saima told him as they walked outside.

'Yeah, yeah,' he said. 'Okay, where do you want to go?'

Glebe Point Road streamed with cars, buses and people conversing loudly in groups.

Saima took a second to look up and down the main strip, her arms folded across her chest. Kal took in what she was wearing for the first time, a kurta over skinny jeans – a perfect mix of her heritage, now that he thought about it.

'What do you feel like?' she asked.

'I'm starving, so something fast would be good.'

'There's this little Malaysian place down towards Broadway,' she suggested. 'It's just around the corner. They do the best laksa, and they're quick.'

'Perfect.'

They headed in the direction of Broadway. As they rounded the corner onto the busy thoroughfare, the roar of six lanes of traffic made conversation impossible, but Kal was quickly working out that Saima didn't mind the silences. The rain had cleared up, leaving in its wake a fresh, warm night, a subtle petrichor wafting over from Victoria Park across the road.

They soon arrived at the busy canteen-style restaurant, filled with milling students. 'I remember this place!' Kal said with pleasure. 'We used to come here from uni a lot.' He grabbed a number from the brusque hostess who barely looked up.

'Wait in line,' she said in a bored drawl.

'Ask her if she's a fan of Riz Ahmed,' Saima whispered, and Kal shook his head and stifled a laugh.

Pretty soon, they had ordered two chicken laksas and were seated at a communal table with a group of students excitedly chattering and sharing videos on their phones.

'It's a bit noisy here,' Kal said.

'I think they call it ambience,' she called back.

He looked around with a grin.

'What's so funny?'

'This place . . . it hasn't changed a bit,' he said and she nodded.

'Since uni days,' she said. 'Are you a Sydney guy or UTS?'

'The latter. You?'

'UWS,' she returned. 'Westie through and through.'

'But you live here now?'

'You should know,' she said, eyebrows raised.

'The Uber app's down, there have been some system errors recently,' he replied. She laughed loudly as their food arrived.

'Anyway, yes,' she said, doling out napkins and cutlery from the silver bucket in the middle of the table, 'I'm in Ultimo now. I've become a bit of a regular here when cooking dinner is a bit too much to think about.'

'Fair enough.' They dug into their laksas.

'Do you cook much?' she asked between mouthfuls.

'Not that much. I'm just never at home to cook, and when I am, it seems silly to cook for just one person. When Krista stayed over, though, I'd sometimes make dinner for her.' He stopped short, feeling awkward for bringing Krista up. It was a dick move, talking about past relationships on the first date. Though, *was* this a date? It seemed to be a mix of interview, date and just hanging out with a friend.

'So you *can* cook,' Saima said, seeming not to be fazed at all by his mention of Krista.

'Yeah, kind of. Stir-fries, roasts, schnitzel. I'm still working on the perfect steak. It all depends on the cut of meat, apparently.'

'Did Krista like your cooking?'

He didn't particularly want to answer that. *Yes*, he wanted to say. Krista had always said it was a big turn-on whenever he cooked for her. Usually they were barely done eating when things would escalate and they'd be making out on the dining table. Sometimes they didn't even make it to the bedroom. He'd lost count of how many times dinner had been left unfinished after they'd leaped onto each other for dessert. It turned out to be a great incentive to be a better cook.

Literally none of this was appropriate conversation for this maybe/maybe-not date. Saima was still looking at him expectantly, so he hummed noncommittally and scooped up a fat golden chunk of bean curd.

Laksa isn't a particularly sexy meal to eat, he thought as he slurped up a noodle. *But by god, it's a satisfying one.*

'I've got to come back here and eat again,' he mumbled. 'I'd forgotten just how good it is.'

'I think this laksa is a human right,' Saima said. The steam wafted from her bowl and onto her face, making it glisten.

117

'Freedom, justice and Hokkien noodles?' he asked.

She sat back with a satisfied sigh. 'And just the right amount of chilli, of course.' A spot of soup clung to her chin.

Without thinking, Kal grabbed his napkin and reached over to dab it clean.

Saima looked as startled as he felt at the move. She quickly took the napkin from him, their fingers briefly touching as she did. 'I must look a mess,' she said with a self-conscious chuckle.

'No, you're all good. Anyway, you can't say you truly enjoyed laksa without leaving a memento somewhere on your person.'

'And yet somehow you've managed to remain spotless,' she observed. 'Must be that Hollywood magic.'

'I'm pretty nifty with my chopsticks,' he said, with a shrug.

'But what about your fingers?' she asked and then blushed rosily. 'Oh god. I mean, how well do you eat with your hands?'

He tried not to laugh, but a smirk slipped out nonetheless. 'I'm pretty good with those too.'

She made a face. 'Modest, too.' And Kal lost his half-hearted battle with the guffaw that had bubbled up in his chest.

Saima tried to insist on paying the bill because, as she said, 'I owe you for the unsolicited orange juice.' They battled it out at the till in front of the bored hostess until Kal managed to tap the machine first.

'If the guilt is too much for you,' he said, 'you can get the ice cream. That is, if you've still got room after all that.'

She scoffed. 'Dessert goes into another stomach, everyone knows that.'

They headed towards a new gelato place near Railway Square that he'd heard good things about, falling into step as they walked, talking about some of their other greatest eatery hits around Sydney. Kal usually didn't venture beyond the Lower North Shore and the city, whereas Saima liberally sampled from the West, where she'd grown up and still worked, to Strathfield ('hands down, best Korean barbecue'), Newtown ('there's a place that just does lamingtons, it's wild') and Redfern ('converted me into a ramen fiend'). Kal, who was often in Melbourne for work, waxed lyrical about his favourite Argentinian steakhouse, after which talk naturally turned to favourite places to travel.

'Oh, my bucket list is about three metres long,' Saima exclaimed. 'But I've never had the time to just pick up and go, you know?'

'It was a bit different for me,' Kal said, and described how he spent much of his childhood trailing after his father on business trips, seeing the world but rarely appreciating it.

As they spoke, he marvelled at how completely at ease he felt. Around her he didn't feel like he had to appear a certain way, talk a certain way, laugh a certain way. It felt – he didn't want to say *easy*, but it was different. A nice different.

At the gelato place, he got a scoop of tiramisu and she got mango sorbet.

'Mango,' she told him, 'is my favourite fruit. Especially Pakistani mango. They're quite hard to come by in Australia, but my mum somehow manages to get her hands on a box every summer. Black-market contacts in the community, probably. Anyway, she says they're much better than the Australian mangoes.'

'Next time she gets a box, let me know. I want to try a Pakistani mango. I don't think I've had one since I was a kid,' he said. 'I'll pay top black-market dollar for them and everything.'

'Sure,' she said. They sat at a small table in the corner of the gelato shop, and she took a deep breath. 'So, all night I've been thinking about how to apologise for what I said last time we met.' She was focused on her sorbet as she spoke. 'I've figured simple and direct is best. It was uncalled for, and I'm sorry.'

When she finally did meet his eyes, butterflies fluttered unexpectedly in his belly. He didn't even notice the ice cream melting down his hand.

She blinked and looked down at his fingers. 'I'll get some napkins.' She calmly wiped the ice cream from the table then looked at the mess in his hand. 'You're going to have to either eat your ice cream or throw it away, because it's not going to stop dripping if you just sit there like that.'

If she had been another girl, he might have reached over and offered her a taste of his cone, maybe stolen a spoonful of hers. And if she had been this other girl, maybe she would laugh and they would share a perfectly ice-creamy kiss.

But she was not this imaginary girl, and he still didn't know if this was a date. He got up and threw the soggy ice-cream cone into the bin.

'Do you mind if I ask you what happened with you and Krista?' she asked him when he got back to the table. His heart thumped in his chest.

'As far as I'm concerned, we've broken up,' he said. 'Though it's possible that she might think there's something to salvage here.' He waited for the inevitable comment about how complicated that all sounded.

'Have you thought of going out with desi girls before?' she surprised him by asking. She was once again focusing on her sorbet cup and so didn't notice his slight start. Kal edged forward on his stool, once again feeling like he was on the verge of something vitally important. 'I've got lots of girls on my client list who I think would be ideal for you.'

He abruptly crashed back to reality. '*Your client list?*'

'Well, yes.'

He was suddenly annoyed. 'That makes it sound like you run an escort agency.'

'Oh, come on, it's not like that,' she said, refusing to be drawn into an argument. 'I probably do a great deal more research than an escort agency might.' She smiled as she said that but he was in no mood to laugh.

'Is that what this has been tonight?' Kal said, feeling hurt without knowing why. 'Research?'

Saima blinked. 'Um, yes. What did you think it was?'

He couldn't answer her without feeling like a fool.

'Okay, let's get back on track here,' she said. 'I just thought that maybe it would be nice for you to meet a girl who understood you and your background. And—' she added hastily as he opened his mouth to reply, '—I don't just mean your Pakistani background. I mean being a third culture kid, like you said in your text. You're not the only one who's travelled to lots of places, leaving you feeling like you don't belong. I know quite a few women who've experienced the same. It's why they've found it hard to meet the right person to settle down with.'

'And what about you?' he snapped. 'Or are you too good to settle down with anyone?'

'What have I got to do with anything?' she asked, nonplussed.

'Forget it.' He got up, ready to call it a night. Her voice stopped him.

'Do you realise that we end up fighting whenever we meet? And then you run away from me?' She said this calmly as she picked up her handbag, but he saw her hand shake a little. So she wasn't as unmoved by their evening as she appeared.

Good, he thought irrationally. 'I believe the first time we met, it was *you* who ran off into the night.'

She nodded. 'Yes, that's true. But I don't want us to end all our meetings with a fight. I really am sorry about how our last conversation went down.'

'Well, maybe if there are no more meetings there will be no more fights.' Kal regretted the words as soon as they came out of his mouth.

'I'm sorry you feel that way.' She stopped, looked at him for a second and walked out of the gelato shop. He followed closely behind, turning right where she turned left and striding a few steps in the opposite direction. Then he stopped. Before his brain connected to his feet, he turned around and loped back to her side.

They stood less than an arm's length apart, not speaking. He could have bent his head to lay his lips softly on hers as he wrapped his arms around her waist.

Except, of course, he couldn't. Not with her.

'I didn't mean that about no more meetings,' he finally said.

'Okay,' she said.

'And I get it, you're not looking for a relationship right now, and that's your business. I understand.'

'Okay,' she said again.

'I should go,' he said. 'Do you want me to order you an Uber?'

'My business . . .' she said suddenly. 'Kal, my business isn't doing that great. There are a bunch of reasons why, but I don't have it in me to get into them now. But if you could meet some of the girls on my list it would make a huge difference, especially to their parents. You're a good catch, which you must know. Having you as a client – it could completely turn things around for me.'

'Why do I feel this is the first time you're being totally honest with me?' he said.

She looked away. 'It's not just about saving my business,' she said softly. 'Because I do think meeting some of my clients could

122

be good for you, Kal. I do. Nobody's booking a nikkah or anything if you meet them. But maybe it could give you another perspective that could help you turn things around?'

'Who said I needed things turned around?' he blurted. Was the strange crisis that gripped him so obvious to everybody?

'Nobody,' she answered, a fraction too quickly. 'I just – I had a feeling, that's all.'

He regarded her steadily for a moment more, waiting to see if she'd say anything else, but she didn't.

'Okay, fine' he said at last. 'Let me think about it. If that's what you really want?'

A huge smile beamed across her face, so bright it almost hurt to look at it. She reached out and gripped his arm, squeezing tightly once, twice, then let go. 'Thank you,' she said. 'You won't regret it.'

Chapter 11

Saima sat at her desk, going through the names of women she could set Kal up with, but recollections of the evening they spent together kept popping into her mind, distracting her from the task at hand. Like when he had reached over and dabbed at her chin with the napkin, how she'd felt embarrassed but also didn't mind the warmth of his fingers; how his eyes were so bright and open as they fell into a comfortable conversation; the look of shock, almost hurt, on his face when she had brought the conversation around to matchmaking. How wrong it had felt to do so. Was that because she felt guilty about his parents' secret involvement? Or was there something more to it? She stared out of the window as the rain pattered down outside, decided to push it all into the Too-Hard Basket, and turned her full attention to her shortlist.

It had been a few days since they'd spoken, and Kal hadn't yet committed to meeting anyone, but she figured showing him actual options might be a better way to bring him onto her client list. She pulled up the profile of one of her newer clients, Shayla Irfan.

Saima quickly skimmed through her private notes on her client, which she separated out from the formal biodatas she shared with potential matches.

Shayla Irfan: 30-year-old lawyer. Born and bred in Sydney, younger daughter of Reza and Fatima Irfan, two practising GPs. Career-focused, not interested in unambitious men who don't share similar career drive. Has had a couple of boyfriends in the past, but nothing serious. Likes shopping, brunches, going to bars on the weekend, designer labels. Not afraid to splash her cash, doesn't want to be with someone overly careful with money. Wants to have children at some point but isn't too hung up on it right now; too busy with work and social life. Says looks are important.

In an ideal world, she would have a similar bank of notes on Kal, but she only had their meeting the other night to go by, since she hadn't formally interviewed him as she usually would. But on paper, at least, Shayla looked perfect. She texted Kal.

Are you ready to meet the perfect woman yet?

Is there any such thing? he responded almost immediately.

Saima smiled and started typing. About as much as there's any such thing as the perfect man.

I am shocked and offended.

K, let me rephrase. Are you ready to meet YOUR perfect woman?

Interested to know what you think that is.

For one thing, someone who won't squabble with you.

Squabble. I like that word. Will challenge myself to use it in conversation with someone today.

It works well in Scrabble, too.

I suck at Scrabble. Well, I did when I used to play as a kid. My sister always beat me.

She sounds smart.

Hey, I'm smart too!

Never said you weren't. And if you were REALLY smart, you'd go out with this girl.

He didn't respond after that.

When the following morning Kal still hadn't replied, Saima wandered into Jess's office.

'On the whole, would you say I'm a pushy person?' she asked.

Her friend gazed at her, considering. 'Not really. Why?'

Saima's phone pinged before she could answer.

Used squabble on my friend Tom at work. He thought it was a rugby term like scrum.

Saima leaned against Jess's wall as her fingers flew across her phone. Try tiff next time. Almost as good as squabble. So what do you think about the date?

Is that what you call them? I thought they'd be more like meet and greets. Would there be a chaperone?

Pretty sure Shayla will be happy to meet you one on one. Meet and greet sounds too formal.

And yet date is too casual for what this is. Appointment then?

Feels too medical.

Rendezvous?

Too French.

Mulaqat?

Saima did a double-take. You speak Urdu?

Googled it. And now you're judging me for losing my mother tongue.

I don't speak it well enough myself to judge anyone. Anyway, you could've just pretended you were fluent.

That would be a lie, though. Feels like a bad place to start a relationship.

Kal's last text pulled Saima up short as her conscience twinged again. Was she lying to him by omitting his parents' involvement? Had she poisoned this relationship or friendship – or whatever this was – by concealing the full truth from Kal? If he found a match

126

and fell in love via her services, then at the end of the day what would it matter if it was his parents who were the ones to hire her? She would have helped him just as much as he had helped her.

I'll set up the date then, she texted. He didn't reply.

'Okay, I *have* to know what's going on.' Jess's voice made Saima jump – she had forgotten for a moment where she was. 'You've been standing there for the past few minutes lost in your phone, and *what* is that look on your face, woman?'

'There's no look on my face,' Saima said, hastily pocketing her phone.

'Who were you texting?'

'Just a client.'

'Girl, that was no "just" anything. Do you realise you had a goofy smile on your face basically the whole time? Until whatever happened at the end there, where you looked like you were about to shoot a puppy.'

'What, I'm not allowed to smile now?'

Jess crossed her arms and gave her an unimpressed look. 'I don't think you're supposed to smile like *that* about clients. If it's *not* a client, though, you need to tell Aunty Jess about it immediately or face my wrath.'

'It was a client, promise.'

'Mmm-hmm.'

In her pocket Saima felt her phone buzz. She pulled it out to see it was Kal texting back with a simple OK – making a smile creep across her face.

Jess eyeballed her.

'If you must know, it's that rich couple's son,' Saima said, looking back at her.

Jess leaped out of her chair and charged towards Saima. '*WHAT?* You reeled in the big fish and *you didn't tell me?*'

'Oh my god, would you relax?' Saima exclaimed, as Jess shook her. 'It literally just happened!'

'What, like right now?'

'Yes!'

'Just like that? As you were standing there? Out of the blue? After you yelled at him last week or whenever it was?'

'Well . . .' Saima hedged. 'Not exactly out of the blue.'

'Aha! I knew it! You've been up to something! If – and *only* if – you tell me everything right this minute, I might just forgive you for leaving me out of what was obviously some top-quality scheming.'

'Woman, you seriously need to chill. There was no scheming. I asked him out for a coffee—'

'A *scheming* coffee?'

'—a *regular* coffee, and then I gave him the sales pitch and he agreed to consider it.' Saima decided on the spot not to go into the details of Laksa Night because it would get Jess more excited for exactly the wrong reasons.

Jess looked deflated. 'Oh. That's far less juicy than I thought it was going to be.'

'Which is what I've been telling you!'

'What was with the smile, then?'

'Look, if there was a smile – and I'm not accepting that there was, mind you – then it was because the big fish has just agreed to go on a . . . on a date with one of my other clients.'

'That's amazing news!' Jess squeezed her arm with excitement.

'Yes, it is!' Saima grinned. 'And now, if you've calmed down at last, I need to go and call her to share that good news.'

Shayla's warm reception to Saima's call was multiplied when she saw the photograph in Kal's biodata. 'Sounds promising, hun,' she said. 'Set us up and let me know the deets, gotta go, mwah!'

With Shayla and Kal's busy schedules, Saima managed to squeeze in their first meeting a couple of weeks later, on a Sunday afternoon at Circular Quay. It was a tried and tested setting for a lot of her couples – it was neutral ground, casual and conducive to getting to know one another, with plenty of different activities to suit a variety of tastes, from cafés and bars, walking along the waterfront or into the Botanic Garden, avoiding the bin chickens, to people-watching, ferry rides and, of course, the MCA.

When she texted Kal the time and place, he was silent for a time and didn't answer her follow-up phone call. He texted back a day later. Yeah, all right.

You're meeting opposite Wharf 4, just outside City Extra. I told her to look for a cross between Dev Patel and Riz Ahmed, she wrote.

Sunday afternoon came and went. Saima busied herself with chores and was scrubbing the shower grout with a toothbrush before she admitted to herself how uncharacteristically nervous she was about the date's progress.

By five o'clock, she hadn't heard from either Shayla or Kal. She assumed they were still on their date. *No news is good news*, she tried to convince herself. She got started on an unnecessarily elaborate dinner to pass the time. It was while she was finely chopping some broccoli that her phone finally rang. She quickly dropped the knife, wiped her hands on a kitchen towel and picked up the phone.

Kal.

'Hey! How was the date?'

'I'm not sure date is the right word for it.' He sounded a bit flat.

'Okay, appointment, then? Mulaqat?' Saima tried to keep things light and upbeat, but he clearly wasn't in the mood.

'I thought we could go for a walk, but it wasn't possible.'

'Why not?'

'She turned up in stiletto heels.'

'Maybe she prefers to walk in heels.'

'She didn't.'

'So what did you end up doing?'

'We went to Opera Bar.' He fell silent, like he was trying to figure out what to say.

'Were you two able to get to know one another?' Saima asked gently.

'I mean, sort of? It was pretty loud there, there was a band playing. And it wasn't exactly easy. She kept going on her phone.'

'Maybe it was urgent?'

'I don't think so.' Kal sighed. 'Look, Saima. I know we talked about me meeting someone different through your matchmaking service. But I have to tell you, aside from being Pakistani, Shayla could have been anyone I'd have met at a bar.'

'There's a certain amount of trial and error with this sort of thing, Kal,' Saima tried to reassure him. 'Usually clients average around six or seven meet-ups before they find someone they like. The fact you could have met Shayla at a bar was one of the reasons I thought she might be a match, but it's totally okay that you didn't click. We learn from that and move on. Next time, it'll be someone who's a better fit.'

'Not sure about a next time. Sorry.'

'Kal, please. Give it another try.'

He sighed again. 'How much trouble is your business really in?'

Saima didn't know how to answer that. 'Don't worry about the business. I don't want you doing this just to help me out. Give it a chance for your own sake. Please?'

He went silent again.

'Are you home now?' she asked him.

'I got back an hour ago, yeah. I think she kicked on with some friends. She asked if I wanted to join, but even if we'd hit it off, I'm honestly beat. We're the same age, but I think she'd probably consider me some kind of fuddy-duddy.'

'Oh, fuddy-duddy is a word you don't hear often,' Saima said with a smile. 'My turn to try and slip it into conversation.'

'Fuddy-duddy is the best, especially because I think you have to be one to use the word.' Kal seemed to have perked up for the first time in the conversation. 'I may as well embrace it, then, hey? Tom's always saying I've turned into a grandpa.'

'Well, if you're a fuddy-duddy, then I'm not sure what I am. Never been the partying type.'

'I bet you're a star on the dance floor, though.' She could hear the smile in his voice.

'I have been known to show off some moves in my time, at various weddings.'

'*Really?*' He sounded very intrigued now. '"Weddings" means that there'll be video evidence of this somewhere. Care to share some footage?'

'Not a chance!'

'Not even when I tell you my mum enrolled me in jazz and tap lessons when I was a kid?'

'No way!'

He laughed. 'I'll tell you what else, Saima Khan. I was *good* at it too. Like, *recital* good.'

'Now I know you're lying – no Pakistani mum would ever take her son to a dance recital.'

'Maybe you don't know desis as well as you think you do?' He chuckled. 'I promise you, there were recitals.'

'Hm, I can't picture it.'

'Fine . . . I know I'm going to regret this but let me send you some photographic evidence.' His voice muffled as he must have been searching his phone. 'It's here somewhere . . . got it!'

Saima's phone pinged with his incoming message. She opened it to see a sullen Kal, about ten or eleven years old, hair spiked, wearing sleeveless black dancewear under a sequinned red vest and bow tie. A beaming Ruby stood beside him.

'Oh, this . . . This is the best!' she said, unable to suppress her laugh.

'I think the look on my face says it all. Mum took about a hundred photos, which got shared far and wide. My sister likes to post that one to my Facebook wall every birthday.'

'Why did you go along with it?' she asked. 'If you didn't like doing the lessons?'

There was a rustle, and she pictured him shrugging. 'You know how it is,' he said nonchalantly. 'Ammy was very excited about the whole thing, so I went along with it.'

'But you clearly applied yourself to it if you were at recitals. I mean, even for migrant excellence, that's amazing.'

His laugh this time was softer, more thoughtful. 'Honestly? It was nice to spend the time with Ammy. We weren't really into family activities, but she got fully into the dance stuff, and I can't tell you how much she loved seeing me onstage. Plus, it kinda helped me later in life. When my friends and I hit the clubs, they hung out on the sidelines while I had the confidence to actually take the floor. Which, you know . . .'

'Made you a knockout with the girls,' Saima said, finishing his sentence.

'Well, I don't want to brag . . .'

'So really, you should be thanking your mum,' she said.

'Ah, I don't think I can mention the dance lessons even now without her grumbling about it. She was quite disappointed I stopped.'

'Why did you stop, if you don't mind my asking?'

He fell silent.

'I'm sorry, I didn't mean to—' she began.

'I don't know, I guess I started getting more into team sports with my friends . . . It's easier to be one of the boys when you do rugby rather than dance. Which now, in hindsight, sounds like a stupid thing to admit.'

'Yeah, but I guess it goes back to trying to fit in, right?'

'I guess . . . Bet you didn't change yourself to fit in, though.'

'Me? Nah, I accepted my life as a person on the fringes. I was the weirdo who was never quite like the others.'

'Saima the weirdo . . . Hmm . . .'

'Hey! Not that you can go around saying that!'

He laughed. 'I wouldn't dare!'

They were both quiet for a moment.

'This conversation helped,' Kal said at last. 'After the afternoon I had.'

'I'm glad,' she said. 'And next time it'll be better.'

'You don't let up, do you?'

'Nope!' Saima replied. 'But I've got to say, that dance recital pic was a happy bonus.'

'Now it's only fair that you share footage of yourself on the dance floor!'

'I work hard to ensure there is no evidence,' she said, laughing.

'Oh, I bet there's something out there,' he said. 'I'll have to search it out.'

'Don't go to the trouble. I'm too much of a fuddy-duddy,' she said, unable to hide the smile in her voice.

'Ha! You used it in a sentence,' he said, laughing along with her.

Saima rang Shayla for a debrief the following day.

'Look, no offence, hun,' Shayla began. 'But he didn't do it for me. He's a hottie, sure, but he kinda seemed like he didn't want to be there.'

Saima paced across her office. 'No offence taken. He mentioned something similar.'

'Well, I knew pretty quickly that he wasn't going to be a keeper, so I kinda checked out,' Shayla admitted. 'I know I can be a bit much for people,' she said, her usually breezy tone now serious. 'You've got no idea how many times guys have said that and dipped, and I'm not going to let them bring me down just because they can't handle all of this.'

'Nor should you,' said Saima. 'Was Kal as bad as all that?'

'Look, he didn't say it to my face and he wasn't a dick. But we weren't vibing, and that's fine. I'm just not interested in putting in work to make something happen where it's clearly not the guy's priority from the jump. It's why I came to you in the first place, right?'

'Fair enough,' said Saima. 'And please, the last thing I want to do is make you feel bad because things didn't work out. I'm here to listen and learn, and hopefully bring something great for you out of that.'

'Totally!' Shayla's voice bounced right back to its usual perkiness. 'And hun, you nailed the stud category!'

Saima laughed. 'Got it, the stud factor is on point, it's the vibe check we need to work on.'

'Yeah, totally! Okay, love you, girl, but gotta run. Talk soon, mwah!'

Saima decided to give Kal some space after the unsuccessful date with Shayla. It was important, she always thought, for clients to come to any potential match with a positive mindset, and she didn't want the previous unsuccessful attempt to cloud the next potential match. It was a couple of weeks before she pulled out her shortlist and ran through it once again.

She thought about what he had said, about meeting someone different from the people he normally associated with. Perhaps a more traditional woman would suit him better, one with close ties to her heritage and family but a modern outlook on what she wanted out of life. She knew just the woman who would fit the bill.

Mariam Hamid: 25 years old, born in Hyderabad, India. Moved to Sydney at 14 with her parents, Naima (teacher) and Arshad Hamid (bank manager). Studied accounting at uni, currently working in a community group to promote migrant women's health in Western Sydney. Passionate about women's rights. Never dated. Bit of a homebody. Likes to bake, read books, helps her grandmother with gardening on the weekends.

Mariam was a conservative choice, true, but Saima thought that Kal might gel with her earnestness and empathy. She rang Mr and Mrs Hamid to propose the match.

'This Khalid,' said Mr Hamid, a little dubiously. 'Do you think he will look after our Mariam? He seems very modern, very hi-fi. Will our Mariam be enough for him?'

'Absolutely, Uncle,' Saima assured him. 'Let them meet, see if there is a connection. If not, no harm done.'

'Beti, with our community, there is no such thing as no harm done,' said Mrs Hamid. 'There is always talk. There must be a chaperone at the meeting to observe the niceties. We cannot have any talk that Mariam is a fast girl, meeting ladkas on her own. You know, we have been hearing some things about some of your approaches, and you understand that we are a good Muslim family . . .'

'Yes, of course,' Saima replied quickly.

She hadn't anticipated this, and briefly wondered how Kal would feel about a third wheel. He'd asked the question about chaperones once already, so she took a gamble that he would roll with it pretty comfortably.

'It's okay, Aunty, I understand. Leave it with me, and I will arrange things.'

Tracking Kal down took longer than Saima expected. Her texts went read but unanswered, and she had left him enough voicemails to be considered a nuisance. After nearly two weeks of being ghosted, it was obvious that he was avoiding her – which, on top of the fact she'd had a couple of prospective clients cancel meetings with her last minute without any explanation, had put her on edge.

Then, out of nowhere one afternoon, the parents of a client called her to say they wanted their daughter taken off her books. When she pleaded with them to explain why, they hung up on her.

'Ack!' She'd cried out so loudly at the end of the call that Jess had come running to check if she was okay.

'Do something to distract yourself,' Jess made Saima promise as they were leaving work.

Easier said than done, Saima said to herself that evening, when she got home. *Imagine caring what some random aunty thinks over your child's happiness*, she thought, as she slammed a glass of water so hard on the counter that much of it spilled out. As she cleaned up, she figured she should do something to relax. There was no option but to put on her favourite crime podcast. Nothing more soothing than listening to the dulcet tones of someone narrating a murder. Just as she was settling into it, her phone pinged.

Sorry just saw your last text. Work's had me beat, deadline looming, no time to respond before. It was Kal.

Her heart began to race but she still persevered with the podcast. It was just getting to the good bit, after all.

All work and no play . . . she texted back quickly.

Ha! I said that to someone a few months back. I pulled back on work for a bit after that. But now it's pulled me back in.

You need other things to distract you.

Let me guess. A client of yours is the answer?

She hadn't been thinking of that, but now that he mentioned it, she swiftly pulled her head out of the podcast, hit 'Pause' and put her business hat on.

You must be psychic. It's a very impressive skill, I'll add it to your biodata, she texted back.

Let me see if I can psychically tell you how I feel about this.

Sorry, wearing my tinfoil hat, can't receive any transmissions.

LOL.

Listen, Kal, what have you got to lose except for a couple of hours one afternoon? Do you fancy doing some gardening?

What?

This client, Mariam, she's great. Her family's a bit more traditional though and they'd prefer a chaperone. I thought you could go meet her at her nani's place.

Even as she texted the words, she knew that Kal wasn't going to buy it. The dots appeared on her screen to show he was typing something. They remained for ages, before disappearing without a text.

OK, maybe it's a bit out there but also something different? she wrote.

He didn't respond.

What the hell, she thought, and dialled his number. He picked up after the second ring.

'I scared you off,' she said.

'Nah, I'm just tired.' He certainly sounded it. 'Got a big deadline coming, so it's been a long week.'

'Maybe we should chat in the morning, then?'

'Maybe,' he said. 'Though I'm in meetings pretty much all day tomorrow.'

'Is this what it's usually like for you at work?'

'Yeah, I guess,' he said. 'It's always busier when there's a big project due. When I turned thirty, I thought I'd focus on things other than work. But you know what I ended up doing? Nothing. It was just the gym, catching up with friends, some video games. It seemed pointless, so work's taken up more of my time again.'

'Maybe you could get a hobby,' she suggested.

'Don't say gardening. A certain nani could teach me?'

She laughed.

'So, how's work going on your end?' he asked. 'I mean, aside from persuading me to go on dates.'

'Oh, you know . . . It has good moments and bad. Like any job, I guess.'

'Something happen?'

'Let's just say it's complicated,' she said.

'Is this something to do with the "bunch of reasons" you mentioned on Laksa Night?'

She hesitated. 'Some of the families are a little put off by my methods.'

'Well, you are persistent!' he said lightly.

'I haven't had to be this persistent with anyone but you, actually. Anyway, it's not that. I mean, is it that bad I want my couples to get to know each other before they marry? Six months isn't too much to ask when you're considering spending a lifetime with someone, is it? But clearly some people think it is! And just because I don't match my clients based on status, community pressures, that sort of stuff, doesn't mean I'm going to put them with someone they're not suited to.'

'Sounds reasonable—'

'Except you know what our community is like,' she continued. 'Some families only want other upper- or middle-class matches for their children. Or professionals only. But I don't operate like that. And then there are the cultural biases. The prospect can't be too dark-skinned. They can't have underlying conditions, like health stuff . . . One family freaked out because the bride was allergic to nuts. "Will her children also be allergic?" they asked me. Honestly!' She stopped and took a breath, letting the anger seep out of her. 'Sorry, didn't mean to offload on you like that. I just had a tough day at the office.'

'No, it's fine. Of course there'll be pushback when you're trying to break convention the way you are. It must be hard.'

'Yeah. I'm just so over the talk. Some families are refusing to come see me now.' She let this slip without meaning to.

'Which is why your business is in trouble?'

'Yeah, that's one of the reasons.'

'I'm sorry.'

'It's not your fault.'

'Have you thought any more about expanding your base?' he asked. 'Move away from the restrictions of one community?'

'What, and land myself in all the complications of a whole bunch of different communities that I don't know? Anyway, where would I even begin? It would mean starting at the bottom all over again. I don't think I have the energy.'

'Would it be more or less energy than fighting back against the talk you mentioned?'

She thought about it. 'I'm not sure. It'd be a fight, either way.'

'Yeah, but you strike me as a fighter,' he said, and she could hear the grin in his voice. 'You've dragged me kicking and screaming this far, after all.'

'A little less kicking and screaming would be very much appreciated,' she replied.

'Then what on earth would we talk about?' he joked. 'My dance lessons again?'

'Yes please!' Saima said, smiling.

'How about I tell you instead what an amazing union star I was going to be?'

'No thanks!'

'What's wrong with rugby?'

'Whatever I say here will probably be the wrong thing, except I don't think I've known a single desi guy who played rugby union!'

'We went on a world tour and everything,' he said, a little proudly.

'God, you really are a North Shore boy! I think the most exciting school trip we went on was to Old Sydney Town, and there you go, trotting the globe.'

'Well, if it helps, I'm still hearing from my father about how much that trip cost,' Kal replied dryly.

'So, going back to the topic of meeting the girl,' she broached, carefully. 'What do you think about a catch-up with Bachelorette Number Two?'

He paused for moment, clearly adjusting to the sudden shift in gear. 'Which one's the bachelorette? The girl or her nani?'

Saima laughed. 'They're a package deal.'

'What makes you think she'd be a better fit for me than your last candidate?'

She thought about it for a minute. 'Look, I'm not going to lie, she comes from a family that's far more conservative than yours. And she's Indian, not Pakistani—'

'—I'm sensing another "but"—'

'—*but* her family are lovely and you can't help but be swept up in their homely vibe. Can you believe they all get together to cook? Every Sunday. How sweet is that? I thought it might be a nice change of pace.'

'What else?'

'And yes, she's traditional, but that doesn't mean she's some kind of village girl. She's passionate about the things that matter. You should hear her talk about improving health outcomes for migrant women. I couldn't help but be impressed.'

'You're doing a great sales pitch here.'

Saima grinned to herself. 'But wait, there's more! She is incredibly empathetic. And though she's on the quiet side, I got the impression that a quieter, slower pace of life was something you might welcome. And you just said you were looking for something other than work to fill your life.'

Kal paused again. Then, apropos of nothing, 'Are you seeing anyone?'

The sudden question caught her off guard. 'I don't – I'm not—'

'Why does the matchmaker not matchmake for herself?'

'It's easier being single in my line of work,' she replied briskly. 'I can fully focus on my clients, no distractions. If I were married, I'd spend half my time managing my own relationship.'

'Yes, I'm sure that's what you tell everyone. What's the real reason? Come on, you can tell me.'

Saima stopped. She found herself uncharacteristically trusting someone with the truth. 'My parents had a seriously dysfunctional marriage that ended very badly. I guess I've never wanted to take that risk myself,' she admitted.

He was quiet for a moment. 'I'm sorry to hear about your folks.'

'It was a long time ago.' She recited her usual response to any sympathy.

'But you know, just because it happened a certain way with them doesn't mean it'll happen the same with you. We don't have to repeat our parents' mistakes.'

'Oof, that sounds very deep,' she said trying to keep her voice light.

'Well, I'm not just a shallow North Shore boy, you know.'

'I've never thought of you as shallow,' she said quietly.

'Okay, good,' he said. 'Though to be honest, it's hard for me to figure out what you're thinking half the time.'

'What do you mean by that?'

'I don't know . . . Let's just say you're hard to read. You'd probably make a good poker player.'

'How d'you know I'm not?'

'Are you?'

'No,' she said, smiling to herself as she swatted away an errant thought about how much she enjoyed talking to him.

'And I shouldn't have asked you about matchmaking for yourself. But . . . On a personal level, what's there for you? *Who's* there for you?'

Saima closed her eyes and pictured that future. '*I'm* there for me,' she said firmly. But for the first time, there was someone else there too, just out of focus. She mentally brushed him aside, but he came back, coalescing like steam curling up from a bowl of laksa.

'Just you?' Did he sound disappointed or was she making that up?

'Things are easier to achieve when you're only relying on yourself, Kal.'

He sighed. 'I think maybe your parents cast a long shadow.'

'Maybe. Or maybe I prefer self-sufficiency.' This whole conversation was getting strangely maudlin, and it was time to move on. 'It's funny,' she joked, 'I get my clients to tell me their deepest secrets but none of them have ever turned around and asked me for mine. I'm not sure I like it.'

'Well, not all clients are the same.'

'Yep, you're definitely a special case. Anyway, the way I see it, there's not a lot I can do to change the past, so I'm not going to dwell on it, just put it aside and move on. But the future? That I can change. Like Mariam Hamid and her nani. Will you meet them?'

'Back to business, I see.'

'You did say I was persistent!'

Kal was silent for what seemed like an eternity.

'Let me think about it,' he eventually said.

She groaned. 'Okay, fine. But don't think I'm not going to follow up.'

'I would never.' Kal went quiet again. 'And Saima, don't let the bastards get you down. Though I probably shouldn't call them bastards. But I mean the people who don't agree with your methods. Don't let them put a dent in your side. Keep going, okay? It's a good thing that you're persistent.'

'I appreciate that,' she said, meaning it.

'Goodnight, Saima.'

After Kal hung up, Saima stared at the darkened screen for a minute before putting her phone down beside her.

Chapter 12

Kal was waiting for Lachie and Nicole outside Bondi Pavilion. After weeks of gentle reminders, Nicole had at last demanded his presence at a long-delayed meeting with Krista to finally hash things out. His friends were running late, so he walked down onto the beach, taking off his shoes to let his toes sink deep into the sand. A cold wind was whipping off the waves, heralding the impending winter. He watched a couple of surfers in the distance. The sound of the waves crashing on the rocks blended with screeching seagulls; a handful of British tourists lay shivering on beach towels nearby, discussing dinner options.

He closed his eyes for a moment, basking in the weak rays of the autumn sun, and had a sudden flash of a memory – the call of a street vendor in Karachi. 'Bun kabab! Garam aur taza!' The man had been selling bun kebabs on a cart that he wheeled around the neighbourhood. His calls were punctuated by goats bleating. Kal tried to expand the recollection but could remember little else. Maybe it was a memory from a Qurbani Eid Kal had spent there, when he was six or seven.

What struck Kal was that at this moment, those sounds from his childhood felt more like home than the sounds of this city, and he couldn't quite figure out why.

'Kal!' He turned to see Lachie and Nicole standing outside the Pavilion. They looked happy, side by side, holding hands.

'You seemed deep in thought,' Nicole said as he gave her a hug.

'I was about to lob my thong at your head,' Lachie added. Lachie wore thongs even at the height of winter. Today he was wearing a thick jumper, but there were still thongs on his feet.

'Your outfit makes zero seasonal sense, mate,' Kal commented.

'Don't even start. I tried getting him to put actual shoes on, but in the end it was thongs or not leaving the house at all.' Nicole shook her head. 'Pick your battles, am I right?'

'Where've you been, mate?' Lachie asked, slapping him on the shoulder. 'The last time we saw you was, what, more than two months ago?'

'Damn, didn't think it had been that long,' Kal said. 'Guess the constant group chats make it easy to forget about real-life contact.'

'See what happens when work sucks you back in? All work and no play . . .'

'Yeah, yeah. So what's new with you guys?'

Lachie puffed up proudly. 'Nicole,' he announced, 'just made staff specialist at the hospital.'

'Holy shit, no way!' Kal exclaimed. He hugged a blushing Nicole again. 'That's bloody amazing, well done!'

'Thanks,' she said. 'I tell you what, I won't be sorry to see the back of those exams.'

He nudged her affectionately. 'Like you didn't go and ace them anyway.' He looked over at Lachie. 'You're batting *way* above your average now, mate. Better lift your game.'

'Nah.' Lachie shook his head. 'She's the star, I'm the backup singer.'

'You'd never convince him to do anything other than be a kindy teacher,' Nicole said with a smile.

145

'I like working with people on my level,' he replied, and Kal chuckled.

'We'll have to celebrate soon,' he said.

Lachie smirked. 'If we can fit into your busy schedule.'

'At least we finally pinned you down for this lunch with Krista,' Nicole said.

'Yeah, you kept postponing it.' Lachie, as usual, had to state the obvious.

'I hoped you guys would take the hint' was Kal's dry reply.

'Stop it, we want a positive mindset only today,' Nicole said firmly, as they started walking to the café. 'I need you to sort this out once and for all so I don't need to hear about it again. Anyway, Krista was the one who was pushing for it. She's still keen on you, in case you were wondering.'

'I wasn't.' Kal raised his hands as Nicole frowned at him. 'Genuinely not being negative!' he said hastily. 'Just being honest. Krista and I are over as far as I'm concerned, and I told her so months ago. I've been seeing some other girls.'

His friends stopped in their tracks and looked at him with surprise.

'So it's not all been work then!' exclaimed Lachie. 'I might have guessed.'

'Don't get too excited. I just thought I might try something different. Go out with some desi girls for a change.'

'And?' Nicole prodded. 'Was it a change for the better?'

Kal shrugged. 'I think I was too boring for the first. And the second one was sweet, but I got on more with her nani than her.'

'Her nani?' Nicole was intrigued.

'Yeah, her grandmother. The family wanted her to have a chaperone on our date, so the nani stepped in. I enjoyed meeting her.'

'The girl or the nani?' Lachie asked.

Kal laughed. 'Both, but probably the nani more. I never got to know my grandparents since I only saw them on the rare trips we made back to Pakistan. This girl's nani taught me quite a bit about gardening. I reckon I might even get a pot plant for my balcony one day.'

'Don't go overboard now!' Nicole said.

'So how are you meeting these girls?' Lachie asked.

'If I tell you, you'll rip me to shreds,' Kal said.

'Excellent.' Lachie rubbed his hands together. 'Come on, spill.'

Kal took a deep breath. 'Basically, it's through a matchmaker,' he said, and braced himself for the barrage of wisecracks to come.

'Oh, like someone who arranges marriages?' Nicole asked. 'Why would we rib you about that? If it means you can bypass the randoms you meet on Tinder, then why not? Especially if you're looking to settle down. I reckon a lot of people would be into it.'

'Yeah, I told her she should broaden her client base,' Kal said. 'But I think Saima wants to stick within the desi community for now.'

'Saima? Is that the matchmaker's name?'

'Yeah.'

Lachie and Nicole both gave him a funny look.

'What?' he asked.

'You only smile like that when you're keen on a girl,' Lachie said.

'What? You mean Saima?'

'See, there, you did it again. Smiling when you say her name. What's going on?'

'It's nothing.' Kal shrugged, trying to keep whatever smile they were talking about off his face. 'What, am I not allowed to smile anymore?'

'You can smile all you want to,' Nicole answered slowly, looking curiously at him. 'Just not sure *that* smile should apply to the person who's setting you up on dates with *other* women . . .' She looked at her watch. 'Anyway, come on, we're late.'

They arrived at the café Krista had nominated for their meeting. She was already at their table, her annoyance obvious before they even sat down.

'The staff gave me a hard time because our whole party wasn't here. I told you in the text, remember, 2 pm sharp,' she said severely to Nicole.

'It's only 2.15,' Nicole protested. 'I'm sorry you were waiting a little bit—'

'We're lucky they even gave us the table,' Krista interrupted.

'Hi, Krista,' Kal said quickly, to defuse the situation. 'Nice to see you.'

She offered him her cheek and, as he courteously kissed it, he caught the scent of her perfume. It hit his gut and then made its way further south. She had worn it on the night they'd had outrageous car sex after dinner, and he – Kal shook the image of sex with Krista out of his head. *This is what happens after months of a dry spell*, he thought.

He focused instead on the menu, handed to him by a waiter who looked like a soap star waiting for his next gig. He took their drink order and strode cinematically away.

'Wow, twenty-five dollars for cereal,' Kal said under his breath.

'It's not cereal, it's a bliss bowl,' Krista hissed.

Another waiter with a jawline so sharp it could cut ice brought them their drinks.

'Can we order the food now as well?' Nicole asked him.

Lachie leaned back in his chair, his be-thonged feet sticking out from under the table. *What would it take to be as relaxed as Lachie?* Kal wondered, discreetly trying to stretch the tension out of his neck. Lachie met Kal's gaze and gave him a wry, reassuring shrug and smile, which Kal returned.

'What are you both smiling about?' Krista asked.

'Kal's been doing a lot of smiling today,' Nicole said, grinning cheekily to herself as she sipped her chai.

'Oh yes?' Krista edged forward in her seat to look Kal in the eye. 'How come?'

'No reason,' Kal replied.

'You're looking well,' she said next.

'Thanks.'

'Been hitting the gym?'

'No, the opposite. I haven't been going as much.'

'I get that,' she said. 'I've not been myself since we last saw each other either.' He opened his mouth to correct her assumption, then snapped it closed again. 'And,' she continued, clearing her throat and taking a deep breath, 'I've been thinking. I wanted to say that I didn't mean what I said when I last saw you.'

Oh god. After months of ignoring the painful scrape that memory still made in his brain, Kal was caught off guard by Krista's sudden mention of it.

'What did you say when you last saw him?' Nicole asked curiously when he didn't respond.

'I said – well, I'm not proud of it – I said a family like his should be proud to welcome a girl like me into the fold.'

'Actually, you said a *Pakistani* family like mine should be proud to welcome an *Aussie* girl like you,' Kal interjected flatly. He didn't want to go into this, not right now with his friends watching, but she had pushed him and it spilled out.

After the argument, Kal had first blamed himself for not introducing her to his parents or taking her to that wedding. Then he'd blamed the horrible costume she'd bought to wear to the wedding. But all along, her words, uttered with such contempt, ate away at him. In that moment, he had known exactly what she thought of him: that he was the outsider, the migrant who should be grateful a girl like her was even interested in lowering herself to his level.

'Ugh.' The sound escaped Lachie's mouth without him realising it.

'No, it came out wrong,' Krista said, tears starting in her eyes. 'You took it wrong. I didn't mean it the way you said it.'

'How should I have taken it?' Kal asked politely.

'*You* were the one who said you didn't want to introduce me to your family because they were Pakistani, even though your father calls himself *George*, for god's sake. I know you've dated white girls before, so what was so wrong with *me* that you didn't want me to meet them?' Her face was red. Lachie and Nicole looked away, clearly uncomfortable. Kal searched for the right words to say.

A cheerful waiter arrived with an armful of plates.

'Oh, what a load of glum faces we have here!' he said with a bright smile. 'Hopefully the food will cheer you all up!' He began to place the dishes on the table. 'Now, who's having the scrambled eggs?'

Kal raised his hand.

'Here you go, Dev Patel!' the waiter said merrily, with a wink.

Lachie snorted loudly before letting out a big guffaw. He set Kal off as well, and before long, the two of them were in hysterics. Nicole grinned and shook her head.

'Well, I'm glad I was able to cheer you all up!' The waiter headed off.

'There's nothing wrong with you,' Kal finally said to Krista. 'I wanted to protect you. They haven't been particularly kind to the other girls who *have* met them.'

They dug in to their meals, and talk turned to the more genial topics of Nicole's new job and an upcoming trip Krista had planned. Eventually, Nicole tossed her napkin onto the table.

'Well, it's been lovely to catch up with you both,' she said. 'Lachie and I have to head off to my sister's baby shower now, but you guys can stay on? We'll sort out the bill so you can just chill.' She got up and Lachie followed.

'I don't mind staying on, if you're okay to,' Krista said to Kal. He decided it was the least he could do.

'Yeah, sure,' he said.

'Have fun,' Lachie said as they left.

After their friends were gone, Krista said, 'Do you think there's really a baby shower?'

Kal laughed and ordered them a couple of bloody marys. 'If there is, Lachie's overdressed with his thongs.'

As they waited for their drinks, they chatted about their mutual friends and stuff that had happened at work. It was only when her glass was clutched tightly in her hand that Krista sat forward earnestly. 'Seriously, Kal, the last thing I would *ever* want you to think was that I'm a racist. I'm so sorry if you thought that's what I was implying.'

Kal sighed inwardly. 'Don't worry about it, Krista.' It showed him once again the worst thing you could call a white person was a racist, as if that insinuation was worse than the casual racism itself. 'It's water under the bridge. And I'm sorry that I made you think I was ashamed to introduce you to my parents. It wasn't my reason, I promise you.'

'You wanted to protect me?'

'I did.'

She reached over and grabbed his hand, startling him. When he looked at her, she was biting her lip. He quickly glanced away. He knew what it meant when she did that.

'I'm *so* glad we were finally able to meet after so long apart,' she said. 'I'd hate to have left things the way we did.'

Kal cleared his throat. 'Yep, always good to clear up any mis-understandings.'

'But we had something good going there, don't you think?'

He moved his hand from under hers.

'Look, Krista, I'm trying to work some stuff out. I'm not sure it was ever a good fit—'

'It's not like this with everyone, you know?' she interjected.

'No, it's not,' he agreed. *Sometimes it's better.* The thought melted into his mind like mango sorbet.

'I get that you want to sow your wild oats and play the field and all that.'

'It's the opposite, actually. I think I'm done with that sort of stuff. But I don't know what I want next.'

'C'mon, Kal, that's what all guys say. Do you even know how much of a cliché it is to tell a woman that you don't know what you're looking for? I'm trying here. Are you really going to pull the "It's not you, it's me" line on me?'

'Krista, what is it you want me to say?' Kal asked at last. 'It's not going to work out between me and you. There are probably a hundred reasons why we're not a good fit for each other, even if we hadn't had that fight.'

Krista's face flushed. 'Seriously, you never change.' She got up, grabbed her bag, and stormed out.

Her words remained with Kal as he paid for the drinks at the till and made his way back to the beach. He turned them over in his mind as he sat on the sand to watch the waves slowly turn a darker shade of blue as the sun started to set. For a brief moment, he was angry at Krista for forcing yet another confrontation. Fresh on the heels of that anger, though, he understood where she was coming from. There had been something about their connection, after all, otherwise he wouldn't have started toying with the idea of settling down with her. Their physical chemistry had been off the charts, and he had been generally fine to let Krista call most of the shots when it came to couple decisions, so on the whole it had been an easy relationship. Thinking about it now, Kal realised that the big argument had probably happened because it had been the first time he'd resisted something Krista wanted.

As he was trying to sift through his thoughts, his phone buzzed.

I may have found the woman of your dreams, the text said.

He groaned, but then smiled, because even thinking about Saima made him feel lighter, happier. Clearly his friends could see that too. He would never have agreed to go on these dates if anyone else had asked him, yet here he was. And he was enjoying himself. Not so much on the dates themselves, though certainly the afternoon with Mariam and her nani had been a pleasant enough way to pass the time. But it was the conversations with Saima afterwards that he most looked forward to. He hadn't seen her in a few months, but during those conversations it felt like she was only a heartbeat away.

He shook his head. Of all the relationships he'd had, the one with his matchmaker was probably the most messed up.

Nah, he texted back, still smiling.

Please, just for once make this easy for me and don't play hard to get.

Who says I'm playing?

OK, fine. So we're going to pretend you're not interested and I'm going to have to chase you for weeks. Let me clear my schedule.

I'm seriously not interested, Saima.

But she's wonderful. I promise. And there's no nani involved.

I liked spending time with Nani on my last date.

You liked her in a maternal way, or should I try and get some more mature ladies on my client list?

You'd do it, too, wouldn't you? No client is unmatchable for Saima Khan.

He couldn't wipe the grin off his face.

I'll get you to put that in a testimonial after you're happily married. So, is that a yes to Bachelorette Number Three? Will you meet her?

Will you meet me? he wanted to text back. Instead, he stared for a moment longer at the darkening water before replying.

OK.

Chapter 13

After the unsuccessful dates with Shayla and Mariam, Saima knew she needed to up her game if she wanted to add Kal to her list of successful matches. Based on the date with Shayla, she was looking for someone ready to settle into their early thirties but not necessarily launch straight into domestic life, as Mariam was keen to do. She combed through her files once, twice, a third time. She simply couldn't see any of her clients with Kal. Whenever she pictured him with a partner, that person was a shadowy blob she couldn't quite focus on.

She was going to have to call in the big guns.

Uncle Malik was the go-to accountant and tax agent for half the Pakistanis in Sydney and had been so for decades. He knew everyone and everyone knew him, and since his preferred method of filing tax returns was to have a long afternoon of gupshup and chai with a sprinkling of financial services thrown in, he also knew *everything* there was to know about everyone. When it came to news about the comings and goings within the community, he was an absolute goldmine, which was the reason Saima found herself calling him.

'Accha, Saima beti, you still need to send me your receipts for last financial year' was the first thing Uncle Malik said when he answered the phone.

'Assalaamu alaykum, Uncle-ji. Yes, I know I'm running late. Things have been a bit complicated and I'm trying to get it all in order.'

'Okay, but you can always come to me for advice, beti, you know this, yes? Your Uncle Malik is always here to help you or your ammy, any time.'

'Yes, Uncle, of course.' It was true, Uncle Malik had helped her set up the whole business and would still bring her news from time to time of potential clients. He'd watched with pride as her business grew, and was probably the best publicist she had never asked for but appreciated immensely. 'Uncle-ji, I'm not calling about my tax return today. I was hoping you could help me with some information. I'm looking for a girl.'

'Oh, is-liye tum ne mujhe call kiya!' he said with a deep laugh. She could picture him relaxing into his armchair on the other end of the line. 'Tell me all about it.'

Saima went through her criteria.

'Hmmm. And who is the boy you are matchmaking for?' Uncle asked.

'The Alis, up in Gordon, Uncle.'

Uncle Malik tsked loudly. 'Yeh ladka trouble hai, beti,' he said. 'He will never settle with one of our girls. Always out with goris. But you will have no trouble finding families to put their daughters forward to meet him.'

'He's not that bad, Uncle, and I think he might be ready to reconnect with the community. I think much of what people think about him is based on idle talk.'

'But idle talk is what we Pakistanis do best,' he joked merrily. 'Anyway, let me make some calls, have a think.'

'Thank you, Uncle.'

A couple of hours later, as he always tended to do, Uncle Malik called her back with precious intel.

'The girl, Ayesha, is very beautiful, or so I hear. She finished a Masters in Marketing at Yale University in America. You know Yale?'

'Yes, of course.' Saima rolled her eyes, smiling to herself.

'Anyway, so she is smart, comes from a wealthy family. She wanted to stay and work in America, but some visa problems got in the way, so she came back here. Her abbu is a businessman in Melbourne, but the family has recently relocated to Sydney. Bare admi hain. She sounds like the sort of girl that shiftless boy may consider stringing along for a few dates.'

'Come on, Uncle-ji, he's not shiftless.'

'To be honest, I almost feel bad suggesting her, but I think when it doesn't work out with Kal, she will be good to have on your books.'

Saima gave an exasperated laugh. 'Shukria, Uncle.'

'Okay, I will send you her ammy's details now and let them know you'll be calling them, yes?'

'Perfect, Uncle-ji, thank you again.'

'It's nothing,' Uncle Malik said expansively. 'Always happy to help. Okay, my salaams to your ammy, and khuda hafiz.'

After a brief chat on the phone, Saima lined up a chai date with Ayesha's mother on the weekend. The family were still house-hunting after their recent move and were temporarily renting a serviced penthouse apartment opposite Hyde Park, complete with a snooty concierge who greeted Saima suspiciously when she entered the building.

Ayesha's mother Gulnar opened their apartment door and invited Saima in.

'Assalaamu alaykum, Aunty,' Saima said politely as she removed her shoes.

'Wa-alaikum as-salam,' Gulnar replied. 'Ayesha will come out soon. Won't you please come through.' She led the way to a light-filled living room.

The apartment was decked out with generic executive furniture – lots of greys and neutral colours and dark wood, very different from most of the family homes Saima was accustomed to visiting.

'Please, sit down,' Gulnar said. She appeared nervous, and there was an odd, almost fevered glint in her eyes.

Saima sat on a cream-coloured leather couch that faced a floor-to-ceiling window overlooking the park, the sunlight glinting off the pool in front of the war memorial far below. 'The views here are incredible, Aunty,' she said.

'Yes, I suppose so.' Gulnar took a seat across from Saima, but leaped up immediately. 'Oh, I should've asked if you would like something to drink! Chai, coffee, soda or just water?'

'I'll wait for Ayesha in case she also wants some chai.'

'Ayesha doesn't drink chai. She'll have an espresso, but she doesn't trust the coffee machine they have in the kitchen. We also have orange juice, if you would prefer that?' Gulnar suggested.

'No, no orange juice for me, thank you, Aunty.' Saima recalled the unsolicited orange juice on Laksa Night, and smiled.

'So, chai then?'

She realised that Gulnar wanted her to choose something to drink so she'd have an excuse to escape into the kitchen, away from the awkwardness of meeting a new person in a new city, who happened to be a matchmaker to boot. 'Chai would be lovely, thank you, Aunty. Shall I come and help?' It was bad form to sit by and let one's elders take care of basic hospitality, but Saima didn't want to impose on what was clearly already an uncomfortable situation.

'No, no, please. You sit and wait for Ayesha.' Gulnar left her on the couch and drifted off. For a while, Saima admired the view. When she had worked in an office in the city, she would often walk to the park to have her lunch, putting off having to go back to a job she loathed. Sitting here now, with a different view of the park, she reflected on how far she had come, from that first desk job she hated, to working for herself. It hadn't been easy by any stretch, but even with the recent uncertainty and pressure, it brought her an enormous sense of achievement watching her successful matches start their lives together.

Fifteen minutes went by, and there was no sign of Gulnar or Ayesha. Eventually, Saima had no option but to get up and go looking for them. She walked into a corridor of closed doors.

'Hello?' Saima called. There was no response. She tried again. 'Aunty?' Only her voice echoed faintly back to her. For a frenzied second, she wondered if she'd walked into a horror film. She decided to follow the length of the corridor, assuming it would lead her to the kitchen, where she hoped Gulnar would be.

The corridor did in fact open up into a large kitchen. Gulnar sat straight-backed at the kitchen table, gazing out another window. There were no signs that she had attempted to make tea, or do anything there at all.

'Aunty?' Saima asked cautiously. 'Is everything okay?' Gulnar didn't respond.

'Yeah, everything's fine,' said a voice with a slight American twang behind her.

Saima turned to see a tall, slim young woman wearing glasses, standing in the doorway with her arms folded across her chest.

'Are you the matchmaker?' the woman asked.

'Yes, I'm Saima. You must be Ayesha?'

'That's me.'

As they spoke, Gulnar didn't turn around and acknowledge their presence.

'Is your ammy okay?' Saima asked.

'Yep,' said Ayesha shortly. 'Come on, then. Let's get this over with.'

This wasn't exactly a promising start.

The two of them went back to the living room, sitting this time at the glass dining table. Saima sat at one end and Ayesha at the other. She crossed her arms as she appraised Saima.

'I get the feeling that you're not keen to be matched,' Saima began.

'What makes you say that?' Ayesha asked, a slight furrow between her brows.

'Okay, maybe I'm leaping to conclusions,' Saima said, 'but you said you wanted to get this over with. That's not exactly ringing with enthusiasm.'

'Well, what did you want me to say? That I'm so excited you're here? That all I've wanted my whole life was an arranged marriage?'

'I don't want you to say anything other than what you feel,' Saima reassured her. 'But I also want you to know that I only work with people who want to get married and want to explore the matchmaking process. If you're here under duress or something, we don't have to go ahead with it.'

'I've never been coerced into anything in my life,' Ayesha declared. 'But I'm also realistic. I'm twenty-seven now, so that makes me ancient by our standards, right? In many ways, it's already too late for me. One of my cousins in Pakistan who's my age is pregnant with her third already, as my father likes to remind me.'

'That doesn't mean you need to do the same,' Saima said. 'You're educated and connected, both big advantages if you want to focus

160

on your career. I heard you looked for work in America after grad-
uating, but some visa issues got in the way?'

'Where did you hear that?' Ayesha waved off her answer before
she could even offer it. 'Never mind, stupid question. Everyone
knows everyone's business here, right?'

'Either way, if you're not keen to get married right now, there's
nothing stopping you from looking for work here. A Yale graduate
and all, you've got so many more options than simply following in
your cousin's footsteps.'

Ayesha watched her silently for a moment. 'You're terrible at
sales patter,' she commented.

'So I've heard.'

'It wasn't visa issues that brought me back to Australia. It was
my mum. We just told people that to avoid the inevitable questions.
She's not well, as you can see. I only agreed to meet you because of
her, because it seemed to make her happy.'

Saima hesitated, but Ayesha answered her anyway.

'Mum's been having these episodes. We thought she'd had
a stroke or a brain tumour or something, but it turns out she is
clinically depressed. Dad's found it hard to accept that her problem
was "just a mental one", as he calls it. She's on some fairly heavy
medication, which is why she spaces out like that.'

'Oh, I'm sorry.'

'Sorry for what? Like you said, we've got it better than most
people. Imagine if my mum had been diagnosed in Pakistan. They'd
have put her in an asylum or something. Or worse, they wouldn't have
believed there was anything even wrong with her, or would have just
hidden her away. I hate how we can't even talk about mental health in
our community. I'm pretty sure one of the main reasons Dad's relocated to Sydney is to get away from the gossip in Melbourne. Like it
doesn't follow you anyway,' she said, with a bitter laugh. 'If you go to

the States, more than half the people you meet have a therapist or are on some kind of medication. And they're so proud of it, they tell you as soon as you meet them – "So my therapist said this and that" – like they're talking about their hairdresser or something. But us immigrants? We're taught to shove all that deep down, right? The best way to deal with a problem is to ignore it, pretend it doesn't exist.' Rant over, Ayesha gazed at Saima with a set jaw, like she was ready for a fight. Saima's heart went out to her.

'That's definitely been my approach,' she said, as lightly as possible. 'I shove anything I don't want to deal with into the Too-Hard Basket, or so I've been told.'

Ayesha grinned suddenly. 'I always say, "That's Tomorrow-Ayesha's problem".'

Saima laughed. 'Exactly.'

'You know what? I think I like you, matchmaker lady,' Ayesha said, leaning back in her chair.

'It's Saima, and cheers,' Saima said with a smile.

'I've got a good feeling about you, Saima. So, let's do this, why not? Who's the guy you want me to meet, then?'

Saima perked up. 'He's a lovely guy, honestly. But I do want you to think about whether this is right for you at this point in your life. You seem to have a lot on your plate.'

'Saima, seriously, do you even make money doing what you do? Like, you seem to want to talk me out of this or something. Don't you get paid if I agree to go on this date? Listen, I'm in marketing, and I gotta tell you, it's cutthroat out there. I learned that when I was in the States. You should straight up say: "This is the deal – you need to pay me this much for doing this and then extra for doing anything else." Here, heaps of people still seem to be stuck in some kind of honour system, where talking about money is embarrassing.'

'I thought I would talk about the money side of things with your parents,' Saima said. 'That's usually how these things go.'

'Nah, you can talk about it with me. I say, whatever you're charging, triple it – hell, *quadruple* it. And get the biggest instalment on signing rather than delivery; that way you're not going to be holding out for my wedding day. Dad won't mind paying. He probably won't even notice, probably just expense it or something. He'll be so happy I'm going out with a Pakistani guy and it'll at least get him off my back for a bit.'

Saima looked at her, considering. 'I have a friend I think you'd get on with.'

'Oh, do you do friendship matchmaking too?' Ayesha said with a snarky grin.

'Ha, no, she's just been on my case to up my rates for months now.'

'Sounds like a good friend.'

Saima thought of Jess. 'Yeah, the best.' She brought her mind back to business. 'Okay, as weird as it feels, I'll boost my fees. Shall we talk about the guy I'm thinking of matching you with?'

'Just give me the basics. It gives me something to talk to him about if I don't already have his entire life history. Is he cute?'

'He's good-looking . . . I'd go so far as to say he's hot. I'll send you a photo so you recognise him when you meet. His name's Khalid, but he goes by Kal.'

Ayesha snorted. 'Oh, I see. He's a coconut.'

Saima laughed. 'Honestly?' she said. 'I'd have said the same when I first met him. But I think it's more a case that his family's not particularly traditional and he's grown up in Australia, so he's a little bit adrift when it comes to cultural identity. His parents are keen to get him back to his roots, though. I thought you might appreciate what that's like.'

'What makes you say that?'

Saima looked at her steadily. 'Oh, I don't know. You were born and brought up here, you lived and studied in America, your mum's mental health has removed you from the community a fair bit, but your dad's keen to settle you down with a Pakistani boy. Have I missed something?'

Ayesha sighed. 'Yeah, right.'

'Look, there's no pressure if you meet and there's nothing there. But trust me, Ayesha, he's a great guy. You might be doing this to get your dad off your back, but just give it a chance to be something more.' She smiled. 'And if you need further proof that you're a good match, I gave him basically the same speech.'

'All right, fine.' Ayesha eyed her curiously. 'Aren't you tempted to snap any of these guys up for yourself? I'm guessing you're not married, by the absence of a wedding ring.'

Tempted? The word wove into her thoughts and she remembered the indistinct person in her mind's eye. Saima shook her head firmly. 'I'm a professional, it goes against my ethics.'

'Wow, a matchmaker with ethics. You really mustn't be in this for the money.'

'I'm not looking for a man, in any case,' Saima said.

'I guess it's a good thing some of us are, or you'd be out of business,' Ayesha said, getting up and walking Saima to the door.

Saima texted Kal as soon as she left Ayesha's place.

I may have found the woman of your dreams.

Chapter 14

Laila had gone all out for what Saima thought would be a quick midweek lunch. There was idli and sambar, dosa with spiced aloo, a coconut chutney along with a mint and coriander one, and if that hadn't been enough, there was chana daal and fried zucchini on the side, all served with a stack of fluffy rotis.

Saima had managed to put off this meeting for months, but Rahat finally skewered her. 'Saima, Laila has done so much for us. The least you can do is join me for one lunch with her,' she had started, as usual. But this time, when Saima gave her go-to answer of 'Go ahead without me', Rahat responded, 'I can't face walking into that house by myself.'

And that, basically, was that. It wasn't often that Rahat opted for bare honesty, but god, it was effective when she did. So here they were, sitting in Laila's backyard as she whipped out an array of delicious food like a magician.

Laila's weatherboard home in Auburn had clearly seen better days, but the backyard was still the fairy garden Saima remembered. A jungle of potted plants and herbs surrounded a concrete court-yard, with a large vegetable patch still occupying pride of place at the rear of the garden, framed by a couple of lime trees whose fruit would be pickled to make achar every year. It would be where Laila had grown most of the vegetables she was serving them for lunch. As a girl, Saima had helped Laila pick those vegies, learning which ones were ripe for harvest and which ones still needed a bit more time in the sun.

'I was hoping the kaddu would be ripe enough for me to cook it for you, but unfortunately, as you can see, it's still a bit small,' Laila said to her now with a smile, pointing at the underripe pumpkin still on the vine. 'But everything else is fresh and organic,' she continued with pride. 'I don't use any pesticides, even though it's hard when the slugs and aphids want to eat into all of my plants! I had such a time last year with curl grubs eating my roots, but I think this spring will be much better.'

They tucked into the feast. 'You're enjoying this, yes?' Laila asked Saima as she piled another couple of idli onto her plate. 'Remember when you were young and didn't like my idli? You kept asking your ammy to take you home so you could eat lamb and chicken again.' Laila had always run a strict vegetarian household due to her South Indian upbringing.

'It's delicious, Aunty, thank you,' Saima replied.

'I think you soon got used to my cooking, though, maybe even liked it. The chana daal I made especially for you today because it was your favourite back when you stayed with me,' Laila told her.

Despite her affection for Laila and her hospitality, Saima couldn't help but wish she'd stop bringing up the past that Saima had wrestled with so hard to make permanently go away. She'd be happy to just focus on their lunch now, the delicious food, the early winter sunshine dappling the courtyard. But even thinking about the time they had lived with Laila made it hard for Saima to swallow.

When Laila went to the kitchen to refill some of the dishes, Rahat looked at her daughter understandingly and said, 'Laila talks as much as she always did.'

Saima forced a shrug. 'I always liked the fact that Laila Aunty talked so much.' In the women's shelter, before they moved to Laila's house, Rahat had said very little. Saima had had so many questions but all she remembered was Rahat refusing to tell her much about what had happened. Laila's chatter had been like heaven in comparison. While Laila never spoke about why her mother had left her father or what exactly had happened, she had filled the silences with other things, insignificant things, and Saima had basked in the ordinariness of her words.

'How is Yusuf? And the bacche?' Rahat asked when Laila returned to the table.

'They're all well,' Laila answered with a broad smile. 'Zana has two children now, can you imagine? And Faiza has three of her own.'

'MashAllah,' Rahat said. 'You must be a very happy nani! And Yusuf is busy with his work, as always?'

Laila's smile took on an odd cast. 'Not as busy as when you were both staying with us. Rahat, I feel that maybe he gave you the wrong impression back then.'

Saima stopped eating. She looked at her mother.

'No wrong impression at all,' Rahat replied stiffly. 'I understood, and it made sense we were getting in his way.'

'You walked in on us at a bad time. I asked him not to talk so loudly.'

'Wait, what happened?' Saima asked with a full mouth, as though she were a child again, left out of the conversation of adults.

'Nothing,' Rahat said, turning back to her food.

'Your mother overheard us having a little argument in the kitchen about how long you two were going to be staying with us,' Laila explained, even now looking a little sad about what had passed. 'But these little arguments happen all the time in a household. I didn't expect her to suddenly announce she was going to move out.'

Unbidden, Saima recalled the day her mother told her abruptly that they would need to leave Laila's house and move back to the shelter, especially if she couldn't find a job. Saima had burst into tears, and a stone-faced Rahat had sternly told her to keep quiet in case the others in the household heard her crying. 'Tears help no-one,' she had said.

When she thought about it rationally, it must have been quite an intrusion for Laila's family to have a stranger and her child come stay with them. Laila's daughters were in their teens at the time, and Saima had always felt as if she was getting in their way.

'I so enjoyed having you stay with us,' Laila was saying now, as she flipped more dosa onto their plates. 'The girls still talk about how fun it was to have a little sister to play with when you were here, Saima. Remember when Zana dressed you up like a doll?' Saima had no memory of that. 'And you, Rahat, having you here was like having one of my sisters from India with me again.'

Rahat smiled politely. 'I'm lucky that Mark offered me the job at the clinic before we had to move out of your place.'

'But you didn't *have* to move out,' Laila said.

Rahat waved her hand to indicate they should move on. 'In any case, I will never forget your kindness, Laila. All these years, I've thought about how to repay you.'

'Oh no, don't be silly! Seeing you land on your own two feet was something so special to behold. I mention you often to other women, you know. Look what Rahat did, look what a success she became.'

'Success?' Rahat repeated incredulously. She turned the word over in her head, a smile working its way across her lips.

'Bilkul! What else can you call it? You picked yourself up in a matter of months, found a job, a flat, raised a lovely, accomplished daughter, all on your own!'

'It wasn't on my own,' Rahat pointed out, but Saima could see, perhaps for the first time, an appreciation of her own accomplishments blooming in her mother. 'There were many in the community who helped.'

Laila sniffed. 'And many more who did not,' she said. 'I have always been thankful to have been able to assist you, but more than that, I've been so proud of everything you've managed to do on your own.'

Perhaps, after all, this lunch was worth waiting for, Saima thought. Her mother was not in the habit of maintaining any close friendships, but the isolation had definitely deprived Rahat of some important perspective.

The two older women chatted some more, and Saima let her thoughts drift to some of the other things Laila had mentioned. Why didn't she remember playing with Zana, but recalled with perfect clarity the scowl on Faiza's face when she'd found Saima playing in the sunroom that doubled as the girls' study?

What was it that Jess had said? *You tend to fixate on the negative.* Maybe there was more truth in Jess's words than she had wanted to admit at the time. Maybe she shot things down before they had the chance to sour and disappoint her because she expected that they *would* disappoint her, and was always looking for evidence to prove herself right, which now she began to realise might have been self-fulfilling.

'Do you still hear from Zubair at all?' Laila said out of the blue. 'I wondered if maybe he contacted you on birthdays, anniversaries and such.' There was nothing but genuine curiosity on her face.

'He's never in touch anymore,' Rahat answered shortly.

'Anymore?' Saima asked. 'So he *used* to be in touch?' This was the first time Rahat had mentioned her husband since Saima was seven years old. She had wanted to ask about him countless times, wanted to know what had happened, but never felt she could bring it up. Her parents had always fought – she had grown up listening to the soundtrack of their arguments – but she could never put her finger on why they had escalated to the point of Rahat's flight and her father's abandonment.

'He used to, yes, for a time,' Rahat said, not meeting Saima's eyes. 'And then he moved on with his life in Pakistan.'

'And your mother was left to fend for herself. You know how divorced women get treated by our community, Saima,' Laila added.

'But Ammy, you never told me he was in touch,' Saima persisted.

'Arre nahin, Rahat, you didn't tell her?' Laila exclaimed. 'Oh, but you should have done! It would've been good for Saima to get to know him. None of it was her fault.'

Rahat abruptly got up and started to clear the dishes from their half-eaten lunch.

'I think we should be leaving now,' she said quickly.

'Oh no, please stay! You didn't eat dessert! I made your favourite, Rahat – gajar ka halwa,' Laila said, in a placating voice. She patted Rahat reassuringly on the arm and uncovered the dessert dish. 'And I wanted to ask how your business was going, Saima.'

'It's going great,' Saima answered automatically. She was still eyeing her mother, who would not meet her gaze.

'Good, I'm glad to hear it. We need more people like you in our community, changing things up. The way some people think is very old-fashioned,' Laila said as she spooned the halwa into a dessert bowl for Rahat. 'I heard how you've pushed back when people try to force you to make your matches in the old ways.'

Saima wanted to ask Laila what else she had heard, but she was fixated on what her mother had inadvertently revealed. Her father had tried to get in touch and Rahat had never mentioned it. What else hadn't she told her?

'I see her sending texts to one of her clients when she comes to my place,' Rahat said, clearly relieved at the topic change. 'She always glows when she messages this person.'

'And who is this client?' Laila asked, eyebrow arched.

'No-one,' Saima replied, feeling more and more like a child.

'He doesn't *seem* like a no-one,' her mother teased.

'Accha, it's a "he"!' Laila played along. 'And you are interested in him yourself?'

'How could I be interested in one of my clients?' Saima snapped.

'If he's the right fit, he's the right fit, beti. You know, Saima, getting married doesn't mean you are letting your mother down,' Laila said, suddenly serious. 'In fact, quite the opposite.'

'My being unmarried doesn't have anything to do with Ammy.'

'My youngest sister back home never got married because she was the only one left to look after our parents when they got old. The rest of us got married and left, but she kept saying her duty was to them.' Laila turned to Rahat. 'We told her our parents would be fine but she didn't listen. Now she is old, and alone. So sad.'

Rahat looked at Saima in dawning realisation. 'You're not married because of me?'

'Ammy, I literally just said that wasn't the case.'

'But it makes sense. Of course it makes sense!' Rahat exclaimed. 'All this time, your duty to me has tied you down.'

'Let's not get sidetracked by something that isn't true,' Saima said firmly. 'First of all, nobody is going to give me any awards for "Most Dutiful Daughter", so you can put it out of your head that some sense of duty to you is holding me back. And second, women can choose to not get married or have children. It's not unusual here. It isn't something to pity. If anything, it gives me freedom, it's not "tying me down".'

'But you are tied down! You are tied down to me!' Rahat looked devastated.

'Ammy, I *promise* you, you're not the reason I'm not married.'

'You're just saying that to make me feel better. And what if it's not just me? What if it's also your father?'

'Of course.' Laila nodded sagely, and Saima squashed the urge to scowl at her. 'A father has *such* a big influence on his daughter.'

'We ruined her life,' Rahat said, more to herself than anyone else, and shook her head. 'Our daughter watched our marriage collapse and thought the same thing would happen to her.'

Though Saima had wanted to hear more about her father, now she wished everyone would just stop talking. 'Please, both of you, stop this. I'm not a child, I'm not assuming just because you got divorced, I'm cursed or something.'

'Saima, not all men are like your father,' Laila told her, completely ignoring what she'd just said. 'Just because your mother went through what she did doesn't mean that you will.'

'But it wasn't her father's fault!' Rahat interjected. 'It was mine.'

Every other thought flew out of Saima's head. 'I'm sorry, what?'

'He was as much to blame as anyone, running away like that!' Laila said.

Running away? Saima inhaled too quickly and proceeded to have a coughing fit. By the time water and thumps on the back had been administered, Laila and Rahat both seemed to have put the subject of her father behind them.

'My daughters complain that I put too much chilli in my food.' Laila tsked. 'I thought you could eat spice.'

The moment had well and truly passed, and neither Laila nor her mother seemed inclined to address the chaos bombs they had just lobbed into Saima's life. She wanted to drag them back on topic, but before she had the chance to marshal her thoughts and her hundreds of questions, Rahat stood up to leave. A few minutes later, they were saying goodbye.

Saima gave Laila a hug. 'Thank you for a delicious meal, Aunty. It was so good to see you again.' *Even if you've been frustratingly vague about everything,* she added silently.

'Don't let it be so many years until the next time,' Laila said, kissing both her cheeks. 'Come again soon, accha? Khuda hafiz.'

She left Rahat and Laila to exchange a few private words on the front porch. Her mother joined her a little later, and they walked the short distance to the bus stop in silence.

'That was nice,' Rahat finally said. 'And I said to Laila, "I think Saima has a man in her life."' She was still avoiding Saima's gaze.

'Ammy.'

'I want you to know I can look after myself. You don't have to worry about me. You've spent your whole life worrying about me, enough is enough. If there is someone you like, don't set your heart against it, especially not because of me.'

'Ammy, can we please talk about what you said back there?'

'No use hiding yourself from life,' Rahat steamrolled on. 'It's my fault. It all is. I thought I was protecting you, but instead I was ruining you. You are so scared to let people in.'

'Ammy, enough. I don't know where all of this is coming from, but it's nonsense.' There was so much she wanted to ask her mother, but Rahat had snapped back to her default of never discussing her marriage or her ex-husband, and Saima, it seemed, wasn't allowed to bring it up either. She sighed as she spied the bus headed down Parramatta Road towards them.

'You okay to catch the train home from Parramatta?' Saima asked.

'What a question.' Rahat sniffed. 'When have I not been okay?'

As she got up to hail the bus, Rahat stood as well, leaning slightly into her as she did. It was her way of hugging Saima. The two of them rarely embraced, but feeling the slight weight of her mother's body against her, a surge of love filled Saima. *You've never been a burden to me*, she wanted to tell her mother. But she said nothing.

They got onto the bus and rode the short journey to Parramatta in complete silence, their bodies leaning into each other as they sat side by side.

Chapter 15

On the evening of Kal's first date with Ayesha, Saima was at the Jamal-Mirza wedding, held in the upstairs banquet room of a popular Indian restaurant in Harris Park. Between the steady decline of her client list and the cooler weather, it had been a slow few months for weddings, and Saima had actually been looking forward to this one. Now, after some hours sitting at the increasingly chaotic venue, she was beginning to remember why she always capped her services at matchmaking, never wedding planning.

As was usual at these events, everything was running extremely behind schedule. The bride was cordoned off in a small anteroom at the back of the restaurant, out of sight of the guests, and waiting, like everyone else, for the Imam to arrive to officiate the nikkah. It was already past 8 pm, and the ceremony could go for up to an hour depending on how many passages of the Quran the Imam wanted to read before the qabools were exchanged. Saima estimated that at this rate, dinner wouldn't be served any time before 10 pm.

A few children whose parents hadn't come prepared with snacks or pre-packed dinners had begun to fret with hunger, and one of the uncles was scrolling through a delivery app to see if he could order something in a hurry. The room was smoky from the tandoor working overtime in the restaurant downstairs. Around each table were eight or nine white plastic chairs, though most people were now gathering in groups in the corners of the room. Unlike the glitzier weddings Saima had been to, there was no seating plan tonight.

She was beginning to feel the closeness of the stuffy room, and started to plan a polite exit. She'd already done the rounds, mingling and making small talk with guests.

'You make weddings sound kind of boring,' Jess had complained. Had her friend been here right now, Saima would have turned to her and said, 'Look, some weddings are fun, but most desi weddings involve a lot of sitting around while the families run around trying to get their shit together, even though most of these weddings are months if not years in the making. For some reason, there are still always last-minute changes taking place. *Always.* Often in real time, during the wedding itself.'

'The Imam is still in Lakemba,' an aunty at her table announced to her husband, who let out an audible groan.

'Even if he leaves now, he won't be here for at least half an hour, and that's in good traffic!' He got up and walked out of the room, presumably to join the gaggle of uncles muttering, complaining or smoking on the pavement outside.

'He was at another wedding before this one,' the aunty told Saima, who was now the only other person left at the table. 'Did they not have much time to organise the wedding?'

Time had probably not been the problem factor, Saima privately mused. It was almost eighteen months since Rukhsana and Asif had blissfully told Saima that they were getting married. They were both the youngest in their large families – Asif was the youngest of six, Rukhsana the youngest of eight. Perhaps that was one of the things the two of them had bonded over – it had certainly been one of Saima's considerations when she'd matched them.

'I'm not sure,' Saima now said to the aunty.

'I heard the families didn't help them organise tonight,' the aunty said in the low familiar and conspiratorial tones of someone sharing gossip to bring others down. 'No wonder it's like this. At least put a bit of money aside when your last child is about to get married, or don't have eight children in the first place, I say.'

Not everyone has tens of thousands of dollars to spend on their wedding, Saima wanted to snap at her. Some of the best, most genuine and heartfelt weddings she'd attended had been held in small venues like this one. Ultimately, though, she decided not to respond. It was as classic a part of desi weddings as the groom's pagri that at least half the guests would be criticising and complaining about the event while attending it.

A group of children decided to play tag in the room, and one of them kicked Saima's shin as he ran past. Their squeals, along with the growing murmur of discontent and the smoke from the tandoor, made the room feel oppressively small. Saima glanced at her phone again. It was still only 8.30 pm.

Asif popped into the room. 'Assalaamu alaykum, aunties and uncles!' he called loudly. 'We've just heard from the Imam that he's on his way, so thank you so much for your patience. InshAllah, we'll be able to get started soon.' He darted away as quickly as he had arrived.

'Couldn't he have got one of his brothers to make the announce-ment rather than doing it himself?' Saima's table-mate sniped. 'Bechara baccha, he looks so panicked.' She seemed more satisfied than sympathetic.

Another half-hour dragged past. With nothing else to occupy her mind, Saima began to wonder how Kal and Ayesha's date was going. Ayesha had rejected the formality of a dinner and nominated a low-key CBD Italian wine bar instead for their first meeting.

Kal had agreed with the suggestion because he'd heard a lot about the venue's wine list.

She eyed her phone again. Would it be weird to follow up with them so quickly?

She decided promptly that yes, it would. Her attention then turned to the thing she had been avoiding thinking about for days – her mother, and the tantalising bombshell about the history of her parents' marriage. Saima still hadn't decided whether she was going to push for more information. Certainly her mother's demeanour as she had accompanied her back to Parramatta didn't exactly invite further questions. Jess had been of the opinion, when Saima mentioned it to her, that Rahat wouldn't be offering anything more without quite a push.

'Honestly, your mum could write the book on repression, Saima,' she had said. 'And not only have you always let her get away with keeping everything to herself, you've learned everything from that book as well.'

'I'm not repressed,' Saima had protested.

'Girl, look at your mum, and you're looking at your future. You are so good at not thinking about shit you don't want to deal with. I'm impressed your brain has any room left to do basic things like have a conversation, with all the stuff it's constantly suppressing. Maybe that's why your mum doesn't talk much.'

'I don't—' Saima began to argue, then stopped. 'Wait, do you really think so?'

Jess had shrugged. 'My psychology degree is from the university of Buzzfeed quizzes, so who knows? Anyway, I reckon if your mum's going to tell you anything, she's going to need help digging up those ghosts.'

Just then a child burst into the room and announced, 'The Imam is almost here!'

'We've been hearing that for the last hour,' someone at the back of the room grumbled loudly. The discontented murmuring increased.

'Saima Aunty.' The boy ignored everyone else and sidled up to her. 'Can you please come with me? Rukhsana baji wants you to be with her in the back room.'

'Me?' The bridal room where the nikkah was officiated was usually a place for a handful of close relatives and friends who were there to offer moral support as the bride took her marriage vows. 'Are you sure?'

The boy shrugged and grabbed her hand, leading her down a corridor, past a bustling upstairs kitchen where some men were mixing a large amount of dough in a steel pot on the ground. The boy came to a halt outside a door and knocked.

'Come in,' a voice said.

The bride sat by herself inside, feverishly dabbing at her tears before they could ruin her make-up. As soon as Rukhsana saw Saima, the tears began to overwhelm the soggy tissues in her hand. Saima stepped swiftly into the stuffy room and closed the door behind her.

'It's all a mess! This whole day! I want this night to be over!' Rukhsana wailed.

Oh god, Saima thought. *This is not part of my remit.* Her phone buzzed in her purse.

If Rukhsana had been panicking alone in this room all night, she thought pragmatically, sympathy might actually tip her over the edge. 'Every wedding since the history of weddings for our people is always a mess,' Saima said kindly but briskly. 'It feels like the end of the world right now, I know. But trust me, once it's done, you won't even remember the details. The Imam will be here soon, and then you can get on with the event, and everything will come right, I promise. I've seen it a hundred times before. Now, is there someone I can get for you?'

'No! There's no-one. They've all abandoned me because Azra Apa is having her baby. She chose tonight of all nights to go into labour! I swear to god! And I didn't tell you before, but Abbu isn't very happy about the marriage. He thinks that Asif is spoiled goods because he's got epilepsy. Abbu said that you or Asif's family should have told us when we were first matched, and Asif feels so bad that he didn't think to mention it himself. And anyway, he manages his condition just fine! But sometimes when he's stressed, he can have a seizure. So all night I'm thinking, what if he has a seizure tonight? His family aren't being that great either – they're mad at my family because they think we think they're beneath us. But *I* don't think that! I love Asif!' By the end of this speech, Rukhsana was practically hyperventilating.

'Okay, Rukhsana, you're panicking, and it's making everything feel even worse,' Saima said in her calmest voice. 'Take a deep breath – *slowly* – now another. Good. Okay. Here, drink some water.' She poured Rukhsana a glass of water while fuming inside that the bride's family had left her there to deal with her wedding alone. The callousness was beyond belief. 'So, no-one is here?' she asked gently.

Rukhsana sniffled and gulped down some water. 'I think some of them are,' she said uncertainly. 'It's hard to keep track of so many people, you know. I've been sitting here alone all night! I thought to myself, Rukhsana, who can you ask to come sit with you? And then I thought of you.'

That was very sweet, but at the same time, Saima wasn't sure what she was meant to do in this situation.

'The Imam's on his way,' she repeated feebly.

'He's been on his way for hours, baji! What if he never comes? Who will we get to do the ceremony?'

'Asif's dad can do it, if it comes to that,' Saima said. 'Or some other elder. I was once at a wedding where the Imam got terrible food poisoning and the bride's taya stepped in.' Her phone buzzed again, and she took it out to see Ayesha's name on the display. 'Rukhsana, I need to take this call. Will you be all right for a sec?'

'It's okay, baji, you can leave. You seem busy,' Rukhsana said pitifully. Saima held up one finger as she walked to the corner of the room.

'Ayesha, what's up?'

'Well, I'm kind of chickening out here,' Ayesha said on the other end. 'I've been telling myself, don't be ridiculous, Ayesha, just go in, for god's sake, if nothing else you can shut your father up and give your mum a break!'

Saima checked the time on her phone. 'Hang on. You were meant to meet at eight.'

'I know! First I was running late so I asked him if we could reschedule to 8.30. Anyway, I'm outside the bar now.'

'Ayesha, it's five past nine.'

'I know! He probably thinks I'm never turning up! But my feet are refusing to move. I'm not sure I can do it . . .'

Saima eyed Rukhsana across the room. It was turning into a far more dramatic night than she had been expecting. 'Okay, Ayesha, listen to me,' she said, in the same brisk tone she had used earlier on Rukhsana. 'You can do it. I promise you, you can. Where's that gung-ho Yankee attitude you gave me when we first met? Just walk up to the door and go inside. That's all. If you can't think of anything to talk about, let him do the work.'

'I don't know,' Ayesha said.

'Or text him. Ask him to come outside and meet you. It might be easier than walking in to find him, anyway. And then maybe you can just decide on somewhere else to go, where you feel more comfortable.'

Ayesha thought about this for a minute. 'Okay, fine. I'm going to do it. If you don't hear from me, it's because I'm with him.' She hung up.

After she had put her phone away, Saima looked up to find Rukhsana staring at her, wide-eyed. 'I had no idea you had to fight so many fires in your job,' the younger woman said in an awed voice.

Saima shook her head and looked around the room. 'Talking about fires, it's like a literal tandoor in here. Let's cool things down a bit,' she said. She manhandled the window in the corner open before collaring one of the cooks in the upstairs kitchen to request a fan. The man managed to magically procure one. Rukhsana now looked calmer, so Saima went outside to get some fresh air and call Rukhsana's mother, whose eldest daughter Azra had just delivered a sixth grandchild at Westmead Hospital.

'I will be there in ten minutes,' she assured Saima.

Saima turned to find the flustered-looking Imam entering the restaurant.

'Assalaamu alaykum! I'm so sorry! The other wedding was running over time, and they wouldn't listen to me when I said I had to leave!' He looked so genuinely harried that Saima couldn't feel the slightest annoyance.

'Wa-alaikum as-salam, Sheikh, it's okay. Let's take you up to see the bride.' Saima led him inside and delivered him into the hands of Asif's eldest brother, Ayman, who then took charge of the proceedings.

'Baji, will you sit with Rukhsana during the nikkah, please?' Ayman asked. 'She's all by herself,' he added sheepishly.

'Her ammy is on her way, if we can wait ten more minutes?' Saima asked.

'I think she'd like to have you there as well, baji,' he said.

And so, Saima ended up as a witness at the nikkah. As the Imam asked Rukhsana three times if she took Asif to be her husband, Saima swallowed the lump in her throat. This was why she did the work that she did. Here, in this smoky restaurant, two people who probably never would have met were it not for a gentle push from a matchmaker were about to start a life together.

Forty minutes later, at 10.20 pm, the couple were married and dinner was finally served. Aluminium trays of gosht, biryani, chawal, tandoori chicken and naan were brought in by weary waiters, who barely had time to place the platters on the trestle tables set up at one end of the room before the guests swarmed for the food. A few of Asif's relatives tried to maintain order.

'We know, bhai, dinner is late, but please don't push past the children. They're also hungry,' one of Asif's brothers told an uncle, who promptly ignored him and kept piling his plate high with chicken.

'There's plenty more food on its way, please be patient!' a cousin called from the other end of the buffet. Soon, the queue snaked its way around the periphery of the room.

As she sat down with a plate of food, Saima finally had the time to enjoy the proceedings around her. There were no wedding speeches and no entertainment as such, save for a Bollywood movie wedding mix that played on repeat. A stage had been set up in one corner of the room where the newlyweds sat on upholstered chairs adorned with flowers, where some of the guests, many still holding plates of food, stood patiently in line to get their photos taken with them. A toddler, probably high on a sugar rush, began dancing in the middle of the room, his oversized shalwar getting caught between his feet. A few adults clapped along, encouraging him to keep going, but he got shy and ran back to his mother. Saima was filled with a bittersweet joy. These were her people, even when they weren't. As intense as some of these events could be, she found that they refilled some inner reservoir almost every time, like she was a solar cell, soaking up the sunlight.

People eventually began to take their leave, too full of the admittedly excellent dinner to eat the rasgulla and jalebi desserts laid out. At midnight, Saima thought she too could finally say goodbye.

Rukhsana clutched Saima's hands tightly as she was leaving. 'Thank you so much, baji, for everything that you did tonight.'

'It was my pleasure, but I did what anyone would do,' Saima said with a smile. It was the truth. Throughout her life, different members of the community had stepped up for her and her mother, and she would not think twice about doing the same. For all the gossip, snobbery and complicated traditions and social conventions, she couldn't imagine belonging to a more big-hearted community.

'Please know that you are family now,' Rukhsana said. 'You're like my big sister, apa, truly.'

Saima laughed and kissed both her cheeks. 'I would have thought you had enough sisters, Rukhsana! But I'm honoured and touched, thank you.' She wished Rukhsana and Asif her very best and headed off home.

It was close to one in the morning when Saima unlocked the door of her studio and headed straight for the couch. She would eventually wipe off her make-up and take out her hair, but for now, all she wanted to do was close her eyes and crash.

She sat unmoving for a good few minutes before her thoughts turned to Kal and Ayesha. There had been no messages or calls from either of them.

This is a good sign, she told herself. *They must have hit it off.* But on the heels of that thought, there was a twinge in the pit of her stomach.

An image from the night she had met up with Kal arose from nowhere. But rather than shoving it straight into the Too-Hard Basket, Jess's words about repression rang in her ears, and she let herself drift with it for a bit. The two of them walking side by side,

184

a river of headlights on Broadway streaming beside them, trying to talk over the noise of the traffic. She hardly recognised the person she had felt like at that moment, possibly the happiest version of her usual self. Wait, no. 'Happy' wasn't the right word. What was it? She'd felt at ease. Content.

Yes. Content. And every conversation they'd had since had amplified that feeling, even when he'd prompted some uncomfortable introspection from her.

On a whim, she dialled his number. It was well past a normal hour to call, but if he didn't pick up after two rings, she would hang up.

He picked up after the first.

'You're up,' she said with surprise. She couldn't hear anything in the background.

'So are you,' he replied.

'Late wedding.'

'Where was it?'

'Oh, probably nowhere you've been to. A small restaurant in Harris Park.'

'Why is it that you always want to make out like I'm some kind of snob?' He sounded hurt or exasperated, she couldn't tell which.

'I'm sorry,' she said. 'It was a bad attempt to lighten the mood.'

'What makes you think my mood needs lightening?'

'I don't know. It's late. Maybe I don't know what I'm saying.' Perhaps calling him after midnight wasn't such a good idea.

'You always know what you're saying, Saima. It's why we all trust you.'

And yet she didn't know what to say to that.

'Ayesha said it too,' Kal continued. 'She trusts you implicitly, just like I do. You make quite an impression on people, did you know that?'

'And what else did Ayesha say?'

185

He was quiet for a moment. 'So are you just calling to fish for information? I should've guessed.'

'No, not fishing. I thought I'd ask you first before calling Ayesha tomorrow.'

'She'll say she loved me, of course.'

'Get over yourself!'

'No? She told me you went on about how good-looking I was.'

'I did not go on about it!'

'Hot, eh?' She could hear the beginning of a smile in his voice.

'It was just part of my sales pitch,' she said loftily, trying to ignore the feeling of her cheeks flushing.

'Is that what I am, then? A product to pitch?'

Saima wished for a moment that she could see him to understand the odd tone in his voice.

'None of my clients are products to me,' she answered. 'You're just souls waiting for connection.'

'That's a brilliant slogan.'

'So how did it go?' she finally asked.

'What do you want me to say? She was nice. She drank a mocktail and I drank a lemonade. We talked for a bit, and then I walked her to her building and we said goodbye.'

'Okay, what did you talk about? Did you land on anything you have in common?'

'We have *you* in common.'

The flutter in her stomach was back. 'What about me?'

'I told Ayesha that she'd straight up find it hard to meet a more frustrating, infuriating individual than you,' he said.

'Rude,' she quipped, but he wasn't done.

'I told her that Saima's voice lights up so much when she's happy, you would do anything to make her feel like that.'

She sat up in alarm. 'Kal.'

'And she's so passionate about people, about their feelings, and she wants everyone to feel love and be loved. It makes you wish you could be even half as passionate about anything in your own life.'

'Stop it.'

'And when her attention turns to something she's passionate about, it's like a laser, and it makes you jealous of whatever she's focused on, and you start to wonder what you can do to make her focus like that on *you*.'

They were both quiet. The feeling in her stomach had moved up to close tightly around Saima's heart. She shut her eyes, but his words swam in front of them anyway, like the aftermath of a blinding flash of light.

'You didn't say those things to Ayesha,' she said at last.

'Didn't I?'

'And you drank more than just lemonade tonight.'

His only response was a sigh. Then, very quietly, 'Goodnight, Saima.' He hung up.

For a long time, Saima sat in the dark with her phone in her hand. She wanted to call him back and tell him his words were the most beautiful thing that anyone had ever said to her. She wanted to go back to that night outside the gelato shop, to the moment that had been lurking in her Too-Hard Basket ever since and now flooded to the front of her mind, when she'd thought for a wild second that she could have just tipped up onto her toes and kissed him. She wanted to let that figure in her mind come into focus, because she was pretty sure she knew who it would be when it did. She wanted – she *wanted*.

She threw her phone onto the other end of the couch, then got up to wash her face and got ready for bed, slamming the lid closed on all those thoughts.

187

Chapter 16

Kal found Ayesha standing outside the bar, poised as if ready to make a break for it.

I'm outside and I'm not sure I can come in, she'd texted.

He approached her carefully. 'Hello? Ayesha? I'm Kal.' He debated whether to extend his hand, then second-guessed himself and ended up settling for an awkward wave.

In the end, it was probably the wave that did it. She visibly relaxed, then grimaced at him comically. 'Hi. Sorry, I'm not really a fan of noisy places.'

'Yeah, I'd hoped it would be quieter but I guess everyone's discovered it,' he said. 'Do you want to maybe walk down to the harbourfront? Cockle Bay Wharf is just a few blocks that way.'

'Sure – I mean, that sounds nice.'

They started walking down Druitt Street. Ayesha gave him a sidelong glance.

'I'm sorry I was so late,' she offered.

'Not a problem. So, how are you finding Sydney?'

'There's not a lot to find yet, to be honest. We haven't had the time to go sightseeing or anything.'

'Sightseeing's the worst way to get to know a city anyway,' he said, with a shrug. 'Have you guys decided where you'll be settling?'

'Not that I know of. Abbu's been busy setting up the business side of things, and my sister's still in Melbourne for the time being, so I don't think he's even thought about it.'

'And your mum?'

An odd look crossed her face. 'She'll happily leave the decision to him.'

'Do *you* have a preference?'

Her turn to shrug. 'I don't know enough about the place to have any opinion.'

He cast around for something else to talk about. 'So Yale, huh?'

'Yep, Yale.'

'How was that?'

'Good. Great.'

'You didn't stay on in the States?'

She shrugged again. 'My mum's not been well, so it was the right decision to come home.'

'Oh, I'm sorry to hear that.'

'It is what it is.'

Well, there was nothing to say to that. They walked the remaining distance in silence, across the wooden footbridge and into Darling Harbour. The twinkling lights of the city and the slowly rotating Ferris wheel across the water reflected on the gently rolling swell of the harbour, while above, the velvety black sky was dotted with stars.

'I never get tired of this.' Kal gestured across the view. 'Doesn't matter how many times I see it.'

Ayesha seemed unmoved. 'It's nice, but it's no Melbourne.'

He smiled. 'That's a very Melburnian response. Are you telling me the Yarra is prettier than this?' She didn't reply. 'Is it Melburnian or Melbournite?'

'I don't know,' she said politely. Another excruciating silence followed. Kal began to wonder when he might respectfully call it a night.

'In many ways, I feel more American than anything this country has to offer me,' Ayesha suddenly said.

Looking over at her curiously, Kal nodded. 'I get that. Though I don't think I feel particularly Australian or Pakistani. America is strange in many ways to me.'

'If you keep politics out of it and find your tribe, then it's a great place to be. Especially the East Coast.'

America turned out to be a passion she could talk about at length. She spoke of visiting Manhattan for the first time and then discovering that the best places to hang out were actually in Brooklyn. She spoke of her friends, about the pressure of studying at an Ivy League college, especially as an international student, because most people assumed she had paid her way in, and though, yes, her father had paid handsomely for her to study there, she still had to get good grades of her own to get admission. She spoke of the issues she'd run into when trying to find a job, and then having to abandon her job search altogether so she could come home to be with her mum.

'She's not well,' she said again, and Kal didn't prod her for more information. But he found he wanted to get to know this vibrant, enthusiastic version of her. There was something oddly familiar about it.

'There's a rooftop café-bar place just over that way,' he said, pointing. 'Do you want to sit down and get that drink? It's much quieter than the bar we were meeting at.'

'Sure thing,' she said, and followed his lead.

'I have to give you props,' he said, as they made their way up to the rooftop terrace. 'Unfamiliar city, unfamiliar guy, and you're going along with everything I'm suggesting.'

She waited until they were seated at one of the tables with a view out across Darling Harbour before eyeing him frankly. 'Saima said you were cool.'

He grinned. 'You know, I first met Saima when she jumped into my car thinking it was an Uber.'

Ayesha smiled at that, the first smile she'd given all night. 'I thought your parents had gone to her for help.'

'Oh, trust me, my parents have been at me about getting married pretty much from the time I graduated university. But I think they've learned by now to stop hassling me. They'll be shocked to find out I've agreed to be set up by a desi matchmaker.'

'They'll probably be excited by it, to be honest. Excited and proud.'

'True.' Kal smiled. 'They'll save their shock for if I settle down with someone she introduces me to.'

'*If* you settle down? You don't think you will?'

'Saima told me to be open to the process, so this is me being open to the process,' he said. 'I don't know whether she's going to introduce me to my soulmate or anything.'

'Ha, she gave me the same speech, you know. So why *did* you ask her to set you up?' Ayesha asked as their drinks arrived.

He took a long sip as he considered his answer. 'I didn't, to be honest.'

'So then . . . how'd you wind up here, with me?'

'Tell you what, I'll think about my answer while you give me yours. Shaadi doesn't seem to be high on your list of priorities right now, if you'll pardon my saying so.'

'The truth?' She looked away across the water. 'I mean, the basic truth is that my dad's been on my case about settling down, which is no big surprise. And then a random uncle recommended Saima not long after we'd moved here.'

'That's it?'

191

'Well, she made a terrible sales pitch for the business, but a great one for herself as a person. Also, she said you were hot.'

'She did not!' he said, stifling a laugh.

'She totally did,' Ayesha said with a grin. 'I don't know, after I talked to Saima, it felt like the right thing to do.'

Kal nodded. 'I know that feeling. And that's basically why I signed on with her too, though I don't think we ever did anything so formal as signing on. She gives the impression that she *gets* it, she gets you. She *sees* you. And you just know that she'll make it her mission to make magic happen.'

'You trust her?'

'Yeah, I do. As do you, I'm guessing.'

'I wouldn't be here if I didn't,' she said.

'Funny how she has this ability to make you feel . . .' He searched for the right word. *Like you've come home*, his brain supplied. No, he couldn't say that. He stared into his drink for a minute. 'Content.'

Ayesha gave him an odd look. 'Yeah.'

They turned to more casual topics and the conversation flowed like water. Ayesha was a pop culture fiend and they spent a happy half-hour revisiting their favourite shows and films, then she began to work in earnest to convert him to podcasts.

'I just feel like I missed the boat on podcasts,' he protested at one point.

She scoffed. 'That's like saying you missed the boat on cars because you don't have a Model T, for god's sake.'

As they talked, he began to realise what it was about Ayesha that felt familiar. She reminded him of his sister, or at least a version of her where they had the time to sit down and connect. He and Amna had never been particularly close. Their personalities were too different and their lives too busy, even as children. While he threw himself into

sport when he was younger, his sister had more scholarly interests –
she studied languages, spoke perfect French at twelve, and learned
Mandarin and Spanish at HSC level. Urdu she spoke poorly by her
own exacting standards. Their parents had been so proud when she
got into SOAS University of London. Kal had been proud of her too,
but it was a distant kind of pride. She never seemed to stop for long
enough for them to get to know each other, and she was so fiercely
intelligent that she rarely had the patience for people who couldn't keep
up with her. Once, when he was about ten or eleven, he'd wandered
into her room just to hang out and she had tolerated his presence for
only a few moments before saying, 'Can you just go now?'

Looking at Ayesha, he recognised that same restlessness and
impatience. When she eventually began to fidget, he had an instinct
for what she was thinking.

'Shall we go now?' he asked.

She nodded with a smile, looking relieved.

They slowly walked back in the direction of her apartment
building, up and over the pedestrian bridge to a deserted Market
Street and on past the Queen Victoria Building. The night was cold
but dry, and they fell silent once again as they walked, but this time
it was a comfortable silence. At the door to her building, he paused
for moment, unsure what to say.

Ayesha shook his hand firmly. 'This wasn't as bad as I thought it
would be,' she said frankly.

He grinned wryly. 'Cheers. I'll go so far as to say that it was
actually pretty nice.'

'Ha! Yes, turns out Saima knows what she's on about, after all.'
Ayesha swiped her entry pass outside the doorway and looked back
at him. 'I guess we'll be in touch?'

'Yep. Goodnight, Ayesha. And thanks for a "not as bad as you
thought it would be" night.'

'You too.' She smiled and walked into the building.

As he sat in the taxi taking him back over the Harbour Bridge, Kal wondered whether this time he would tell his parents that he'd been out with a Pakistani girl. Out of the three dates Saima had arranged, Ayesha had been the one he'd connected with the most. But then he examined that connection more deeply. They'd gotten along well, yes. He'd enjoyed most of it, really, and he wouldn't say no to catching up again in the future – in fact, he'd feel lucky if he could eventually count Ayesha as a friend. She made him aware for the first time how much he'd missed out on the relationship he could and should have had with his sister.

The indisputable fact, though, was that of all the girls he had met this year, only one made him feel like he'd finally stumbled onto the sense of belonging, of homecoming, that he hadn't even known he was looking for. And the feeling, as far as he could make out, was not mutual.

He was lying awake a couple of hours later when his phone rang, and set his heart pounding when he saw the caller ID. He hit the answer button straight away.

'Did you land on anything you have in common?' Saima prodded.

Maybe it was the late hour that made him more bloody-minded than usual, but Kal gave in to the urge to see if all his churning emotions were as one-sided as he'd assumed.

'I told her that Saima's voice lights up so much when she's happy, you would do anything to make her feel like that.'

Was it his imagination, or had her breath hitched for a moment there?

'And she's so passionate about people, about their feelings, and she wants everyone to feel love and be loved. It makes you wish you could be even half as passionate about anything in your own life.'

'Stop it.'

'And when her attention turns to something she's passionate about, it's like a laser, and it makes you jealous of whatever she's focused on, and you start to wonder what you can do to make her focus like that on *you*.'

Neither of them spoke for what seemed like an age. Once again, as so often happened with Saima, he felt like he was on the very edge of something incredibly elusive and important. If he could just reach out and—

'You didn't say those things to Ayesha,' she finally said.

Defeat coursed through him.

'Goodnight, Saima.'

The following morning, Kal lay groggily awake, his mind churning, delaying getting out of bed, but keenly aware he had agreed to go for lunch at his parents' place. Although he desperately wanted to take a raincheck, he'd missed their lunch dates for several months running, and he didn't want to let his parents down again.

He started shuffling around the bedroom, almost knocking over the small potted plant he'd gotten the week prior. It was looking a bit limp. Was it weird to ask Mariam's nani to diagnose what he was doing wrong? A text pinged on his phone as he tried shifting the plant to a sunnier location.

I was a good boy and didn't go out last night. Got up early to try surfing, Tom wrote.

Who even surfs in winter? Kal replied, and then Tom rang him.

'Only the hardiest of real men,' he said.

Kal could hear the waves crashing on the beach in the background. 'So, how was it?'

'I got dumped, looked like a complete fool, froze my arse to death, but yeah, I think I love it,' Tom said. He sounded winded and exhilarated.

'Sounds amazing,' Kal said, laughing. 'Well, surfers like to get up at dawn to catch the best waves, so you might have to pick between your new love and your old one, because I don't know that partying and early-morning water sports are compatible.'

'Meh, I'm still young, old man!'

'Can't hear you over my warm cup of cocoa.'

Tom sniggered. 'So where were you last night? I called.'

'I was on a date.'

'Oh yeah? Another Pakistani girl?'

'Yeah.'

'How was this one? Did she bring her grandmother along?'

'No, no grandmothers or stilettos. She was nice. Bit scary.'

'Yeah?'

'Just incredibly switched on, you know?'

Tom laughed. 'Smart women are super hot, bro.'

'She's definitely smart. But it's probably not a good thing she reminded me of my sister.'

'Ha! Yeah, that'd be hard to move past, however hot someone is. So you gonna see her again? Or have you got the matchmaker looking for more girls?'

Kal thought about the strained phone call with Saima. At what point did he admit that he was only in this so he had an excuse to be around her? Stringing her along wasn't fair on her, and definitely wasn't fair on the women he'd met. 'Nah, I reckon I'm over it,' he said slowly.

'Yeah, but mate, you're over a lot of things right now. I've seen you dragging your arse to work.'

'And here I was hoping no one would notice,' Kal murmured.

'Hard not to, it's been going on for months now.'

That much was true. Kal had tipped into actively disliking his job over the past few weeks, and try as he might to hide it, the pall that fell over him whenever he sat at his desk was probably obvious to someone who knew him as well as Tom did.

'I dunno. Kinda feel it's all a bit boring,' Kal said, hoping that would satisfy Tom.

'Mate, you're thirty, not fifteen. Life is boring. That's why we go out and party. Though even that's stopped with you recently.'

'Maybe I'll take up surfing.'

'Stop dicking around for a second and be serious,' Tom said with uncharacteristic sternness. 'Look, Kal, you're one of my best mates, but you never tell anyone what you're thinking. It's okay to tell someone what's really going on.'

Kal thought about Saima's call last night, how he had *willed* her to give him an opening to finally tell her how he felt about her, and how she'd shut that down faster than a steel trap. 'Trust me, people don't want to know what's really going on.'

'I'm not talking about "people", mate,' Tom said. 'No-one's telling you to start writing a blog about your problems. I'm just saying, you have actual *friends* who care about you, and you shut them out as well. It doesn't have to be me, but I'm here if you want to talk. Have you thought that maybe you're depressed?'

He hadn't ever considered that as a possibility.

'Dad went through a bad depression when I was a kid, especially after Mum left,' Tom continued. 'It was tough seeing him go through that. There were days he couldn't even speak to us. I had to look out for my younger brother, make sure he got to school and that. So I get it, I get how shit it can be.'

In all the years Kal had known him, Tom had never revealed this much about his family. Kal had always assumed he'd had a bog-standard childhood, but perhaps no-one actually had one of those.

'I'm sorry to hear that,' he said. 'It sounds awful and I hope your dad eventually got help.'

'Yeah, we sorted it out in the end, even though it wasn't easy with him being your typically stoic old Japanese man, you know? But I can tell you that it only gets harder to tackle the longer you try to muddle it out on your own.'

Kal sighed. 'I appreciate it, mate, I do. But I don't think I'm depressed. I think it's, like, existential angst.'

'Come off it!' Tom let out a short laugh.

'I mean, the partying and stuff, I genuinely think I'm just at an age where I want to go somewhere where I can actually *talk* with the people I care about. It's not fun anymore to head to some noisy bar to get wasted or pick up. I want to know more about *you*, for example. All these years we've been friends and you've never mentioned how you grew up.'

'Ah, stop it,' Tom said. 'Didn't mean to make you gush.'

'Sure you did, you're just waiting for me to give you a best friends necklace so you can lord it over Lachie.'

Tom guffawed. 'Mate, if you give me a best friends necklace, you better believe I'll never let Lachie forget it.'

'And I promise, if I'm feeling bad, I'll tell you,' Kal said, as his phone buzzed with a calendar reminder. 'Anyway, I gotta run, I have to head up to Gordon for lunch.'

'Say hi to your folks for me.'

'Will do. And Tom?'

'Yeah?'

'Thanks, man. For real, jokes aside. I appreciate the chat.'

'I'm not just a pretty face, I keep telling you.'

'Yeah, yeah. Anyway, try not to drown out there, and I'll see you at work on Monday. I'll try to be livelier!'

The thought of eating his mum's cooking certainly perked Kal up. Ruby had made Pakistani food all the time when they were children, but as they got older, she started reserving her dishes for special occasions only. It was easier to make what she called 'no-fuss dishes' – pasta, meatballs, roasts – and then she began to order meals from a delivery service instead.

Kal inhaled deeply as he walked up his parents' driveway to the house he'd grown up in. It was positioned on the high side of the street, surrounded by mature trees, with a long driveway running alongside a manicured lawn that was still maintained by the gardener his mum had employed since Kal was a kid. The street was quiet, respectable and, as far as Kal was concerned, boring as hell. For years they were the only non-white family living in the neighbourhood, until a quiet Taiwanese family moved in across the road when Kal was a teenager. But other than that excitement, the place seemed stuck in time. It was one of the reasons why Kal hadn't been able to get out of there quick enough as soon as he started university.

When he let himself in the front door, the house smelled of lemons and furniture polish, as always. 'Assalaamu alaykum, Ammy, Papa,' he called.

'We're in the living room,' George called back.

Kal wandered over to where his mother sat scowling over her glasses at an iPad screen and kissed her cheek. 'Fresh from the salon, Ammy? You look nice.'

She eyed him appraisingly. 'You need a haircut yourself, Khalid.'

'I'm thinking of growing it long enough for a man bun,' he said with a grin. 'Go for the real hipster look.'

'Chee!' she exclaimed.

He laughed, then went to sit on the sofa across from her. 'I thought you were going to make salan,' he said.

'Salan? What sort of salan? When did you last want to eat my salan?' Ruby asked.

In fairness, he couldn't remember the last time he'd asked his mother to make one of her curries, and he guessed she had noticed.

'Your mother hardly cooks nowadays,' his father muttered, briefly looking up from his newspaper before retreating behind it.

'Why should I cook when no-one likes to eat my food?' Ruby asked. 'Last time I spent all day making nihari, the two of you barely ate any of it. I ended up having to throw it all away.'

'You know it gives me indigestion,' George said, his eyes fixed on the paper.

'Yes, but then you will happily eat a fried steak with no problem,' Ruby said. George knew better than to respond.

Kal couldn't remember why he hadn't eaten his mother's nihari in the past. She would simmer the thick spicy stew for hours, till the goat meat was falling off the bone, then she'd pour the curry into bowls, garnishing it with sliced ginger, green chilli, coriander and a generous squeeze of fresh lemon. There would always be hot, fresh naan on the side, perfect for soaking up the gravy. Just the thought of it right now made his mouth water.

'Are you sure I didn't want to eat it?' he made the mistake of asking.

'Am I sure? *Am I sure?* Do you think I would forget throwing away food I spent all day preparing? I even went to a special butcher to buy the goat meat. And then your father with his indigestion, and you carrying on about how you were cutting down on meat and carbs and whatever. What is it with you young people these days? When I was young, I ate anything and everything!'

'When you were his age, you already had two children,' George said dryly. 'And you were on a permanent diet.'

'Bakwas band karo!' Ruby exclaimed, and left the room.

'Your mother is in a bit of a mood, in case you haven't noticed,' George said.

'What's happened?' Kal asked. 'What did you do?'

'God knows. Do you think I want to find out? Anyway, what makes you think *I* did something?'

'Because Ammy never flies off the handle at random, whereas *you* love to push her buttons for no reason. You could at least try to find out why she's upset.'

George shrugged. 'Trust me, son, when you have a wife, you will learn very quickly to keep your mouth shut.'

Ah. As usual, the conversation somehow came back to him finding a wife.

'Any news on that front?' George asked, folding his paper and finally looking him in the eye.

'What, the wife front? Are you kidding me?'

'Well, a father likes to know. Are you going out with anyone? Well, anyone worth us knowing about?'

Kal ran a hand through his hair, unsure of how much to reveal to his father. The conversation with Tom at the front of his mind, he took a breath. 'Okay, don't get too excited, all right?' he said quickly. 'But I met this woman. She's a matchmaker. And she put me in touch with this Pakistani girl. Well, three of them. I met one of them last night. She was probably the best of the three. Anyway, what I'm trying to say is that I think I've met someone who feels right, you know? But—'

George threw down the paper and shouted for his wife. 'Ruby! Come in here!'

Kal flinched. He should've just kept his mouth shut.

'This will make your ammy feel so much better. I just know it,' George said.

Ruby hurried into the room. 'Why are you shouting? What's the matter?'

'Kal here has just been telling me that he met a matchmaker who has set him up with some Pakistani girls and the one he went out with last night feels right—'

'Wait, I didn't say that . . . Not the one last night . . . I meant . . .' Kal stammered, but they weren't listening.

Ruby's face changed in an instant, transforming from fed up to sheer joy. For a moment, Kal wondered what she would look like if he told her he was getting married. She'd probably explode with happiness.

The rapid-fire questions began immediately. 'Why didn't you say anything before? How long have you been going out with these girls? You should have told me! And the one you like, from last night – who is she? And her family, do we know them? What do they do? Does she work? Where do they live? Where in Pakistan are they from?'

'Whoa, just chill out, Ammy!' he exclaimed. 'I just met the last girl yesterday and it was nice but brief. I don't know that anything will come of it.'

'Why? What's wrong with the girl? If the matchmaker was as good as you said she was, she would have chosen a proper match.'

'I never said anything about the matchmaker being good,' Kal said.

'Arre, your mother was just assuming she was good, beta,' George said, getting up from his seat and coming over to him. 'We're just excited that you agreed to go out with some Pakistani girls at all. And then to find someone you connected with, well, that's very exciting.'

'I didn't say—' Kal started, but Ruby spoke over him.

'Yes, of course. The matchmaker must be good, otherwise why would you even agree to use her services?' she said, looking, for some reason, at her husband.

'Why are you both being so weird about the matchmaker?' Kal asked. 'Have you met her? Oh, you might have. She was at that wedding I was supposed to be at earlier this year, remember? The one in Bexley?'

'Wedding? Which wedding? We've been to so many weddings.' Ruby let out a short laugh.

'You've probably heard of her, now that I think about it. Her name is Saima Khan. I'm guessing there aren't many matchmakers like her in the community,' Kal said.

'Arre, beta, why are we talking about this matchmaker when we should be talking about the girl you went out with last night? Now tell us, what's her name?' George asked. 'And you, Ruby, sit down and calm down.'

'Well, her name is Ayesha,' relented Kal, eyeing his mother dubiously as she plopped down on the sofa, looking for all the world like she'd been told off. 'Her father runs a business in Melbourne but they've recently relocated to Sydney.'

'Oh yes, what sort of business? What's his surname? I might know him,' George said.

'It doesn't matter what his surname is, Papa. I've been trying to tell you – I don't think me and Ayesha are a good match,' Kal said.

'What? Why?' Ruby cried.

'Well, for one thing, I think she'd rather be back at Yale than in Sydney.'

'Yale!' his parents exclaimed in unison.

'The girl went to Yale?' Ruby repeated.

'Where in Sydney are they staying?' George asked.

'In a penthouse in the city,' Kal said. 'Until they find somewhere permanent.'

'Penthouse? That matchmaker must be *good*,' Ruby said.

'Stop talking about the matchmaker!'

'Okay, okay, beta, I'm sorry,' she said soothingly. 'But going back to Ayesha, you need to give it a bit of time. The first time you meet someone is never going to be perfect.'

He thought about the first time he met Saima. No, he wouldn't describe that as perfect. But it somehow seemed perfect in hindsight, even if he hadn't felt that way at the time.

'The first time I met your mother, I thought my father had lost his mind introducing me to a skinny, worried-looking girl like that,' George said.

'You never told me that!' Ruby protested. 'You said you knew I was the one from the first moment you laid eyes on me!'

'Arre, bhai, I'm trying to help the boy out here and you keep ruining it with your talk!' George said, exasperated.

His wife gave him a look that promised retribution, then turned back to her son. 'Your father is right. It's never perfect the first time round. Give the girl time. Is she pretty?'

Kal thought about it. 'Yeah, she's definitely pretty.'

Ruby seemed satisfied.

'Okay, let's stop harassing the poor boy,' George said, trying to defuse the tension, before pulling out his phone. 'Anyway, I'm hungry, and I'm sure Kal is too. Shall we figure out what to eat?'

They ended up ordering Portuguese chicken, extra spicy. As they ate their lunch Ruby wondered out loud, 'Does Ayesha also like spicy food?'

'I don't know,' Kal said.

'Well, next time, you can ask her and find out.' And Kal didn't have the heart to tell her there wouldn't be a next time, at least not in the way she meant, and once again he thought how he should have kept his mouth shut. Though maybe it meant something that his parents had gotten the wrong end of the stick about the woman he'd felt a connection with. His thoughts turned to Saima, as they increasingly seemed to do, and he remembered that on their not-date, she had asked for extra chilli to pour over her laksa. She could definitely eat his mum's nihari without any problems, even with the fresh green chilli on top.

'Look at him, smiling to himself like that,' Ruby said to George. The two of them beamed. 'Hamara beta kithna piyara hai!'

Chapter 17

Linda was moving through reception when Kal walked in on Monday. *This is a sign*, he thought to himself. The night before, he had lain awake for hours, trying to figure out how to start making work less of the slog it had recently become. Though the attempt to open up to his parents probably could have gone better, maybe Tom's advice would work out more in a work setting.

'Morning, sunshine,' Linda said as she briskly walked past him.

'Actually, Linda, do you have a sec?' he asked quickly, before he had a chance to talk himself out of it.

She was clearly surprised at the request, but without hesitation motioned for him to follow her into a meeting room and shut the door behind them. The room had no windows and Kal immediately felt boxed in.

'What's up?' she asked, casually taking the seat beside him. Kal wished she had sat opposite him, across the table. Her proximity brought back the uncomfortable memory of his stupidity at the Christmas party two years ago, when, in the time-honoured tradition of work functions with an open bar, he'd drunkenly decided to flirt with Linda. It had been a colossally juvenile move.

'Linda, I'm not, um, I'm not feeling the job as much these days,' he started.

'"Feeling the job"?' she repeated. 'You're going to have to explain what that means.'

Kal bit the bullet and gave her the untarnished truth. 'I guess I'm not very motivated lately by what I'm doing.'

Linda paled noticeably. 'You're planning to quit? Because, if so, that's going to stuff me up no end. We've got the Stewart account coming up, and you know it's going to be all hands on deck.'

'No, no, I'm not thinking of leaving.' Though now that he thought about it, *should* he be manoeuvring to leave? His father would never forgive him if he resigned purely based on 'not feeling it', but then, maybe that was reason enough to consider it.

'Is everything okay with you? I mean, at home?' Linda leaned forward, clasping her hands on the table in front of them.

He hid his discomfort with a short laugh. 'At home? I don't exactly have a home life, Linda. And this has never struck me as a workplace that really wants to know about our lives outside office hours.' All he knew about Linda, for example, was that she had a couple of children in primary school and a husband that nobody ever saw. 'Anyway, everything's fine.'

'I wondered if it had something to do with your father. You seemed worried about him, that time you took off midmorning to see him.'

'I wasn't worried—'

'Look, it's none of my business. Though I could say as your manager, what you do on company time *is* my business, and I'm sort of responsible for you, especially if it's impacting your job. Is the work not as interesting as before?'

'The work itself hasn't changed,' Kal told her. 'I think that's the problem. I've been here, what, seven years now? There's been one promotion in that time, and it's been the same work over and over. I know that I'm capable of doing more.'

'Like what?'

'That's the thing, Linda – I've not had a chance to figure that out, because we're not exactly given the space to take the initiative and learn other sides of the business, are we?'

'So you're angling for *my* job?' Linda asked, leaning back slightly.

He blinked. 'Absolutely not,' he said quickly. 'I'm not talking about managing people, I'm talking about broader remits, creative accounts, something a bit more innovative, that sort of thing. With the greatest respect, I don't have it in me to keep the sharp eye you have on our productivity on top of the accounts that *you* manage. Frankly, I don't know how you have enough hours in the day. Don't you ever miss spending time with the family?' As soon as the question left his lips, Kal wanted to drag it back in. It was a shitty thing to ask any working mother, let alone one who worked in a male-dominated industry like theirs.

Linda raised her eyebrows. 'Yes, of course I miss them,' she said. 'And they miss me. I haven't taken my entire annual leave entitlement in years. But what choice do you think a woman with young kids has in this environment? I have to work twice as hard as any of you to prove my worth to this company.'

'Listen, I get that,' Kal said. 'But—'

'Do you?' she interrupted. 'You're still young. You have lots of opportunities ahead of you. And I would hate to lose you. We all would. But if you decided to quit, I'd understand. Maybe starting afresh somewhere is the right move for you.'

'I'm not trying to quit,' Kal repeated. 'I'm just pointing out that as far as career progression and job satisfaction go, things aren't great here right now, not like they used to be.'

The two of them sat quietly for a moment. Kal looked across at Linda and noticed a weariness creep across her features. He thought about the encounter they'd had at the Christmas party and how they had danced, their hips almost touching before the music changed and the two of them immediately came to their senses, stumbling away apologetically. He wondered if she had been lonely then, and again, how she managed all the time at work with the demands at home.

'So what's the solution here, Kal?' she asked. 'Are you asking for a promotion? For different accounts? To move teams? You know I'm on your side, but I have to tell you, there's already been talk about your performance, and now probably isn't the right time to be raising your head above the battlements.'

'My performance?' he said incredulously. 'My *performance* has been up to its usual high standard, Linda, and you know that. Every single account Tom and I manage is doing brilliantly – we have the feedback to prove it. And as for solutions, I'm asking *you* what's possible here. I'm not the one who calls the shots.' He could hear the frustration creeping into his voice and reined in the angry words lining up on his tongue. 'Look, maybe I should take a couple days off and work through things.'

'That's up to you. Though you should know, Charles will be doing his employee evaluations soon, if *that* matters to you at all. The Stewart Group wants to launch by mid-August, too, so that work's going to pile up if you're not going to pull your weight.' She looked deflated as she spoke, as if Kal's imminent resignation meant she could not take her own foot off the pedal. Ultimately, his leaving would mean more work would fall on her shoulders.

'Let me just think about it, okay?'

Well, that achieved a grand total of nothing, he thought, as he retreated from the room. By the time he got to his desk, he'd lost all motivation to do any work. Within minutes, Tom had popped up like a jack-in-the-box.

'Hey, don't forget the meeting with Charles at ten.'

Kal groaned. 'Dude, I don't think I'm going to make it.'

'What? It's a meeting with *Charles*. You know, your manager's manager? Sometimes you need to go to things you don't want to. Even if they are boring.' When Kal shrugged, Tom bent down to eye level. 'Oi, what happened to "I'll try to be livelier"?' He studied his friend with concern. 'Like I told you, I'm here to help if you need,' he added quietly.

'I know, man, and I appreciate it so much,' Kal said, squeezing Tom's shoulder. 'I just – I need some space, okay? I told Linda I was going to take some days off.'

Tom returned the gesture. 'Sure, mate, I'll cover for you, no worries,' he said. 'And I reckon some time off might do you a world of good. But if I don't hear from you every day, I'm going to call your mum and tell her you're about to run away with a Russian gangster, or maybe someone else more to your liking?' he said with a wink.

'Thanks, mate. And don't worry, I'll keep in touch.'

After Tom left, Kal turned off his computer, shoved the few personal items he had on his desk into his bag and walked out of the office, unsure in that moment whether he would ever return. As he made his way out of the building, he was flooded with a sense of liberation he hadn't felt in a long time. Some actual time off! He was free to do whatever he wanted. But when he thought about it, he wasn't sure what it was he actually wanted to do. He even suppressed an urge to run back to his desk. *Oh shit, do I have Stockholm syndrome?* he wondered.

Before he could head back into captivity, Kal found himself pulling out his wallet and staring at the dog-eared card that had sat in there for months. Saima's office address gleamed back at him, embossed in gold. An overwhelming impulse seized him to go to that address. He didn't want to think about what he was doing. He was just going to do it. He was free, and if he didn't act now, another ten years would go by and he would be in the same job until he was scrapped for a younger, hungrier upgrade, and he'd have wasted another decade on fruitless pursuits with nothing to show for it. He wanted to feel challenged and energised. He wanted to feel the certainty and peace of knowing that he was exactly where he was supposed to be and all the pieces around him fitted perfectly. He wanted to feel alive and *happy*. And in his mind, clear as crystal, he knew exactly when he most felt that way.

He had to tell her.

Chapter 18

The new barista at her usual café needed to stop burning the beans so much, Saima thought as she took a sip of her usual order and stifled a grimace on her way to the office. The excitement hit almost immediately as she walked in the door. Dave quickly shuffled up as she was closing it behind her.

'There's a man in your—' he whispered, before Jess, almost running down the corridor, interrupted him.

'Thank you, Dave, but I'll let Saima know.' She grabbed Saima by the arm and frogmarched her down the corridor. 'Is this the guy you've been exchanging all those texts and calls with?' she hissed.

'What guy?' Saima asked.

'The one in your office!'

'There's a man in my office?'

'That's what I'm telling you!'

'Why is everyone freaking out? I've had men in my office before.'

'*Not like this.* What have you been up to, you saucy minx?'

The ill-advised late-night call with Kal bubbled immediately to the top of Saima's mind. 'Nothing!'

Jess pounced. 'Aha! You said that way too quickly!'

'Shhhh! You still haven't explained why you're losing your mind over whoever is in my office. What do you mean, "not like this"?'

'For one thing,' Jess said, 'he's *hot*. No offence to your other clients—'

'—always offensive—'

'—but none of them look like freaking Dev Patel.'

Oh no.

'I'd like to know the exciting news too. Is it about the handsome man?' Dave asked, having quietly followed behind them.

'Not now, Dave,' Jess said, rolling her eyes.

'He's just a client,' Saima told him, trying to calm her racing heart.

'So you *do* know who's in there!' Jess exclaimed. 'Gotcha!'

'Can you stop acting like a hyperactive Miss Marple and calm down, please?' The pang in Saima's stomach was back.

'Well, if he needs a cup of tea or anything, I don't mind being the receptionist for clients like him,' Dave said.

'Dave!' Jess's exclamations were getting louder and louder. 'Anyway, I already asked the handsome man if he wanted a drink but he said no. Then I asked him if there was anything else I could do to help and he said he'd just wait. And then I ran out of things to ask him so I just stood there like a fool until I heard you come in!'

'This office is far too thirsty this morning,' Saima muttered. 'I'm assuming from your melodramatic descriptions that his name is Kal.'

'The handsome man?' Jess clarified.

'Yes, the handsome man! And if you two are done acting like teenagers, I should go see why he's here. He doesn't have an appointment.'

'Men like that don't need appointments,' Dave said with a broad grin, before he ambled off towards the kitchen.

'He's turning out to be a bit of a dark horse, isn't he?' Jess said, as she watched Dave leave. 'But back to more important things – is there something going on between you and the Dev Patel hottie currently sitting in your office?'

'No, why would you say that?'

'Because you, my unflappable friend, are beginning to look extremely flapped. Anyway, if there is, you should go for it. And if there isn't, you should still totally go for it, because if you don't, Dave will.' Jess was grinning, but her eyes were serious, even watchful.

'It doesn't matter if there is or isn't something going on,' Saima hissed. 'He's the son of that rich couple who came here. Remember them?'

Jess looked disappointed at the news.

'And my professional reputation and the future of my business hang on me finding Kal a good desi wife.'

Jess perked back up. 'But don't you see? It could be you! *You* could be the good desi wife!'

'I'm not a good desi, and I definitely won't be a good wife,' Saima said. She finally pulled her arm out of her friend's grip. 'I set him up on a date at the weekend, and I'm guessing he's here to talk to me about that.' *And not what he said to me after*, she prayed. She hadn't decided what to do about *that* conversation, which had been banging around in her brain, shaking loose a whole lot of other emotions that she usually repressed.

She had already spoken to Ayesha earlier this morning – it was why she'd walked into the office a little later than usual.

'He's a decent guy, Saima,' Ayesha had said.

'Did you like him? Enough to see him again and consider something more long-term?' Saima found herself holding her breath for Ayesha's answer.

'Look, you were right about us hitting it off.'

'Was I?' Her stomach dropped.

'Yeah, totally. My parents were super happy I went out with a nice Pakistani boy. Even Ammy told me how pleased she was. I think you've got great instincts about people.'

'Thank you. And?'

Ayesha hummed for a second. 'Less of an "and" and more of a "but". I think we'd be better off as friends.'

'Oh, I'm sorry to hear that.'

'Anyway, I don't think it matters who you set him up with. He's not going to end up with any of them, because my guess is that none of them will make him feel content, like—' She stopped abruptly.

'Like what?'

'Ask him,' Ayesha said, and then moved on to other chitchat.

Now, outside her office, Saima composed herself after the frantic whispering in the corridor. 'Okay, I'm going in.'

Kal stood up as soon as she came in. 'Hey!' He looked slightly jumpy, restless, but his face lit up at the sight of her.

'Hi yourself,' she said cautiously. 'I wasn't expecting to see you today.' *After you said all those terrible, wonderful things*, she added silently.

'I—' Kal broke off as he caught sight of Jess, still lurking in the corridor.

Her friend smiled toothily when Saima turned to glare at her.

'Um, fancy a walk?' she asked him quickly. There was no way Dave and Jess were going to resist eavesdropping, if their behaviour this morning was anything to go by.

'Oh yeah, sure.' Kal grabbed his bag.

They walked silently side by side to the Parramatta River fore-shore.

'Have you been here before?' Saima asked at last, when he still hadn't spoken.

'Yes, Saima, I have been to the West before,' Kal said, with a little grin.

'All right, North Shore boy,' she retorted, and he laughed.

The paved walkway wound its way along the riverbank, past apartment buildings, cafés and a busy playground. Saima watched the parents clutch their takeaway coffee cups and chat as their kids threw themselves across the equipment.

They walked until they found a quiet bench under the branches of a large eucalyptus tree, where they stopped and sat. She caught a drift of his aftershave. Like trees after rain.

'Petrichor,' she said suddenly.

He eyed her with a bemused smile. 'Great word. Funny you mention it. It reminds me of the night we walked along Broadway, the smell from the park after the rain.'

'It's one of my favourite smells.'

'I've just realised we haven't seen each other since that night,' he said.

'Not like we haven't spoken since then, though,' she replied.

He didn't seem to clock her leading tone, and carried on watching the brown water flowing downstream. She, on the other hand, watched his face, trying to decipher the odd light in his eyes. His face was more unshaven, his hair more overgrown than when she had last seen it. Without thinking, she reached out to push back a strand that was hanging loose over his eyes.

Her touch caught both of them off guard.

'I'm sorry,' she blurted. 'Your hair was in your eyes.' Oh god, she could feel the scalding blush overtaking her face. Shit, shit, shit, why had she done that?

Kal was looking at her like she had both lost her head and also handed him something precious and unexpected, like the moon.

He suddenly seemed so much closer, close enough for her to just lean forward the last few inches and—

He looked away, back at the water, and she felt a palpable sense of loss.

'Kal, why are you here?' she asked, a touch more severely than she had intended.

'I almost quit my job today,' he replied.

'What? What does that mean, "almost"?'

He shook his head. 'It doesn't matter.'

'Okay, so you almost quit your job but it doesn't matter,' she repeated. 'Neither of those comments answer my question, though.'

'I know, sorry – I didn't think through what I was going to say when I got here, to be honest,' he admitted. 'Just – give me a moment. Please?'

'Okay . . .'

He paused, visibly collecting his thoughts. 'Okay, so I almost quit my job today, like I said. And there have been a few other things that have happened this year – I won't go into them, they're probably pretty boring to hear about – but I feel like everything has been pushing me somewhere lately.'

'Pushing you where?'

'Home.' He finally met her eyes and she felt a jolt. 'Like the puzzle piece that fits exactly where it should be.' They stared at each other for a second. 'You have a weird effect on me,' he said, unexpectedly.

'I do?'

'From the beginning, yes. I know, I know, it's such a cliché,' he said when her eyebrow twitched upwards. 'But that doesn't stop it from being true.'

The pang low in her belly was back.

'Honestly, even when I thought things were a bit challenging in my life, they always came too easily,' Kal continued. 'You were right

217

when we first met, even if I didn't react so well to what you were saying at the time. Whenever anything got complicated, I tended to move on. But you know that static shock you get when you're wearing a woolly jumper? Meeting you, speaking with you – I think it woke me up.'

'Woke you up to what?'

'I don't know if I have the words for it,' he admitted with a short laugh. 'It's like I didn't know that I was looking for something until I found it.'

'And what did you find?' she whispered. The tightness was clenching around her heart now.

He simply looked at her. 'Saima. Are you even going to mention our last conversation? Or are you going to pretend it never happened?'

It was her turn to look away. A voice slid into her mind from the Too-Hard Basket. *That's right, repress it. You're turning into your mother.*

No. She took a breath and took the plunge. 'Kal, what you said . . . Those were some of the loveliest things I've ever heard. And remember that I've heard a *lot* of wedding vows.'

His eyes lit up. 'They were?'

'But what do you want me to say?' she asked, as kindly as she could.

Kal shook his head. 'I don't need you to say anything. And I get it. I know it's important to you, your standing in the community, your ethics, and I would never want to jeopardise those or your business. I just wanted you to know how I feel.' He gave another short laugh. 'A good friend of mine – Tom, you'd love him – has been telling me that I need to open up more, and this felt like the most important thing to say. *You* felt like the person I had to be most honest with.'

'There seems to be a rash of people telling both of us to open up more, then,' she muttered.

'Oh yeah?' he asked. 'Do you ever wonder whether the way we were brought up taught us to stay quiet about the things that matter?'

'Culturally, you mean?'

'Yeah, or maybe open conversation wasn't really our parents' forte.'

'Quite likely,' she agreed. 'But then they too have learned that behaviour from *their* upbringings and life experiences.'

He ran a hand through his hair. 'So does that mean we're just doomed to echo our ancestors' hang-ups?'

'Or perhaps it means that we could learn from them and the people around us to live better lives,' she said, as much to herself as to him.

He smiled gently. 'I think I like that definition of third culture more than any other I've found.' They fell silent once again, companionable and warm in the weak sunlight reflecting off the river. Saima was once again overtaken by that feeling of being the most at-ease version of her usual self. She thought of everything Kal had said, and what he had not yet said, leaving whatever happened next between them completely in her hands.

Kiss him, you blithering fool, she told herself. An animal had revealed itself inside of her that she didn't even know existed, and it was igniting a warmth in her body that she hadn't felt before. All she wanted, needed, was to feel his lips.

She quickly shut this feeling down.

'I can set up more dates for you,' she said instead, though the thought made her want to scream.

'No, god no,' he said quickly. 'And I mean it this time.'

She had the sense of something significant slipping through her fingers before she'd had the chance to hold it properly. If she didn't think carefully about her next words, the two of them would go their separate ways and never cross paths again.

When she looked back at him, he was gripping the edge of the bench, his face contorted into a look of confusion while keeping his eyes firmly on the water washing around in gentle eddies at the edge of the riverbank. Kal had been honest with her. She hadn't been at all honest with him, and she didn't think this was the right time to mention her arrangement with George and Ruby, particularly when she didn't know where things stood between him and his parents. But maybe she could give him some of the truth.

'Kal, the night we met, I don't think I can pretend that I felt the kind of connection that you've mentioned,' she began. He met her eyes before quickly returning them to the river, swallowing sharply as he did.

But still he said nothing, only listened closely, as he always did.

'After Laksa Night, though, I started to realise that whenever I'm around you, whenever we've talked or texted, I've always felt . . .' She trailed off, searching for the words, then remembered Ayesha's cryptic words over the phone. 'Content.'

For a minute, he didn't react. Then, slowly, a smile spread across his face and he turned to look at her. 'Content.'

She shrugged awkwardly. 'It's the only word I could think of. Ayesha mentioned it this morning, and I guess it stuck.'

He laughed, looking once again like she'd handed him something precious. 'She's a smart girl, that one. Far too smart for me.'

'Well, she did go to Yale,' Saima pointed out, returning his smile. 'Anyway, I think the only reason you think you're closed off is because you haven't looked inside my head. I thought if I avoided thinking about it, if I didn't give it oxygen, it would snuff out.'

'What would?'

'If you're not going to say it, then I'm certainly not going to.'

'Did I not say it?' he asked in surprise. 'I genuinely meant to. Let me say it now. I like you, Saima. I think you're smart and funny and kind, and incredibly sexy, and I respect the hell out of you. And if I'm honest, the biggest – and lately the only – reason I agreed to be your client was because of *you*. If I'd acknowledged that sooner, I definitely wouldn't have wasted Shayla's and Mariam's time. Though it was nice to have met Ayesha, if only as a reminder that a part of me misses my sister,' he added.

Saima marvelled at how easily he laid it all on the table. 'Okay, you're better at this than I am, clearly,' she said. 'So I don't know that I'm going to say anything half as lovely as any of that. But I think I like you too, Kal.'

'I already know you think I'm super hot,' he said, with a grin.

'Oh, totally, like a cross between Dev Patel and Riz Ahmed.' She chuckled. 'How could I resist those Hollywood looks?' They beamed at each other for a moment.

'So what are we saying, Saima?' he pushed, gently. 'Are we going to give this a go at last?'

Do it. It's right there. Take it. But on the heels of those thoughts, caution flowed in.

'I would like to,' she told him earnestly.

'But?'

'What you said about my standing in the community? That's also true. And I can't jeopardise my business by being seen with you.'

The light went out of his eyes, and he nodded once, sharply. 'Right. Yes, of course, I can't ask you to—'

'Kal, no, what I mean is, if we're going to do this, we're going to need to be careful. Desis are literally everywhere, especially around here, and since things are already shaky with the community, all it will take is a whisper that I'm behaving inappropriately for everything to go to shit.'

'So what does that mean? We went on an almost-date on Laksa Night. That was okay?'

'One time I can get away with – I'm courting a client. After that, every conversation happens in my office or over the phone, and everyone else knows that. And everyone also knows you're already a client, so I have no excuse to be seen with you.'

'What about right now?'

'I'm living on the wild side under a very big, very shady gum tree.'

He thought about it for a little while. 'I could – you could – do you want to have dinner at my place?'

'Your place?' she repeated.

'I know, I know,' he said quickly. 'It's a big step and I don't want to impose—'

She interrupted. 'You place would be perfect.'

He stopped. 'It would?'

'And I already know you can cook; you said as much on Laksa Night. Unless that was just to impress me?' she added with mock severity.

He laughed, the deepest, warmest laugh she had heard from him yet, and it stole around her heart like a soft blanket. 'Name the day and prepare to be blown away by my MasterChef prowess.'

'Tonight? Or is that too soon?' she asked, and he smiled, his eyes twinkling.

Kal walked her back to the cottage, all the way to the front door. Dave popped out of his office, obviously delighted to see him again. Kal smiled and waved goodbye as he left.

'Don't be a stranger now,' Dave called after him.

'Settle down, Dave,' Saima said, with a laugh.

Seconds later, Jess grabbed her arm and dragged her into her office. 'Tell me everything!'

'There's nothing to tell.'

'Nope, you're not going to fob me off, or I'll ask Mum to put her evil eye on you, and her curses are creative and terrifying.'

'Well, we're having dinner tonight,' Saima admitted. She could feel her face melting into an uncontrollably swoony expression.

'What? You go, girl! And I remember that look,' Jess said. 'I looked the same for months when Rob and I first started going out. So I'm guessing things are heading in the right direction.'

'The right direction?' Saima repeated. She wasn't sure if that was what this was, just that it *felt* right.

'You know, you're on the road to being the good desi wife.'

'Whoa, okay, I'm not at wife level yet. But we're going to see where this goes.'

'Yessss, this is everything I need!' Jess crowed. 'I saw the way he looked at you, and more to the point, I *definitely* saw the way you looked at him. So, did you tell him about his parents and all that?'

Saima immediately felt the warm glow of the morning dim.

'You *didn't*?' Jess asked. 'Is that a good idea?'

'I thought about it,' Saima said. 'I did. But I don't know how things are between him and his parents. From our conversations in the past, I'm not sure if they speak much to each other about this sort of thing, or if he's close to them. It felt like a mistake to lob a grenade into a situation I'm yet to figure out.'

'But should you be dating him without clearing that up?'

'I don't know if this is a date, exactly,' she hedged.

'Babe, if you could have seen your face when you walked back inside, you wouldn't think for a second I'd buy that.'

Saima exhaled. 'Okay, honestly? It was really hard to even make myself vulnerable enough today to face what's going on between Kal and me. I don't think I had it in me to add to the mess with his parents in the mix. But I'm going to tell him. I am. Sooner rather than later, as soon as I can suss out where things stand with them all. As for dinner, I just want to enjoy the moment for a second before tackling that. Is that so bad?'

Jess smiled gently. 'I totally get that. And I don't want to be the killjoy in this situation, but—'

'I know,' Saima groaned.

'—*but*, like you said earlier, what about his parents?' Jess continued doggedly. 'Are they going to expect a refund if you end up with their son? Or, like, do you get to keep it because you still matched him up with someone, even if that was you? Isn't that double dipping? And how will this affect your business in the end?'

'Jess, *I know*. Believe me, I'm obsessing over it.'

Jess's phone buzzed in her pocket. 'I hate that I have to get back to work, but I'm so happy for you, even if—' She stopped short.

'Even if it doesn't work out in the end,' Saima completed her sentence.

'No, I was going to say, even if it's been difficult getting here. Don't expect the worst before you've even begun the relationship,' Jess said. 'Like I keep telling you – don't fixate on the negative. Just be honest with him, with yourself. No excuses about how you're not a good desi or whatnot. And Saima' – she paused in the doorway and threw her a wicked grin – 'have *fun* tonight!'

Chapter 19

'Wait, let me get this straight,' Nicole said over the phone. 'The *matchmaker* is coming to dinner? Wasn't she the one meant to be finding you the dates?'

'Yeah, it's weird, I know. But I like her. I have done since I met her.'

'I knew it!' she exclaimed. 'No wonder you couldn't wipe that smile from your face when you told us about her. Lachie! I was right!' Lachie murmured something in the background. 'Lachie wants to know if you're grinning like a fool right now – his words, not mine.' And then Kal realised he had a huge smile on his face again.

'Tell him to shut his damn mouth,' he said, and Nicole laughed with delight.

'He *is*!' she said to Lachie.

'Anyway, stop fixating about me smiling and help me out, please. I can't figure out what to make for dinner,' he said.

'Aw, you're overthinking things. That's so sweet! And so unlike you!'

'Saima's made me feel quite unlike myself, I guess. Or maybe more like myself than I've ever been. I honestly can't tell if that's a good or bad thing. I'm even considering whether or not I should be quitting work.'

'No way! Not Kal the workaholic!' Nicole teased. 'But look, it's probably good to shake things up with work – you've been there how long now, must be at least six or seven years? So I don't think it's the disaster scenario you're imagining, even if you do leave.'

'Yeah . . .' He hadn't thought about the work situation, what with everything that had happened with Saima afterwards.

'And as for dinner,' she continued, 'I say go for something simple. How about some grilled salmon with roasted potatoes and steamed greens? Easy to buy what you need, easy to do – there's no way you could mess that one up.'

'That's such a white meal to suggest, Nicole!' he joked.

'Look, I've got plenty of other recipes that are more complicated if you want to spend the next six hours wandering around a specialist grocer.'

'Okay, sorry, fish and veg it is.'

'Thought you'd say that. And have you considered what you want to make for dessert? I could text you my chocolate mousse recipe.'

'As long as it's super simple. You know desserts aren't my forte.'

'Look, even Lachie can make it.'

'Oi!' he heard Lachie shout.

'And you remember that birthday cake he made me that actually broke the knife when we tried to cut it,' she said loudly, as much to Lachie as to him.

Kal cackled. 'Oh my god, the Chocolate Knife Cake! I'd forgotten.'

'Okay, so, salmon, spuds. Some fresh herbs – maybe some dill would be good, and I'm assuming you've got the basics: garlic, ginger, et cetera. You could jazz it up with some soy sauce if you want. And then for greens, go with bok choy maybe.'

'Right, yes,' Kal muttered. 'Bok choy.'

'Wait, are you writing all this down?'

'So what if I am?'

'I have to say, I've never heard you this ruffled before, Kal.' He could hear the smile in her voice. 'She must be something special.'

'Yeah.' Butterflies flapped in his belly as he remembered everything that had happened on the bench by the river earlier today. When she'd touched his hair, he had been a heartbeat away from kissing her but his brain had caught up with his body just in time. And thank god for that, because what if someone from the community had spotted them? It seemed to him there was always someone in the community with their eyes and ears looking out to catch every Pakistani in Australia doing something they shouldn't.

'Hey, don't forget about the music,' Nicole was saying. 'Don't go too sexy on the first date.'

'I was just going to go with my standard RnB playlist.'

She hummed. 'Mm. I'd opt for the SmoothFM vibe, if I were you.'

'Ugh, really?'

'Let the man have his sexy tunes, Nicole.' Lachie had seized the phone. 'And you, Kal, stop being a wet blanket. She already knows you, and she obviously likes you or she wouldn't be coming to dinner.'

'Thanks for the pep talk, mate.'

'Any time. Be yourself, follow Nic's recipes properly, and don't fuck this up, because we want to meet Mystery Woman and that's gonna be awkward if she hates your guts.'

Kal laughed, thanked them both and hung up.

He grabbed what he needed from the local supermarket under his building and got started on his plans for the evening. He would sort out dinner just before they ate, since it wasn't food he could cook in advance. He made the dessert – Nicole was right, the mousse was simple but decadent – tidied up as best he could, lit some candles and streamed the toned-down version of his Spotify playlist. Perfect.

And then he waited. For a brief moment, he felt a slight panic that she'd have second thoughts and cancel their evening. But at 7 pm on the dot, the intercom buzzer went off and his heart quickened.

He opened the front door, and there she was. She'd changed into a silky black shirt over her usual jeans.

'Hey.' He beamed at her and she grinned back.

'Hi.'

'You came.'

'Did you think I wouldn't?'

'The thought did cross my mind,' he admitted. He stepped back with a wave of his arm. 'Please, come in.'

Her eyes sparkled as she stepped into his domain and looked around. 'Oh, this is nice!'

'Yeah, it's all right.' He tried to see the apartment through her eyes, with its minimalist furnishings and neutral tones. 'Not exactly cosy, but I like it.'

'I'm in a tiny studio myself, so I can tell you cosy is overrated,' she said, with a laugh. 'Shoes on or off?'

'Off, please. My mum would have a heart attack if I started wearing shoes in the house,' he said. 'It might be the final straw in going full coconut.'

'God forbid!' She toed off her shoes and handed her coat and bag over to him. 'Thank you.'

'Do you want anything to drink?' he asked over his shoulder as he moved to hang her belongings in the hall cupboard.

'Some sparkling water would be nice, if you have it?'

'Sure thing. Please, take a seat.'

Instead, while he headed to the fridge for the water, she wandered over to his bookshelf, looking not so much at the books as the framed photos there.

'Your sister?' She pointed at a family portrait taken at his sister's wedding. He nodded and gave her the water. 'Thank you.'

'Yeah, that was at Amna's wedding.'

'When was that?'

'Three? No, four years ago.'

'In London, right?'

He glanced at her, distracted. 'Oh, have I mentioned her before?'

'You must have done,' she said, her attention fixed on the photograph.

'Yeah, must have. Anyway, yeah, they met and married in London. Faheem's a nice guy, from what I could gather.'

'You didn't get a chance to find out for sure?'

He grimaced slightly. 'Amna and I aren't exactly close, and work was pretty busy as usual. I think I flew in for three days and flew out before the jet lag even caught up with me.'

She looked at him thoughtfully. 'That's a pity. Family weddings can be a great time to reconnect.' She laughed shortly. 'Or for things to fall completely apart, too, if I'm honest.'

'I bet you have some war stories,' he said lightly. 'Anyway, they're still together, still happy, by all accounts. Amna's not the type to suffer fools, so at the very least Faheem's not a fool.'

'What more can a woman ask for?' she quipped, then moved on to one of his favourite photos. 'And who are these happy folks?'

It had been taken at Nicole's graduation five years ago, at the big surprise dinner they had planned for her at a Lebanese restaurant in Surry Hills. She'd done her medical degree postgrad, so he, Tom and Lachie, who were already out in the world working, had the pay cheques to go all out to celebrate. In the picture, they were all at least half-drunk, draped over one another and beaming happily at the camera. He grinned widely at the memory. 'Those would be my best mates. That's Tom, that's Nicole in the middle, and the one who looks like he's about to fall over is Lachie, her partner.'

'You all went to uni together?'

'No, only Lachie and I did. Tom and I met at work and instantly connected. Nic met Lachie at a pub crawl between Sydney Uni and UTS in first year.'

'They're still together, that's lovely,' she said with delight.

'Yeah. And very keen to meet you, by the way.'

Saima smiled at that as she sipped her water, but didn't say anything. 'You're a skier?' she asked next. She was looking at a photo of the family ski trip to Japan, when he and Amna had been in their late teens. It had been a great trip, though he supposed they had been their happiest because they each spent much of their time on the trip apart pursuing their separate interests.

'Yeah.' It occurred to him that she was repeating the same pattern of conversation from most of their previous chats, deflecting any focus on herself by asking a lot of questions about him. He touched her elbow to direct her away from the photos. 'Have you ever tried it?'

'I've only seen snow once in my life,' she answered, turning around to look at him. 'I was twelve, I think. Ammy and I took the bus to Jindabyne. It look so long to get there, and when we arrived the snow was slushy and not the best, but it was still snow, which made it so magical in my eyes. Though Ammy didn't like how it made her feet wet, and she slipped when she walked.'

'You need to wear proper snow boots,' he said.

'We aren't the sort of people to have snow boots.'

The comment struck him the wrong way. Saima always seemed to draw a barrier between the sort of person she was compared to him, like she was from the wrong side of the tracks. Rather than argue the point so early in the night, he quietly headed to the kitchen to start dinner.

A moment later she followed him.

'I said the wrong thing,' she said. 'I'm sorry.'

'No, it's okay,' he said, busying himself getting things out of the fridge. 'I do wish, though, that you wouldn't make us out to be so different from each other.'

'But we are different,' she said. 'You have a nice happy family. It's just me and my ammy.'

'You decided I had a happy family life based off of a few old pictures?' he asked.

She didn't respond. When he glanced at her, she looked a little bit stricken.

'You weren't happy?' Saima finally asked.

'I wouldn't say that. It's complicated, the way most families are. I guess if you're still on speaking terms with your family, though, things aren't all that bad between you, right?'

'I guess. I speak to my mother almost every day. But I haven't seen or spoken to my father since I was a child, ever since he went back to Pakistan.'

Kal was silent. 'You ever think about reconnecting with him?' he asked casually.

'Not really. But I just found out he had been in touch with my mother after he left. She never told me about that.'

'You didn't ask her why?'

'I haven't had the chance to yet. But to be honest, we don't have a super communicative relationship about these big life things. Most of the time, I appreciate that she gives me the space to do what I want. Unlike many Pakistani mums!'

'Like mine!' Kal laughed. 'She's all right, though, I guess. Don't let her intimidate you when you meet her. She'll give it a red-hot go, I don't think she can help herself.'

Saima gave him an odd look. 'Are you close to your mum? To your parents?' she ventured, as she picked up a knife and began trimming the ends of the bok choy.

'Depends what you mean by close, I suppose,' he said, momentarily distracted by how naturally they moved around each other in the kitchen, as if they had lived together for years. 'We try to have lunch together at least once a month, but they're not the first people I turn to with most life things. I think we've gotten a little closer in the last few months, though.'

'Oh yes?'

The pans clanged as he put them on the stove. 'Yeah, we've had some semi-decent conversations recently. I don't see eye to eye with them about a lot of stuff, and some of their choices are frankly ridiculous, but I think I understand them better than I've ever done. And I think, I *hope*, that the feeling's mutual. My dad, if you can believe it, has started seeing a psychologist.'

'No way!' She handed him the bowl of greens. 'A desi uncle seeking psych help?'

'I know, I don't think I've processed that information properly yet,' he said with a chuckle. 'But whoever he's seeing, they're *good*. I hardly recognise some of the things he's said and, more to the point, what he's not said recently.'

'Like what?' she asked curiously.

'Like marriage, funnily enough.'

Saima had just picked up the platter of salmon to pass to him, but it slipped from her hand at this moment. 'Oh, sorry!' He seized it before it could drop to the ground.

'No stress. And you don't have to help, seriously. Very happy for you to just sit and enjoy the show. I did promise you a MasterChef special.'

She grimaced comically. 'You're just asking me to go away because I nearly dropped dinner all over the floor.'

'Well, I didn't want to say . . .' he said, and laughed when she wrinkled her nose at him. Rather than moving to the other side of the kitchen island as a spectator, she came to stand beside him at the stove as he laid the salmon onto the sizzling pan.

'I'm kind of glad you decided not to make any desi food, because Ammy has set the bar impossibly high,' she joked. 'I would have had to be polite and tell you it was good.'

'I expect you would have told me exactly how bad it was,' he responded lightly.

'Hey, if you want to live the MasterChef dream, you have to get used to criticism.'

Her eyes twinkled with mischief. Kal was overcome with a sense of contentedness standing there, the faint spice of her shampoo in the air as she leaned ever so slightly towards him.

Slowly and carefully, hardly daring to breathe, Kal did what his soul had been crying out to do for months. He bent his head and pressed his lips against hers. She inhaled sharply once, perhaps with surprise, and then she was kissing him back, soft-lipped, joyous. He almost expected to taste mango sorbet as he slipped his hand over the cool silk of her cheek. She speared her fingers through his hair, pulling him closer with a murmur, and he grasped her waist, pulling her closer still, urging her soft curves against him, one of her hands moving slowly down his back, wanting, needing, marvelling all the while at the wholeness, the completeness of this moment when everything in the world felt *right*.

'I think the salmon's burning,' she whispered.

'I don't care,' he said, and dived headlong into another kiss, and another. Her fingers crept to the edge of his shirt, then under it just once, fluttering over the skin at his waist before darting back so quickly he almost thought he'd imagined it. 'Is this okay?' he murmured, as his lips lightly traced her jaw.

'It couldn't be more perfect,' she breathed.

The smoke alarm screamed overhead.

With a muffled laugh, he reluctantly unwound his arms from her and turned off the stove, pulling the pan of blackened, smouldering fish off the heat. He blinked through the haze, only partly due to the smoke filling the kitchen. Saima seized a kitchen towel and frantically flapped it underneath the alarm, and Kal slid open the balcony door to clear the room before the sprinkler system could engage and thoroughly douse their evening.

When at last the alarm was silent, they stood there on opposite sides of the room. Saima looked like Kal felt, dazed and happy, as she took in the carnage in the kitchen. 'At least we've got some bread?'

They ended up ordering pizza from an Italian place down the road, eating it sitting on the floor around his coffee table. As they chatted effortlessly, he would look over every so often and catch a sight of her, her face soft and happy as she pulled strings of melted cheese off the pizza. She finally caught him at it when she was wiping her fingers clean.

'What?'

'What?'

'You're looking at me funny.'

'Am I?' He reached over and picked up her hand, drawing her over to his side of the table. She edged her body closer until their sides were touching, and let her head rest on his shoulder. The simple act flooded him with warmth. They sat that way for what felt like ages, silently enjoying each other's company.

'So how come you never got married?' he asked her eventually.

'You sound like my mother,' she said, and he could hear the smile in her voice.

'It's a genuine question, with no judgement,' he added. 'You're a woman who is devoted to arranging other people's happiness – I'm just curious why that happiness never extended to yourself.'

Saima bit her lip. 'I guess I never found the right guy,' she finally said. 'Though maybe it's more complicated than that. I don't associate marriage with my own happiness. I may have mentioned that my parents' marriage was a mess by any standard. While it lasted, the two of them fought a lot. It's kind of all I remember of them.'

'I'm sorry.'

She shrugged, awkwardly. 'And then one day, my mother left my father. She woke me early in the morning and our bags were already packed. She didn't explain anything. Just bundled me into a taxi and we made our way to a women's shelter, where we spent some time before an aunty took us in. I never saw him again.' She stopped talking and he realised that her grip on his hand had tightened. 'My friend Jess reckons that I've developed the habit of pre-emptively shutting anything down that has even the smallest potential to go wrong, and relationships definitely fall under that description.'

He didn't say anything, just ran his thumb gently back and forth over her hand. Her previous distance from him made a lot of sense now.

She pulled away at last and started stacking the dishes in front of them, avoiding his gaze. 'I don't want you to feel bad for me.'

'Not at all,' he said.

'No, I mean it. Please don't pity me.'

He wished he could see her face, but she picked up the remains of their dinner and carried them to the kitchen without another word. He belatedly leaped to his feet and followed her. 'Please, Saima, leave it.'

They faced each other across the kitchen island.

'What are you thinking?' he asked, unable to decipher her expression.

She eyed him for a moment. 'That I want you to kiss me again.'

He laughed. 'I already kissed you.'

'That's why I said "again".'

He shook his head, unable to keep from smirking. 'No.'

'Kiss me, please?' she tried.

'No,' he repeated. '*You* kiss *me*.'

She blushed so rosily that he didn't think she'd do it, but he should have known better than to underestimate a fighter like Saima. She rounded the island in a heartbeat, grasped the back of his neck and pulled him towards her.

'Are you playing hard to get or something?' she whispered incredulously.

'Would serve you right if I was,' he returned.

'I could destroy you in a minute, you know.'

'Come and destroy me, then.'

She gently tugged his hair. 'You're so cheesy.'

'Well, we just had pizza. Come and taste how cheesy I am.'

With a laugh, she closed the last few inches between their lips.

This time, they were ravenous, Saima hitching her hips high against him until Kal hoisted her onto the counter, their hands roaming freely. He could feel his heart – or was it hers? – pounding away as they held each other.

'Okay,' she said when they came up for air. 'What's for dessert?'

'I thought you were.'

She thwacked him on the thigh with a grin. 'So cheesy.'

Chapter 20

There was a feeling now as she walked, like her feet were not fully touching the ground. All her senses were awake and she experienced every sensation acutely. The touch of a passing breeze, the smell of a neighbour's cooking, the sharpness of the sun first thing in the morning. The world seemed to be waking up before her and she was finally coming to understand how beautiful things truly were.

Your cheesiness is contagious, Saima wanted to text Kal but she stopped herself. Maybe it was a good thing to let her cynical side drop once in a while, she thought. After all, this man had convinced her that love didn't need to be only something she arranged for others. It could be for her too. Though perhaps calling it love at this juncture was getting ahead of herself.

After a heavenly first date – burned dinner and all – life had truly got in the way of everything. It started with Tom sending Kal an SOS from work. The Stewart Group had to bring its big launch forward and Linda was freaking out. Kal went back to work, not only because his work ethic wouldn't let him ignore the shitstorm brewing, but because he could never let Tom down. Before he knew it he was back to his runs of eighty-hour weeks.

This, along with working at opposite ends of Sydney, Saima found, meant that dropping by for a quick coffee or lunch date was out of the question, so their interactions returned to phone dates.

'Ah, now this feels familiar,' Kal joked the first time she called him as he was about to sit down to eat an unappetising desk sandwich.

'I figure we can have a meal together in some way or another, even if you're being very busy and important right now,' Saima said.

'What do you mean, "right now"?' he asked loftily. 'I'm *always* busy and important.'

They could talk about anything and everything. But after a month of chats and texts sneaked in around meetings and late nights, during the last of which Kal had managed to fall asleep – it had been close to 2 am – Saima decided to risk it and take advantage of a quiet day at the office to head out to meet Kal for a quick lunch. It was past time to tell Kal about the situation with his parents; Jess was not letting up about it and she wasn't about to do that over the phone. So she steeled herself and headed into the city.

'God, I've missed you,' he groaned as they stole a kiss in a shadowed loading bay in the lane behind his office building. He jumped as the siren above blared, for a car approaching the driveway. 'If alarms keep going off every time I get my hands on you, I'm going to start getting wildly and inappropriately turned on when I hear one. It'll make the next emergency drill at work extremely awkward.'

Saima laughed. 'Come on, let's get out of here and into some sunshine.'

'I don't think I can handle it,' he bleated, shading his eyes as they headed into Barangaroo Reserve. 'I haven't seen the sun in weeks, and I feel like I'm turning into one of those slimy white frogs that live in dark caves.'

238

'That's fine, then, because I just kissed you, and you know what happens when you kiss a frog.'

'I don't remember, we better make out again to jog my memory.' He pulled her enthusiastically into the shade of a cluster of trees.

She leaned into him, her hands over his heart, and murmured, 'If this one doesn't turn you into a prince, I'm going to be *so* disappointed.'

Their lips were just about to meet when her ears picked up the unmistakable cadence of conversational Urdu approaching. She shoved Kal aside, sending him crashing backwards into the bushy undergrowth mere seconds before a figure emerged on the stairs to Stargazer Lawn, speaking quickly on the phone.

'. . . Ammy, abhi thak kuch nahin hua. Okay, khuda hafiz, love you.' The woman slung her phone into her handbag and continued at a rapid clip towards Saima, who was trying to stand casually, just in front of where she'd flung Kal. Her vaguely familiar gaze met Saima's and she did a double-take.

'Oh! Hello!'

'Hello?' Saima answered cautiously. She tried to place the woman.

'Seema, right? We met last year at that engagement party?'

Ding. Sara Irfan, Shayla's elder sister. 'Lovely to see you again, Sara. It's Saima.'

'Oh yes, of course, sorry, I'm so bad with names. How are you? Talk about a small world, running into you here. How've you been? What brings you to these parts?'

'I'm well, thanks. I'm, uh, just meeting a client.'

'Anyone I know?' Sara smiled brightly at her.

'Not sure . . .' Saima shrugged, changing the topic. 'How are you doing? How are things with' – she cast her mind back for a name – 'Adnan?'

'Oh, well remembered, well done,' Sara said, with a laugh. 'He's fabulous, thanks so much for asking. He *very* subtly asked Shay to find out my favourite gemstone a few weeks ago, so I think he might be about to propose, the sweetheart.'

'That's great news! Can I offer an early congratulations?'

'Thank you, but let's hope he's not just looking for some nice earrings for my birthday or something!'

They chatted for a couple more minutes, Saima shifting uneasily at the thought of Kal lying low in the bushes nearby. He hadn't made a single noise – was he all right? At last, Sara checked her watch and exclaimed, 'Oh, I'm going to be late! So lovely to see you, Saima, let's catch up properly sometime, yes? I'll get your number from Shay, okay, bye!' And she whirled away. Saima waited until Sara had rounded the corner before cautiously making her way back to the bushes.

'Kal?' she whispered. 'You okay?'

There was no answer.

'Kal?' she hissed again, poking through the undergrowth until she found him lying on his back, eyes closed. 'Oh shit, Kal!' She crouched beside him and lay her hand on his chest.

He opened one eye. 'This prince is going to need another kiss to bring him back to life.'

'Prince? I thought you were more the frog?' She smiled before kissing him quickly on the lips and then dragging him back up to his feet.

Kal rubbed his back and chest. 'That was one big push you gave me. I hope I didn't break any bones,' he said, pouting a little.

'I think you'll be just fine. But that was a little reminder of what I meant with the eyes of the community always being around.'

'Uh-huh – I gathered as much. Which is why I was quiet as a mouse. Gave me a chance to grab a quick nap, too.'

She looked over at his face and saw rings of dark circles beneath his eyes.

'Don't push yourself too hard,' she said, placing a hand on the side of his face. His skin was warm against her fingers. She wanted to tell him he felt like home. Instead, she quickly withdrew her hand.

'I know. I didn't expect for it to be like this going back to work. Was hoping it'd be different somehow . . . I don't know why.'

'Well, some things are different,' she said, smiling at him tenderly.

'That they are,' he said, looking to go in for another kiss before stopping himself. 'Nothing like the eyes of the community to keep you on your toes, huh?'

It's not just the community, it's also you and your parents, she wanted to respond. Not seeing Kal for a month meant she'd been able to shove thoughts of how to tell him the truth about how she'd been hired by his parents in the Too-Hard Basket. But now that he stood in front of her, his eyes shining, a hint of vulnerability in the way he spoke, she wanted to come clean right there and then. But she couldn't. The words refused to form in her mouth.

'Yep.' She shrugged instead.

Just then his phone began to ring. 'Ah, crap,' he said, glancing at the display. 'It's Tom. Give me one sec?' After a terse few words, he hung up and turned back to her, grimacing. 'I'm so sorry—'

'You have to head back,' she said, nodding. 'It's okay, I understand.'

'And after all the trouble you went to, coming here in the first place.'

Saima caught his hand. 'Kal, seriously. It's okay. I'll take a raincheck on that lunch, and we can have a proper date when you're done with this busy patch. And this time I'll cook.'

'That sounds perfect. It'll only be like this for a few more days, I swear. After this Stewart launch is behind us, I'll be all yours.'

'I'll hold you to that,' she said, with a smile. *And then I'll tell you the whole truth*, she silently promised herself as they swiftly walked back towards his building, exchanging a furtive kiss before parting ways.

The surprise meeting with Sara, not to mention seeing Kal again, had brought home to Saima how she had to speak to the Alis about the whole situation with Kal. She shuddered at what could have happened if she hadn't heard Sara approaching – she would've been spotted in a very compromising position with Kal, and it wouldn't have been long before the whole community was aware, and then imagine how the tongues would wag! If not with Kal, she needed to get things straight with the Alis.

So that Friday, Saima headed up to Gordon. Despite her nervousness, she took resolute steps on the short walk from the train station to the Alis' house. There was a good chance things would get ugly and messy after they heard what was happening between her and their son. She was under no illusion about how unhappy they would be that Kal had decided to pursue a relationship with someone with her background, who was also older than him, if only by a few years. But Saima was determined that the prospect of a negative outcome was not going to stop her from taking action. Not this time.

After she had dealt with the Alis, she could then tell Kal that his parents had hired her. In the grander scheme of things, she figured, it wasn't a terrible lie. She'd had everyone's best interests at heart, and had never intended for this to happen. But yes, he would probably be upset, she didn't doubt that, though after everything was said and done, surely they would find a way to get past it, maybe even laugh about it.

And she would tell them all that she would return the Alis' money, even if that meant some sacrifices for the business.

Lost in her thoughts, Saima almost walked straight past the Alis' home, but pulled herself up at just the right time, stopping outside the large house. This place was exactly where she had imagined George and Ruby would live. The manicured lawns and hedges were clearly maintained by a professional gardener – Ruby did not at all strike her as the gardening type, and she expected George wouldn't be caught dead pushing a lawnmower. They had wealth enough to pay people to resolve the situation for them, just as they had thrown money at the issue of their single son. Money, it seemed, provided them with solutions. Except this time, the solution may not be to their liking.

Taking a deep breath, she walked up the sandstone steps of their entranceway and rang the doorbell. Ruby answered, dressed impeccably and perfectly coiffed as always, and invited Saima in with a big smile, into a foyer that seemed to be finished floor to ceiling in imported marble.

'I'm so happy you came to see me,' Ruby said. 'Though you needn't have come all this way. I could have come to you. George and I were just saying we needed to catch up.'

'It's okay, Mrs Ali, it was no trouble at all,' Saima said.

'Arre, beti, I've told you, don't bother with Mrs Ali and whatnot. Just call me Ruby. Do you want anything to drink? Tea, coffee? I was just about to pour my morning chai.'

'Chai would be lovely, Ruby, thank you. Can I help?'

'No, no, but come and sit in the kitchen and we can have a cosy chat.'

The sleek luxury kitchen was imposing rather than cosy, but Saima took a seat at the gleaming breakfast bar and silently wondered what Ruby would want to be called after Saima came clean about the situation with Kal. They'd probably not be on a first-name basis after that. At least for a little while.

'Where's Mr Ali?' she asked, as Ruby fussed around with a tea set.

'Oh, George is taking a meeting in the study,' Ruby said. 'He's working from home a lot these days. When the children were growing up, he never worked from home. Not once. In fact, he was hardly home. And now, all the time he's here, getting in my way. I would much rather he be in the office now, and give me some space.'

Amused, Saima accepted her tea with thanks, also privately relieved that she only had to speak to Ruby right now and not George as well.

'So Kal told me about the girl from Yale.' Ruby settled comfortably in her seat.

'Oh, yes, Ayesha.'

'I can't believe you found him a girl like that! You should have told me that he had agreed to go on dates with some desi girls. I don't know how you managed to convince him!'

'Yes, but Ruby—'

'A lot of times I wanted to ring you to check on how you were getting on with Kal,' Ruby prattled on. 'But George said to let you be – "see how successful Saima's been without you interfering", he told me. It was hard, let me tell you, to not call. But I suppose George's instincts were right.'

'Well, I appreciate you giving me the space I needed, but I—'

'No buts. I know that boy must have told you much the same as he told me – that Ayesha wasn't right for him. But at the start, it's always like this, no? In your line of work, you must see it all the time. No-one is perfect to begin with. He needs to give it time to fit.'

'Yes, but—'

'Again with the buts!' Ruby said. 'Stop being so argumentative and pass me that bag over there, please, beti.' Saima walked over to the handbag Ruby had indicated, fighting the urge to ask how someone could be argumentative when they were not permitted to finish a sentence.

'Shukria,' Ruby said, as she pulled out the chequebook Saima was now all too familiar with.

'No, Ruby, please,' she protested. 'There's no need for this.'

'You need to become a better businesswoman, Saima. I mean it. But don't worry, I know why you came here. I know your business has been in some trouble. Don't think I didn't hear about that. Some people in our community don't want to move with the times. But you're leading some of the changes and I want to support that.'

In another context, Saima would have liked how strong-minded and forthright Ruby was.

'It's very kind of you to want to support me, Ruby, but there's no need. Your recommendations are all the help I need as I'm looking at ways to grow the business. Kal even suggested that I should expand my client base.'

Ruby stopped writing and eyed Saima over her glasses. 'He told you that?'

'Yes, my business woes are a very badly kept secret, I suppose,' Saima said.

'That's my Khalid,' Ruby said, 'Always looking out for people in trouble. He's a good boy. A sensitive one, too. And he has a keen business eye. He's doing great things at work. Won't be long before he's running the place.'

Saima tried to not let the comments annoy her. When Ruby and George had first come to see her, they had called their son a bewaqoof, a fool. Sometimes it was hard not to be cynical about what fairweather friends desi parents could be. There was a noise out in the foyer and she tensed. Any moment now, she figured, George would join them, and this conversation would get even harder.

'Here, take this.' Ruby tore out the cheque. 'You deserve it, even purely for making my son see that Pakistani women can be as attractive and intelligent as any gori can.'

Saima's hand automatically reached out to take the cheque, even as she blurted out at least some of what she had come here to say. 'Ruby, we need to tell Kal that you hired me.' Something clattered behind her.

She turned around, expecting to see George.

It wasn't George.

'Hi?' Kal's hands were in his pockets, but his stance was anything but relaxed.

The cheque trembled in Saima's suddenly nerveless fingers.

'You two have met, of course,' Ruby was saying, but Saima couldn't hear her over the rushing in her ears.

'Yeah . . .' Kal replied. 'But I didn't know *you* two had met.'

'Guess it's time for us to come clean, huh?' Ruby jovially nudged Saima as though nothing untoward had happened. In Ruby's eyes, Saima supposed, it was inevitable that her son would find out that they had hired a matchmaker, and now was as good a time as any.

'Yes, Saima,' Kal said, his tone arctic. 'Time to come clean.' He finally met her eyes and she flinched at the hardness there. There was no twinkle, no customary warmth, not the slightest suggestion that they were going to work this out.

'Arre, why are you acting like this?' Ruby asked. 'Yes, so we asked Saima here to find you a nice desi girl, and look at what a good job she did!'

He laughed harshly. '*Such* a good job she did!'

'Khalid, you know if we asked you to come see a matchmaker with us, you never would have done it,' Ruby reasoned, in soothing tones.

246

But Kal wasn't listening to his mother. His eyes were focused on Saima. 'You've been going behind my back to see my parents? You've been working for them?' Saima had never heard him speak like this. Even Ruby looked alarmed.

'It's not what you think,' Saima started, but her tongue felt thick and heavy in her mouth.

Kal strode forward. 'And how much have they been paying you to do their dirty work?'

Saima had forgotten she still held the cheque. She instinctively crushed the paper, rolling it hard into her fist.

'You're terrifying the girl,' Ruby intervened. 'You need to calm down.' She came over and put her arm around Saima's shoulders.

'So this has all just been a big scheme to get me to date desi girls? Did they pay you extra to do what you did at my place?' Kal's face twisted into an expression she didn't recognise, and for a moment, Saima wondered whether she knew the man standing before her at all. Then her own anger flooded into the numbness in her mind.

'What *I* did?' she repeated, incredulous.

Ruby's arm dropped. 'What is he talking about?' she asked sharply. 'What did you do? Why were you at Kal's house?'

'What's all the noise in here?' George walked into the kitchen. 'I'm trying to write an email and all I can hear are raised voices.' He stopped talking abruptly and took in the scene. 'Wow, what happened?' When no-one responded, he turned to Kal. 'I wasn't expecting you to come over today, beta. That's a nice surprise.'

'But you were expecting her?' Kal gestured at Saima.

'The matchmaker? No, were we expecting her, Ruby? I thought we were going to go and visit her office . . .?' And then the penny dropped. 'Oh, I understand. He's found out that we hired her.' George turned to Kal. 'Beta, no need to get angry about this. Your mother and I were just trying to get you to meet girls from your own culture, so you could see how perhaps they would be a better fit than the goris you usually associate with.'

'Was it all an act?' Kal asked Saima.

'What was an act? What has been going on, beta?' Ruby's eyes had narrowed suspiciously.

'How can you *ask* me that?' Saima hissed through gritted teeth. 'After everything we talked about, everything we've been through? You have to know I lo—' She swallowed her words, horrified, angry tears starting in her eyes.

'Oh god,' she heard George quietly say.

'*Love*?' Kal snarled. 'You're really going to try that, are you? And yet all these months, you never once thought to tell me the truth about my parents hiring you? You could've told me at any point—'

'Oh yes, and what would have happened if I had just told you the truth from the beginning?' Saima returned. 'You expect me to believe that you wouldn't have just run off like a spoiled child?' He didn't answer.

'I wasn't paying *you* to fall in love with my son,' Ruby interjected shrilly. 'Was that your plan all along? To take our money and then trap him so you could get to his money, too? I should've seen it coming.'

Saima was shocked at the accusation and inadvertently looked over to Kal for support. He looked away. 'Of course not!' she exclaimed. 'I don't want your money, Ruby! Not *everyone* wants your money!'

'I've seen girls like you before,' Ruby snapped. 'Though calling you a girl is a stretch.' She looked Saima up and down, her lip curled. 'You're, what, over thirty now? Getting old – and desperate too, I imagine. You saw a good boy like my son, and I suppose you did what you had to do to get his attention.'

'*Excuse* me? *You* came to *me*, remember? I didn't do anything!'

248

'So what is he talking about at his house?'

Saima couldn't fight the flush that burned across her cheeks at the thought of their date. Ruby clocked her expression. 'Do women like you have no shame? I suppose coming from a broken home like you, with a single mother, who knows what sort of things you saw growing up.'

'Enough!' George said. 'There's no need to sink to such depths, Ruby. What happened, happened between the two of them. They are both grown adults. Your boy is no angel, as you well know.'

'Yes, and she knows how to trap a man!' Ruby shrieked. 'You all end up thinking from one part of your body when it comes down to it.'

'Rubaiyah!' George barked.

'It's true.' Ruby was on a roll now. 'And for this woman to even *think* that she would be good enough for our son! Look at how *old* she is, and with *nothing* to her name, not even a proper family behind her.'

Saima wanted to let Ruby have it. To scream and shout at the disrespect the older woman was throwing her way. But she refused to say anything, because at the end of the day, it always seemed to be the women who ended up tearing each other apart while the men stood around and watched. And Saima wasn't going to be a part of it.

'Are you going to say anything?' she finally asked Kal, trying to keep her voice as even as possible.

'What do you want me to say?' he asked, stony-faced.

'You honestly think I would do what your mother is accusing me of? You know me. You know what sort of person I am.'

'Do I?'

Saima flinched. *Keep your head held high*, her mother's voice whispered. *Tears help no-one*. She set her jaw and grabbed her

249

bag, dropping the crushed cheque on the ground, and ran out the door.

There was nothing more left to say.

When she was far enough away from the Alis' house, after she had given up hope that she would hear Kal's footsteps running up behind her, asking her to forgive him, she found a bench in an overgrown reserve with a lone swing set and nothing but a few magpies pecking around in the undergrowth for company. She dropped her head into her lap and cried and cried. The tears came out of her in a big violent gush. How could he not defend her? she kept thinking. Everything that Ruby had said cut to the bone. It was as if all Saima's worst fears had manifested at once. Someone had openly pointed out that she wasn't good enough, that she was somehow less than everyone else.

It had been her fault, of course. She had led herself to believe that she too could find love. When all along, she knew, it wasn't worth it. This pain she was feeling now wasn't worth it. Opening herself, her true self, to someone else, being vulnerable and raw, had been the biggest mistake she had made in her life. Perhaps some women got lucky, but it seemed in their family, Saima and her mother only attracted men who would hurt them. That was her destiny. The thought made her cry some more.

After a while, when it seemed she had exhausted her supply of tears, Saima stopped crying, but made no move to wipe her face. Instead she looked up at the sky and let the air brush over the wetness. It was okay, she decided then, to live in the greys. Not everything in life had to be felt acutely. The sun would come up as it always did, she just wouldn't experience its sharp brightness. The smells of life, too, would be dulled again and she would live with that.

Chapter 21

The moment the front door swung closed behind Saima, Kal wanted to run after her, to shout, to demand an explanation, to apologise. Ruby reached out and gripped his arm, anchoring him to her. And he let himself be anchored, his feet feeling like they were encased in cement.

George stood silently for a few moments, scrubbing his fingers through his hair. 'Well . . .' he said eventually. The word hung in the air.

Kal's mind churned chaotically, and his ears were still ringing as if from a sudden heavy blow. Maybe it was the unexpected plummet from the dizzying heights of happiness to the sheer misery and confusion in his mother's kitchen over a few horrible moments.

Are you going to say anything?

What had she wanted him to say? He had believed in Saima, completely trusted her, opened up to her as he had never done to anybody before.

And she had done the same for you.

He pushed the insidious thought away. She'd manipulated him with her uncanny ability to draw people in. He wasn't imagining it– Ayesha had observed that same ability herself. And she'd wielded it simply for his parents' pay cheque. When he'd said he didn't want to meet any more of her clients, she must have pulled out the big guns to keep him on the hook. That was why she'd agreed to their date – *that was why she remained unmarried. She was her own top agent—*

She's not an evil genius, and you're being a bloody fool.

The thought pulled him back from the spiral of wretched self-pity he was about to dive headfirst into. Facts. Focus on the facts. His parents had gone to her for help to get him to consider desi women as future partners. She had approached him as a job, as a client.

You knew that. She always told you that.

She hadn't, however, told him about his parents' involvement.

It's not like she was double-dipping. She never mentioned payment to you.

That was true. He couldn't believe that he'd never considered why she hadn't billed him for anything, even when she admitted her business was struggling.

If anything, it's a lie of omission and nobody needed to be the wiser as long as you were happy and Ammy and Papa were happy, his brain rationalised. *Hardly the worst thing in the world – barely unethical, really.*

His heart, which had been thudding leadenly in his chest all this time, now flared up with angry hurt. However and wherever this whole charade had started, the *fact* was that it had ended up with long, passionate kisses and unspoken promises, and through it all, Saima had never mentioned the truth. And his shell-shocked heart couldn't understand *why*. *Come and destroy me, then*, he'd said to Saima. Well, as with all her clients, she'd delivered. He felt obliterated.

'Shall we order takeaway for lunch or go out somewhere to eat?' Ruby was asking. She still held his arm in a vice-like grip and towed him into the living room as he came crashing back down to earth.

'What?' His voice shook.

'The boy is still upset, can't you see?' George's voice was pla-catory as he walked over to the sofa and sat down. He patted the spot beside him. Ruby, thinking he was gesturing for her to sit down next to him, went over and did so. George looked annoyed, but said nothing.

Kal remained standing and stared at his parents. They seemed suddenly aged. Even though they were both fit and healthy, they looked smaller than he remembered them being when he was growing up. As if they had shrunken into their bodies. His mother had lost some weight, and her face looked more hollowed-out and drawn. His father too had now gone from being a towering figure in Kal's life to a slightly stooped, worn man. If either ever learned that their son thought of them as old, they'd have a fit.

Old or not, George and Ruby weren't fools, and they were certainly well aware of what they were doing. And despite everything, despite whatever the truth ended up being, Saima hadn't deserved his mother's cruel words.

'You need to apologise to Saima,' he said to his mother.

'For what?' Ruby looked appalled.

'Ammy. You said awful, unforgivable things to her.'

'The woman took my money and had her way with you! Didn't she?'

'Ammy, I'm thirty years old. No woman is having her way with me unless I want her to.'

'Tawba, tawba,' Ruby muttered, touching each cheek with her right hand. 'The way you speak to your parents these days. Besharam.'

'You want to talk about shame?' he snapped. 'Let's talk about how you went behind my back to hire a matchmaker. Who even does that? What's the *matter* with you two?'

'We had to do something, Kal.' George sounded tired, but matter-of-fact. 'You're stuck in a rut. Or haven't you noticed? Your life isn't moving forward. You aren't achieving your full potential.'

'Maybe this *is* my full potential – a jobless, single loser. That's what you've always thought of me, isn't it?' Kal's voice was harsh and overly loud in his ears.

'Jobless?' his father repeated.

'I'm thinking of quitting my job.' Throughout the past hectic month, Kal had grown ever more conscious that work would never change. Saying it out loud when he saw Saima in that harried lunchbreak had confirmed it. All those days grabbing sandwiches at his desk and working late into the night – he was conscious that, if he let it, work would rob him of his only chance to get closer to the woman he had started to feel he could spend the rest of his life with. He couldn't let work do that. He had no option but to think about moving on. He'd come here to tell his parents this, hoping to soften the blow of his imminent resignation with news about the incredible, wonderful, maddening woman he'd met.

'Oh, but that's great news! That job has always been so beneath you,' George said.

For a moment, Kal was lost for words. He had expected recriminations and rebukes from George, not this response. Ruby took the opportunity to get up and hug him.

'We don't think of you as a loser, beta,' she said. 'We just want you to have the best that life can offer you.' She led him over to the couch, seating him between them. They looked at him with love and concern. 'It's been quite the time for you.' Ruby's voice was like silk. 'And yes, maybe I got a bit too angry at Saima. I didn't expect to hear that you two had a fling.'

'It wasn't a fling,' Kal said.

'Maybe we were rushing things by trying to get you married. You're a young man. You need more time to sow your wild oats and whatnot,' George said.

'I don't. I think . . . I love Saima, too,' Kal said. As soon as he spoke the words aloud, his heart did a flip and his stomach clenched. His mother's grip on his arm became stronger and her jaw tightened.

'You are saying things in the heat of the moment right now. You need time to cool down,' she said, her voice soft and soothing.

'I do. But I don't think that will change what I just said.' He pulled his arm from her grasp. 'Ammy, I need you to apologise to Saima for what you said to her.'

'But beta, do you really love Saima? Have you even known her that long? Just recently you were telling us about Ayesha. And now all of a sudden you say you're in love with the matchmaker?' Ruby was trying to keep her voice even, but a hint of shrillness entered it now.

'We've gotten to know each other pretty well these past few months,' he said.

'Saima is a sweet girl. I understand why you may think you love her, Khalid,' Ruby said, bringing back that smooth voice of hers. 'It's that sensitive side of you. You've never been able to turn your back on someone having a hard time. And she no doubt just did what she had to, to keep her business going.'

'Who can blame her? Bechari,' George said. 'Imagine having no father and an old mother to take care of.'

'Still, it's no excuse,' Ruby said.

'No, of course not. Imagine thinking she could end up with our Khalid.' George shook his head. 'But she is not our concern. You, beta, need to forget about that girl and sort yourself out. In fact, maybe it's thinking about these girls that's made you lose focus at work.'

'I thought you were happy I was quitting!' Kal retorted.

'Arre, don't bring up work just now, George,' Ruby said, tut-tutting at her husband. 'Kal, you met a girl from Yale who you yourself said you got on with. And then wasn't there also a gori before her? So much going on in your life, Khalid. No wonder you're confused about your own feelings.'

'I'm not confused.' The anger that had subsided under the weight of his dazed hurt now came surging back up Kal's throat. Saima had made a fool out of him, but she hadn't acted alone. He was sitting between the two architects of his misery right now.

'But you *are* confused, my son,' George said. 'I should know. It was only after I started seeing the psychologist that I realised that I was confused about my priorities. Maybe she could help you, too. Help you to understand that whatever it is you think you feel for Saima is just a distraction from the lack of focus in your life. That isn't *love*, beta.'

Kal shot to his feet.

'You know what I need?' he said to them quietly and fiercely. 'I need you' – pointing at his mother – 'to apologise to Saima for the completely foul things you said.'

'But—' she started. For once he would not let her talk over him.

'I need you both to stop meddling based on whatever ideas you have about where my life should be heading. That's not your decision, it's mine. And I need you to *back the hell off*, because I can't even look at you right now.'

He slammed the door behind him as he stormed out of the house, thinking, *No more! No more of them and their meddling ways.*

Chapter 22

Kal lay awake on Sunday night, still stewing over everything that had happened a couple of days earlier. Though he could never talk himself around to approving of his parents' ridiculous scheme, he did on some level understand it. He even understood why Saima might have agreed to it. For one thing, he knew what a persuasive force his mother could be when she set her mind to something. He and Saima had also talked at length a few times about her struggle to maintain her business when the community started turning against it. But the thing he simply couldn't move past was that she hadn't told him the truth when their relationship changed, not on the bench beside the river, and especially not on *that* night.

You should ask her why.
She could have told you why.
If she felt the way you did, would she not have stayed and fought for you?
The way you fought for her?

Such thoughts churned inside his head over and over again with no clear answer or explanation that would give him any peace.

It was why sleep had been so elusive since that fateful day at his parents' place.

'Mmph.' The person beside him mumbled in her sleep. Unlike Kal, she slept like she didn't have a care in the world.

Krista. She was lying on his arm and it had gone numb. Perhaps, he thought, he should stop fighting her. Maybe the key to long-lasting relationships was not to allow them to become too close, maybe even expect them to be a little boring, easy and predictable. He'd tried to be challenged and open, and all that had gotten him was a pounding skull, insomnia and a heart that felt like it was being skewered over and over with hot knives.

Predictable was probably what he had been looking for when, after a weekend spent drowning his sorrows alone, he decided to answer the phone when Krista rang, as she had intermittently done every few weeks since they had broken up. He had no memory of what they had said to each other, but it had ended, as it always did, in bed. Hers this time.

Krista's hair tickled his nose and he tried to shift his face away. His arm had succumbed to the inevitable pins and needles under her head, and he tried to gently nudge her back onto her side of the bed.

'What's the matter?' she mumbled.

'Sorry,' he whispered. 'Just go back to sleep.'

'Mmph, it's hard to sleep when you keep moving around like that.' She was fully awake now, peering at him in the darkness.

'Just got a lot on my mind,' he said, staring up at the ceiling.

'Is that why you couldn't get it up before?'

He recoiled from her question, for there was no way to answer it honestly without being an absolute shit. There had been no chance of intimacy, however drunk and lonely he was. She smelled wrong, she felt wrong, she looked wrong. And then it had occurred to him that it wasn't her, it was him. *He* was wrong. This was wrong.

'We could try again?' Krista said now as she let her fingers trail down his stomach. He stopped her before they reached their mark. 'Oh, don't be like that,' she purred.

'I'm in love with someone else.' Saying the words aloud set his pulse racing so fast he felt like he was going to throw up. Or maybe that was the booze.

'You – you fucking *what*?'

'I—'

'You're such an arsehole!' she shouted. 'Why did you come home with *me*, then?'

'I don't know!' he said, more frustrated at himself than ever. 'I don't know why I'm doing *anything*!'

'I'll tell you why,' she hissed, springing from the bed and furiously pulling her clothes on. 'Your head has gone so far up your own arse, you can't see night from day! And I don't know why I let it happen when I clearly should know better!'

'I'm sorry. I really am,' said Kal, struggling upright. 'I'm not with her, if that makes it any better,' he said.

'It doesn't.' She flung his jeans into his face. 'Get the fuck up.'

'I don't know if we will ever be together,' he continued doggedly as he dragged them on. 'She hates me, I think.'

'Her and me both. You're amassing quite the collection of women who hate your guts, Kal!' Krista stalked around her bedroom, hurling his clothes at him. 'It's my fault,' she muttered, mostly to herself. 'I should've listened to my instincts. I kept telling myself, "Krista, don't make that call. He doesn't deserve you."'

His shirt whipped him in the face. 'I don't,' he mumbled. One shoe, then another thudded onto the bed. 'Shit, Krista, I'm so sorry. I shouldn't have – please don't leave it like this,' he said, as she stomped out into her living room.

'Why? What more could you possibly need to say before I throw your arse out of here?' She was standing by the door, her hand hovering over the handle.

'I'm sorry . . .' he started.

'Stop repeating those empty words that mean nothing!'

'You've been my longest relationship to date,' he said. 'And there was something comforting about that. And if things had maybe gone differently, I think I was prepared to go all in for a future with you, but I think that was more because of, I don't know, like a comfortable familiarity than us actually being right for each other.'

Krista folded her arms across her chest. She looked suddenly very young and lost. 'You were my longest relationship, too.'

'Shouldn't we have had longer runs by this age? Isn't it strange that we haven't?'

'I don't know . . . Maybe our expectations are too high.'

'Maybe that's the problem,' he said. 'Maybe they're so high that when people do something human, we feel massively let down.'

'Like how I always feel let down by you,' she said, thinking about this for a moment. 'But it's more than that. Maybe we're drawn to each other because we don't know what we want. Because we're similar.' She looked sad. 'And because we're so fucking *lonely*. I'm so sick of the single life.'

Kal put on his shoes. 'I really am sorry.'

She opened the apartment door. 'Get out,' she said, without heat, without any emotion at all. 'I don't care how lonely you might feel. And trust me, I won't make this mistake again. Just – get out. And close the door behind you.' She didn't look at him again as she returned to her bedroom and softly shut the door.

He awoke very late the following morning to a loud banging at his front door. He stumbled out to open it a crack and Tom burst in, nearly mowing him down.

'Why haven't you been answering my calls? I thought we were supposed to hang out Friday night, and then you just disappeared. Where've you been the last couple of days?' he demanded at once.

'How did you get in?' Kal asked, nonplussed and not yet quite awake.

Tom shrugged. 'I lurked outside till someone went out, then I charmed one of your neighbours into buzzing me up the lift. Where the hell have you been? Is it the girl? The matchmaker? What's her name, Saima? Oh shit, is she here?'

'Wait, how did you know about her?'

'I was talking to Lachie yesterday and he told me you two were dating or something. Which you *didn't* tell me, by the way.' He waved away whatever explanation Kal had been about to make. 'Doesn't matter, things have been mad, it's not like we've had the chance to breathe, let alone catch up. Anyway, stoked to hear that you finally got your shit together with her. How did it go?' Whatever Tom saw in Kal's face drained the slight smirk from his own. 'Are you okay?' he asked, his eyes now full of concern.

Kal took a deep breath. 'I, uh, I broke up with Krista and Saima.'

'What? Krista *and* Saima? You weren't even with Krista. I thought you guys already broke up? And you were barely with Saima.'

'Things got very complicated very quickly.' He couldn't meet Tom's gaze and headed to the kitchen to get a glass of water. Tom followed behind.

'Do you need to talk? Can I help? Is that why you disappeared? You can't just disappear when things go wrong, Kal, we talked about this.'

'I'm sorry, man, I should've gotten back to you. I just shut down.'

SAMAN SHAD

'Shutting down is the worst thing you can do. You know I'm here for you. So is Lachie. You know that, right?' Tom spoke with a rare earnestness. Half-hungover, feeling bruised inside and out, Kal couldn't hide the sheen of sudden tears in his eyes.

'Oh, mate, I had no idea things were this bad.' Tom squeezed Kal's shoulders tightly.

'I appreciate you being here, man,' Kal said, swiping at his face with the back of his hand and clearing his throat.

'Of course I'm here. Jesus Christ, what *happened?*' Tom swept him into a bear hug and Kal found his face squashed soggily and comfortingly into his brawny shoulder.

'I don't think I'm ready to talk about it yet. I don't think I've made sense of it myself.'

'Do you need to find someone to talk to?' Tom said as he pulled away.

Kal thought about it seriously for once. 'Yeah, I think I should,' he agreed, knuckling his eyes. 'Sorry about crying on you like that.'

'There's nothing wrong with a bit of crying to take the edge off. I may not look like the kind of guy that does, but I'm quite fond of a good cry every now and then.'

'You are? When? Why are you only telling me this now?'

'I cry at soppy movies, but I'm not going to call you to say "Kal, I bawled my eyes out in *Marley & Me*", am I? Man, I couldn't even make it through *Endgame*.'

Kal squeezed his arm. 'I appreciate you coming around, man. And I just appreciate you.'

'Does this mean I'll be getting that charm necklace at last?' Tom quipped with a gentle grin. 'I prefer silver to gold, by the way.'

Kal gave a slightly waterlogged laugh as his phone buzzed on the counter. He picked it up to find a text from Linda.

Charles has requested a meeting this afternoon and I need to tell him whether you're coming in or not.

I'll be there, Kal responded.

'Oh, yeah. That was why I was trying to track you down when you didn't turn up for work this morning,' Tom said, reading over his shoulder. 'Charles came past your desk saying he wanted to grab you for a meeting but you weren't there. I did my best to cover for you, mate, told him you were taking time off in lieu for all the long hours we've been pulling. I tried to call you, but you weren't picking up, so as soon as he left I jumped in an Uber and headed over here.'

'Thanks for that. Maybe it's time I go have a chat with him, I've been putting it off. Give me five minutes to get ready?' Kal asked.

'Take all the time you need,' Tom said. 'I'm going to help myself to whatever is happening in your fridge.'

Just over an hour later, Kal was back in the office, trying his best to avoid Linda's disapproving gaze. He wasn't ready to pick up where *that* conversation had left off, so he busied himself until it was time for Charles's requested meeting. As the clock ticked over to three, he steeled his nerves, straightened up his suit and walked into the boardroom, where Charles sat beside Anjelo, the stony-faced HR representative, whom Kal always found a little unnerving and never got on with. A pile of documents and a sealed brown envelope sat on the table in front of them. Kal smiled at the two men, but he couldn't help thinking that it was never a good sign when the HR rep was in the room. He tried to get a grasp of the tone of the room. Anjelo's face was sombre, but Charles, a man in his fifties with a sharply receding hairline, seemed almost cheerful.

'Kal! Nice to finally get the chance to talk one on one,' he said, reaching out for a handshake as Kal took his seat across from the two men. 'And I do need to apologise that we haven't had the opportunity to do this earlier.'

Anjelo shuffled some papers, then passed them over to Charles.

'You've been doing well, judging by your past performance reviews, but I've also been keeping an eye on you for the last few months. So, anyway, to get to the point, we've been doing a bit of restructuring in the department,' Charles continued, and Kal almost held his breath. 'And we've noticed that as a firm we aren't innovating as much as we should. We need fresh blood, a different way of thinking.'

Oh god, maybe Linda's snide remarks about his performance weren't empty threats after all, he thought. 'I'm sorry, am I fired?' Kal blurted. After the last couple of days, his filters were at an all-time low.

Charles looked startled. 'What? No! The very opposite, in fact. I wanted to talk to you about whether you were interested in heading up a new department. It was why we had been paying close attention to your performance these past few months, and all in all I can say I'm very impressed. Though perhaps I shouldn't be calling it a department, when really it'll just be a small team made up of you and maybe Tom Sato, as you both seem to work so well together. Plus a couple of others, maybe some new hires. I'll leave the team make-up to you. We thought we'd call it our Agility Lab, but of course that's up for discussion. You'll be working with some of our newer, smaller clients to figure out how they can be more agile and innovative in their own firms. You know, some proper advisory consulting, some real value-add, cutting-edge thinking. It'll be a new direction for our company, but I think we could trial it for twelve months. It's something different to help us stand out among the big players who don't have time for the little guys anymore. I've seen how organically you and Tom work together, and I've been impressed with what you've come up with over the past few months. What do you think?'

Kal felt almost frozen with surprise and relief.

'I'm happy to take feedback about how we can best run this little experiment,' Charles continued, with a determined smile. 'And yes, if your silence is hesitance, we can look at making it a permanent fixture?'

Kal remained silent.

'Kal?'

He shook himself. 'Sorry, Charles, it's been a strange few days on a personal level.'

'Oh, I'm sorry to hear that,' Charles said. 'Please take any time that you need to, especially before jumping into a new role. If you want to accept it, that is? We don't need your answer right now. You can sleep on it.' He smiled benignly while Anjelo eyed Kal with caution.

Kal finally relaxed enough to smile back at Charles. He thought about the past few days. About how he'd found and lost the love of his life, about how his relationship with his parents seemed irreparably broken, but here was something positive, something unexpected. This new role sounded promising, and hopefully it would change how he felt about work. And in any case, if he left his job now, what else would he do with himself? The prospect of lonely, empty days stretching out before him made him shudder.

'This is one of the few things I don't need to think about,' he said. 'I'd love to accept.'

Chapter 23

Lying on her mother's frayed floral couch, eating Bhuja mix from the packet and streaming Indian TV shows had become Saima's new normal.

In the first two weeks following the horrendous encounter in the Alis' kitchen, she had prioritised scraping together the repayment for the two instalments that she had accepted from them. The sooner she could return all of that money, the sooner she could repress the entire episode and move on. She was by habit a frugal person, and her office lease was paid off for at least the next few months thanks to Ayesha signing on as a client, so the only real outgoings she still had to cover were her studio rent and living expenses. And so, against her better judgement, she did the only thing she could think of to remove those costs, and the one thing she had dreaded doing ever since she had moved out. She terminated her lease, sold off whatever she could on Gumtree and moved back in with Rahat.

Keeping busy with life admin was a tried and tested method for Saima, allowing her to avoid all the bubbling anger and sorrow that kept threatening to overtake her. After an evening spent on Jess's living room floor, during which they shared a therapeutic rant about the unfairness of everything, the shittiness of men and the outrageous hypocrisy of Ruby in particular, Saima decided that putting the business on hiatus was the best move while she waited to see what the fallout might be from losing the Alis' favour.

'You think that bitch is going to drag you in public?' Jess had asked. 'Won't it make *her* look bad?'

'Definitely not. She'll be able to play the role of the mother who just cares too much and was taken in by a jezebel like me,' Saima said.

'Ugh, kill me.' Jess finished her drink and slammed the bottle down, rattling the others cluttering the coffee table. 'I hate her and her blingy face. And I hate whatshisname, that prick.'

Even though Jess called him a prick, a term Saima wholeheartedly agreed with, the distant mention of Kal made Saima's heart sink. *If only . . .* The words that had been threatening her from the moment she had gone to see the Alis cropped up in her head. *If only*, they persisted, *you had spoken to Kal first.*

Saima grizzled at the thought. Yes, she had made a mistake, but perhaps it was for the best. He had shown his true colours. He was bound to show them sooner or later; better he did it before she invested any more of herself in the relationship.

'Anyway,' Saima said a little loudly, to silence the thoughts running through her head. 'The clients I've got left on my books aren't in any massive hurry or anything. The only ones who've stuck with me that aren't already matched are the ones who could honestly take or leave my services. So it's not like I'm keeping them hanging, I guess.'

Jess blinked rapidly, looking like she was about to cry. 'But you could have introduced them to their soulmate.'

'They'll have to find their soulmate without my help,' Saima replied, her throat tight. 'Maybe they'll have better luck.'

'Don't say that!' Jess lurched over and flung her arms around her friend. 'You have been responsible for so much happiness, Saima, you're like – you're like a love godmother or something!'

'I am! I was! Not anymore!' The instant she had allowed herself to fall in love with a man, her whole business had fallen apart. She had no-one else to blame but herself.

With her business now finished, how else was she meant to spend her days?

The soaps were all merging into one histrionic mess in her head. The one she was watching right now reminded her of the showdown at the Alis' place – dramatic showdowns were a clear staple of these dramas. Maybe that was where Ruby had learned some of those barbs that had been perfectly designed to wound her. Or perhaps the writers on these shows knew that all South Asian mothers were overly protective of their sons and lashed out at any woman who would dare to shift their sons' attention away from them.

Her mother's key turned in the lock and the front door opened. 'Assalaamu alaykum, Ammy,' she mumbled, her eyes still on the TV.

'I see you haven't moved from where I left you this morning,' Rahat said.

'I have moved,' Saima protested. 'I brushed my teeth, went to the kitchen, went to the bathroom, got something to eat . . . Lots of moving.' She turned at last to see her mother laden with grocery bags.

'You went shopping? You should've told me, I could have helped.'

'Could you?' Rahat asked.

'What do you mean?'

'Can you please just get up and help me with these now?' her mother said wearily.

Saima hoisted herself off the couch to haul some of the bags into the kitchen.

Rahat had neither been pleased nor unhappy at the news of Saima moving back in, she just tacitly knew that her daughter needed her, and welcomed her back quietly and without question.

When her mother wielded her silences, however, Saima usually talked too much to fill the gap.

'What's the point of you in your place, me in mine, both by ourselves, when we could be under the same roof?' she'd babbled. 'It makes moral and economic sense.' And Rahat had simply nodded without responding.

When Saima had started wearing her pyjamas as her daily uniform, even when she was sent out to the shops, Rahat, again, said nothing.

Then, a couple of weeks later, when cleaning up after a meal began to feel like too much effort, Saima had suggested they eat from paper plates so they didn't have to worry about the washing-up. Rahat had nodded at that too, before getting out her real crockery and cutlery and setting the table in silence. Saima had nattered for what felt like an hour about water shortages and waste.

Now, watching her daughter carelessly put away the groceries, Rahat couldn't hold her tongue any longer.

'Saima, come help me with dinner,' she said.

'Can't we just get takeaway? I think I've got a voucher for a discount at that burger place.' Saima pulled out her phone and began to scroll through her emails.

'No burgers. No takeaway. Proper home-cooked food. Okay?' Rahat said.

'Fine,' Saima said, putting her phone away and wandering back to the couch.

Rahat picked up the remote control and turned the TV off.

'I was watching that!' Saima protested.

'You've been "watching that" almost nonstop for weeks. Enough.'

'I guess I take after my dear mother, watching this trash nonstop. You should be so proud.'

SAMAN SHAD

'I would say you're acting like a twelve-year-old, but I remember you at twelve, and you were far more mature than you are behaving now.'

'What does *that* mean?'

'What does it mean? Look at you! Never in my life have I seen you behave like this.'

'Yeah, well, maybe you were never paying attention when I was,' Saima said. 'That's a specialty of yours, isn't it? To bury your head in the sand?' She regretted the words as soon as she'd said them. 'I'm sorry, Ammy. I didn't mean that.'

'No, no, please, tell me what else you've been meaning to tell me!'

'Forget it. Can I please have the remote back?'

'No, no more TV. In fact, no more lying around here doing nothing. I want you to get up, have a shower, take your things and go back home.'

'You're kicking me out?'

'I'm not kicking you out. But at least when you're in your own place, you're doing what you are meant to do – going to work, seeing your friends, paying your bills, having a life – all the normal things you do. Things that make you happier.'

'Well, this is my new normal now.'

'What?'

Saima sighed and finally told her mother what she'd avoided mentioning for weeks. 'There *is* no work. And if there's no work, then there's no seeing friends, no bills, no life. There's definitely nowhere you can kick me out *to*, either. I vacated my flat.'

'But I thought you were living here temporarily. To see if it would work out with us under the same roof. And your business was doing well! You seemed so busy,' Rahat said, bewildered.

'I was busy, but now I'm not. Not anymore. And I don't think I'm likely to be in the future, either.' She could feel the burn of tears

270

behind her eyes, and tipped her head back onto the couch to stare at the ceiling. A thought fought its way through the fug in her brain. 'Hang on, did you really believe I moved here temporarily? What did you think I was doing?'

Rahat sat across from her. 'I assumed it had something to do with a boy.'

'You think I just threw in the towel with work and everything for a boy?' Saima asked incredulously.

'Did you not?'

For a moment Saima didn't reply, weighing up how much she wanted to reveal about Kal.

'There's no boy, Ammy,' she finally said. 'There's no *man*, either.' She didn't know who she was being snarky about, her mother or Kal.

'I'm a simple woman but even I know when I'm being lied to, especially by my only daughter.' Rahat folded her arms across her chest. 'Tell me, what happened with this man?'

'Nothing happened.'

'Is *that* why you're here?'

'No, Ammy!'

'Saima,' her mother said in a stern tone she hadn't heard since she was a child. 'Do not lie to me.'

'Fine! There *was* a man, okay? Was. Past tense. We are cursed, you and me. You can't deny it. My father was a bad man and I guess I attract men like him.'

'Your father wasn't a bad man,' Rahat said.

Saima let out a short derisive laugh.

'No, listen, he wasn't,' Rahat insisted, sitting forward with urgency.

'Right, so you took off without a word because he was just an average guy, right?' Saima said sarcastically.

'He didn't want to live in Australia,' her mother said sadly. 'He was never happy here. He had family and influence back home, and here he was nobody, a man who worked in a shop, where no-one could say his name properly, and people shouted at us in the street simply because of the way we looked. He wanted us to move back home to Pakistan. I said no. We fought a lot about it. But, beti,' she reached forward and clasped Saima's hand tightly, 'he wasn't a bad man.'

Saima stared at her in shock, before asking, 'Why did you say no?'

'To going back to Pakistan?' Rahat looked at her incredulously. 'Because there was nothing for me there. My parents had died, my brother had moved away and never cared to see if I was okay. And a part of me knew that my marriage wasn't working anyway . . .' She sighed and sat back in her seat. 'Moving back would mean your father would have more rights than me when it came to you. I couldn't lose you, don't you see?'

Saima opened her mouth to speak but couldn't find the words.

'I finally left him after a big argument,' her mother said, looking at her hands as she did.

'I remember the fighting,' Saima said. 'What did he do to make you leave, Ammy? It's okay, you can tell me.'

'When I look back on it, it seems silly. He told me I was stubborn because I didn't go back with him for the holiday.' Rahat squeezed her eyes shut for a moment. Saima knew this was hard for her mother, but she needed to know the whole truth and she wasn't going to let go of this opportunity.

'Holiday? What do you mean?' Saima asked.

'He was in Pakistan. Don't you remember?' Rahat said.

'Is that what Laila Aunty meant by running away?'

'He wasn't running away. He went there for a holiday, or so he said, but I knew it was to see if we could fit back into life there,' Rahat explained.

'I thought he was here. The fight, that day we left, when everything changed . . . I thought he said something, did something . . .' Saima was finding it hard to form full sentences.

Rahat sighed. 'You were so young. We left because he told me on the phone he was going to stop paying the rent on the place we were living in. I think he was hoping it would convince me to go and be with him. But you know your mother, Saima. I'm a stubborn woman. So I said, fine, do what you need to. But I won't leave Sydney and move to Pakistan.'

'All this time I thought he had done something horrible, and that was why we left like we did.'

'I wasn't thinking straight back then,' Rahat said. 'I grabbed all that I could and walked out of our little flat. I didn't want to ask anyone for help. I didn't want to admit that I needed it. Or maybe I was embarrassed. I suppose I worried more about what people would say or think rather than how it would affect my child.' Rahat covered her face with her hands. 'Only now I can see how much this has affected you. I wish I hadn't got in the way of you and him. He adored you so much, which is why he tried to reach out to you. But I burned his letters, I didn't take his calls . . . And that holiday he took became something more permanent. He never came back.' Tears began to roll down Rahat's sunken cheeks. 'I think I went crazy for a while there. Maybe I lost my mind. But he wasn't a bad man.'

'Did he know we stayed at the shelter?' Saima asked, her voice cracking as she did.

Rahat shook her head. 'No one knew, until Laila found out and came to get us.'

Saima sat, frozen with shock, nausea rising inexorably.

'I wanted to tell you the truth before, but I was afraid that I would lose you too. You adored your father so much when you were a child. I thought you would rather go back to Pakistan with him than be with me. And then, at last, he stopped trying to contact me. Eventually, I heard he had a new family in Pakistan. You might even have some other brothers and sisters. I shouldn't have got in the way of all that. I should have told you.'

Saima dashed to the bathroom and threw up. And when she was done, she kept gagging, even when there was nothing left to bring up. She wished something more from inside of her would come out that would magically make her feel better, but nothing came, so she sat, her head resting on the toilet seat, and wept.

A while later, mother and daughter stood in the kitchen. Rahat had begun to cook dinner and Saima wordlessly chopped the onions and washed the rice.

'I would never have left you,' she said at last, as the onions fried in hot oil. 'You're the only family I need, Ammy.' But Rahat didn't respond. They moved around the kitchen silently.

When finally they sat down to eat, Saima said, 'I think I'll go back to work tomorrow.'

Rahat nodded. 'You need to fix your business. I know you can do it,' she said. 'And you can stay here as long as you need. I would never kick you out.'

They ate the rest of their meal in silence, even though thoughts about her father swirled in Saima's head. *How could he not come back and find me? Why didn't he fight for me if he loved me as much as Ammy says he did?* She batted these thoughts away – only her mother would know the answers, and as she watched Rahat quietly pop morsels of food in her mouth, she knew that she was not ready to talk. One day soon, Saima thought, perhaps when they were both less emotionally strung out than they were right now, she could learn more about her father and think about reconnecting with him. In the meantime, there was plenty else she needed to do.

She was surprisingly nervous heading back to the cottage after weeks away. Spring was well and truly here as she quietly let herself in to the building. A peaceful return to normal, however, was not on the cards.

'Don't ever leave me again!' Jess exclaimed, snatching her immediately into a tight hug. She pulled back to study Saima's face intently. 'You okay? I got the feeling you weren't letting on how you *really* were whenever I texted you.'

'I'm not a hundred per cent,' Saima admitted. 'But I'm getting there.'

Dave shuffled out of his room with a plate of biscuits he had baked.

'Oh, thanks, Dave. I never knew you baked so well,' Saima said, taking a bite of a delicious oatmeal cookie.

'I'm a man of many surprises,' Dave said, before wandering back to his office, blowing into his mug of probably-Horlicks. 'Good to have you back,' he called over his shoulder.

Saima laughed. She was already feeling a lot closer to normal and wondered why she had kept herself away from a place that felt more like home than anywhere else.

'So, what's on the cards today?' Jess said as they walked together into her office.

'Oh, you know, the usual,' Saima said, feeling lighter with every step, closing the door behind her. 'Big plans.'

'Yessss, I love your big plans,' Jess said, as she flopped down into the plastic chair next to Saima's desk, 'Tell me more.'

'Well, you know how many in my community are giving me the cold shoulder and, well, I can't rely on the goodwill and recommendations from the remaining others to keep this business running. So I started thinking about what K—' She found it hard to say Kal's name out loud. She decided she didn't need to, even though he had given her the initial idea. 'Basically, would people outside the desi community pay for a matchmaker to help them find someone to settle down with?'

'Yes!!' Jess said immediately. 'A hundred percent yes! I bet even Dave will agree.'

And he did, hearing everything through the thin wall, with the caveat, 'Although I do all right myself without any help.' Which made Jess shout back, 'Okay, for weeks you've had next to nothing to say, and *now* you come through with a comment like that?'

Saima smiled. It was all the push she needed to go ahead with her plan.

She spent the rest of the week designing and sending out a market research survey to everyone she could think of in her network outside the desi community. Though quite a few responded positively to the concept of a matchmaker, most participants mentioned that they usually turned to the apps. Here was where she came unstuck. Her knowledge of the apps and social media was flimsy at best, and she couldn't for the life of her think of how to carve out a space for face-to-face bespoke matchmaking services in a world of swiping left and right.

She called the only person she could think of to help.

Ayesha sounded surprised to hear from Saima, but also pleased.

'I've been so bored!' she said. 'I've had to spend most days at home with my mum, and I think it's starting to do my head in! I need to get out more.'

276

Saima laughed. 'I know what that's like – I've been back at home with my mum, too.'

'Oh, how come?' Ayesha asked.

'Kal and I . . .' Saima began, without meaning to. 'It's complicated. Was complicated.'

'So he didn't tell you – I thought you both would . . .' Ayesha trailed off with rare uncertainty.

'We decided it wasn't meant to be,' Saima said.

'That's a shame. He seemed so keen on you.'

'Yeah, well, it's probably for the best.'

'So why are you back with your mum?'

'Now this is a longer story,' Saima said, and laid out the situation with her business.

Ayesha groaned with frustration. 'Oh yes, I know how that goes. One of the reasons Abbu packed up and moved us here was because the gossip around Ammy's mental health was starting to affect his work. I'm sorry, Saima, that absolutely blows.'

'It does, but I'm comforting myself with the thought that I'm only staying with Ammy temporarily, till my finances are back in better shape,' Saima said, before changing the topic. 'But I didn't call you to speak about Kal or about the small-mindedness of people. I'm actually calling you about a work thing.'

'I'm intrigued.'

'Okay, so obviously it's no longer feasible for me to keep my clientele within our community, so I'm looking to expand my business.'

'You mean to goras?'

'Goras and anyone else who is looking to settle down and maybe would like a more personalised one-on-one service than what the apps offer. I've done some research.' She laid out the plan that had slowly coalesced over the past week, but she hadn't even finished giving Ayesha the full spiel before the younger woman interrupted.

'I'm in. When can I start?'

'Oh, it isn't a job,' Saima hastened to explain. 'More like a consultancy, I guess? A very budget-limited one, I'm sorry to say. Like *no* budget . . .'

'It's an internship,' Ayesha said firmly. 'With a view to a staff position.'

'Wait, no, I can't pay you a salary, Ayesha.'

'Look, if I were back in the States, I'd be slogging through some unpaid internship or another at this stage, just to try and get my foot in the door at one of the big firms. I'd much rather be doing that with you, honestly.'

'But don't you need to be with your mum? I thought that was why you hadn't gotten a job here already?'

'Yeah, but my dad and sister just came up permanently from Melbourne at last, so I'm finally free.'

'So won't you start on the job hunt now?'

'Frankly, Saima, I don't need the money, since Abbu's still happy to support me. And to be honest, I'm not that motivated to do the whole job hunt thing. I'm bored, and I'd much rather help out a friend with a solid commercial idea than slog around with job applications.'

'It's sweet that you think of me as a friend, Ayesha, but I need to pay you.'

'Are you feeling bad? Stop feeling bad, girl! Do you think those big organisations pulling in millions of dollars of profit feel bad for hiring unpaid interns? No!'

'I'd like to think I'm a little bit more ethical than an exploitative corporation,' Saima answered dryly.

Ayesha sighed dramatically. 'Okay, *fine*, if you're going to be weird about it. I'll be your consultant, so I'll bill you for my hours.'

'You'll bill me at a *normal* rate,' Saima insisted.

'Don't be ridiculous, I'll bill you at mates rates, linked to outcomes,' Ayesha said breezily. 'Shall I come over now?'

And so began Love Masala – their matchmaking agency. Within a couple of weeks, they both started to reach out to other businesses. Ayesha began cold-calling dating start-ups and events management companies, looking for potential partnerships, while Saima focused on interviewing the couples she had already matched up in order to create a policy document and a code of conduct for the new business, working out how her skills and experience could complement the specialised start-up dating apps.

Their focus on building partnerships led to a meeting with a Muslim dating start-up.

It didn't take much to convince the team to work with them, especially when the app founders learned that they shared Saima's values, wanting their clients to be matched without cultural biases and prejudice. Saima's offering essentially became a premium product for any users who wanted to consult with a professional matchmaker instead of simply trawling the app.

'Excellent, this means we've got access to their existing database instead of you having to do all that groundwork yourself,' Ayesha said.

After a few false starts and a stressful afternoon trawling Word-Press, Ayesha built a website that included glowing testimonials from an array of Saima's success stories. After months of feeling the sting of ostracism and weeks spent focusing outside the desi community, she was once more humbled by how quickly so many in that community wanted to help. When word got out among the couples she had matched, everyone pitched in. One client turned out to be a budding graphic designer and overwhelmed them with gorgeous logo options. Uncle Malik was typically ready to help with all the additional accounting; Faisal insisted on helping

Saima further develop their basic web presence and took over the management and admin of the Love Masala site, much to her relief. Rukhsana, whom Saima had last seen in that stuffy Harris Park restaurant, turned out to be a savvy social media strategist and dedicated herself to setting up and growing the Love Masala accounts across Facebook, Instagram and TikTok. Thankfully, they all agreed to charge her mates rates, though Saima promised she would pay them all properly once the funds started rolling in.

One blessedly quiet afternoon found Saima, Jess and Ayesha sitting with cups of tea in her office, surrounded by boxes of freshly printed flyers. Uncle Malik's wife, Aunty Rehana, had sent a container of homemade assorted mithai to celebrate their burgeoning success, and it lay open on the desk between them.

Ayesha looked around with smug satisfaction. 'I knew we'd get here.'

'We're not quite there yet, but it's a start,' Saima said.

'Yes, I know, but it's okay to celebrate our milestones, even if they aren't the big ones,' Ayesha countered, and Saima nodded in agreement as she took a bite of a gulab jamun, winking at Jess as she did.

'Oi, is that some kind of dig at how many of those I've consumed?' Jess asked.

'No, not at all!' Saima laughed.

'Anyway, I'm just here to partake in the celebrations,' Jess said, picking up another gulab jamun and nudging it against Saima's. 'Cheers!'

'We've met a lot of the short-term goals I had in mind,' Ayesha said, thoughtfully chewing on a barfi. 'I'm keen to see how the long-term ones shape up.'

Saima started laughing. 'You had short-term *and* long-term goals? Ayesha, you're terrifying.'

'You mean to tell me that you don't?' Ayesha returned.

'Short-term is my specialty,' Saima admitted, and Jess nodded emphatically. 'All right, you don't have to agree *quite* so quickly,' Saima told her.

'Saima doesn't *do* long-term,' Jess told Ayesha. 'She's got this whole thing about any long-term planning going to shit.'

Ayesha eyed Saima, considering. 'Okay, then. Give me one long-term goal, right here, right now. Imagine anything is possible. And I won't judge if you say your goal is taking over the world. I'd much rather *you* do it than some billionaire white guy.'

Saima lingered over her answer for a time, resolutely not thinking about the last time someone had asked her to picture an ideal future. 'I've always wanted to be able to buy my mother the apartment she lives in.'

Ayesha grinned. 'Even with the property prices in this ridiculous city, I honestly don't think it would take us that long to reach that goal.' She said it with such confidence that Saima had no option but to believe her completely.

'As easy as that?' she asked.

'As easy as that.'

Saima laughed again and finished off her gulab jamun, affectionately basking in the company of both her old friend and her new one. 'Okay,' she said.

Maybe, as Jess had said all those months ago, she needed to stop expecting the worst. Maybe, just maybe, some good could happen, too. Lots and lots of good.

Chapter 24

'You're depressed.' Lachie stated this before they'd even ordered drinks.

'You need to call the girl you don't like to talk about but who you're obviously still obsessing about,' Tom said. 'The one whose name we're not allowed to mention.'

'Yeah, the one who's got you moping around like a lost puppy.'

'More like a sick puppy, judging by the look of him.'

'You two are worse than my parents.' Kal got up to fetch the first round.

'No-one's lining up to watch you waste away, mate,' Lachie said, when he returned with their drinks. 'First night I've come out with you lot in ages, and here you are, looking like dead meat before we've even started.'

'Cheers,' Kal replied sardonically.

'I'm just saying, you look like a marionette whose strings have been cut.'

Tom looked at Lachie, impressed. 'Dude, that's perfect. That's *exactly* what he looks like.'

'Yeah, we started doing a bunch on puppets this term, and one of the kids got a bit happy with the scissors. Thought of Kal immediately when I saw that mess,' Lachie said.

'Are you finished?' asked Kal.

Tom thumped him heavily between the shoulder blades. 'You, my friend, need to get your spark back. That's what we're saying. Just call her.'

'I'm not going to get my spark back by calling her.'

'Aha!' Lachie waved his finger in front of Kal's nose. 'So you admit that you do need to get the spark back, though?'

'I've asked you heaps of times to come surfing with me,' Tom added.

'I've hated every time I've gone out with you,' Kal said flatly.

'You've just got to give it time. The early mornings out on the waves, you can't beat it.'

'Sorry, man, it's not for me. I could just hang out at home and waterboard myself for the same effect.'

'So then find something else you're into,' Lachie said.

'I've been busy at work,' Kal began.

'Don't even try it. Charles asked you to ease back in,' Tom interjected.

'He's asked all of us to do that,' Kal retorted. 'Not like he made a special case just for workaholic me.'

Charles had turned out to be a popular manager who championed a healthy work-life balance. Part of that meant no-one was allowed to work on weekends, and overtime was supposed to be a rarity. Kal finally had the scope for the lifestyle he'd wanted – with no lifestyle to fill up the time.

'Oh, Nicole wanted me to ask you if you made that eggplant recipe she sent you last week,' Lachie said. 'She said you never texted her back.'

'Uh . . .'

'You didn't, did you?'

'Sorry. Not much into cooking right now.'

'Anyway,' Tom said. 'It doesn't have to be surfing or cooking, but we're older now, and we need to have a more well-rounded perspective on living. You can't just keep pouring it all into work, either. Something's gotta change.'

'Honestly, do you even hear yourself these days? Surfing's made you a fuddy-duddy,' Kal said, smiling to himself at the term.

'Krista's engaged,' Lachie blurted suddenly.

'Engaged? To who?' Kal asked.

'Some Russian dude who runs an "import-export" business,' Lachie said. 'Sounds dodgy as.'

'I hope she's happy,' Kal said, and he meant it.

'Seemed pretty stoked when Nic was talking to her.'

'See?' Tom said. 'Change is good, my friend. Gotta embrace it. How's the therapy going?'

'Yeah, all right. Slow going, but I guess it's helping.'

'Well, that's great, isn't it?' Lachie said jovially.

Kal rolled his eyes. 'Lachie, I'm not one of your kindergarteners. But yes, it's great.'

'Has the psych told you to call the girl we're not supposed to talk about?' Tom asked.

'She hasn't, no. So give it a rest.'

'Listen. Mate.' Lachie exchanged a glance with Tom. 'Jokes aside. We want to see you move past this. You won't even tell us what happened, and that's fine, but it's been ages. You went out for what, a month? What's so bad that you can't move on from it, and how can we help?'

'Genuinely? You can help by talking about something else. Please. What's going on with you?' Kal asked, looking at Lachie, and injected a lighter tone into his voice. 'Are you going to make an honest woman out of Nicole or what?'

'One step ahead of you,' Lachie said, with a grin. 'Or rather, Nicole's one step ahead of you and me both. She came out and told me the other day that we should get married because it makes financial sense. We're going shopping for engagement rings together on Saturday.'

'You're engaged?' Kal and Tom said in unison.

'Well, I'm still planning to surprise her with a proper proposal, but yeah, I guess.' Lachie was beaming with pride. 'It's why I wanted to see you both tonight.'

'Congrats, man!' Kal said, wrapping him in a hug. 'So happy for you.'

'This is amazing news!' Tom exclaimed. 'We need to celebrate.' He hightailed it back to the bar.

Lachie was watching Kal carefully. 'You okay? We didn't know if telling you now was going to make things worse.'

Kal didn't even need to think about his answer. 'Absolutely, mate. This is the best news in ages. And I'm sorry I've been so down in the dumps lately that you had to worry about me instead of just celebrating. I couldn't be happier for you. We should do something, all of us together, as soon as Nic's free.'

Tom manoeuvred three tumblers onto their table. 'Okay, so who's going to be your best man? I reckon I look better in a suit than our friend Dev Patel over here.'

'While clearly I tell much better jokes,' Kal sniped back.

Sitting there, trading barbs with the men he'd always thought of as brothers and celebrating his friends moving on to the next stage of their lives, he felt the warm glow of joy defrosting the grey slump he'd been in for months after things had so spectacularly imploded with Saima.

Saima. Whenever he let his guard down just a little, flashes of their time together would invade his head and amplify the gnawing emptiness in his gut. It felt like a relationship that had gone on for years before ending in the fireball at his parents' house, rather than just the actual month they were together.

At his therapist's behest, he'd tried to view the situation from a distance, with some level of detachment. But while he could recall Laksa Night, and their many conversations, even their one and a half dates with a smile, he lost any hope of aloofness when he got to the memory of her standing in his mother's kitchen, aghast, upset and so very guilty. It was the guilt he couldn't detach from – neither hers nor his own, sitting deep inside his heart.

The night out with Tom and Lachie ended far earlier than it used to. Another sign of their changing priorities, he supposed. And change, as they both kept saying, was good.

A couple of days later, sitting at his desk, Kal found himself looking at the business card that he just couldn't get rid of. It was definitely looking worse for wear after several months folded up in his wallet. *Move past this*, Lachie had said. *Detach*, his therapist had said.

He was so very tired of being a miserable bastard.

What the hell, he thought, and dialled the number. It rang a couple of times before he realised he hadn't thought about what he was going to say to her. He panicked and hung up just as it connected. *That went well.*

Okay, what was he going to say? He was going to ask for an explanation, he supposed. Yes, that's what he was going to do. Calmly and reasonably, he was going to find out once and for all what had happened, why she'd let it happen, and most importantly of all, why she had kept the truth from him. Yes. Great. That was the plan.

He hit redial.

Charles walked out of his office and made a beeline for Kal's desk, and Kal hurriedly hung up yet again. *Jesus Christ.*

'Kal!' his boss exclaimed. 'Have you seen this excellent feedback that just came through from the Stewart Group?'

'Yeah, Linda sent it over this morning. Looks great, doesn't it?'

Charles congratulated him on a job well done, and left.

He picked up his mobile again. Third time lucky.

His office phone rang precisely two and a half seconds after he pressed redial. By the time he had sorted out the non-question one of the juniors had rung him for, Kal felt on the verge of a nervous breakdown. Maybe this was a sign, he thought. Before he could talk himself out of it, he hurried to an empty meeting room, closed the door and dialled the number a fourth time. This time, the call was answered before the first ring had even finished.

'Listen, mouth-breather, enough with this bullshit. If you call and hang up again, I'm going to call the police. Also, for a spammer, you're terrible. Aren't you meant to be trying to sell me an energy plan or warn me that there's a warrant out for my arrest instead of chickening out?'

'Ayesha?' Kal asked, startled. He'd registered the slight American twang of her accent.

'Who is this?'

'It's Kal.'

She was quiet for a long time. Then, 'Did you call to speak to Saima?'

Having amped himself up into a complete state at the prospect of speaking with Saima again, Kal was now completely thrown.

'Uh, no, it's okay, I was just calling to see how she was doing,' he stuttered. 'So, how is she doing?'

'So you *didn't* call Saima's number to speak with Saima?' she asked in that familiar impatient tone.

He cleared his throat. 'What are *you* doing answering Saima's phone?'

'Her mobile redirects to the office phone while she's at an appointment.'

'That clarifies nothing,' he said.

'I-am-in-Saima's-office,' she said slowly, enunciating every word. 'Saima-is-not-here. I-am-answering-her-calls. Do-you-understand-me?'

'*Why*-are-you-in-Saima's-office?' he asked, mimicking her.

'Oh, I work here,' she said in her normal voice.

'You what?'

'Well, *technically* I'm interning as a consultant at Love Masala, but basically I work here. Business is booming, by the way. No thanks to you.'

'What do you mean?' he asked, startled.

'Well, she had to work hard to get out of the hole the debt to your parents put her in. What did you do that made her return all that money? She definitely could have used it.'

'I didn't, I mean – did she say something?'

'No, she didn't say anything. Well, not to me, anyway. I think Jess might know, but Saima refuses to talk about it again. I'm guessing that you were a bastard to her, though. Jess gets all mad whenever you or your parents come up in conversation, but Saima just looks a bit sad and changes the subject.'

'It was a misunderstanding,' he began, then pulled himself up short. He had not made this call to defend himself, particularly not to Ayesha.

'Have you thought about clearing things up? Or do you want to keep going with everyone thinking you're a dickhead?'

'Who thinks I'm a dickhead? And anyway, I'm not the one who needs to clear things up!' he said, throwing any attempt to keep his cool out the window. 'My parents hired her behind my back, and I caught her taking money from them. I didn't do anything wrong. It was a shock, to say the least.'

'Oh shit,' Ayesha said.

He regretted telling her any of this.

'Wait,' Ayesha said. 'Why did she return all your parents' money, then?'

'I didn't know she'd done that,' he said.

'They didn't tell you?'

'I haven't spoken to them in a while.'

'And Saima's not been in touch at all?'

'No. I didn't expect she would, to be honest. She was pretty upset where we left things.' Perhaps it was Ayesha's brisk approach, but Kal found himself admitting for the first time aloud, 'Maybe it was my fault. My mum – she said some horrible things. I should've stood up for Saima and said something.'

'God, this sounds like some major drama. I had no idea.' She thought for a minute. 'So how come you were calling today? Do you want me to pass on a message to her?'

'I thought—' He stopped abruptly as his brain finally caught up with his heart. 'I thought I was going to ask her for an explanation. But I think I already know that she must have had a good one, or she wouldn't have done any of it.'

'Oh, a hundred per cent,' Ayesha said. 'I have no clue what was going on, but that doesn't for a second change the fact that Saima's one of the most principled people I've ever met.'

'I miss her,' he blurted. 'I think that's why I called. And to say I'm sorry. For everything.'

'Then tell her!'

But Kal had come to a decision in the last couple of minutes. Saima not answering her phone had definitely been a sign, and the fact that she hadn't reached out to him in almost three months made it perfectly clear that she'd put him well and truly behind her. 'No, she doesn't need me walking back into her life. She seems busy with the business, and I'm happy to hear that. She's probably moved on.'

'I won't lie, she's incredibly busy. But I don't think she's moved on. I've caught her a number of times just staring at nothing, and then Jess always says, "Stop thinking about that prick." Sorry.'

'No, it's okay.'

'She's all right, though. In case you were worried. She's a fighter.'

He smiled. 'I know.'

'But I'd like her to be happy, you know?' Ayesha said. 'She deserves it. And I think she's still hurting too much to be properly happy right now.'

'She does deserve it. Did it at least help when my mum apologised to her?'

'Your mum? When was that supposed to happen?'

Kal hadn't been able to be in his parents' presence since that July morning – which now seemed like a lifetime ago. But he'd still spoken to them over the phone, and he'd made a point to call his mother a couple of weeks ago to check if she'd apologised like he'd asked.

'Ammy said she spoke to Saima in September,' he said.

'Nope,' Ayesha replied. 'I've been here since then, and I'm pretty sure I would have remembered that.' There was a clatter and muffled voices on her end of the line, and she swore softly. 'Shit, sorry, that's the electrician. Listen, Kal, I've got to go. But my advice is that you should square things with Saima properly, whether you're going to give whatever you had another go or not. You need to talk it through. You both deserve that.' And she hung up before he had the chance to say another word.

That evening, after work, Kal headed to his parents' house.

'Oh, Kal!' Ruby answered the door dressed head to toe in matching athleisure wear, behaving for all the world like he was regularly dropping by. 'I'm heading out to pilates. Your papa is in his study playing chess online with someone, maybe a computer, I don't know.'

'Did you apologise to Saima?' Kal demanded.

'What? Yes, I told you I did.' She busied herself with the carry straps on her exercise mat.

'And what did she say? After you apologised?'

'She said, okay, thank you. And then I left. The end.'

'When was this?' he pressed. 'Give me the exact date and time. And tell me precisely what you said, word for word.'

'Kal, what's gotten into you? I don't remember the specifics. It was last month, maybe.'

'No, you would remember. If you had done what you said, you'd remember. And you know why, Ammy? Because you never apologise. Never. Not even when you're at fault.'

Ruby stared at him for a moment, clearly assessing whether she could brazen her way out of this conversation. At last, she sighed. 'Honestly, I think one of the worst decisions I made was hiring that matchmaker. I see it now. We should have just left it to you to find someone for yourself. Lesson learned.'

'Why didn't you go and apologise, Ammy?' Kal's voice was soft. 'You know it's the right thing to do.'

Ruby ran her gaze up and down her son, appraising him for the first time in a long while. 'You're wasting away,' she observed.

'So I've heard.'

She pursed her lips. 'All because of this girl?'

Kal looked away. 'Of course not.'

Ruby's hand landed gently on his chin, bringing his gaze back to her. 'She's not right for you, my son,' she whispered.

He closed his eyes against a wave of longing and regret. 'She was the only one who was right for me, Ammy. That's why I should have kept running after her, not remained still when it mattered most.'

When he opened his eyes again, his mother was watching him with compassion and sorrow all over her face. 'It was never my intention to hurt you, beta.'

He nodded. 'I know.'

'And what I said to her . . . I was angry. I was unwise and unkind with my words because I saw she had hurt you.'

'I know, Ammy. I hurt her too, though.'

'I think, perhaps, we all did a great deal of nuksaan to one another that day.'

'Just speak to her, Ammy,' he said. 'Please. We have to make this right.'

Ruby smiled sadly. 'I'll talk to her, beta,' she said. 'I can see this is important to you. I'm sorry I didn't do it before.'

Chapter 25

The three of them were standing around in the kitchen. Ayesha and Jess were talking about the Pump class they were going to that evening and Saima had tuned them out, as she usually did when they spoke about their mutual passion for working out. Unfortunately, as they still did with depressing regularity, her thoughts turned to Kal. The laksa they ate, the gelato, the smell of petrichor and those late-night conversations over the phone. But it was the thoughts of the two of them in his apartment that were the most persistent: Kal's face as he was cooking, the feeling of his hands on her body, the way she felt as she rested her head on his chest. Just then she let herself remember the feeling of her skin on his, the warmth that spread from her face to the rest of her body.

'The water's boiled, Saima,' Ayesha stated, making her jump. 'Are you going to make the tea, or are you going to stand there?'

'Just call him,' Jess said.

'Call who?' Saima asked. She busied herself pouring the water from the kettle.

Jess scoffed. 'Oh please. We know that look.'

'There's no look.'

'You should call Kal,' Ayesha interrupted before an argument broke out. 'I'm sure he's thinking about you, too.'

'He's not.'

'I'm not so sure of that,' Jess said, accepting her tea with a nod of thanks.

Saima glared at her. 'Why are you backing Kal all of a sudden? You couldn't even say his name without spitting before.'

'Because, babe, you need to move on, and you can't do that while you're still stewing over all the stuff you didn't say to him. At least you can tell him the things you didn't get a chance to before.'

'It wouldn't change what happened.'

'Nothing can change what happened. But you can change how you feel about it,' Ayesha piped up.

'I see Jess has been at you with her motivational Instagram posts.'

Jess threw her hands up in defeat. 'Fine, joke about it. But you know we're right. Listen, Saima' – she came to stand in front of her friend – 'you've done so much in the last couple of months. You guys have completely slayed and it's time to be excited and looking forward to the future. Don't let this hold you back.'

'I am looking forward to it!' Saima exclaimed. 'I even used "girlboss" as a verb the other day. Unironically!'

Ayesha shuddered. 'Please let's never talk about *that* again.'

'But you're still carrying around all that garbage with Kal and his folks,' Jess continued. 'And I hate seeing that it's standing in the way of you fully enjoying this moment.'

'Look, I'll think about it, okay?' Saima conceded at last. 'I can't say that I'm in any hurry to speak to his mum again, though.'

'The only thing you need to say to his mum is tell her to fu—' Jess stopped as Dave called out down the corridor.

'Visitor incoming!'

'Yes, thank you, but I don't need announcing.' The last voice Saima was expecting to hear reached them in the kitchen. Jess and Saima stared at each other, aghast.

'I know you're getting good at manifesting your goals but this is next level,' Jess said to Saima, her eyes wide.

'Ayesha,' Saima hissed. 'Stick your head out for a second and tell us who's in the hallway right now.'

Ayesha was eyeing them like they had both gone mad, but she obligingly peered around the corner. 'There's a woman there,' she reported back.

'What does she look like?' Saima asked.

'She looks like a Real Housewife.'

Jess sniggered, then grabbed Saima by the arm. 'Okay, girl, this is your chance. Go out there and tell that cow where to stick it.'

'I think I'm going to throw up,' Saima replied.

'Then let me at her. I will throw some *hands*.'

Ayesha had finally caught up. 'Oh shit, is that *Kal's* mum?' She let out a horrified laugh.

'Ruby.' Saima didn't mean to say the name out loud, and Jess shushed her.

'Maybe she's like Candyman! How many times did you say her name out loud?' Jess asked, on the verge of frantic snickering.

The three of them started laughing and alternately shushing each other.

'Hello?' Ruby called down the corridor. 'Is anyone there?'

Saima wiped her streaming eyes. 'Oh god, I needed that.' She brushed down her top and blew out a breath. 'Okay. I should go see what she wants. Wish me luck.'

'Call us for backup if you need it,' Ayesha whispered.

Saima stepped out into the corridor, spotting Ruby standing in her office doorway. 'Assalaamu alaykum, Mrs Ali,' she said, her words coming out coldly formal without effort as she approached the older woman. 'I don't believe we had an appointment for you today.'

'Nice,' she heard Jess mutter, as she and Ayesha clattered into Jess's office.

'Won't you step into my office?' she asked. She followed Ruby inside and closed the door firmly behind them. 'You should have received your full refund by now.'

'Refund?' Ruby repeated. 'I didn't come about the money. And you needn't have refunded us. You did the job we asked.'

'So, what can I do for you today?' Saima settled into her seat, glad to have her desk between them.

Ruby regarded her mutely for a moment. For the first time since she'd met her, Saima saw her struggling for the right words to say.

'I've come to apologise,' she said at last. 'I didn't mean to say what I did when we last met.' She said the words quickly, her eyes averted.

This was the last thing Saima was expecting to hear, and she couldn't think of any response. A clearly uncomfortable Ruby leaped to fill the silence.

'You must understand, it was a very great shock for me to learn that you and Kal – that you and he—' She finally looked at Saima and baldly stated, 'You are not the person I imagined for my son.'

'I am not who I imagined for your son, either,' Saima snapped. 'And I certainly didn't set out to extend my relationship with you or him. As far as apologies go, Mrs Ali, yours could do with a little more work.'

Ruby inhaled sharply, furiously. 'I see the past months haven't impacted *you*,' she said, eyeing Saima up and down. 'You're looking rather well for someone who claims to love the man they've been separated from.'

Saima's pulse quickened at what Ruby's words implied, that Kal had not been well. She couldn't bring herself to ask, though. 'Life is not a Bollywood serial, Mrs Ali,' she said, wanting this conversation to be over. 'People don't fall apart after every setback.'

'You said you loved him,' Ruby pressed. 'Did you mean it?'

Saima tried to maintain an expression of polite detachment. 'I don't know what you expect me to say.'

They both stared at each other across the cluttered expanse of her desk, squaring off like two fighters.

'I think,' Ruby said quietly, almost as though she was talking to herself, 'that we could both stand to tell each other the truth for once.'

'You didn't blacken my name in the community,' Saima said. 'You could have. You could have crushed me completely. Why didn't you?'

'Do you still love my son?' Ruby said, avoiding the subject.

Saima closed her eyes briefly. 'If you answer my question, I will answer yours.'

'Very well. I admit the thought occurred to me once or twice. But every time, I asked myself, "Ruby, what will you achieve with this?" You see, as I told you before, I did my research before we came to see you earlier this year. And yes, while there was some gossip, some talk, mostly people said they found happiness and fulfilment, because of *you*.' She glanced over at Saima's pinboard, reassembled and still in pride of place on her wall. 'You are very dedicated to the happiness of others, aren't you, beti?'

'I wouldn't do this if I wasn't.'

'And so. Why would I act to take away the happiness of others simply because I was unhappy myself?' She leaned forward. 'Now, it is your turn. Truth.'

Saima searched for the right words. 'Mrs Ali, your son . . .' She sighed. 'Did he ever tell you how we first met?'

'No. Why?'

She shook her head. 'It doesn't matter. Suffice it to say that we didn't exactly get off to a great start. I'll admit I found him attractive, yes, but that was it. I'm telling you this because I need you to

297

understand that I wasn't interested in your son when you and I first spoke, nor for months later.'

'But something changed?'

'Yes. The long and short of it is that I got to know him. And the distance I've always kept between my personal life and my professional one – well, with him, there wasn't any distance at all.'

'He told me he was the one who pursued you.'

'The most he did was urge me to face the feelings that I'd been keeping hidden. Nobody pursued anyone. We just found each other. It wasn't planned, and was certainly unexpected.'

'You still haven't answered my question.'

Saima's throat felt thick with tears. 'Yes, I meant it.'

'Do you mean it still?'

'Is there any use if I did?'

'Arre, that's not what I'm asking. You think I go around apologising to people left, right and centre?' Ruby asked. 'Not once have I done this. But today I had to, and you, my girl, will answer me, please.'

'I don't know that you actually apologised today,' Saima replied curtly.

Ruby's eyes narrowed. 'Yes, I did.'

'You absolutely did not.'

Ruby glanced away for a moment and muttered something under her breath. 'Commit this to your memory, then, Saima, because I will not be repeating myself.' She looked Saima dead in the eye. 'I should not have said any of the harsh things I said to you that day,' she enunciated clearly. 'And I am very sorry that I did. And I also extend my apologies to your mother, because I tried to shame her with my words as well, and mother to mother, I know she has raised a child who is a credit to her.' She leaned back. 'Bas. Khatam.'

Saima was stunned. 'Thank you,' she managed.

'When I said truth, I meant it,' Ruby said. She got up and wandered over to the pin board, running the lacquered tips of her fingernails across the invitations there. 'Do you still love my son?'

Saima paused. 'Yes.'

Ruby nodded once, satisfied. 'Will you speak to him?'

'Why?'

'Why do you think?' Ruby turned back to her. 'I believe he thinks you hate him. Or at least that you will never forgive him, and that is eating away at him inside. A mother knows. This is why I came today, because I know I played a part in breaking my son's heart.'

'You didn't break his heart. He made a choice, as we all did, and that's his responsibility. Not yours and not mine. And I notice *he* hasn't made any effort to speak to me, either'

'But he's a man. Don't you see? They are bewaqoof. They don't know what they are doing half the time.'

'I'm sorry, Mrs Ali, I don't buy that for a second.'

'I think your life has faced some difficulties,' Ruby mused contemplatively. 'And you've hardened your heart as a result.' She reached over and patted Saima's hand once. 'But darling, don't harden it too much or there will be no room for the joy you deserve.'

And with that, she sailed to the door and left.

Saima remained where she was, turning the whole conversation over in her mind. She looked up when Jess and Ayesha peered into her office. 'You heard everything,' she said. It wasn't a question, but both her friends had the grace to look at least a little abashed.

'He did call,' Ayesha blurted.

'What?'

'He called. Yesterday, when you were at the dentist.'

'*What?*'

'I told her to tell you immediately!' Jess exclaimed.

'*You* knew?'

'I didn't know what to do about it,' Ayesha explained. 'I didn't know your history. So I asked Jess.'

'And I told her to tell you,' Jess repeated.

'Then we got busy in the afternoon, and I figured I'd tell you today. But then in the kitchen this morning, you didn't want to talk about it and I started wondering whether I should leave it alone. And then his mum turned up.'

Saima got up and began pacing the room. 'He called yesterday.'

'Yep.'

'Well, what did he say?'

'That he missed you and he was so sorry about everything.'

'You're making this up.'

'No.' Ayesha shook her head. 'I swear. But then—' She hesitated.

'But what?'

When Ayesha still didn't speak, Jess nudged her. 'You've got to tell her.'

'I told him to speak to you. And he didn't want to. He said he thought you'd moved on and you didn't need him coming back into your life.'

Saima stopped pacing and closed her eyes against the shaft of pain this information sent through her heart.

'I've fucked up,' Ayesha said to Jess.

'No.' Saima looked at her friends, who were watching her sympathetically. 'No, you haven't. I've wasted months wondering what he was thinking, wondering whether we could somehow get back to where we were. Or whether we could move past this. You've just answered my question. He's not interested in us being together, and I am certainly not going to beg.'

'You don't need to beg,' Jess pointed out quietly. 'You could try just meeting him halfway.'

Chapter 26

Kal appraised his reflection. It had been many months since he had last worn this particular suit, which he usually reserved for weddings, funerals and other big life events, and it just didn't fit him well anymore. There hadn't been much call for it since one memorably strange night in Bexley.

'Clean yourself up and get a haircut,' Ruby had said over the phone when she'd demanded his presence at tonight's wedding. 'The dulhan's abbu is a very important associate of your father's and I won't have you slumping in looking like a hippie.'

'Ammy, I look nothing like a hippie.'

'And make sure you shave beforehand, too!' she had instructed, ignoring him. 'None of that designer stubble nonsense you keep trying to sell me.'

He had groaned. 'Why do I have to go tonight, anyway? I thought we agreed that I don't do weddings with you anymore.'

'Khalid! Did you not hear me when I said that Farooq Uncle is Papa's good friend?'

'You said he was an associate. You never said friend.'

'Arre, friend, associate, it's the same thing. Why are you arguing with me? You must attend tonight, and that's the end of it.

And don't even think about disappearing like you did last time. Papa even booked parking for you.'

At that point, it had been easier to just go along with whatever it was Ruby said, which was why he now stood in front of the most forgotten corner of his closet, shrugging on his jacket and looking for a pair of shoes to match the outfit. He moved a few boxes out of the way to pull out the slightly-too-stiff shoes that were only ever unearthed along with this suit, and that was when a dull sparkle caught his eye – a pair of strappy shiny heels.

He had forgotten that he'd thrown them in there all those months ago. The sight of them now made his heart do a flip. Were they a sign? He'd spent days trying to decide whether he should listen to Ayesha and speak to Saima properly, or whether he should just leave the situation alone. Deep down he knew that he only considered the latter option because in many ways it was the easiest one. Speaking to Saima would mean confronting his fear that she had truly moved on without him; that no matter what he said it would have no impact on her.

Strangely, the shoes gave him hope. If nothing else, they were a reason to see her again, to return them, and to take the opportunity to lay his heart back down at her feet. Maybe that would give him the excuse he needed to drive back out to Parramatta to drop them off. Lest he forget them again, he scooped them up now and took them with him to his car. He tossed them in the back seat, the diamantés on the straps sparkling even under the strip lighting of his apartment car park.

Haniya and Faisal's wedding had been a long time in the making since they had dropped by Saima's office back in February. But as much as she loved them both, after a very long week, a wedding was the last place that Saima wanted to spend her Saturday evening.

'Do you maybe want to go instead?' she asked Ayesha over the phone.

'You can't be serious. After everything they've done . . .'

'Maybe I can just call Haniya now and take them out to dinner another day.'

'Don't be ridiculous, you know you can't do that. You're just wasting time instead of getting dolled up.'

Saima groaned. 'I definitely don't have the energy for getting dolled up.'

'What are you talking about? You've got to look spectacular tonight,' Ayesha insisted.

'Why?'

'Listen, Saima, it's *Haniya* and *Faisal*. Like, I can't believe I have to remind you of this, but her dad's done all our legal work *pro bono*, and Faisal's done actual magic with our website. And didn't he gift you that new phone? You're not just going to some random clients' wedding, they're practically family at this point.'

'Okay, okay. I know, you're right. I'm sorry I'm being such a pain,' Saima said.

'I'm always right.' Ayesha hung up.

When Saima had left her mother's place to move into her new apartment, Rahat had demanded that she take with her the notorious bridal suitcase. 'You're a much more important figure now, and you must look the part at these functions, and what use is it sitting under my bed anyway?' she had said. While Saima privately thought her mother was probably jumping the gun a bit in terms of how important she was, she was grateful now to be able to pull out a vibrant, shimmering turquoise shalwar suit from Rahat's collection. She ran a straightener through her hair and went in search of a matching pair of shoes. It was only when she was looking in her cupboard for the right pair that she remembered the sequined heels she had worn on the night she met Kal. They had murdered her feet that night, but right now they would have been perfect, and she recalled them with a fond smile. She had never gotten around to asking him what he'd done with them.

She shrugged to herself, still smiling. She realised that it was the first time in months she had thought of her history with Kal with nothing but a smile. Following Ruby's visit and Ayesha's revelation of Kal's phone call last week, Saima had decided to suggest he meet her somewhere on neutral territory and hash out everything that had happened. Maybe she could ask him to return her shoes. Whatever the result of that conversation might be, she would leave it up to Jess's all-providing universe. This year had taught her all too well the damage done by things left unsaid, and she wasn't going to relive the old patterns forged by pride and repression anymore. She just had to build up the courage to call him to arrange the meeting.

Meanwhile, she pulled on a sensible pair of wedges which would allow her to comfortably stand and mingle with the other guests. And most importantly, if she did end up wanting to make a quick getaway, she was unlikely to take them off and leave them in a stranger's car.

Typical Sydney traffic meant that Kal was running late getting into the city. His parents had been uncharacteristically texting him for the past half-hour to see where he was. He sent up a hasty thanks to his father for the parking he had booked in the Sussex Street multi-storey just across from the hotel where the wedding was being held. He parked his car, legged it to the plush lobby and up the carpeted stairs to the ballroom. The noise hit him before he'd even pulled open the doors.

Inside was the usual chaos of a Big Fat Desi Wedding. A DJ was loudly playing Bollywood hits, while groups of guests sat at lavishly decorated tables or milled around the room. There were easily three hundred people present, probably more. He'd clearly missed the bride and groom's entrance, for they were seated at the high table, which had been ornately bedecked like something out of an *Arabian Nights* fever dream. He scanned the room, looking for his parents.

'Khalid! I haven't seen you in years!' a vaguely familiar uncle exclaimed, thumping him vigorously on the back. 'Good to see you, beta, good to see you.'

'Salaam, Uncle,' Kal replied automatically, incredibly glad that the uncle and aunty honorifics made it so easy to conceal the fact that he remembered nobody's name. He searched for his parents among the crowd. Perhaps he should go out again and look for the seating plan.

'Arre, Khalid, MashAllah, how handsome you look!' an aunty cried, pinching his cheek.

'Salaam, Aunty.'

'Khalid! Heard about the promotion – congratulations, beta!' another uncle said.

'Shukria.'

'Accha, Khalid, you are here? How are you? How is your ammy?'

'Wah, Khalid, kaise ho?'

'Khalid Ali! How are you, my boy?'

'Khalid, bohat ache lag rahe ho!'

As Kal wheeled through the beaming guests, he realised that in spite of the distance he had imposed between his parents' heritage and his own, he had deeply missed this feeling of being accepted and embraced. Perhaps this was what kept Saima so firmly rooted within their community despite the damage it had occasionally done her.

'Salaam, Khalid, I've been meaning to talk to your abbu. Perhaps you could tell him to call me . . .'

He turned to respond to the uncle who had been speaking. The crowd parted, and then all at once the noise stopped, all except the steady thud of his own heartbeat echoing loudly in his ears.

She was bending down to talk to an aunty who had grabbed her hand as she walked past. He found himself drifting towards her and caught a snippet of their conversation.

'Arre, Saima, what is your secret? You are looking radiant,' the aunty was saying.

Saima crouched beside her and laughed. 'Shukria, Aunty-ji, but it's just make-up.'

Aunty shook her head emphatically. 'I know what it is,' she said. 'You aren't married. That's why you are looking so well. That's why we ladies get so dressed up on our wedding days, as a final reminder to everyone of what we looked like before we get a husband.'

Saima laughed again as Kal strained to hear her answer. 'Nonsense, you're looking so good too, Aunty, MashAllah.'

'So tell me your secret,' Aunty said. 'Are you doing keto? I've been thinking of cutting down on carbs.' She continued at length but Saima suddenly looked flushed, as though someone was staring at her. She looked up.

To Kal, everything felt like it was happening in slow motion. He moved as though he was wading through syrup as she stood up and walked towards him, her eyes bearing an expression that he couldn't quite read.

They met halfway across the crowded dance floor.

'I'm sorry,' they both said in unison, the words sounding overly loud in a gap between the DJ's tracks.

'No, I'm sorry,' they tried again, talking over one another. With a small grimace, Kal gestured to Saima to go first.

'I didn't expect to see you here,' she called over the music.

'I came with my parents,' he shouted back.

She thought for a moment that he was joking. 'Wait, seriously? Your parents aren't here.'

'What?'

'Your parents. They're not invited,' she repeated.

'What do you mean? How do you know?'

'Your dad and Farooq Uncle,' she explained. 'They famously don't get along. I thought everyone knew that?'

Kal was speechless for a moment, then he shook his head and began to laugh. Saima watched him, a slightly confused smile on her face.

'What's funny?' she asked.

'My parents,' Kal gasped. 'They never learn.'

Realisation dawned on Saima. 'Ruby's been scheming again.'

'I don't think she can stop,' he admitted, laughing.

She remembered Ayesha's odd insistence this afternoon and told him, 'I think in this case, she had some help.' And they laughed some more.

'I'm sorry,' he said, after a moment. 'I should have gone after you.'

She shook her head. 'I should have told you about your parents long before we got involved. *I'm* sorry.'

'Why didn't you?'

'I don't know. It never felt like the right time, and I wasn't sure how it was between you and them. I didn't want to cause some

307

massive drama between you all, even though that's exactly what ended up happening. I panicked.'

'Okay.'

'No, Kal,' she continued. 'I swear. I came out to your work that day wanting to tell you in person, and, well, you remember how that went. Then I was at your parents' house because I wanted to let them know the truth about us . . .'

'Saima—' he moved to touch her hand, then quickly looked around, remembering where they were, and pulled it back. 'I mean it, it's okay. I believe you. And like I said, I should have come after you, I should have defended you when my mum flew off the handle.'

'Why didn't you?'

'Truthfully? Because I was angry and hurt and a bit shocked. I never expected to see you at their place.' He closed his eyes for a moment before opening them. There was a sheen of sadness in them. 'I've spent months beating myself up over how I acted.'

'You shouldn't have beaten yourself up. We were both at fault. The least I could've done was reach out to you to explain,' Saima said, looking at the ground. 'But I was so hurt. You don't know how hard it was for me to open up to someone like I did with you.'

'I know,' he said, his eyes filling with warmth.

'At least you tried to reach out to me.'

'I should have called you again after I spoke to Ayesha. But she did tell me about Love Masala. You seem to be doing amazingly well!'

Saima flushed a little. 'There's a way to go, but it's really exciting,' she said, unable to keep the grin off her face.

'I'm so happy for you.'

They stood gazing at each other for a heartbeat longer. Kal looked like he was summoning up every last bit of courage he had, before asking, 'So what do you think, Saima? Can we give this another go?'

'Ladies and gentlemen, uncles, aunties, bhais and bajis,' the emcee boomed into his microphone. 'If you could please clear the dance floor, the bride and groom and their friends have prepared a special dance for you all!'

The guests surged to the edges of the parquetry. Saima darted forward to grip Kal's hand as the room darkened and a smoke machine began to spray out plumes in which purple, pink and orange spotlights danced. Kal curled his fingers around hers, hidden among the folds of her dupatta.

'*Ishq haiiiiiiiii.*'

The opening strains of 'Salaam-E-Ishq' filled the ballroom and Haniya and Faisal's sisters and friends assembled at one end of the dance floor in formation. Haniya swiftly ran down from the high table, slipping off her shoes to take the central position, while Faisal and his groomsmen faced them off on the other side. With a great deal of clapping, whistling and cheering, the thumping beat of the song overhead, they began a perfectly imperfect choreographed dance, making up with enthusiasm and joy what they may have lacked in coordination.

Saima looked up at Kal, who was watching the show with a huge grin of enjoyment like everyone else around them. She took him all in – his brown eyes, his black hair, which was longer, his stubbled chin. For a second she wanted to throw caution to the wind and kiss him right there and then.

'Ladies and gentlemen, please make your way to the dance floor to join the bridal party!' the emcee bellowed into the microphone.

Kal looked back down at Saima, with a sly smile at his lips. 'This might be my chance to see those infamous dance moves of yours.'

Before she could overthink things, Saima let herself be guided onto the dance floor by Kal. Her feet couldn't help but follow and it didn't take long for those very feet to get into the rhythm of things.

Soon a crowd of aunts and uncles, teenagers and toddlers, and a swarm of excited men and women from the bridal party were raising their arms in the air, hollering while moving to the beat. It was easy to get swept up in their enthusiasm. So Saima threw her head back and danced, her hands waving, her hair swishing from side to side. She was thankful she'd worn those wedges, so she could dance without wincing in pain.

It took a moment before she noticed Kal wasn't by her side. Instead, he was standing back and watching her, his eyes shining brightly.

'So you do have the moves, matchmaker,' he said coming up to her. His fingers quickly grazed the side of her face before he whisked them away.

As fun as the dancing had been, she had better ideas of what she wanted to be doing right there and then.

'Let's get out of here?' Saima asked, tipping up onto her toes and whispering in his ear. 'You still owe me that MasterChef dinner.'

Kal laughed elatedly. He grabbed her hand once more and this time towed her away from the dance floor, towards the exit.

'Wait, my bag!' she protested giddily, swiping the clutch from her table in a quick detour.

They didn't stop outside the ballroom, in the lobby or on the street outside the hotel.

Only when they were in the car park, safe from the inquisitive eyes of any lingering guests, did Kal release Saima's hand and turn to face her. He cupped her cheeks gently.

'I love you.' She beat him to it.

He pulled her close, his hands now in her hair, and her own reaching up to his. They came together with breathless laughs, shivering despite the humid November night, and everything in the world shifted, tilted, until it was *right* once more. At last Kal raised his head, the colour high on his cheeks, and lay his forehead against hers. 'I love you too.'

She gave a happy sigh as he opened the passenger door of his car. He got in behind the wheel and started the car engine, while she clicked her seatbelt into place.

As she turned to look at him a sparkle caught the corner of her eye. There in the back seat she saw them – her shoes.

He looked over at her with a grin. 'I think they might be my good luck charms.'

She leaned back in her seat and closed her eyes. 'Home, please,' she said. 'I don't mind which route you take, but I usually go via the Eastern Distributor.'

It took him a moment to remember what she was referring to. He took his foot off the brake with a blissful laugh and started to drive, their destination clear in his mind. 'Home it is,' he said.

She opened the window a little, letting the warm humid air brush across her face, feeling better than she ever had before.

Acknowledgements

There are a number of people who helped take this book from a concept to publication. First of all, to my agent Tara Wynne, thank you for listening to my ideas and for encouraging me to keep at it before we landed on this book concept. I appreciate all your help in making this idea become a reality.

Radhiah Chowdhury, who brought this book to Penguin Random House and who championed it from the very beginning, thank you! Your help in taking my broad idea and honing it down with your scrupulous notes and edits was a great learning experience and made this book what it is today.

Meredith Curnow, your belief in this book and its place at Penguin Random House has been so reassuring. Thank you for all your support and for keeping me in the loop during all the various steps towards publication.

Kalhari Jayaweera, it was so heartening for this writer to hear how you connected with this book. I'm grateful for your encouraging notes, for your many reads of my manuscript and the copyedits.

I know it takes a number of people to make any book a reality, so for the team working behind the scenes at Penguin Random House, even though we may not have met, this debut novelist is forever grateful for all your hard work.

Only a handful of people truly know how long and tumultuous this writing journey has been for me. But the one who knows it best is my husband Matt, who has been a part of this journey from the very beginning. Thank you, Matt, for supporting me by listening to my many ideas, for reading drafts, for taking care of the multitude of tasks that come with running a household of five and for telling me all those years ago when we first met that you would support me in becoming a writer no matter what it took.

To my wonderful children, Milan, Kaiden and Nyle. You three are amazing and you've been so understanding when I needed to spend time away from you to write this book. Your enthusiasm for my work and for me is honestly what helps me keep writing even when it becomes really, really hard. I don't think a mum could ask for better children – I mean it!

For the Shads – my ammy Yasmeen, my abou Ashraf and my brother Arsalan. Thanks for keeping me humble always – ha! But also for giving me inspiration and for supporting me no matter what I decide to do.

For Mehfooz Begum, my nani, who all those decades ago made the choices that allowed her children, grandchildren and great-grandchildren to live out their dreams.

And to you, dear reader, if you've read this far. Thank you for supporting someone who started dreaming about being a writer back when she was eight and had no idea of the many hurdles she would have to overcome to get there. Here's to persevering, despite it all.

Saman Shad is a writer, editor, journalist and teller of stories. Much of her work is inspired by her experiences as a third culture kid, growing up and living in Pakistan, the Middle East, the UK and Australia. Her writing credits span mediums, including radio scriptwriting for the BBC in the UK and the ABC in Australia, and playwriting, with works commissioned by theatres across London and Sydney. She is a regular writer for several publications, including the *Guardian*, *Sydney Morning Herald* and SBS. She has also worked on screen projects, including developing the feature film *One of Us* with funding from Screen Australia. She is currently working as a screenwriter on a number of upcoming projects. Saman is a proud mum of three children and lives with them and her husband in Sydney.